About the Author

Nick B. Ponter was born near Windsor, England in 1968. His interesting career started as a carpenter, then the army and foreign service, during which time he lived in Asia for six years. A school prize in English was an early indicator of his interest in writing fantasy and his storytelling is also influenced by contemporary issues. He has a bachelor's degree in International Studies and today is a business English trainer and prepares students for exams. Nick narrated his first book as an audiobook. He is inspired by outdoor activities, heavy metal and travelling.

By the Same Author

Connor Jackson and the Memory Thieves

CONNOR JACKSON
AND THE
QUEST FOR AZOTH

Nick B. Ponter

CONNOR JACKSON
AND THE
QUEST FOR AZOTH

Pegasus

PEGASUS PAPERBACK

© Copyright 2024
Nick B. Ponter

A CIP catalogue record for this title is
available from the British Library

ISBN 978 1 80468 018 6

*Pegasus is an imprint of
Pegasus Elliot MacKenzie Publishers Ltd.*
www.pegasuspublishers.com

First Published in 2024

**Pegasus
Sheraton House Castle Park
Cambridge CB3 0AX England**

Printed & Bound in Great Britain

Dedication

For the animal world and moles who continue to give me great
inspiration.

Acknowledgements

To family and friends who supported me during the planning, writing, editing and listening to my creative ideas. To all people who bought *Connor Jackson and the Memory Thieves* who gave me great reviews and the motivation to write the sequel. Most of this story was written on location in Thailand, so a huge thanks goes to the wonderful country and people who greatly inspired me during my travels.

Prologue

The block of salt glistened in the star-laden night, a strong metal cage protecting it from frequent and unexplained thefts. It was atop a wooden post and just the right height for deer to lick, offering a perfect target. A second block was at the bottom in yet another cage, this one suitable for wild boar. The crosshairs of the hunter's telescopic sight rose and fell with his controlled breathing, fully focused as he eagerly awaited his prey.

"A perfect night for hunting," he whispered, with a smirk on his face.

But then, his concentrated face changed to confusion as he reflected on an annoying experience. The meticulously organised hunter always laid his clothes on the couch before going to bed, but on getting up early this morning, found one of his socks missing even though he had definitely put both out. And this was not the first time. What happened to his darn socks?

A rustling sound shook him out of his thoughts. Yes, wild boars were coming his way, so he moved his aim to the lower block, levelled his crosshairs, controlled himself, applied a little pressure to the trigger and waited. He heard hooves trampling loudly through the forest and the snapping of twigs as they approached. And then there was nothing. Just silence. Not wanting to give away the slightest of noises, he sat motionless, but his impatience got the better of him. After remaining in this posture for what seemed an age, he peered above his sights to survey the clearing. Still nothing.

Then something caught his attention at the edge of the forest. He looked through his sights for a clearer view, briefly forgetting about the wild boar and, to his amazement, a man dressed in an orange robe came into view. The hunter sat there in the silence of the trees, completely bemused. A Buddhist monk was looking directly at him!

Suddenly, thrashing directly below broke the peace, followed by a loud crash as something smashed into his wooden perch. Wild boars! The jarring impact threw him out of his seat, and he had to hold on to the frame tightly as the structure swayed erratically.

"What's going on?" he yelled in shock, his eyes shooting down at the forest floor.

A large, hairy wild boar looked up at the hunter, grinned, then barked just like a dog. He dropped his rifle with a loud clatter, completely shocked at this bizarre experience, then sat down on his chair with a thud and scratched his head, wondering how a boar could make such a noise. He looked down again to check he was not imagining things and saw the boar retreating into the darkness of the forest. The confused hunter remained seated for a while, head in hands, before composing himself. He picked up the rifle, adjusted his position, looked through the sights and aimed at the block. The metal cage had been prised open, and the salt was gone.

***

Ormerod Forsythe-Twyke was sitting at a rooftop bar, a wide-brimmed hat protecting him from the unrelenting sun. The smog below smothered the buildings like a thick layer of gauze with skyscrapers poking out in search of air. The crescendo of noise from the busy streets couldn't be blocked out as a permanent orchestra of tooting horns and the distinct high-pitched noise of two-stroke engines squealed in the rat race. Holes in the gauze revealed a river teeming with boats and also the golden pinnacles of a grand palace glinting in some of the sun's rays which managed to penetrate the smog. On the other side of the river, a tall white spire with four similar structures at each corner clearly stole the show amongst the majestic buildings.

He was the younger brother of Felicity Forsythe-Twyke, the mayoress of the Molehamptons and owner of the Food Factory. He dabbed the sweat from his tanned, leathery face with a spotted handkerchief and picked up his phone, revealing a tattoo on his forearm. Two snakes wound around a winged staff—the caduceus.

"Yes, Father. A bit hot where you are, I think."

"I didn't call to chit chat about the weather. Now, down to business. The last trace of our *target* was here, but the trail has now gone cold," he explained, moving his phone around to show the Bangkok skyline.

"So that's where he's hiding, and with the secret technology. Our secret technology!"

"I didn't say *the target* was here. I just said the trail went cold here," replied Ormerod curtly. "

Ormerod had a prominent position in the British Secret Service and used its assets for his personal use. But his real master was the Cult of Azoth. His quest for the Head of the Eternity Project, allegedly custodian of the secrets of Azoth, had been his one and only task for many years and he successfully managed to infiltrate the organisation's upper echelons. But even there nobody knew who the head was, not even if it was a man or a woman, such were the layers of security protecting *the target*. He had suspected quite a few people over the years, but all his investigations ended up in a dead end. But one day, he must have got close as his *target* suddenly disappeared, making sure Ormerod knew about it. Control over the Eternity Project was now done from afar. Over the years, he was fed with pictures and names of multiple identities *the target* used, keeping Ormerod and his agents busy. The latest was a picture at Bangkok Airport.

"So, now you know *the target* is a man, and you surely have the name he is using."

"Bartholomew, a name yes, but not much use as it is obviously fake, and he is for sure using another one now. You have to understand he is the master of disguise. But by giving away his location, he is sending me a message—he wants me to go after him and lead me into a trap."

"But why not go after him? You are much better."

"And ruin everything I've been doing all these years? To track down my father's three missing sisters and their offspring. They took on new identities and were never seen again. Annabelle took over the reins of the Eternity Project then passed control to her eldest child—*the target*. He is not only Head of the Eternity Project but undoubtedly holds the key to the identities of his missing aunties too. I don't need him disappearing again. Oh, we will go after him, but on my terms."

"Is it time, father? All is in place and disorder is ripe below the Molehamptons."

"Trigger our plan, and do it immediately," said Ormerod, barking out his orders to his son. "We also need bait, and it's now time to reveal my secret half-sister."

"Secret half-sister. But I never knew about this."

"Of course not, you twit. That's why it's a secret and even my sister, Felicity, doesn't know about her. My father, George, had a social entanglement with one of the servants from that rabble at Lower Molehampton, and the result was a baby girl. She was brought up in another town and has no idea who she is related to. I am the only person in the family who knows about it, but that is about to change, and it will certainly put the cat amongst the pigeons."

Bartholomew swallowed in shock at the news. "Well, this will startle the family, and I still don't understand why you kept her identity under wraps for all these years."

"It's not for you to question, so just leave the thinking to me. Just remember what my great-grandfather used to say: power lies with the unscrupulous manipulation and possession of information. And that, Bartholomew, is exactly what I am now doing. Just know, I have meticulously planned everything and left nothing to chance."

"And what about your sister's best friend, Jemima Kingston?"

"She doesn't know who her real father is. But we do! It's time to send her the picture. She will have no idea where it came from, and it will get her mind racing. Then send the file about her husband and make sure my name is seen as the chief investigating officer. If all goes as I planned, she will start looking into our family, and that's exactly what we want. She will get the memory thief to investigate us. He is already suspicious of Felicity's involvement in our attempted acquisition of Professor Wingnut, but he will need some prods from us to push him in the right direction. Start with the photograph and the notes at good intervals. We need to feed him the right information and this is this is where Vanessa will come into play. The memory thief's job is to find *the target* and lead me to him."

"Yes, the memory thief can do our work. That pesky man, Connor Jackson!"

Chapter One
Change, Friends … and Rabbits

Pesky man! Yes, I knew that's what the Forsythe-Twykes call me after scuppering their plans to steal Professor Wingnut's memory. They also call me the memory thief and I suppose I am, Professor Wingnut's glass jar kept safely under lock and key in my house!

But what do you call me? The normal man? Connor Jackson the boring analyst? You probably know me as a rather ordinary person working at the government's secret listening station in the Molehamptons. My job means utmost secrecy and nobody in the villages knows what I do, believing me to be only a bland paper pusher. Would you believe it if I told you I had a mischievous streak? Well, I do. It gives me immense pleasure to play with my colleagues' computers when they are foolish enough to leave them logged on, unattended. Changing the default font to white is one of my favourites and inviting people to a party at the unsuspecting host's house is a real hoot. My best was only the other day when I called the home number of a completely innocent male colleague sitting opposite me. On the third ring, and just before his voice message played, I transferred the call to the angriest woman I have ever met. She works in the adjacent office and only needs a gentle prod to send her into mad tirades of abuse. Seconds later, I heard a volcanic eruption as she exploded in rage and stormed into our office demanding to know why he had called her with a stupid message. My poor colleague didn't know what hit him as she stood there imparting an intense torrent of her wrath, like a dragon burning its victim to fine ash.

But enough of this, as I now have the most curious story to tell you. By now, you might know of the secret world of moles right below our feet in the Molehamptons. I certainly do, and in this world, I discovered moles administer all creatures. Yes, all creatures including humans. They store memories in jam jars and reprogram those who pass through for future assignments on the surface. Were you to lie down on the grass next to a molehill and listen carefully, you may well hear strange noises coming from below. Try it at night-time and you might also see flashing lights shining out of the top of these mounds. It was down in this strange underground world where I really questioned the true meaning of good and bad. Were the moles who were trying to steal Professor Wingnut's memory bad, or were the ones protecting the system good? I couldn't decide, and it all came down to perspective. At the end of the day, whichever side they were on, the crafty moles weren't to be trusted.

I would love to tell you more, but I have just been stopped by four rabbits bouncing through the centre of Lower Molehampton, their large ears flapping around like wings. They were Flemish giant rabbits – the largest domestic ones known, and about one metre long. The sight of these enormous rabbits thumping their way along the pavement without a care in the world made the local residents stop in their tracks and dogs cower behind their masters in fear. Sergeant Dawson was not far behind.

Also, I often caught people looking at me in the street, surreptitiously pointing in my direction, and hushed conversations about how strange I had become. They thought I didn't notice, but it was really no surprise when you think about the bizarre events in Upper and Lower Molehampton when I planned my escape from the moles. You would have thought the strange incidents at the County Cup football match and the disappearances of players were long forgotten. But no. Not in the Molehamptons. Just the sight of me walking along the street was enough to arouse interest, and not only by the human inhabitants.

The rabbits were now standing in front of me, and we entered into a hearty discussion about the newly constructed bridge and bypass when suddenly, and in mid-sentence, the rabbits bounced off leaving me staring at an empty space on the pavement.

"Are you OK, Mr Jackson?" Sergeant Dawson was now standing in front of me, genuinely concerned.

"Yes, of course, Sergeant. What on earth could be wrong on such a lovely day?" I declared, looking up at the clear blue sky in a petty attempt to conceal my behaviour. I was sure the rabbits had just set me up for a bit of fun.

"Well, it just looked as if you were talking to those rabbits, and I just wondered …"

"If I was sane?" I finished his sentence.

"Oh no. I was not suggesting anything of the kind, just enquiring about your well-being."

"That is very kind of you, indeed. But there's no need to be alarmed. I was just lost in my thoughts and daydreaming. I have always been a bit of a dreamer, Sergeant. Please don't make a mountain out of a molehill," I added sarcastically.

My eyes darted away from the Sergeant as for the briefest of seconds I saw a Buddhist monk in an orange robe walking down an alley. I stared intensively, lost in my thoughts and I suddenly had the same feeling of being watched after finding Professor Wingnut's glass jar. He disappeared between a shop and a garage door, *VoleWeb* painted on the front.

"What is it?"

"Oh, it's nothing. Just thought I saw something, but maybe I was mistaken."

Sergeant Dawson was just about to speak when a deep rumbling sound came from below the pavement, followed by aggressive vibrations. It sounded like a construction crew was digging up the road, but there was no work going on. The sound moved further up the street with shop windows rattling in their frames and pedestrians looking at the ground in puzzlement.

"Strange," he said before starting what he wanted to say. "You are aware people talk about you? It appears you've been seen a few times speaking to animals, in particular rabbits, which is madness, and impossible of course. I don't believe any of it."

"Speaking to rabbits? Me? Impossible, Sergeant, and I couldn't agree with you more," I made an attempt to sound convincing. "Oh, just look at the time. I must dash. Goodbye, Sergeant." I turned on my heel and darted off quickly, leaving a rather baffled Sergeant Dawson gazing at me.

He was right of course. Not only about me speaking to animals but getting caught in the act too. Ever since my return from the mole world, I have been able to speak to all creatures, an extraordinary gift to possess

I must admit. Humans wrongly, and perhaps arrogantly, presume spoken communication is only an ability possessed by us alone. But unknown to people, all creatures share only one language, unrecognisable to humans, allowing them all to easily communicate with each other whilst we are separated by hundreds of languages. This causes great amusement in the animal world, and to me now as well, so I often take full advantage of this special ability. Unfortunately, I often get carried away and forget what seems perfectly normal to me is, in fact, extremely strange for my fellow residents of Lower Molehampton.

I have this incredible ability because down below the ground I was given one of just a few special tablets designed by Professor Wingnut allowing me to resume my life on the surface. And I wasn't alone. Three exceptionally good friends I made in the mole world joined my escape: Ludwig, Basil and Vanesa.

***

"Ludwig! Ludwig! Come here now," Mr Rye hollered across the fields. "Darn, dozy dog. Where is he when I need him?"

Mr Rye was dressed for hunting with his shotgun open, hanging over his arm. He needed Ludwig to fetch his prey, hence the reason he had a retriever.

"I bet he's sleeping under the willow tree again," he grumbled and stomped across the field towards the River Angler, shouting for Ludwig at the top of his voice.

Mr Rye was naturally correct, and Ludwig was lying under the low-hanging branches of the willow tree, but not sleeping. On the contrary, he was alert with pricked-up ears, as if he was guarding something valuable. Ludwig for sure heard Mr Rye but decided to stay put and disobey him. The river life needed more protection than his master his retrieving skills. He turned his head towards something splashing in the river. A beautiful duck with a green head and a bright yellow beak sat majestically on the water, basking in the glorious sun of the late summer day. Every now and then it would break its rest and dive briefly below the surface in search of food. Then it emerged and paddled slowly upstream and traversed the river until it reached the roots and bushes on the inside bend. It spent some time waiting, then disappeared under the hanging foliage. Apart from some birds sitting on a bush, the duck was alone. After exploring the riverbank, the duck floated gently back downstream towards his home under the roots of the willow tree, guarded by his best friend.

"Ludwig, Mr Rye is calling for you. He will not be too pleased."

"He's never pleased with me, Basil, and always calls me a dozy dog. If only he knew I can understand him! I will just pretend to be old and sleeping in the tree's shade when he comes down here. He will be ever so angry, but he loves me, and always falls for it especially since I returned from our adventure."

"Adventure? Really? It was a terrible experience, and I would certainly not liken it to an adventure. We died, Ludwig!"

"Well, not really, Basil. Look! Here we are, enjoying life to the full. Anyway, how's the family?"

"We're all fine, Ludwig. Our youngest will start duck school soon and learn the crafts of the water. But that's more than I can say for the rest of the river life. We used to have lots of neighbours here, but there are not many of us left now. The badgers and otters have gone and there are only a few plumps of waterfowl remaining. School classes are small now and even the teacher didn't turn up today. The ducklings were really looking forward to a lesson on river food. I just don't understand what's going on around here. Very sad indeed."

"Mr Rye complains too about changes happening at the moment. He used to supply the Food Factory, but he couldn't keep up with their demand and was too expensive. Apparently, the Food Factory now uses suppliers from far away and at much cheaper prices."

"Quiet now, he's coming," Basil sounded the alarm.

"There you are, you silly dog. Asleep again. Of course, what else? You do know you can sleep at the farmhouse, Ludwig? I really don't know why you come down here lately. Are you keeping someone company? Come on Ludwig, old chap. There's work to be done and I need you."

Ludwig rose ponderously, stretched and walked off at a leisurely pace behind his master, pretending he was having difficulty to keep up whilst Basil floated under the cover of the roots.

***

"Basil? Is that you? Are you home? How was it? Did you meet anyone?"

"So many questions and, no, my dear. All the homes are empty."

"It's sad here, Basil. We used to live in beautiful peace and tranquillity, and now we have a constant rumble of noise from that monstrous bridge. No wonder our neighbours stopped breeding. Why do these awful humans live like this?"

Basil and his wife sat for a while in deep thought, the roots of the willow shaking in unison with the loud mechanical noises from the nearby bridge.

***

And what of Vanessa? The experience below the ground had changed her from a stuck-up spoilt brat into a caring team player. She still remained aloof as her upbringing as a Forsythe-Twyke had taught her to be. But this was just for appearances sake, as she was distrustful about her family's connections to the world below and control over allocations to the Food Factory. We became good friends and met quite often, laughing about our experiences over a few beers, but making sure nobody overheard us. She was a vegetarian now, the thought of eating fellow creatures she met below quite abhorrent to her. But this now put her on a collision course with her mother and would prove to be quite a dilemma for me too.

***

A flock of pigeons flew straight past, circled back then hovered near my window. To the innocent bystander, they appeared to be normal birds, but I knew better. It was a squadron of Mr Tinker's bombing pigeons, an elaborate Special Operations Directorate run by Colonel Pickle far below our feet in the world of moles. Upon closer inspection, one could see that each pigeon had a harness attached under its belly, holding two upside-down glass jars containing white liquid, with mice stood on the platform pointing to potential targets on the ground. The pigeons constantly circled above Mr Tinker's store, just floating on the thermals, but occasionally some groups flew extremely fast, came in hard and low and then suddenly pulled up, splatting their bird droppings all over the place in targeted attacks. Those hit were infiltrated and taken over by a special forces operative disguised as bird poo, and underwent immediate change. It was quite funny to see a human take a direct hit and then leave whatever they were doing with others just looking on in confusion. This is in fact what had happened at the County Cup football match I mentioned earlier. Don't worry – more about this again soon!

I already told you that I have a mischievous streak and these bird droppings were just too tempting. Only the other day, I was talking to Earl Pike outside my house when Mr Singh, the postman, came by. At exactly the same time, a flock of pigeons pulled up above and released their loads. I could have just stepped out of the way, but I cunningly shoved Mr Singh directly into the firing line and watched him run off up the street, leaving his post bicycle behind.

"Wow, Mr Jackson, that was cool," Earl Pike said, quite surprised at what I had just done.

Earl and I had developed a friendship over the last months with the young boy often visiting, intrigued by my childhood possessions I still kept in my garage. My old, red chopper bicycle with a T-bar gear shifter on the top part of the frame fascinated him so much I reluctantly parted company with it. But he wasn't the only one interested in me. Frequently, dogs would appear in our lane. They were obviously part of Colonel Pickle's Special Operations Directorate sent to observe me. That's why I decided to busy them and gave Earl my old remote-control pickup truck with the extra-large wheels. He had immense fun driving it through Trout Lane with dog biscuits in the back and Mr Lawnsworthy's front garden proved a fantastic playground for him, as the truck jumped over his impressive rockery. The dogs soon forgot their mission and spent all their time frantically chasing the vehicle for the treats. Mr Lawnsworthy was in hot pursuit, shouting and cursing at the top of his voice, and the pigeons circled above with great interest at the strange activities. The sight of these birds made me contemplate the adventures I had and how my life had changed.

∗∗∗

The familiar clanking of Mr Cross's ferry had been replaced by a concrete bridge and the constant rumbling of livestock lorries sporting images of happy animals on their way to the Food Factory. Actually, it was only called the Food Factory by local people and its real name was F-T Happy Animals which was clearly contradictory to its plastic-wrapped meat products decorated with joyful looking pigs, cows, sheep, chickens and ducks. The bridge was fed by a new bypass, both of which were a blot on the landscape, and the uninterrupted din of traffic shook the villages to their core. The tourist magnet of this sleepy location had been taken over by an ever-expanding industrial centre based on the Food Factory with its company slogan *Quality Meat at Happy Prices.*

The new giant supermarket on the outskirts of Lower Molehampton was the final nail in the coffin for long-established and family-owned local shops. Although opposed by local residents, the Mayoress, Felicity Forsythe-Twyke, pushed through her policy of modernising the villages without any opposition from local councillors. The discount supermarkets conveniently stocked the Food Factory's products at extremely low prices and local butchers were not able to compete with the cheap vacuum-packed meat as much as people could not resist the temptation. But it wasn't the only thing which went ahead without protest. To extend her power over both villages, Felicity Forsythe-Twyke had successfully merged the mayors' offices of both Upper and Lower Molehampton. Her alleged cost-cutting measures also extended to the police stations with Sergeant Dawson now the only police officer for both villages. Change comes to all of us whether we like it or not, and I certainly don't.

But there were also little flickers of hope, the days of locally sourced delicacies in the local bakers and grocery stores would survive thanks in part to Gertrude Lawnsworthy. Her family had been in the service of the Forsythe-Twykes for generations, but this had come to a bitter end. Her brother Gerald, as well as their late father before, had been the family gardener for many years. He retired some time ago, now only tending his own garden with love and care. Gertrude's service as a cook for the influential family was cut short when an absurd accusation of her thieving ingredients led to her dismissal, as to be expected, without any severance pay. But the Lawnsworthy family were well respected in the local community and not ones to give in. With her meagre savings and the financial support from family and friends, Gertrude turned her living room into a shop and cafe with a truly homely feeling, warmed by her roaring fire in the winter. In Gertrude's Pasty and Pie shop, the frequenters really feasted on genuine home cooking; each dish made by her own loving hands from fresh ingredients she sourced from local farmers, proud to contribute to her recipes as they most certainly felt hard-done by the changes in the Molehamptons. The mouth-watering menu of local delicacies even showed the exact ingredients and their origin. Residents phoned in advance to guarantee not missing out on her scrumptious food and her Shepherd's Pie was an insider tip.

***

Some things thankfully stayed the same, like some of the residents in Trout Lane. The Pike family still lived to my left in house number two. We had escaped back to the surface through the Pike's greenhouse, so they obviously had something to do with the mysterious Eternity Projects. Quite what their role was I do not yet know, and apart from their involvement in our escape, I knew nothing about their organisation. Edward and Edith Pike are recluses and we had never had the opportunity to discuss the matter. Their son, Earl, now sped through Trout Lane on my old red chopper bicycle pretending to be the coolest motorbike rider and often stopped to say hello and have a chat. He quizzed me on literally everything, but strangely never about the four of us coming out of his greenhouse, as if he had orders not to. He was most inquisitive indeed and I had the suspicion his parents were somehow behind all the questioning to find out what I was up to. Who knows?

To my right in number four lived the meticulous Gerald Lawnsworthy. He had successfully stopped the molehill attacks in his front garden by concreting the whole area and covering it in artificial grass, but his back garden remained his pride and joy. During the strange events of my kidnapping, his immaculate lawn was left looking like a bombsite and I had felt quite sorry for him. But now the moles left him in relative peace, and he was able to tend to his lawn once again. Only occasionally, some of these annoying mounds sprung up and he fought them with gas. Mr Lawnsworthy wrongly presumed the gas was poisonous, but the truth was quite the contrary as it was in fact laughing gas to those little creatures below the ground, who used it for their rave parties. The ingenuity of the moles was quite amazing, because they knew all they needed to do was dig a few molehills and he would give them what they desired. As a neighbour, Mr Lawnsworthy was not one for many words and he often looked at me with great suspicion. This was really no surprise after what had happened. I approached him shortly after I escaped from below to ask if he would look after my spare key again. He turned white in the face, became visibly nervous and bade a hasty retreat whilst muttering something incomprehensible under his breath, shaking his head. Now, mostly just a curt nod of the head was about the only communication between us.

The Khans lived at number one. In fact, they had moved in a few months before my kidnapping and were the ones who captured me, but they had been infiltrated by Colonel Pickle's poo bombs and wouldn't have known anything about it. The Khans were extremely polite and chatty people, living with their three children and taking active roles in the community. One day, I was standing outside my house when my nose started tingling. A few deep sniffs were enough to detect an aromatic odour blowing in the air. Intrigued, I started sniffing my way around Trout Lane, trying to find the source until eventually stopping outside number one. I just stood there sucking in as much scent as I could and failed to notice Mr Khan open the door, who was quite amused at what I was doing. He immediately invited me in to join the family sitting round the dinner table. Despite my apologetic protests, the lovely Khans told me they would be offended if I didn't join them for lunch. I am not an adventurous eater, and you will find out more about that later, but I was treated to an amazing spread of food. I found out they originally came from Lahore in Pakistan and the food they served today a local speciality. My taste buds burst alive on the tasty Lahori Chicken Handi, a mouth-watering curry and mopped up with delightful naan bread. It wasn't the last time I sat with them, and we began a very close friendship.

The remaining house in Trout Lane, number five, was resided in by the Kennedy brothers. Apparently, they had moved in just before my kidnapping as well. They were arrested but released on lack of evidence despite intensive questioning by the police. Yes, they also tried to kidnap me and knew nothing at all about it, which was quite true as they had been infiltrated by Colonel Bacon's operatives, Colonel Pickle's counterpart. At the County Cup Final, they were arrested again, caught in the act stealing from the changing rooms. This time they did a short stint in prison before being released, put on a rehabilitation program and allowed to stay in Trout Lane. I knew all of this because Earl Pike questioned everyone in the street and told me all he learnt. However, I was sure the Kennedy brothers were not able to turn over a new leaf and sometimes I saw them sneaking back in at night-time with stolen goods, shortly followed by a visit from Sergeant Dawson.

The River Angler sneaked away from my view out of my bedroom window, meandering gently past the old willow tree and Mr Rye's farm. The beautiful castle ruin was sitting on one side of the River in Upper Molehampton and the rural Lower Molehampton on the river plain on the opposite side. And then there was the ever so popular Angler Arms, the inn next to the village square. Of course, I cannot forget to mention the popular campsite next to the river with smoke rising from the fires and the smell of smoked fish wafting on the breeze over the villages. But there was a small change at the campsite – the addition of brand-new wooden huts for cyclists and hikers to spend the night in right next to the river, proving particularly in demand over the summer months.

***

Oh yes, there were some other changes too, but more peculiar in nature. The rabbits thumping around Trout Lane and its gardens never caused any damage or trouble, but their permanent presence most certainly raised eyebrows, especially from Mr Lawnsworthy. Rabbits usually are jumpy animals – please excuse the pun – and escape from danger rather quickly. But not these ones. These rabbits were like soldiers and seemed to patrol the streets keeping them clear of any threats. In fact, that was exactly what they were doing. During my involuntary stay below, I became good friends with a rabbit. Dusty offered his assistance should I ever need help after my escape. I readily took him up on his offer, and now employed the rabbits as personal bodyguards.

You might wonder why I would need bodyguards? The answer is quite simple. I was still in possession of Professor Wingnut's memory and knew this story was far from over. My house had, in the meantime, been turned into a maximum-security zone, with alarms and cameras covering every possible angle. However, this didn't stop the crafty moles constructing huge observation molehills in my garden with metal periscopes sticking blatantly out of the top, rotating around to observe the surroundings. They didn't even bother trying to hide their activities. Colonel Pickle was keeping a beady eye on me, but who else was watching? The feeling of permanent surveillance was a constant reminder of the power struggle I knew was going on below the ground. And that is why I needed the rabbits to keep any intruders away from my house and inform me on developments in the mole world.

But I still needed my fun, and no doubt Mr Lawnsworthy would have not only seen me talking to animals but also leaving items next to the molehills in my garden. Things I knew they required like my many single socks accumulated over the years. I had no use for them but knew the moles did. They were always gone in the morning! It was also my way of sending messages to Colonel Pickle and keeping the lines of communication open.

The finding of the jar with Professor Wingnut's memory started an incredible chain of events which most people would not believe and led me on an amazing adventure. But still, questions remained to be asked and needed answering. What information did the Professor possess and still needed to reveal? And the Professor wasn't alone in the safe. A memory stick with unknown voices was also kept safe. But who was behind those voices and how were they connected to the plot? There was so much more to be analysed. I was quite sure both the Professor and the stick would expose the ringleaders—the devious Forsythe-Twykes.

Chapter Two
The Devious Forsythe-Twykes

"Vanessa, darling. You know we are having important guests this evening!" screeched Felicity Forsythe-Twyke, looking down her nose at her daughter.

"Just stop it, Mumsie. I dress as I like, and I definitely won't wear these posh uniforms like you and Mrs Kingston. I am in my twenties, not in my sixties. You know everyone calls you the tweed ladies."

"People can call us what they like. I need to keep up appearances as the mayoress of the Molehamptons, you must understand that. As for Jemima. Hmm, she just copies me!"

Vanessa tutted, rolled her eyes and gave up. "So, who's here for our family dinner? I've forgotten."

"Your cousin, Bartholomew. He has just arrived, and I've told you a few times."

"Another Forsythe-Twyke relative. You know mother, every few months you introduce me to yet another family member I've never met. How is that possible?"

"This chap is my dear brother Ormerod's son."

"I'm sure you haven't spoken to your brother for ages," Vanessa quipped sarcastically.

"We must leave some things in the past. Let sleeping dogs lie, as they say."

"Yes, the lovely Forsythe-Twyke family. You all get on so well with each other. Your secrecy about our family is quite intriguing. I wonder why you must have all these secrets?"

"Not now, darling Vanessa. Let us concentrate on the future. Your future."

"My future? Hmm, you need something, or Bartholomew wouldn't be here! What is it?" She asked, looking at her mother sternly.

"Vanessa dear, our company is expanding at an incredible rate, and I need more expertise. Bartholomew is extremely well-connected and I'm looking for a new business consultant."

"Our company?"

"Yes. One day you will take over the reins and I intend to leave you a successful and globally operating company. F-T Happy Animals will be yours."

"But you know I'm a vegetarian. How many times do I have to tell you? A vegetarian running a meat company. How ridiculous!"

"Please grow up, Vanessa. You can't run a business without believing in its product."

"Yes, exactly my point. And, unfortunately, you equate quality with industrial scale slaughter?" Vanessa was now becoming angry at this pointless conversation with her mother who, as usual, completely ignored her comments.

"My dear daughter, we adhere to all government standards as your cousin Bartholomew would assure you. He runs the government's Food Standards Ministry, you know," added Felicity.

"Why doesn't that surprise me? I would be interested to know what his qualifications are, letting him head up such an important committee?"

"Bartholomew is a real pioneer in social issues and a caring man. He used to be a banker and oversaw a program of affordable mortgages to low-income families. Unfortunately, the bank went bankrupt, and he was promoted to a senior government position.

"As I thought, no qualifications for such an important position."

Anyhow, come and meet him now," said Felicity, taking her daughter by her arm.

***

The dining room was elegantly decorated with newly hung portraits of the Forsythe-Twyke family adorning one wall. The table had been laid out immaculately with the cutlery, glasses and plates all perfectly arranged in straight lines like a military parade ground. Crystal glasses glistened under the lights of the beautiful chandelier and the candles on the table. Vanessa stuck out like a sore thumb in her yellow leggings and purple jumper. Her newfound cousin, Bartholomew, was sitting to her right. Her mother seated at the head of the table and her father at the other end. I'll tell you about him soon. Nobody was sitting in the two chairs opposite yet, but the places laid made Vanessa wonder who else might turn up. Her suspicions were soon answered as Clementine and Bill Farrow entered the room and nervously took their places.

"I don't mean to be rude, Mother, but I thought this was a family dinner," whispered Vanessa, looking dubiously at the two new arrivals.

"Oh, it is just that. Let me introduce you to my half-sister, Clementine," Felicity added proudly.

Vanessa choked on her wine and looked at her mother and the Farrows, her eyes flashing around the room to the people now glancing at her with devious looks on their faces.

"Darling Vanessa," started Bartholomew in support of his aunt, "your grandfather added to the population of the village in a rather inappropriate act of socialising. Clementine was born to a servant from this household. In secret of course, as George didn't want to jeopardise his career. She grew up with parents of better standing in another town but was kept under observation and given gainful employment in assisting your mother in certain tasks. Bill's family on the other side has been closely connected with ours for many years. My father, Ormerod, arranged for them to meet and now both Clementine and Bill are sworn to secrecy."

"And, on Ormerod's order, this must stay a family secret until he sees fit to announce it publicly. Not a word to anyone!" Vanessa's mother added, winking at them.

Vanessa just stood there with her mouth open at this bombshell of news. "And you never knew about this?"

"Nothing at all," replied Clementine. "It was an utter shock as Ormerod informed your mother and I only yesterday. Unfortunately, I don't know my real mother, but I am sure Ormerod might be able to reveal this at some stage. But, in the meantime, I'm just delightfully happy to be a Forsythe-Twyke, even if it is only half," she added proudly.

"I wouldn't be so sure about that," quipped Vanessa sarcastically.

Farquhar Forsythe-Twyke had remained silent and expressionless during the whole conversation. Vanessa's father was a quiet and unassuming man, taking a back role in family matters. His wife took the more public role, not only as mayoress but also as the manager of the Food Factory, leaving him pretty much a recluse. He was rarely seen in public and wandered around the house in a strange daze, some believing him to be crazy. He had taken the Forsythe-Twyke family name on marriage, leaving behind his surname of Ogulburt-Dilingbrush. Sadly, for Vanessa, she was unable to forge a meaningful relationship with her father owing to his ailments and strong medication.

"Let's tuck in then, shall we," said Bartholomew in his shrill voice when the butler entered the room to serve succulent steaks, vegetables and potatoes.

"Oh, just how divine," squawked Felicity in delight. "One shouldn't take the credit, but I will. And thank you, Mr, Mr, Mr urrrm," she shouted after the retreating butler who shook his head in amazement.

"What's his name then, Mumsie?" quizzed Vanessa with a mischievous glint in her eyes.

"Oh, darling. How do you expect me to remember the names? This incompetent service agency fills the positions from a constantly changing pool of cooks and butlers. How am I to remember all these names?"

"This steak is absolutely delicious. Where did ..." Bill Farrow started before being cut off loudly by his wife.

"I couldn't agree more Bill but let me do the talking – it's for the best. Just remember what happened at our anniversary dinner. You behaved like a dog."

"Oh, my dear sister, I'm sure Bill just had a funny turn that evening," Felicity said with a nasty smirk on her face. "All forgotten and forgiven now."

"And Bill. Don't forget to use your knife and fork this evening."

Clementine could not help her sarcasm and Bill just sat there, looking at everyone in total bewilderment. On that particular evening he had, in fact, been infiltrated by Ludwig in the course of one of Mr Tinker's bombing missions and the retriever did an absolutely awful job acting like a human. At the dinner table he forgot all about cutlery and stuck his head right into the plate, slurping up his food like a dog usually would. Poor Bill had, of course, no recollection of what had happened but was often reminded about his strange behaviour.

Vanessa banged her knife and fork down on the table, bringing the room to silence. "Dear sister?" she exclaimed, walking across to the wall and looking up at the pictures set out like a formidable family tree. "You are all going on like these family intrigues are good fun! I just wonder how many more family members there are who I've never heard of. How many more secrets and family feuds you are keeping from me. And look at all of these newly hung-up portraits. I haven't even had the chance to look at them."

Montague, Vanessa's great-great-grandfather, led the family tree with his wife Madeline and their only child, Beaumont, who married Florence. The couple allegedly had four children. The three portraits of Annabelle, Agnes, Beatrice were empty though but nevertheless named. The fourth was of George, their youngest child and Vanessa's grandfather.

"Grandfather never mentioned his sisters and neither did you, Mother. And here's the next surprise, my mother next to Ormerod and Clementine. The paint is probably still wet! And here you are," she said, looking at Bartholomew. "Next to your brother, Cromwell. Never heard of him."

"What's wrong, Cousin Vanessa? Not eating this gorgeous steak. I can't believe it, a vegetarian in a meat family," said Bartholomew in a petty attempt to change the subject and to save his Aunt Felicity from further interrogation. "How the devil does that work?"

"I suppose it works the same as leading a bank into bankruptcy by mismanagement and being rewarded with a high position in the Food Standards Ministry," she answered seriously.

"You forgot the mighty fine pension I received for my efforts and success," added Bartholomew, and almost choked on his meat when he noticed his own foolishness.

"Oh, don't worry about her, Bartholomew. She's been acting like this since returning from her trip to the temple. But now it is time for Vanessa to learn her responsibilities about our company and about our family," added Felicity, looking sternly at her daughter. "And Bartholomew is just the person to help, as he is head of the Ministry dealing with food allocation and standards. And did you know …"

Felicity Forsythe-Twyke carried on talking but Vanessa sat there deep in thought as the mention of food allocation brought back memories of what was discovered in Clementine's office at the equestrian centre. She had never told her family about her incredible adventure, and how could she? Instead, she had explained her disappearance with a story of seclusion at a Buddhist temple in Nepal, which was strangely never questioned by her mother. But, in reality, she had ended up in the mole world below. For a training mission to the Equestrian Centre, she had been turned into bird poo allowing her to infiltrate a cat, and, in the office, she overheard a conversation between her mother and Clementine about duck allocations to the meat processing plant. At the time, it made no sense to her. A minister was mentioned too, and influence in return for cooperation. Now that she learnt that the Food Standards Ministry had been in her family's hands for years and her Uncle Ormerod also worked for the government, somehow, the pieces were falling into place. But why would Bartholomew also open a branch for the company in Bangkok? She looked in deep suspicion at her mother and newly-found Aunt Clementine. Her family were really quite devious.

***

Strange things were going on in Upper Molehampton on this moonlit night. A line of newly-dug molehills suddenly sprouted up on the grass verge of the road leading away from the toy shop towards the river, with small antennas and periscopes rotating out of the tops to survey the deserted street. Not long after, strange whirring and ticking broke the silence. The noise got louder until suddenly a convoy of tiny toy cars zig-zagged erratically along the road chased by the watchful cats and dogs patrolling the streets. Invisible to those living above the ground though, these remote-controlled and wind-up cars were operated by scavenging moles sitting in the driver's seat. Bouncing over stones and bumps, the expert drivers weaved their way through the legs of their pursuers like racing car drivers in a mad race for the finish line. Their journey reached the post office where they flew up a small ramp, bounced across the grass and headed directly towards a post box. A rope coming out of the slot was violently yanked upwards and a trap door in the grass opened, just as the cars were about to collide with the post box. The cars hurtled into the depths below and the door banged shut leaving the bemused cats and dogs scratching and sniffing the surface.

***

Sergeant Dawson was sitting in his office. He was the well-loved policeman in the villages and, since very recently, responsible for both Lower and Upper Molehampton. He was popular for his friendly and jovial nature, but he will never be remembered for successfully solving cases. Quite the contrary. Files of unsolved cases had been sitting on his desk for a long time: the mysterious theft of glass jars from the jam jar factory years ago, the kidnapping of Connor Jackson and the disappearance of both Vanessa Forsythe-Twyke as well as Ludwig, Mr Rye's dog. Thankfully, all three returned safely to their homes, but the reasons for their disappearance remain a mystery to him.

At first, the tea in his mug started slopping around and then his toast began vibrating just as he was about to take a bite. He stopped and looked around as a strange noise got closer and his whole office started shaking. It appeared to be coming from directly below him and sounded like high-speed digging with some sort of machinery. The shaking and rumbling crossed from one side of his office to the other and then became quieter until it disappeared. He sat there confused and wondering what on earth this unexplained noise was. And for the second time too.

He shook his head in disbelief and opened his mouth again, the piece of toast about to be devoured when his phone rang. He reluctantly picked up the receiver with a loud tut then listened intently.

"Let me confirm. Your whole stock of toy cars has disappeared from your shop. And no signs of a break in. Yes, this is not the first time these items have vanished into thin air. I know. Yes, I know. I am patrolling more often than I used to and am convinced the Kennedy brothers have nothing to do with it. You have called the insurance company and ordered a new supply of cars. Yes, I can understand your anger, Mr Player, but ..."

Sergeant Dawson had dropped his toast and jotted down notes. Now he glumly looked into the receiver as the line went dead, then threw the notes on top of the other files. This would become file number seven.

"How could this keep on happening in our peaceful Molehamptons?" he asked himself out loud. "It used to be quiet here and now so many odd thefts are reported!"

Earlier in the day, another phone call from the municipality's landfill reported all of the discarded smartphones and other electrical items had been removed from the skips. Most strange indeed. Who would steal waste? And, if that wasn't enough, stolen digging equipment was reported by a local construction company. Case files five and six! Sergeant Dawson contemplated if the digging noise and all of the missing items could somehow be connected. He was just about to tuck into his food again when the door was thrown open.

"Oh, you again, Mr Poacher."

"Yes, it's me again. And if you want to know why I am here, then you should be able to guess," the hunter blurted out angrily.

"Let me think. Your socks are missing, and another block of salt gone too."

"Two blocks of salt. But there's more. I saw a monk in one of those traditional orange robes at the edge of the forest and there's also a tremendous increase in these strange rabbits. They are bouncing through the village freely and I want to know what you are doing about it."

Sergeant Dawson had incidentally spoken to Mr Lawnsworthy earlier today who had also been complaining about these rabbits. The keen gardener had told him they were just standing around in Trout Lane and appeared to be keeping watch over number three. He even claimed the rabbits were up to other strange things and he had witnessed them doing building work at Mr Jackson's house. Rabbits pushing little wheelbarrows with rubble out of the house and returning with freshly mixed concrete. Pure nonsense, but, of course, he wouldn't tell any of this to Mr Poacher.

"I wasn't aware being a monk was a crime but thank you for letting me know. However, I must agree, quite out of place in our serene villages. I'll keep an eye out for him. Regarding the rabbits, Mr Poacher, you're the hunter here so maybe you could give me some expert advice about what to do."

"As they are not damaging any crops, I am not sure if I am allowed to …"

His sentence was cut short by the loud arrival of two women, bursting through the door.

"Your situation will not be solved by the Sergeant here, Mr Poacher. He's always too busy munching toast and slurping tea. Just look at this pile of unsolved cases which have been sitting on his desk for ages. I bet you he still hasn't solved any of them, have you now?"

"Look, Mrs Forsythe-Twyke. That's not quite true. Those who strangely went missing all returned safe and sound."

"Yes, and no thanks to you."

"And what may I do for you today, Mrs Forsythe-Twyke?" sighed the Sergeant in an effort to change the subject.

"As the mayoress, I decided to pay you a quick visit to make sure everything here is shipshape. You are now the police officer for both villages, and I have to know we are all safe. In particular, as my nephew, Bartholomew, will now be spending some time here. He's a government minister and you should be extra vigilant, Sergeant. Oh, there's more. At dinner yesterday evening, we discussed some issues raised by residents. It appears, they are concerned about an unusual number of rabbits running through the streets, especially in the vicinity of Trout Lane. Good you are also here, Mr Poacher, as your services might now be required."

***

The darkness was broken by the flashing and vibrating of a smartphone.

"Yes. Cromwell here," said the Chihuahua, looking at the display.

"Mr Cromwell, it's the Minister, we can put our plan into operation now. Mobilise our troops and start the public unrest," he said spitting the words out in machine gun like bursts.

"Do it, Minister. Set the wheels in motion," whispered Cromwell.

***

"Did you hear that, Felicity?"

"Hear what, Jemima?"

"The voice of course! I heard a voice saying, 'set the wheels in motion'," quipped Jemima.

"I didn't hear anything. Where did this voice come from?"

"From my handbag, Felicity. Most strange. And nobody else heard it?" she asked, looking rather embarrassed at the others.

"Let me check for you." Felicity was the first to break the awkward silence as she stuck her arm out and rudely snatched Jemima's handbag. "And who's this little darling hiding in here?" she said, pulling out Cromwell. "Was that you talking?" asked Felicity sarcastically. "There, there, you beautiful, sweet cutie. I really must take you for walks more often, Cromwell. And you should visit your Aunty Felicity at every opportunity!"

Jemima grabbed her handbag and composed herself, then stomped out of the police station with her friend on her heels. "Felicity, why do you like to borrow my darling Cromwell here so much? Why not get your own dog?"

"Because he is just divine and, as you know, I just love animals. He is the sweetest dog in the village, and we have such a special relationship. One could believe we are family," she laughed.

Suddenly, everyone's attention was distracted by strong vibrations and a loud rumbling sound.

"What's that?" blurted out Jemima and craned over to hear exactly where the noise was coming from. "It sounds like someone is digging right below us."

***

The bare room resembled a heavily reinforced bunker, with only a dull light on the ceiling illuminating a desk, a computer and a telephone. A man in a pin-striped suit grabbed for the receiver and dialled a number.

"Bartholomew Forsythe-Twyke here. Start the next phase and send her the pictures. Also forward the notes for Mr Jackson. It's the right time to trigger him into action."

Mrs Grae de Vole made notes as she carefully listened to his instructions. She smiled and immediately left her office at the equestrian centre. In one of the horse stalls, she cleared away the straw and opened a trap door before retrieving a package. She had chosen a perfect place to keep her secrets. Who would ever suspect the innocent looking Mrs Grae de Vole? Least of all that silly Clementine Farrow. She looked at the two notes and pictures with a mischievous grin and jumped on her bicycle. As always, she was prepared to complete her secretive mission without question and with utmost loyalty. Long had she waited for this.

***

The Forsythe-Twyke mansion was riddled with secret passageways and hidden rooms, concealing the dark plots being hatched. One might presume Felicity Forsythe-Twyke to be the ringleader, but she was merely a pawn in the game. Yes, she was now the mayoress of both Molehamptons and the owner of the Food Factory, but it was, in fact, her brother, Ormerod, who was pulling the strings behind the carefully thought-out plots. He worked in the secret service and had been taught ever so well by his devious father, George. Everything that happened had a reason. Felicity's interest in Cromwell, the covering up of Clementine's true identity and Bartholomew's work with the government. Mrs Grae de Vole also played an important part in the family's spider-web of deceit which went much further than the Molehamptons. She had been assigned by Ormerod to monitor Clementine Farrow until the moment was right to reveal her as the secret sister. What's more, Mrs Grae de Vole was the eyes and ears for Ormerod and also served in the employment of the Cult of Azoth. In her role as marketing manager, she constantly fed back valid information she gleaned from the influential people frequenting the equestrian centre. The Forsythe-Twyke family and their sinister accomplices were more dangerous than one might think.

***

Jemima Kingston was back sitting at her desk, intensively staring at a large, padded envelope marked 'Top Secret' and addressed personally to her. She picked it up and slowly inspected it for signs of who the sender could be.

"Strange. This is not the normal protocol to receive such top-secret material. No sender's name and no document receipt. This is out of the ordinary indeed," she whispered to herself.

It was also curious that the envelope was already sitting on her desk when she returned after visiting Sergeant Dawson, her assistant claiming she knew nothing about it. She carefully prised open the envelope and removed a purple file. It was evidently quite old, well-used and bound with yellow string. When she looked at the first page her eyes opened widely, and the colour immediately drained from her face. She dropped the file as though discarding something evil.

"Oh my God! It can't be."

With tears welling up and visibly in shock, Jemima Kingston put her head in her hands and stared at her desk shaking uncontrollably. It wasn't the first time. Just a few days ago she received an anonymous letter with an old black and white photograph of a young man, now in a frame on her desk. Somebody unauthorised clearly had access to her office and was sending her messages. But why would someone want to rake up her painful past? She managed to recompose herself and picked up her phone in a mixture of shock and anger.

"Mr Jackson. Come to my office and make it quick!"

***

Meanwhile, in the depths of Jemima Kingston's handbag, Cromwell dialled a number and spoke.

"She has fallen for the bait. Make sure you send her the other pictures soon. That should really tip her over the edge."

Chapter Three
The Wheels are Set in Motion

Crossed legged, a monk sat on a small mat deep in meditation. He was bald, as Buddhist monks are, and wore a bright saffron robe. In front of him was an ornately carved wooden chest and far behind him rose a huge spire soaring high into the sky. It had four sides, larger at its base and became narrower as it rose majestically upwards, perfectly symmetrical and covered in thousands of sculptures. The pinnacle was tall and elongated with a trident set on the top. Four smaller spires were at the four corners of this vast structure. The beautiful temple shimmered in a golden colour in the Bangkok night sky.

A small door in the wooden box opened and a mole in a smart suit came out. It stood in front of the meditating monk and looked up towards him.

The mole spoke slowly and clearly. "I have news—the information trail is close to being compromised. We always knew this would eventually happen. Thankfully, my real role down here is still unknown by the other moles, and I trust your fellow monks don't know what you do either."

There was no reaction from the monk, still deep in meditation.

"The enemy must not get there first," spat out the mole. "The prize has to be protected at all costs."

His eyes flickered open, and the monk briefly spoke before returning to his silent state. "We've already sent an observer to the Molehamptons then Mr Jackson will be triggered into action. We have set the wheels in motion."

***

I worked for the government's secret information collection agency and held the highest security clearance possible. So, you think a thorough interrogation would have followed after my kidnapping. But no. Nothing. Instead, a mysterious letter from a government agency found in my house stated I was on a mission. It appeared the organisation I came across, Eternity Projects, had a long reach and in the highest of government circles. Mrs Kingston accepted the circumstances and welcomed me back, no questions asked. I naturally wanted to know more about this Eternity Project, but all searches I made at work just came up with a blank. I had a lot of resources at my disposal and to find no information at all about this ultra-secret organisation was alarming.

Then the strangest of things happened when I was summoned to Mrs Kingston's office.

"Good morning, Mrs Kingston. You sent for me?"

"Ah yes. So nice to see you again," she replied, putting a handkerchief in her sleeve. "Are you well, Mr Jackson?"

"Yeees," I replied slowly, a little wary of the situation, as she had never enquired about my well-being before. I stood there looking around her office and noticed a picture frame on her desk. It was turned on a slight angle and showed a young man, and it definitely wasn't there the last time I was here. Maybe her husband, I thought to myself. I didn't know anything about her personal affairs and had no idea if she was married, as we all kept ourselves private in our department. She was holding a battered purple file and seemed on edge, which was quite out of character. Her eyes were red, and I was sure she had been crying.

She was just about to speak when a bark stopped Mrs Kingston in her tracks. I looked around the room to see where the noise came from.

"Oh, don't worry, Mr Jackson," she said, opening her handbag to reveal a Chihuahua. "It's just Mr Cromwell saying hello."

Cromwell poked his head out of the handbag, flashed his teeth and gnarled at me.

"Now, now, that's no way to treat the nice Mr Jackson." Cromwell and I just stared at each other before Mrs Kingston broke the silence.

"Anybody would think you already know each other," she laughed, shoving an uncomfortable looking Cromwell back into her bag. "Now, down to business, Mr Jackson. I have an important job for you, and for you alone. I am promoting you and, at the same time, putting you in sole charge of a top-secret intelligence gathering operation."

I was taken aback and just managed to stammer a reply to her. "Thank you for your trust in me, Mrs Kingston. This is really quite unexpected to say the least. May I ask who I should gather information on?"

"Mrs Forsythe-Twyke and the rest of her devious family!"

Now I was really shocked. "But I thought you were friends?"

"We are, but please do not question the task, Mr Jackson. You are the most suited for such a secret and sensitive job and you are to report only to me. I don't care how you do it: legal, illegal or costs, as it is all irrelevant. Just find out all you can about them, and I really mean all. You are close to her daughter I hear, so it shouldn't prove too difficult for you to find out some facts."

My boss now appeared agitated and out of sorts, somehow nervous and also sad. Something had happened, and she wasn't letting on.

"And what exactly am I looking for?"

"Everything, Mr Jackson. Anything and everything. In particular, who is in the family. I suggest you delve deep into their secrets."

"When should I begin?"

"Yesterday, Mr Jackson."

"And there's more. Another family member is now here. Bartholomew Forsythe-Twyke, and he is Felicity's nephew. There's something fishy about him, and the timing of his arrival cannot be an accident.

I left the room with Cromwell gnarling at me as Mrs Kingston took him out of her bag to stroke him yet again.

***

I don't lead a normal life and certainly not according to Mr Lawnsworthy. My rabbits kept everyone nattering about me, much to my amusement. Only the other day, some rabbits bounced brazenly down Trout Lane carrying my shopping bags. Mr Lawnsworthy witnessed everything from his living room. But three other weird things happened which were not of my making.

43

Firstly, I received little notes with only one word written on them. The first one was taped to my house door and read *Kloss's*. Another note under the windscreen wiper of my car had *Town* on it. A further note stuck to the handlebars of my bicycle read *Old*. I kept the three random notes in a box in the hallway and often pondered over their possible meaning. The fact someone was trying to communicate with me was quite evident, but I didn't have enough to fathom out this riddle. Also, the messages seemed to come from more than one source as the notes with *Kloss's* and *Old* were written by the same hand and someone else wrote the note with *Town*.

Secondly, I noticed Cleopatra sometimes disappeared in the dead of night. She was an extremely secretive guard dog, and never told me about her former life or activities, so this was not out of character. But what was she up to? I asked Basil and Ludwig if they could follow and, excited at the prospect, readily agreed. They saw Cleopatra approach the village green, extremely carefully, making sure she wasn't being followed, then circling the whole green twice. Ludwig kept his distance, and Basil observed from above. She went to a bench, stuck her snout below the seat and retrieved an envelope, before going to another bench and wedging it in exactly the same position before leaving. About an hour later, a man came and collected the envelope. It was a classic dead drop, and the man was none other than my neighbour, Mr Pike. But this was not the end. I personally went to the village green and sat on the bench used for the Pike's dead drop. Careful not to be noticed, I dropped something on the floor and stooped down to pick it up. There was a small wooden opening built underneath the seat, and on checking, found other benches had them too. Further observation of the village green also uncovered a dead drop for Gertrude Lawnsworthy.

Oh yes, there was something else about Cleopatra—she kept on stealing my well-worn tartan slippers. Without the slightest hint of remorse, she manged to chew holes into them and leave her slimy slobber inside. On challenging her, she informed me that she does it to keep her jaws strong and teeth clean. Another excuse was the moles had programmed her as a dog and I should take the issue up directly with them.

And finally, I have to tell you about what happened only today, alerted by the banging shut of my post flap. Two envelopes were lying on my hallway floor and a person dressed in orange moving outside. I was confronted by a bald man of South Asian origin with a scar on his face. He carried a leather satchel over his shoulder and just stood there staring at me. Why was a Buddhist monk in front of my door? Two rabbits bounced up and stood next to the monk, looking up at him, as though they were just as surprised as I was about his presence. We stood there, just looking at each other for a while before I broke the silence.

"Hello. What can I do for you?"

The monk didn't reply and carried on peering at me without an expression on his face.

"Do you need any help? Are you lost?"

Again, the monk didn't reply and, after a short moment of further silence, he turned around and just walked slowly and purposefully down the street, taking a good look at all the houses. I stared after him, not quite believing what had just happened, shook my head and returned into my house to pick up the letters. While receiving letters is not exciting or out of the ordinary, this was different, as my name had been written ever so stylishly with a fountain pen, which is not very common today. Very personal, I thought to myself as I looked closely at the handwriting and realised the letters had again been sent by two different people. I opened one envelope and found a personally written letter from my bank manager, Mr Pence, asking me to come in and receive a key to a safe deposit box left to me by my late father. He passed away many years ago and his will long since dealt with. I never knew he had such a box or left anything else for me. This was highly peculiar, and I suspected some strange events were about to begin again. I then opened the second envelope to find a grainy black and white photograph of a man who appeared to be going through immigration, possibly at an airport. I turned it over but there was nothing written and no indication who this person was, or better even, why it was sent to me. The picture was evidently from CCTV but the details with date and time had been cut off. However, in the background I made out a blurred sign—*Welcome to Suvarnabhumi Airport*. I picked up the phone and called Mr Pence.

These independent events were not by chance but, I was convinced, somehow connected. The timing was too much of a coincidence; and that I don't believe in. The wheels of something had just been set in motion.

Chapter Four
Sowing the Seeds of Discontent

"Oh, not again. What is it now?" questioned an annoyed mole.

"Mrs Simpson, we've just had another return due to inferior quality issues. We reprogrammed an old dog's processor to go back as a wild boar in the forest. All protocols were followed: the memory extracted, stored, the processor wiped clean and then reprogramed for its new assignment."

"Then, what went wrong, Mr Harris?"

"The reprogramming didn't work properly because the wild boar could only bark. Unfortunately, we only realised this afterwards when it was too late."

"A barking wild boar? Really Mr Harris, I've heard about this problem so often lately, but it never used to happen before. I really don't understand what is happening these days."

"I don't work in the reprogramming department, but I understand they are extremely short-staffed, and the quality therefore affected."

"We are all understaffed these days, Mr Harris, but we have to cope if we do not want to end up in the Food Factory. Those of us in the quality department have an ever-increasing workload with dwindling resources. I really shouldn't talk like that," she said with an element of fear in her voice. "What other issues do we have today?" quickly changing the subject.

"Oh, normal issues which we are used to these days. A golden retriever which couldn't retrieve, a cat scared of heights and also a bald sheep."

"I don't know what this place is coming to, Mr Harris. I fear for the future."

Mr Harris looked kindly at the obviously sad Mrs Simpson. "All I know is if I do not perform one hundred quality checks per day, then the factory it is for me."

"These new performance targets are set far too high. Our numbers are reducing but tasks on the up. It used to be so stable and organised here, but now it appears we're all in competition with one another to achieve continuously increasing targets. This surely cannot end well, Mr Harris."

***

A paw stabbed out towards the screen as a bright, flashing light rudely interrupted the darkness.

"Cromwell here. What can you report, Minister?"

"Mr Cromwell, the increase in allocation for the Food Factory is taking its toll on morale and especially performance. The planned economy has practically ceased to function and been replaced by competition. Nobody wants to end up in the food chain so individual performance is permanently under the spotlight. The teams press-ganging workers into the Food Factory are terribly busy, and also extremely unpopular, as you can imagine. It's just the toxic climate you tasked me to create."

"When can the rioting begin, Minister? I want the government ousted so we can end this corrupt regime. We need to replace the planned economy with the competition of a free market as soon as possible, and this time we will not fail."

"Soon, Mr Cromwell, very soon indeed. I have organised for something to happen which should tip the scales and trigger protests against the regime. The protests will, of course, be peaceful, like most are below the surface, but my teams will infiltrate and ensure violence breaks out, something unheard of down here. The police and military will be powerless to intervene, as they are also disgruntled and understaffed like everyone else. They will sympathise with the protestors. Anyhow, we have enough of our operatives hiding amongst their ranks."

"Good work, Minister, considering you are forced to work with me." Cromwell stabbed at the phone, and the small space where the Chihuahua was speaking returned to darkness.

Clearly sad about what he was doing, the minster dabbed tears from his furry face.

***

The mole, dressed in immaculately pressed military fatigues, stood next to the flipchart, looking at the many empty seats in front of him.

"Sergeant. Where are the scavenging crews?" He barked out.

"I'm afraid this is all we've been sent, and I was informed it is all we will get for the foreseeable future."

"But, Sergeant, we can't possibly scavenge all the things we are ordered to get with so few."

"I totally agree with you, Sir, but you're not going to like this. I was also informed we have to keep records of who collected what and how long they took to complete the scavenging task. The records must be shown openly to encourage competition amongst the crews. Also, everything on the list must be scavenged, regardless of the risk."

"But that means sending the teams out three or four times in one night. Not only is that risky but mistakes will be made. I must speak to higher authority immediately."

"Sir, I would like to advise caution."

The captain, obviously angry, nevertheless started his briefing to a fearful looking group of scavengers. He now had to improvise and adapt his meticulously planned task list on the flipchart. Everyone knew the consequences of failure.

Team one was assigned to collect light bulbs from the electrical shop in Lower. The captain quickly scanned through his list to see what other jobs were close by. A visit to the petrol station for transport shuttle fuel was added along with plastic cutlery from the toy shop. Three stations in one night were risky and a tall order, therefore the captain advised his crews to hide items should they not be able to bring the goods back on time. He briefed the other scavenging crews to bring back every day needed items like blocks of salt from the forest, food, furniture, building materials and, of course, socks. And, finally, he instructed a special team consisting of thirty members to go back to Mr Player's toy shop and steal his latest delivery of toy cars.

***

Sergeant Dawson, known to enjoy a beer in the Anchor Inn after he had finished his duty, was just leaving to walk the short distance home. He was weaving ever so gently and singing something quietly to himself. A rustling sound in the undergrowth made him suddenly stop in his tracks and look. After stooping down, he was amazed to see three stuffed socks moving all by themselves through the grass. This was not the first time he had witnessed moving socks in the village green and, rightly puzzled again, the Sergeant looked to see what was moving them. Socks cannot move by themselves. He immediately suspected some local boys pulling them on strings to fool him, but a feel of his hand in the grass proved otherwise. There was no string and this was not a trick. Eventually they stopped moving. Sergeant Dawson jabbed his hand out and grabbed one of them, but the other two socks immediately jumped forward with a jolt, gathered speed and left for the cover of the bushes. Despite his surprise, he immediately set off in hot pursuit. They became even faster and started to zig-zag across the grass, attempting to get away from him. The last time this happened, he never found out where the socks disappeared to, but this time he was going to win!

"Stop!" he shouted out as he stomped through the village green, the beam of his torch trying to follow the socks.

"Sergeant Dawson. Is that you?"

He stopped, looked up and saw Mr Rye, who he had just been drinking with.

"Why are you running strangely across the village green?" he asked with concern as he approached his friend. "And why do you have a stuffed sock in your hand? You didn't have that when you left a few minutes ago."

"I'm trying to catch these darn socks. I've got one of them and two more are on the loose." He stuffed his captured sock into Mr Rye's hands and waddled away into the darkness.

Mr Rye shook his head in disbelief and then followed suit. The Sergeant was now lying on the ground, one hand holding a sock, his other hand stuck down a molehill.

"What are you doing?"

"As I just said. I'm trying to catch these moving socks and it seems I've been successful as he excitedly pulled the third out of the molehill.

"Are you sure you're OK? We only had a few beers, and I certainly didn't see any moving socks."

"Well, what do I have in my hands then? And there's something in them," he added triumphantly.

"But they must have already been lying there, and you just picked them up. Socks cannot move by themselves, can they? You know we've had a big problem with litter in the village in the last days. Lower has always been so tidy and suddenly people are leaving things all over the place. I even saw a block of salt on the side of the road yesterday. Why would someone leave it there? I don't know what this place is coming to."

"Anyhow, the socks were definitely moving. What do you think I was running after?" He then shook the contents of one sock onto the grass.

Mr Rye bent down to inspect. "What do we have there then? Plastic toy forks and small light bulbs. And what's in this one?" as Mr Rye squeezed out a plastic bottle. "It smells of petrol," he said, sniffing the top.

"But why would anyone put toy cutlery, light bulbs and petrol in socks and then go down this molehill here?"

"And what do you mean by 'anyone'?" Mr Rye asked bemusedly. "There's nobody here apart from us. I suggest we keep this between ourselves and don't write a report. I think you will have difficulty explaining it and, besides, who would believe you?"

Both their heads suddenly turned towards an opening between two shops, illuminated by a streetlight.

"Did you also see that?" asked Sergeant Dawson.

"I saw something orange quickly disappear over there."

"Yes, me too. I am sure it was a person."

***

A cow, a badger and a woman, all of whom appeared quite flustered, entered the briefing room.

"That was a close call!" the first member of team one blurted out, panting heavily.

"What happened?" demanded the captain.

"The goods were scavenged as instructed, but time was against us. We made too much noise trying to get the socks through the undergrowth and back to the molehill. Unfortunately, there was a policeman on the village green, and he gave chase after hearing us. For such a large man, he was really quick, and he even managed to fish one out of the molehill. I'm afraid we've returned empty-handed."

"I'm going to have to write a report about this," said the captain formally while the three members of the scavenging team looked on with resignation, knowing their expected fate.

***

The austere looking mole sat at his desk, staring intently around the walls of his office, adorned with portraits of imposing moles, all wearing the same clothes as the person now admiring them. He was wearing a black pin-striped suit, light pink shirt, black bowler hat and had an umbrella propped up against the side of the lavishly carved wooden desk. The moles illustrated in exquisite golden frames depicted power and prestige, but the mole sitting at his desk portrayed a different image. His grey whiskered face bore the marks of worry, fatigue and sadness, unlike his predecessors, all of whose eyes were now disapprovingly looking down directly towards him. His eyes now hovered over the telephone, sitting on a large leather mat next to a bottle of ink and a quill, as if expecting a call. Eventually, the ringing shattered the silence, and his old hand stretched reluctantly for the receiver.

"The President, speaking."

"Dear Mr President. I have the weekly plan for you."

***

The large conference room was full of moles awaiting the President's entrance, their loud bickering drowning out the click-clack of the umbrella's metal tip as he approached. It wasn't too long ago the conference room epitomised power, style and orderly discipline. The latter, like so many things below, had waned in the last months. Normally, the President's approach was enough to hush the room into a respectful silence, but not today. The noise in the conference room was nearly unbearable, with ministers hurling accusations at each other about lack of staff, shoddy quality control, missing supplies, performance measures and much more.

"Order! Order! Ministers, please!" shouted out the President, but it was to no avail as the loud arguments persisted. It took the President repeated blows of his hammer to eventually bring some sort of peace to the room. "Ministers, let us begin our weekly meeting and may I remind you to treat this occasion with more respect and discipline. Minister for Logistics, what have you to report today?"

The minister stood up with a glum look on his face. "I only have unwelcome news, I'm afraid to say. Owing to the continued lack of replacements, I am unable to keep up with demand. This is not new, and I have been telling you all for months, but I can now say the situation is critical, and we are severely lacking some key supplies." He looked seriously at the President and all the moles, finally settling his gaze on the Minster for Allocations.

Other ministers started shouting their agreement and venting their anger at each other, especially to the Minister for Allocation. The President looked old and frail, appearing to have already lost control of the meeting.

The Minister for Logistics then did something unthinkable not too long ago. He turned towards the President, pointed his finger at him and at the top of his voice shouted, "And Mr President, what are you doing about it?" The room now fell into a hushed silence, knowing the minister had overstepped his mark.

The President was agitated, not accustomed to being challenged in such a fashion. He stood up slowly, cleared his throat and looked long and hard. "Minster for Logistics, I understand your frustration, but the allocations come from higher authority, and we can only implement what we are given. It is not for us to question the system. Our role in this world is to manage allocations, whether we find it correct or not. We strongly trust in our planned economy, and we must also believe just as strongly as those above know what they are doing. Do not blame the Minister for Allocations as he is merely carrying out my orders and I am also following mine. We have to adhere to the plan."

"So, who is this higher authority you often talk about?" the Minister for Education chimed in, followed by a round of banging on the table in agreement.

"I am not at liberty to say. For as long as we have administered memories and the life cycle above, the allocation system has worked like this. I am sure there is a good reason. Only I have contact to higher authority and no President has ever questioned the system."

The Minister for Culture stood up without being invited and expressed his discontent about everyone working in fear of being sent to the Food Factory. Loyalty to the system and good honest graft had been replaced by unrealistic performance checks and dangerous competition.

"And, fellow ministers, some of us sitting here are to blame for this situation," he exclaimed, looking disapprovingly at his colleagues. "One moment you're obeying the President and the next moment plotting against the system."

This was now too much for the cornered President who abruptly closed the meeting and left his bickering ministers as he exited unnoticed. Colonel Pickle dutifully closed the door and took a good look around to check they were alone and not overheard.

"Ah, Colonel, somebody I can trust at last. I believe you should send in your troops to show we are in control and to allay any fears down here. We need to calm things down, and quickly," whispered the President in short erratic bursts.

"I believe that would inflame the already tense situation. It seems an external organisation is orchestrating events and sending in troops would play into their hands."

"It must be connected to the memory thieves, and it is your job to find out."

"Mr President, there are no loose ends and only you and I know what happened," answered Colonel Pickle, lying about most of the facts. He reaffirmed what happened with the memory thieves. Colonel Bacon was the scapegoat for the theft of Professor Wingnut, and decommissioned along with everyone who knew about it, including Mr Jackson and compatriots. The Professor's jar was now stored under high security in the memory warehouse and only the Colonel knew its location. However, the traitorous minster was still at large as well as Mr Cromwell.

"But who, Colonel Pickle? Who?"

"I have some suspicions, but whoever it is, is an expert in deception. Someone on the surface is behind this, Mr President. Of that I am quite sure. They are the ones sowing the seeds of discontent."

"It seems I can only trust you. What do you propose?"

" I should go to the surface on a special operations mission."

Colonel Pickle then explained his plan. He was already investigating some ministers and keeping them under strict surveillance, but whoever it was couldn't be working alone. Support must be coming from humans.

"The culprit must be the one least suspected, and an expert at covering their own tracks down here. The scent might be better picked up on the surface. They will eventually make a mistake and I will be there to pounce."

"Who else to hunt down an expert in espionage than an expert in espionage himself. But Colonel, be quick about it. I don't know how long we can keep a lid on this and when our enemies know you have gone… well, I don't even want to think of it. What will happen to the world if our system is wrestled away by humans. They are naturally greedy and must be kept in check. Animals take only what they need to live, whereas humans take everything. A free market led by humans will be based on greed, competition and ultimate destruction. Mark my words, Colonel. It is our responsibility to stop them."

"Mr President, I suggest you keep a low profile whilst I am away, and you might want to consider a secret hideout with someone to take care of you. You must be prepared for the worst though. You might not survive this, and I believe the time has now come to consider nominating a successor. Someone you can one hundred percent trust," added Colonel Pickle slyly.

The President looked seriously at the Colonel, then his expression changed to one of sadness and he changed the subject. "Colonel, you never knew your parents, but I did. Your father was a Brigadier and died when you were a toddler and your mother, Beatrice, just disappeared off the face of the earth. The military school you went to on the surface became your family. I decided to look out for you when you eventually came down here, and that I have done without your knowledge. I put you into the special operations directorate and then had you converted to a mole, the highest lifeform down here. It was not all down to me, and you deserved your promotions and the position you have."

"Why are you telling me this now?"

"Going to the surface might uncover some things you are not prepared for, and there are deep, dark secrets I know of. Be careful with the truth—if you can find it out there at all. Where will you start?"

"With the devious Forsythe-Twyke family."

Chapter Five
The Wooden Hut

Memorabilia from river life and scenes of the Molehamptons decorated the bar and restaurant. A polished ship's wheel took centre stage behind the counter where Mrs Draught was busy pulling beers for the thirsty guests. I looked out of the window, taking in the beautiful scene with the River Angler gently winding its way down the valley. A huge horn sat on the restaurant's terrace, blown to welcome visiting tourist ships. There were also three wooden huts at the entrance of the campsite, a recent acquisition from the owner for cyclists and canoeists to stay overnight. Today, the huts were empty.

Some rabbits were busy bouncing around on a forklift truck on the road leading to the old ferry crossing. It seemed out of place, as there was no construction work going on. And then, there in the half-light of the evening, I saw the monk again, just standing and looking in my direction. Why on earth was he following me? The smell of a wooden fire and gorgeous smoked fish wafted into the bar. The trout at the campsite was a local delicacy and people came from afar to enjoy the succulent delight.

I was sitting in the campsite bar waiting for Vanessa to arrive, reflecting on what I knew about the Forsythe-Twyke family, and it wasn't much. Either they were exceptionally good at covering their tracks, or there really was nothing interesting to find. Strangely, the records provided little information for such a prominent family.

So, what had I found out until now? Felicity Forsythe-Twyke married Farquhar Ogulburt-Dilingbrush, thankfully taking her surname as nobody was able to pronounce his. However, he was rarely seen, rumoured to be mad and held in the mansion under medical supervision. Felicity's only child was Vanessa, and she also had a brother called Ormerod who married Clarissa Hammonsond-Spike. They had two children: Bartholomew and someone else with no name or records. Apparently, this person died in a tragic accident.

Felicity's father, George, married Isabelle Smythe-Couper. He ran and owned the Food Factory, which he had inherited despite being the youngest of four. Records showed he had three elder sisters, but this is where the trail went cold—no names and all records removed. There must be a darn good reason for it. Even my access to highly classified information proved useless, which meant they were hiding something and, therefore, somebody in power was protecting them.

I then stumbled on a remarkable connection with the Secret Service. Montague Forsythe-Twyke, George's grandfather, had worked in the upper echelons of the Foreign Office and widely believed to have set up the modern-day Secret Service Bureau in 1909. George founded the secret listening station in Upper Molehampton on the first of November 1919, officially known as the Government Code and Cypher School. The history of the organisation I worked for had never interested me, but now it did. And then I found out Ormerod was also listed in the Secret Service, but all searches ended up in a dead-end, as though he only existed as a ghost in the organisation.

I had to find a way to quiz Vanessa about this, but would have to be careful, not wanting to give away what I was doing or even abuse my friendship with her. But the real reason for me sitting here waiting to meet Vanessa started two days ago. Apart from the letter from the bank, a picture of an unknown person and some notes, I then received another message from a quite unexpected source.

***

Colonel Pickle sat alone in his office, staring at the wall in deep concentration, fiddling with a small tablet bottle in his paws. His office was decorated with his proud military past. Squadron pictures, oil paintings depicting famous battles, plaques, swords and different uniforms he had worn. He was brooding over what the President had told him and for the first time thought about his family outside of the military. From a child he knew nothing different apart from college, the officers' academy and military service, unfortunately cut short by a tragic accident. He always believed his death appeared highly odd and somewhat planned. But, of course, it was too late, and he never had any proof, just a lasting suspicion. Fortunately, he was able to carry on with life and his military career down here, and for that he was forever in debt to the President. Special operations followed conversion to a mole, the ultimate aspiration for any life form, and then a steady rise through the ranks eventually becoming the President's right-hand mole. And now the opportunity to be President was tantalisingly close.

His father was a Brigadier and his mother called Beatrice, but he had no information about any other family members. The military was his family. Normally, Colonel Pickle had access to all memories, and he could simply find out more information by interrogating his father's memory. However, the memory interrogation machine had broken down, coincidentally at the same time as Connor Jackson escaped, and was still to be repaired.

The President evidently knew things he did not, and the Colonel had also lied about what happened to Connor Jackson and the Professor's glass jar. Events were now getting out of control and this was disturbing. He looked hard at the bottle in his paws, unscrewed the top and tipped out a tablet onto his desk. This was the last remaining from Professor Wingnut's secret project. Cromwell stole one, Connor Jackson and his team took four, Cleopatra one and the last was lying here. The tablet giving the possibility to pass freely from the mole realm below the ground to the world above as a real and complete life form. The tablet of life and freedom. He had kept it hidden and now the time had come to use it.

But the Colonel had a problem. Cleopatra used constantly changing exit points and, despite the Colonel's position, he did not know where these were. Also, conducting his work secretly and alone was going to be challenging. He looked long and hard at the ceiling and then a sly smile appeared on his face. It was time to take things into his own paws and gain back control of Professor Wingnut at the same time as cutting the communication channel with the Forsythe-Twykes. He had to protect himself and his possible future as President.

***

A glint of something shining at the top of a molehill caught my attention, and it immediately reminded me of the circumstances finding Professor Wingnut's jar which started my adventures. My face turned to disgust as my feet were greeted by wet slobber as I put on my slippers.

"Cleopatra!" I shouted out, annoyed that this keeps happening.

Armed with wet slippers and dressing gown, I ventured out into the garden, with an ever-observant Cleopatra in the bushes. There it was again. Something shiny was twinkling in the sun and I found a small piece of metal just poking out the top of the mound. I picked it up to find a piece of string attached, which I then pulled until a small plastic bag popped out. Inside was a simple hand-written message.

I need to get out. Help! CP.

Colonel Pickle didn't know how to get out and he wanted my help. The greenhouse in the Pikes' garden was removed shortly after our escape and I naturally didn't know of any other exit points. Not wanting to ask the Pikes, the only solution was to call the number on the letter from the mysterious government agency called Eternity Properties. But when I called, found the number no longer existed. Strange! How could such an organisation just disappear. But I had also heard of the Eternity Project and suspected they must be connected, so decided an internet search might reveal something. And it certainly did. The website was simple with only the name of the company, Eternity Projects, and a contact form. My message was short—*How do I extract a pickle from a molehill in an emergency? CJ.*

***

The next day the response came. My doorbell rang, accompanied by loud barking from Cleopatra. I quickly poked my head out and was sure I saw the rear wheel of a bicycle disappear next to the Pikes' house. A piece of paper was sticking out of my post flap which I quickly grabbed whilst nervously checking around to see if anyone else was watching. There he was yet again—the monk in orange robes standing at the entrance of Trout Lane. I hastily retreated back in the house and away from his gaze. The note simply informed me to wait at the campsite bar at ten tomorrow evening. Deep below the ground, Colonel Pickle also received a note. A message for his eyes only, informing him to be at a location in the tunnel system at an exact time.

I pressed a button and the sound of thumping feet soon reverberated through my house as rabbits sprang into my hallway. After passing on my instructions, they bound up Trout Lane before separating—one went to Vanessa, one to Ludwig and the other to Basil. It was time to reconvene.

***

Vanessa sauntered through the door, looked disapprovingly around her with her upper lip curled up before heading in my direction.

"See you haven't changed much, Miss Forsythe-Twyke!"

Cleopatra, sitting dutifully next to my side, gnarled and flashed her teeth in disapproval at her snotty behaviour.

"Just keeping up appearances when I come to this side of the river, Connor. Nice to see you by the way. But why here of all places? We usually meet in Anglerton away from prying eyes."

"This time I really do want prying eyes. It's happening again. Pickle!"

"Oh, stop talking in riddles will you, man. What pickles are you talking about?"

"Not pickles, but the pickle. Colonel Pickle. He wants to get out and contacted me for help. He must need something more, but I don't know what."

"Why involve me? I am just happy to be back on the surface, even though I have to share my life with my strange family and forget that ghastly episode down below."

"Yes, I am sorry, but I fear something is starting again and I don't want to face it alone." I looked out of the window in the direction of the river, with Vanessa following my gaze.

"And you thought you would involve all of us?" she asked, looking at Ludwig and Basil sitting next to each other on the riverbank.

"Yes, strength in numbers. We have an hour to wait so I thought we could chew the fat as it's been a while. But Vanessa, that's not all, as other strange events are going on. I've received small pieces of paper with single words written on them. First was the word *Kloss's*, then *Town*, and then *Old*. And more recently, a fourth note with *China* on it. I have no idea who's sending them and what they mean. The words are just so random. But I know from the handwriting they were sent by two different people, and one of them is old."

"It's a riddle and you are the one to solve it. With such a good analytical brain, I am surprised you haven't worked it out already."

"But there's more, Vanessa," I added quietly and leaning towards her. "I'm being followed by a Buddhist monk!"

"Now I've heard it all. The next thing you are going to tell me is you are a martial arts expert."

"It's true, Vanessa. He appears completely randomly and just observes me. He even came up to my house door and just stared at me. I asked him some questions, but he didn't answer. And do you know what? He's here. Earlier, I saw a glimpse of his orange robes up the road towards the ferry."

Vanessa's face suddenly changed. One moment attentive and the next lost in her thoughts and sad. She changed the subject. "I had an awful family dinner and was introduced to another relative, my cousin Bartholomew. I do not know where she digs them up from. It's strange, Connor, because the dining room now has a wall full of portraits set out like a family tree. I am finding out things I never knew. My grandfather had three sisters and never told me."

My ears pricked up on hearing the three sisters. I frowned with interest at Vanessa. "George's sisters? How interesting. Tell me more. I love hearing about family intrigues."

"Don't mock me, Connor, and since when have you been interested in my family? How do you know my grandfather's name anyhow?" Vanessa replied suspiciously. "Their names are Annabelle, Agnes and Beatrice by the way.

"I am always interested in what you tell me. You could tell me more about your family, the Food Factory and changes in the village. That should keep us busy until Colonel Pickle arrives."

"Where exactly are we to meet him? He's a mole and I can't exactly see him strolling into the bar and sitting down next to us."

"No idea," I said shrugging at her. "The dinner didn't go well?" I asked, attempting to steer the conversation back to her family.

"No, it didn't. I knew the day would come and now it is here. My mum is actively trying to get me to take over some functions at the Factory and I am the next in line, so at some stage I will inherit the horrible place. Apparently, Bartholomew is here to help. He's actually a failed banker then rewarded with a lucrative government position. Apparently, we have new business in Thailand, and he has set up an office in Bangkok. He's a real numpty! But, Connor," she added seriously, "I have such a dilemma. I know they are all scheming and up to no good, but they are my family, and you know blood is thicker than water."

"I can really understand you, but please go on," I prompted with genuine interest.

"I was having a family dinner and guess who walked in and joined us?"

"No idea!"

"Mr and Mrs Farrow. Ormerod, my uncle, kept it secret from the whole family but decided now of all times to let the cat out of the bag."

"What secret?"

"Mrs Farrow is my mother's half-sister and only Ormerod knew. Her mother was one of the household staff, but we don't know who it was. There are family secrets, Connor, and I am sure they are drip feeding me information for some reason. Don't tell anyone though as I have to keep it a secret."

"But I don't understand. Mrs Farrow works with your mother, passing allocations to the moles from her office. You witnessed it when you infiltrated a cat. She may not have known she was your mother's half-sister, but she certainly knows about the world of moles. Why? The plot is getting more complicated, and your mother is up to something."

"Yes, she is scheming, Connor, and I have no idea what she is doing. I have the feeling this is being choreographed, but not by her—she is not clever enough and neither is Bartholomew."

"Why on earth would they keep that a secret and only announce it now? And even the Farrows didn't know. Unbelievable."

"Yes, and Ludwig didn't suspect anything when he infiltrated Bill on our special operations mission. I will never forget what he did when he dressed as a woman and stuck his head in his food at the dinner table. I still remind Ludwig about it, much to his embarrassment!" I said, as we both started laughing.

"You are not the only person to bring it up," explained Vanessa, just managing to control her laughing bouts. "They even mentioned it at the dinner, but Bill naturally had no idea what they were talking about."

"Do you think you have any more relatives hidden away in the closet?" I chuckled trying to keep the conversation going."

"Well, yes. Bartholomew apparently had a brother who died in an accident, but nobody speaks of it. His name is Cromwell."

I now filled in the last gaps in my head.

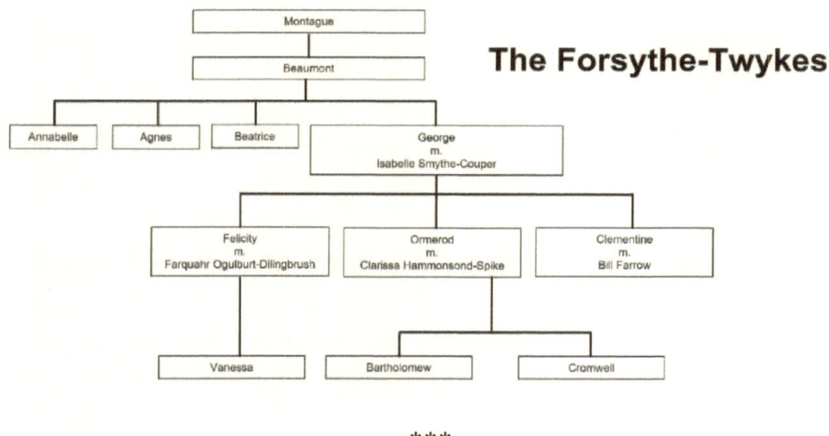

***

The transport shuttle banged its way along the dark tunnel, light only coming from the exhaust flames spewing out the back. Although all shuttle journeys were rather bumpy owing to their high speeds and crazy drivers, this one seemed to be badly driven. There were no passengers, just a solitary driver wearing a leather jacket, flying cap and goggles struggling to keep the contraption under control. With great effort, he pulled the brake lever and the shuttle skewered to a halt in a long-disused station. Colonel Pickle let out a sigh of relief.

The only light in the pitch darkness was his military torch, covered in green paper to dim the beam. After taking off his disguise, Colonel

Pickle proudly stood there in his pristine military uniform. Earlier, he had walked unrecognised through crowds of different animals protesting against the current system. His police and military units stood by as some agitators riled the crowds until violence broke out. Experienced as he was in military operations; he was untrained as a driver and this showed as he commandeered an empty shuttle, unprofessionally steering his way to the given location at the outer reaches of the mole world.

He took out a tablet from his pocket, looked at it long and hard, his face deep in serious concentration, before slowly putting it into his mouth. Using his paws, he carefully scraped away some earth at the end of the tunnel revealing a wooden door, took a look behind to make sure he was really alone before ever so quietly prizing it open. The Colonel was now standing at the bottom of a shaft with a ladder and, clutching his torch in his teeth, went up until his head eventually smacked against something hard. The hatch made a loud creaking noise as he pushed up until his head was poking out in a room with a strong smell of fresh wood. He remained motionless, just observing to see if anyone was there.

After satisfying himself he was alone, he climbed out and found himself standing in a small room, only dimly lit from outside. He was in a wooden hut with two beds, table, chair and windows, one directly above the bed. Even though he was head of Special Operations, he didn't often have the opportunity to come to the surface. The smell of fresh air instantly brought back memories of his former life and he had to pinch himself in order to stay focused.

Using his paws, he pulled himself up the back of the chair and then onto the bed, but he was still too small to look out of the window. Care had to be taken, but he had to be seen by someone as this was his prearranged exit point and Connor Jackson had to be waiting for him somewhere. He heard voices and a door bang shut. Standing on the bed offered him a better overview of the hut. And there it was. Just above the light switch a hand-written note was pinned to the wall with the words 'press here' and an arrow pointing to the light switch. The Colonel walked to the end of the bed but the gap to the table was too large, so had to hang underneath a cable and pull himself across. He dropped onto the table and pressed the switch. The hut was suddenly bathed in bright light, followed by a hissing sound and white gas pumped into the room to start the transformation process. An indescribable strange sensation was happening in his body as his properties changed in a process allowing him to pass freely to the surface and back. Other creatures would feel stretched at this point as they were transformed back to their original height, but Colonel Pickle remained in his original mole size. Below the ground, all creatures were the same size as moles, leaving Colonel Pickle now tiny in comparison to giant humans. It was time for someone to come, and he just hoped it was Connor Jackson.

***

Vanessa and I now sat alone in an empty bar, oblivious to Mrs Draught wanting to close up and go home.

"I thought you said ten o'clock, Connor?"

"I did because that was what I was told. Come on, Vanessa, it's only fifteen minutes past."

Our eyes simultaneously darted towards the hut.

"Look. There's a light on over there. And I can see smoke in there too," whispered Vanessa. "This must be our cue."

The lights in the bar were switched off as we got up to leave. But unknown to us, a squadron of pigeons had taken off from Mr Tinker's ironmonger store and were now hovering above the campsite, the range finding mice looking for their targets.

***

The Kennedy brothers, dressed in their standard red tracksuits, had been sitting in the bushes for some time now, waiting for the right moment. As soon as the lights of the pub were switched off, they made their move. They crept silently towards the forklift, hunched over and careful not to be seen. Joe Kennedy switched the motor on and drove behind Gavin, who walked towards the campsite entrance and directly towards the three wooden huts. Gavin pointed to one of them, oblivious to the fact a light was on, and somebody might be inside. Joe hit the hut with a loud thud, the forks thankfully going directly underneath and, at a thumbs up signal from his brother, lifted it up with a loud cracking and grating noise as it was ripped from its base. The light in the hut was immediately extinguished as the cables flew out of the ground in a flash of sparks. Once it was off the ground, cables hanging loosely underneath, Joe quickly reversed and turned the forklift one hundred and eighty degrees, with the hut hanging precariously above the ground. Gavin jumped onto the back of the forklift, and they drove straight out of the campsite and down the road, with the hut swaying dangerously on the forks. The appearance of a monk dressed in orange robes, who was just standing at the side of the road observing their actions, distracted the brothers as they trundled past.

***

The Colonel was sitting bolt upright on the table with white smoke swirling around him. He had straightened out his immaculately pressed uniform and fixed his gaze on a point on the wall, his peaked hat just covering the top of his eyes. The noise of an approaching engine jolted him out of his concentration.

"And about time too," said the Colonel out loud. "I can't stand unpunctuality."

The noise was now uncomfortably close, so the Colonel stood up, wanting to be ready to get out, but an almighty blow to the hut sent him staggering over and he fell from the table, just catching hold of a cable in time. The hut was now lurching erratically from side to side and up and down before being plunged into darkness. He held on to the cable with all his strength, but another violent shake sent him flying, fortunately right onto the soft bed. The shaking carried on, causing him to bounce up and down on the mattress. He was now going so high he sometimes saw out of the window. On one upwards motion he stuck out his arms and caught hold of the window ledge and was now hanging on with all of his might, just managing to peer out.

What he saw made him shake his head in disbelief. Connor Jackson and Vanessa Forsythe-Twyke running after the hut, closely followed by a dog, a low flying duck, some rabbits and a squadron of pigeons.

***

The Kennedy brothers were yet again out of luck. Sergeant Dawson had received a tip off and was now waiting beside his police car, blocking the road and the Kennedy's escape route. He switched on his blue flashing lights and waited for the shaky hut and forklift to come to a halt.

"Joe Kennedy and Gavin Kennedy, you are both under arrest," he proudly shouted out. He didn't get to do this often.

He walked towards them but tripped over a white block, which seemed to have appeared on the road from nowhere and went sprawling on the road. He pushed his large body up with a groan and straightened his uniform.

"Damn rubbish!" he shouted in shock and looked down. "Salt! Salt! Why is there a large block of salt on the road? I am sure it wasn't there a few minutes ago," he said surprised and bent down to pick it up.

He composed himself then proceeded to read them their rights. "You have the right to remain …What the heck is going on now?" he exclaimed.

A fluffle of rabbits bound along the road and stopped straight in front of him. If that wasn't enough, two people arrived, then a dog followed by a duck flattering down to land next to them. Unseen by Sergeant Dawson, the pigeons were now coming towards him – hard, fast and low!

"Mr Jackson and Miss Forsythe-Twyke! Why are you here? And who is this lot?" indicating to the animals.

"Oh, just going for a walk, Sergeant. Lovely night for a stroll, don't you think?" I replied, walking around the hut, trying to get a look through the window.

"Just come away. This is a crime scene now."

We were interrupted by the sound of approaching sirens followed shortly by a police car screeching to a halt. At exactly the same time, a loud beating of wings made us all look up into the sky. A fatal mistake. The whistling of objects screaming through the sky fixed our gaze upwards as poo bombs started splatting all around us. Thankfully, I was not hit but Ludwig and Basil took direct splats on their heads. A few second later, they turned and ran away, having just been infiltrated by the Special Operation Directorate.

"Ah, Sergeant Dawson. Good to see you caught these two dimwits in the act. Well done!"

"Thank you, Detective Inspector James," he proudly replied.

"We'll take over now, Sergeant. The Kennedy brothers will come with us, and you can make sure the hut is put back where it belongs. File your report to me by first thing in the morning and list everything in the hut too."

"Yes. Yes, of course, ma'am."

"What's that noise?" she suddenly asked, her eyes darting towards the ground.

It was that deep rumbling noise again followed by intense shaking as though someone was digging right below our feet. All our eyes followed the noise from the left to the right before it disappeared away into the distance.

"And another thing, Sergeant," she quipped, getting back on track. "Why is there a Buddhist monk dressed in orange robes observing us?"

Sergeant Dawson looked at Detective Inspector James in astonishment and shrugged his shoulders.

"Look, he's over there," she said turning around and pointing down the road. "Oh. He's gone!" Detective Inspector James was now the one to look surprised and, to avoid any further embarrassment, changed the subject. "And Sergeant. Why are you carrying a block of salt?"

Sergeant Dawson looked down and then returned his gaze to the Detective Inspector.

"No idea," he replied, shrugging his shoulders yet again.

"And get rid of all of these rabbits too!"

Chapter Six
Finding Colonel Pickle

The lights of their head torches reflected brightly off the shimmering white tunnel. But this one was quite unlike the others. It was encased in white crystal-like bricks, forming a square cavity for the two moles to move along. Its smooth shaft seemed to go endlessly into the distance, as if hollowed out of a massive block of white stone. The front mole had a military bearing about him and was using a stick to count his steps. He was dressed in perfectly ironed blue overalls with creases so sharp you could cut paper on them, and his glossy shoes shone like mirrors in the light. The second mole was dressed in a black pin-striped suit, a light pink shirt and a black bowler hat, using an umbrella for support.

"That's it," whispered the front mole.

"Have you found it, Fraser?"

"Yes, I believe I have, Mr President. Exactly 347 steps using this pace stick form the beginning of the shaft. That's what Colonel Pickle told me. He told me to feel the wall when we get to this point so the opening must be somewhere here."

"They all look the same to me," uttered the President, looking frustratingly at the smooth walls.

"To me also, but the Colonel leaves nothing to chance. If he said it is here, then it must be here," exclaimed Fraser confidently.

Fraser started feeling with his hands, slowly stroking the walls up and down until he stopped and went back over a small area.

"Got it," he smiled and pushed the brick gently, making a loud grating sound as it moved. Fraser put all his weight behind it and shoved the white stone as hard as he could. With a thud, it fell down on the other side, leaving a perfectly square hole in the wall. The chamber on the other side had three basic beds, a table, chairs and a large box with food and drinks. It was sparse but functional.

"We should be safe here. Come on, Mr President. Let me help you in," offered Fraser.

"Thank you. What is this place anyhow?"

"This, Mr President, is the salt store. It is a vast hall with hundreds of blocks and a maze of shafts like this one, worming their way through the salt structures. It is so easy to get disoriented down here as each shaft looks exactly the same. Colonel Pickle was right when he said it was the best place to hide if the need arose. And it is. Nobody will find you here," Fraser explained.

"And what happens now?" asked the President.

"You wait," Fraser replied. "Wait until Colonel Pickle comes back for you. It is now too dangerous since the protests turned violent."

"I can't believe it. Violent protests. We've never had such behaviour down here."

"Mr President, it is evidently being orchestrated by other powers. The police just stand to the side and there are agitators egging the crowd on. Someone wants you toppled."

The President, now a shadow of his former self, lent on his umbrella and lowered himself onto a chair. "Fraser, thank you for helping me, but I fear I have failed. There is no hope for us anymore. The power of greed and the free market have unfortunately won."

"It is only over when we are beaten, and whilst we are here, and Colonel Pickle is still out there, then we have a chance. It is not over yet!" Fraser exclaimed defiantly.

The President just looked at the floor in defeat, Fraser's words doing nothing to buck him up.

"Mr President, I'm sorry but I have to go back now, or my absence will be noted," said Fraser sadly, heading to the hole in the wall as he made to leave.

***

"How are we going to get this thing back?" Sergeant Dawson looked questioningly at Vanessa and me.

"Why are you asking me? This is a crime scene, and I can't touch anything," I sarcastically quipped back.

"Oh, gentlemen, you are really quite useless. I'll do it," said Vanessa, tutting at them then climbed into the driver's cabin.

"You?"

"Yes, me, Sergeant Dawson. I once helped out in the warehouse and learnt to drive these things. It was really boring in the house, so I used to escape and do exciting things. Mother never knew of course, and she would have had a fit had she known. And gentlemen, it should stay like that."

Without saying another word, she turned the key and slowly drove the forklift, with the hut still balancing precariously on the forks, back down the road towards the campsite. Her serious face turned into a grin as she saw a mole dressed in a military uniform bouncing up and down on something, appearing in the window every time the hut went over a bump.

"Slowly now, Miss Forsythe-Twyke," ordered Sergeant Dawson, trying to act as if he knew what he was doing. "Left a bit. Down. Gently now."

Vanessa completely ignored him and with great skill and precision placed the hut exactly back down where it was before and got out of the cab.

"What now?" she asked, frowning at them.

"The inventory. I have to take a list of everything in the hut," yawned Sergeant Dawson at them.

"You look tired, Sergeant. Let me do it for you. Just go home, make a tea, eat some biscuits and go to bed. It's late you know, and you still have to write your report," I advised, trying to get rid of him.

"You're up to something, Mr Jackson. I'm not stupid, you know, but I just don't know what. Not yet anyhow. You can both stay here and be useful," he said opening the door of the hut.

Sergeant Dawson shone his torch in front of him, flashing it around. I nervously followed him, watching the torch beam, hoping he wouldn't find Colonel Pickle. The hut was a complete muddle. The table was on its side, chairs fallen over, crockery and cutlery strewn over the floor.

"This is a right mess. Why, in heaven's name, did they want to steal this hut?"

"Oh, probably just for firewood," I replied. "Let's just make a quick list and go."

"Why are you in such a hurry, Mr Jackson? Something to hide?"

Vanessa prodded me hard in the ribs and whispered, "Just shut up you idiot. He's too suspicious."

"Do something useful, Mr Jackson, and please hold my torch so I can see what I am writing," the sergeant said, taking his notebook out of his breast pocket and then started to list all the items.

He was serious when he said listing everything as I showed the way with his torch, getting more nervous as I knew we would soon uncover Colonel Pickle.

"Come on, Mr Jackson, you are not really putting much effort in, are you? Turn everything over and look everywhere."

He was correct, of course, and I was trying to slow things down, knowing I had to be here when he found the Colonel. We looked everywhere, in everything and under everything. But there was no sign of the Colonel.

"Well, I think that's it. It's all listed. Thank you for your help."

Sergeant Dawson put his notebook back in his pocket and started to turn around towards the door when he suddenly stopped.

"Did you see that?"

"See what?" I replied.

"The pillow. It moved."

"Surely not, Sergeant. Must have been the torchlight playing with your eyes."

But there was no stopping him. Sergeant Dawson picked up the pillow to find a mole in an immaculate military uniform lying on the bed. There was a deathly silence in the hut as we all stood motionless, staring at the mole.

"Don't just stand there!" barked the mole, standing up and straightening his uniform. The mole put on its peaked cap and stood on the bed at attention.

"It speaks! The mole can speak," stammered Sergeant Dawson, holding on to the chair for support, his mouth wide open in disbelief.

"Of course, I can speak."

"Erm. I think I can explain this."

"How, Mr Jackson, can you explain why there is a mole in military uniform in this hut? And not only that, but it can also speak!"

"'It' has a name. My name is Colonel Pickle."

***

"Gavin and Joe Kennedy, back with us again I see. You must really like us here!" quizzed Detective Inspector James, looking at them across the table. "Please tell me, why did you want to steal the wooden hut? It's not exactly inconspicuous, and you didn't get far at all."

Joe coughed and looked down at the table in obvious embarrassment at getting caught yet again. "Well, it's like this. A few days ago, someone called me and told us to go to the campsite and get the hut. He told me there was something of value in it and we could have the contents, and the hut itself."

"He. Who is he?"

"Dunno. Just said his name was Cromwell. He sounded kinda important, you know."

"And where were you to take it?"

"Dunno. I had to call the number when we finished the job."

"Dunno? You don't know much. And I don't suppose you have the number, do you?"

"It's in my phone. Last call."

Detective Inspector James picked up Joe's greasy phone with the tips of her fingers and a visible look of disgust on her face.

"Let's find out then," she said as she stabbed at the call button and put the phone close to her ear, making sure there was no physical contact.

***

Sergeant Dawson's face was still ashen as he put down his phone.

"That was Detective Inspector James. Apparently, someone with the name of Cromwell used Mrs Kingston's phone to call Joe Kennedy and told him to steal the hut. Mrs Kingston is on her way here now to give a statement," he rasped out in a trembling voice.

"Cromwell. Did you say Cromwell?" demanded the Colonel.

Sergeant Dawson's mouth opened wide as he sat in shock looking at a talking mole in military uniform. Colonel Pickle was standing between a block of salt and a pile of case files on the Sergeant's desk.

Sergeant Dawson looked down with amazement at Colonel Pickle, still clearly finding it impossible the mole could speak. It took him a while longer to find his words and eventually managed to gasp, "You know this Cromwell?"

"Yes, most certainly. Look, Sergeant Dawson, I understand you have your job to do but I really have important business with Mr Jackson here to attend to. Could you please let us go?"

The Sergeant's eyes grew ever wider, clearly unable to grasp the strange situation. "That I can't do. There's too much going on here and I need to get to the bottom of it," his voice still shaking in shock.

An uneasy silence then followed but didn't last long until the next surprise came. At first, Colonel Pickle's whiskers started fluttering, then Sergeant Dawson's police helmet began wobbling on his desk and finally a whirring and juddering noise came from below the room. It passed from one side of the office to the other before everything quietened down, and normality returned.

"That noise again. What was it?"

"That, Sergeant Dawson, is our moleways, our new transport system currently under construction. We are upgrading our old shuttle system with cars, but of course we need new tunnels and that is what you just heard. Drilling equipment is just much quicker than shovels."

"So, you thieving moles are responsible for all of the missing things recently: Mr Player's toy cars, the electronic devices and drilling equipment?" Sergeant Dawson's face turned even whiter as he struggled to take this in.

"Thieving moles? No, Sergeant. We scavenge and acquire what we need. We are not thieves!"

I thought it now the right time to solve his unsolved cases and explain about Colonel Pickle's world of moles. I sat next to Sergeant Dawson and slowly told him about the glass jar I found in my garden, triggering a series of strange events culminating in my kidnapping and the mysterious disappearance of Vanessa and Mr Rye's dog. We all entered a world right below our feet where the moles administer our memories and life forms on earth. I described the transport shuttles, arrivals process, shops and other facilities and also Colonel Pickle's Special Operations Directorate. The Sergeant's face remained unmoved the whole time with his eyes only flickering when I mentioned the true purpose of Mr Tinker's pigeons, infiltration missions and scavenging. Finally, I told him all about Professor Wingnut, his research and why he was able to understand Colonel Pickle.

"Now you know where your socks and Mr Poacher's salt blocks disappear to. Amongst other things of course!"

Sergeant Dawson moved for the first time since I began talking, a dumfounded look on his face. "And that is why I caught you talking to rabbits. I knew you were," he whispered, still understandably in complete shock.

I looked at his case files. "You could answer some of these too."

"But I can't write that in my reports. Everyone would think me mad."

Vanessa had until now been silent. "I've been thinking, Sergeant. How did you know to be at the campsite at exactly the right time?"

He had now managed to calm down a little and replied. "Easy. I got a tip off," showing Vanessa a slip of paper.

"Campsite. Tonight. Closing time. Kennedy brothers," read out Vanessa.

"Something strange is going on here," I said, looking at the Colonel. "It seems the same organisation which arranged your journey also tipped off the Sergeant. But why? Cromwell, Mrs Kingston, Colonel Pickle, the Kennedy brothers and the news your mother and Mrs Farrow are sisters. I can't believe there's not a connection somewhere here."

"Your mother and Mrs Farrow are sisters!" stammered Sergeant Dawson, his mouth wide open yet again.

"And another thing," added Vanessa, turning to face the Sergeant. "Did you tell Detective Inspector James about the tip off?"

"No. How did she then know to be there and just at the right time?"

"That is another question in this riddle to be solved," I said.

The sound of a car pulling up on the stones made them all look at Colonel Pickle.

"Yes," he muttered slowly, "what is it?"

Sergeant Dawson quickly picked up the Colonel and unceremoniously chucked him in his desk drawer just as the door opened.

"Mrs Kingston. Thank you for coming so quickly," said Sergeant Dawson, trying his best to act normally.

"Mr Jackson, what are you doing here? And with Miss Forsythe-Twyke. You have got nothing to do with this misadventure, have you?"

"Mrs Kingston, it was just pure coincidence we were at the campsite and witnessed everything. Should we leave now so you can give your statement in private?"

"Oh no, I would actually prefer you stayed. I have really nothing to …" she broke off in mid-sentence as a loud banging noise came from the desk. "What's that?"

"Get me out of here," came a muffled voice.

"Who said that?" Mrs Kingston exclaimed, looking around the room, followed by Cromwell poking his head out of her handbag and barking.

Sergeant Dawson kicked his desk. "Who said what?"

"I heard nothing. Did you, Vanessa?"

"No, Connor, no. Nothing at all."

"Hmm. Suspicious," replied Mrs Kingston, looking towards the desk. "And why is there a block of salt on your desk, Sergeant? And look, there's a small military peaked cap. What's more, there's a Buddhist monk wearing orange robes standing outside. Why?"

***

Felicity, Clementine and Bartholomew sat in plush chairs around the fireplace.

"We are nearly there. Total control is now within our grasp."

"Yes, Aunty Felicity. We will soon have full control if we play our cards right. We know where the Professor is, Colonel Pickle is now on the surface and the President in hiding. Our time has now come to wrestle control away from the moles and back to humans."

"Quite right, Bartholomew. We have everyone where we want them, and nobody will ever be able to challenge the Food Factory allocation again. But we are not finished yet as we really need the ingredients for the special tablets.

"Yes, it would have been easier if we'd successfully stolen the Professor and we could have found out from him directly. Now, I am not sure the Professor is of much use so we need to use another method, and I'm sure Mr Jackson will help us achieve our aims. We just need to feed him with the right information and let him do the work for us. Why put ourselves at risk? He will eventually lead us to the prize, of that I am quite sure," added Bartholomew with aplomb. "George and Montague would be extremely proud of us right now."

They all smiled at each other and chinked their glasses in celebration, Clementine not really understanding much about the conversation.

***

"And about time too!" shouted Colonel Pickle angrily as Sergeant Dawson put him back on the desk. He brushed himself off for the umpteenth time today, leaving biscuit crumbs on the surface.

"Have you been eating my biscuits?"

"I don't think you have the right to complain," said the Colonel, looking harshly. "And what happens now?" he barked out, looking around at everyone. "I came to the surface, at great risk to myself and the President, so I could meet Mr Jackson and I don't have time to waste."

"You are part of the crime scene and I have to include you in the inventory. And what's all of this about Cromwell? Who's he? Mrs Kingston is either a good liar or she really doesn't know anything about it."

"Cromwell is the dog in her bag," Colonel Pickle answered.

"A talking dog? Now I've heard it all. A talking dog, calling himself Cromwell, told the Kennedy brothers to steal the hut? And a talking mole. I can't put that in my report."

I coughed to interrupt their conversation. "It appears not, Sergeant. "And I think I know why," I turned my gaze to the Colonel. "They wanted you. Somebody told Cromwell you were coming. He unquestionably has something to do with the plot to steal Professor

78

Wingnut but how and why he is in my boss's handbag is a mystery. Until now I thought Mrs Kingston was an innocent bystander in all of this, but I am now having doubts."

"The mystery deepens and that is the reason why I am here," said the Colonel and then told me about the situation below the ground and how he was protecting the President.

"You are looking for who is behind this unrest and especially who is directing the Food Factory allocation. We don't have to look far. It's obviously something to do with my mother and our secretive family. I just don't know how she is involved. But, Colonel, you have warehouses full of memories, including those of my ancestors, and a machine to interrogate them. Surely, you've been able to puzzle together enough information to find out something credible?"

"Yes, Miss Forsythe-Twyke, you are quite correct. Normally we can do that, and it is exactly what I intended to do. But a crucial part of the memory reading machine went missing, coincidently just at the same time you all left. It has been rendered quite useless," declared the Colonel, looking suspiciously at me.

I just stared at the Colonel with a blank expression on my face.

"There is something more, Mr Jackson, and it is private. My father died when I was young and my mother, Beatrice, mysteriously disappeared. I would very much like to find out who they were and maybe even visit their graves. So, Mr Jackson, I trust you understand the importance of my mission."

"Hmm, I might be able to shed some light about the missing part," I sympathetically replied.

"Go on, Mr Jackson, this is very interesting indeed," exclaimed a visibly excited Sergeant Dawson.

"I took the part," I blurted out. "I took it as my insurance should anyone come for the Professor again. The Professor's memory is useless without the part. And I have both."

"I thought so," said Colonel Pickle, looking at me straight in the eyes.

"Hang on. Did you just say your mother was called Beatrice?"

"Yes, why do you ask Mr Jackson?"

I turned to Vanessa. "You mentioned three missing sisters, one of them called Beatrice. Maybe just a coincidence."

"Do you remember everything I say?"

"Because you mentioned it a short while ago, Vanessa. Don't you think it strange the same name has been used twice today already?"

"I agree and I think you are now imagining things," replied Vanessa with an annoyed look on her face. "And, Connor, why are you so interested in my family?"

I decided to now come clean about my investigations and told her what I had been up to.

"You've been spying on us. Using me. Why not just ask? And our conversation at the campsite tonight, well, you were fishing for information. How could you?"

Sergeant Dawson coughed to attract our attention. "Why, Mr Jackson, would you spy on the Forsythe-Twykes? I thought you were just a civil servant?" asking innocently.

"Enough!" the Colonel shouted. "You can discuss this at another time. We need, as a matter of urgency, to investigate and stop who is behind all of this. And quick. Mr Jackson, be prepared to go back below with the Professor and the part you stole. It is likely he knows who is behind all of this and who the secret minister is. He had himself decommissioned to prevent more technology getting in the wrong hands. But he was stolen, and you know the rest."

"I'm not going anywhere and certainly not back down there."

"I think you will find you have no choice. One of my special ops teams infiltrated your duck friend and he is now below for safekeeping. Basil will be sent to the Food Factory if you do not cooperate—you have your insurance, and I have mine. I will now stay the night with the kind Sergeant, and you have two days to prepare before we go below."

Sergeant Dawson's mouth dropped open again before he managed to ask, "Who's Basil?"

Chapter Seven
The Eternity Project

Colonel Pickle was up to no good! It must have been him who informed all parties he was coming to the surface, and he was in the perfect position to instigate trouble below the ground and imprison the President, allegedly for his own protection. And who best but the Colonel to take over should the President fall. Basil was his bargaining chip for Professor Wingnut's memory as he undoubtedly wanted to secure the secret technology for himself and protect his identity as the secret minister with direct contact to the Forsythe-Twykes. This was my suspicion, and I had two days to prepare with plenty to do.

Taped on my door was yet another note—this time the word *Field* written on it. I ripped it off and put it in the box with the other four notes, picture of the mystery person and letter from Mr Pence. Yes, the safe deposit box also had something to do with this, so off I went to the bank to see what this was all about.

"A pleasure to see you again, Connor, and after such a long time. Please take a seat. Back in a jiffy," added Mr Pence.

I waited for his footsteps to disappear before gingerly opening the box, half expecting something dangerous to jump out, but instead found a handwritten letter from my father.

Dearest son,

You are now reading this letter in the knowledge that death is not what it appears to be. I instructed Mr Pence to release this letter to you only when he receives authorisation from certain friends. This time has now come, and it is up to you to take up the mantle of our cause. Mr Pence is unaware of all matters below the ground and is just following orders. You, however, know more and have either already been below, or been informed about the realm of moles. Whatever happened, you must be back on the surface to read this letter, and for that I am grateful.

Connor, you have only received this letter because our enemy is too strong and is making a move. I'm sorry to involve you, but it is now up to you to stop them. You, or we, have been chosen for this task because we are outside of the family in question, and you know of which family I speak. Also, you possess a wonderful analytical mind and I suspect only you are up to the task of finding **him**. I'm sorry but I cannot tell you who **he** is, and that is because I do not know myself. In fact, nobody does. Our safety net has been set up in such a way the people involved only know parts of the puzzle. It would be far too dangerous if I, or others, know too much. This letter will hopefully set a chain reaction in progress, but only you, Connor, can find the next clues. Your ultimate mission is to find **him** and protect the secrets from the Cult of Azoth. I've followed your career carefully from down here, and I know you are up to it. To begin with, Connor, there is a clue in our house. I have hidden it purposefully so nobody apart from you can see or at least guess its importance. I also expect you to receive more information and prompts from other sources and you will know what to do.

You need to go below, no matter how hard it is, and interrogate two memories: mine and Professor Wingnut's and we will both reveal different information. My memory may be rather hard to find. Sorry, but that is for security reasons. I will say no more now but to wish you luck and success. And, Connor, don't trust anyone, even the people who you believe are close. And some you think are bad, are not. Follow your heart and you can then decide yourself.

Yours with love,

Dad

Some things about my father were beginning to make more sense to me. His strange behaviour when I was a child was connected to the mole world. He had something to do with special operations: collecting of thimbles and doll's house furniture. It was all for use below the ground, and that is exactly where I now had to return.

***

The beeping of a keypad preceded a longer alarm noise and the automatic unlocking of a door. A woman entered and quickly closed it firmly behind her, ensuring the lock was secure again. It was the only entry point into the soundproofed room which resembled a bunker. The desks against the walls were all covered with an array of sophisticated listening equipment and computers, maps of Lower and Upper Molehampton the only decoration on the walls. This was the bunker of one of the sleeper teams in the village.

"Do you have anything for us today?" asked a man, sitting at one of the desks, a younger boy next to him.

"Yes, dear. There was a letter at the dead drop for us."

"Well, darling, let's see what they want this time," taking it from his wife and checking the envelope carefully to see it hadn't been tampered with. He intently read the contents, nodding in understanding, before looking at the boy, "Earl, I have an errand for you."

***

Where would I have hidden it? My father collected many things but also loved maps and reading about other countries. The house was still much like my parents had left it so it must still be here. But where? And why do this alone? With a mischievous grin, I called the rabbits and after a quick briefing, they started pulling my house apart.

Anyone listening would have thought a violent burglary was going on as the sound of thumping feet and the crash of objects was easily heard outside. The contents of each drawer and cupboard were systematically emptied on the floor and all items thoroughly examined for anything out of the ordinary. Discarded items flew through the air and landed in a big pile until the floor was completely full. Despite the rabbits appearing not to pay any attention to careful handling, nothing was actually broken. And infuriatingly, after a thorough search of the rooms my parents used, nothing could be found. They bounced and pulled everything apart until only my bedroom remained unsearched. We started with my huge book collection, opening each one and flicking through in the vague hope of finding something. Ah yes, my world atlas, given to me as a child and now hopelessly out of date. A rabbit leafed through the pages with expert speed, getting quicker and quicker, then suddenly stopped, went back and handed me the atlas. An envelope was glued onto a page and written on the front was one word—*Kloss's*, one of the notes I had mysteriously received. And on which page was it? Bangkok!

***

Time was now of the essence and my investigations sped up as I turned my attention to my boss, Jemima Kingston—she was the one to set this all off with her role a bit of a riddle. What I found was a very sad story indeed. Her husband, or late husband I should say, Robert Kingston, used to be quite high up in the Secret Service and ran the listening station in the Molehamptons. He mysteriously disappeared some years ago and subsequently registered as dead, his body never found and prompting suspicion of foul play. Official records in the case uncovered some startling information. The Chief Investigating Officer into the death of Robert Kingston was none other than Ormerod Forsythe-Twyke. Now the plot was getting thicker.

Unfortunately, Jemima's sad story didn't end there as she was given away for adoption when she was a baby, her real parents choosing to remain anonymous. But when I read who adopted her, the colour drained from my face. Lawrence and Lily Wingnut. Jemima then grew up with her older stepbrother, Reginald, who became the renowned Professor Wingnut. Jemima's unlucky streak wasn't over because Reginald died at a fairly young age, in an accident apparently, directly after completing a research project on genes and cloning.

But there's more! Jemima Wingnut married Robert Kingston and his parents were Martin and Rose. There was information pertaining to Roberts's father, but nothing on Rose's side, not even a maiden name. I then checked the Wingnuts and found exactly the same pattern. There was indeed information on Lawrence Wingnut who married Lily, but as you might now guess, there was no information about her background either. It was as though Rose and Lily just arrived from outer space with no earlier history. So, who were they? I just couldn't connect the dots.

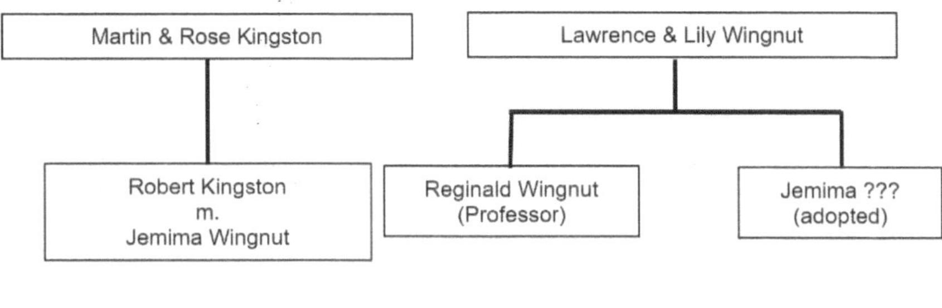

***

"What's happened here?" exclaimed Sergeant Dawson with a shocked expression on his face. "Has someone burgled you?"

Sergeant Dawson, Vanessa and Ludwig stood in my living room perusing the destruction.

But before I could answer, a muffled voice shouted out from somewhere in the room. "Get me out of this awful place."

The Sergeant removed a rather dishevelled Colonel Pickle who he had stuffed in his tall police hat.

"Don't do that again!" he ordered, glowering up at the innocent looking Sergeant.

Ludwig towered over Colonel Pickle, and gnarled, "I really hope for your sake you are looking after my dear friend. Should anything happen to Basil, I will hold you personally responsible."

Ludwig was with Basil when they were both attacked by pigeons with their loads of bird poo bombs. Both had taken direct hits and immediately been infiltrated. Basil went straight into the hands of his ambushers whilst Ludwig strode off aimlessly and sat under a tree. He later recalled the incident and the sensation of being taken over by an infiltrator. He had of course experienced it the other way when he took over Bill Farrow and did a really bad job passing for a human. He remembered being hit by the white slime and numbness slowly took over until he was unable to move. And then suddenly his body was taken over, and he was powerless to intervene. Sometime later, he woke up under a tree, absolutely no recollection of what had happened in the meantime. The numbness had disappeared, leaving him in control of his body again.

"Yes, Colonel, and not only from Ludwig! We will go below and take the Professor with us for interrogation. I trust, for your own safety, you keep your end of the bargain."

"And what exactly do you lot want to achieve down in that hole?" piped up Vanessa, turning around to glare directly at me. She had not uttered a thing since arriving, instead electing to stand away from the rest of us and stare out of the window.

"Achieve? We need to find out what the Professor knows, especially the connection between up here and the secret minister."

"You mean my family! And who will go with you on your crazy mission? Is it your intention to put us all at risk in a badly hatched plan?" By now her face was crunched up as Vanessa's fury was rising at each word she said.

Silence reverberated around the room, everyone observing the confrontation.

Ludwig was the first to break the awkward silence. "I'm going," he added seriously, "and he's coming with me," looking sternly in the Colonel's direction.

"You can't expect me to go after my own mother. I'm out of this," she spat out. "What do you think I can do down there in the world of half death, corruption and an outdated political system? Maybe it's good what's happening, and my mother really does manage to take full control of the Food Factory allocation," she said, looking around the room with a sneer. "My advice is don't be bribed by this disloyal crook," glaring at the Colonel. "Don't go but instead send him packing back to his dank hovel. And as for Basil. Well, he can end up in the Food Factory for all I care. He'll end up there sometime anyhow."

Vanessa turned around, leaving us all in shock at her outburst, and left the house, slamming the door loudly behind her.

Sergeant Dawson rather awkwardly asked, "Shall I make some tea then?"

***

Not even the rustling of trees interrupted the silence of Trout Lane as Cleopatra returned from one of her dead drop missions. Despite her excellent observational skills, she failed to see me waiting in the shadows outside dressed in a red dressing gown and my battered and chewed tartan slippers. I needed to go below the ground, but Colonel Pickle's arrival had been compromised and the greenhouse where I exited from not there anymore. Cleopatra was the only one I could trust and ask for help. I knew she had connections and worked quite separately from Colonel Pickle's organisation. We sat down on the floor of the shed, and I told her some of the things I had learnt, but certainly not all. Cleopatra then explained some amazing things which filled in quite a few gaps about my father, the Eternity Project and the Forsythe-Twykes.

The Eternity Project was set up as the interface between the mole leadership and the humans; the remnants of an old system created by two people: Beaumont Forsythe-Twyke and Oldfield Thomas. We will find out much more about them later. Anyhow, Beaumont was Felicity's grandfather and also father of the three sisters who disappeared—he represented the good side of the family. Sleepers were placed in the Molehamptons, and a dead drop system set up for messages. Cleopatra's job was, and still is, to operate the dead drop system.

Later, the Special Operations Department was set up and Professor Wingnut was involved in secret research to design tablets allowing ultra-secretive operatives to move above the ground in their own form. But the technology wasn't advanced enough, and some sent in the wrong size, others not being able to communicate. The Professor was eventually successful and designed special tablets allowing those below the ground to pass freely to the surface and back at will, retaining their original life form. He only made a few of these and everyone wanted the ingredients.

The attempted theft of the Professor's jar was just the tip of the iceberg and Cleopatra arranged for me to keep the Professor as it was too dangerous for any other side to get him—I should be the protector of his secrets. Nevertheless, she carried on passing messages, believing the sleepers still to be working in utmost secrecy for the good side.

However, the real motive to get hold of the Professor was not only his technical knowledge but who he knows. A secret person, a person really in control of the Eternity Project, and hidden far away, holding the key to the secrets of Azoth. Cleopatra told me the head of the project was only known by a precious few and his or her identity a safely guarded secret. But the Eternity Project was compromised by the Forsythe-Twykes trying to take over the organisation. The weak link in all of this was Professor Wingnut so a political officer was assigned to him to make sure the secrets stayed with the Forsythe-Twykes. And this political officer is none other than Bartholomew's brother who died in extremely strange circumstances. Some even say he was killed by his own family. His name was Cromwell.

The theft of the Professor's jar was part of Cromwell's elaborate plan. He stole a tablet and went to the surface, but it backfired, and I ended up with the jar. Now, he is sitting in my boss's handbag, but what has she got to do with all of this? She might have valuable information which the Forsythe-Twykes need. This is all slowly beginning to make sense and Cromwell can't get any further, so they need me to do it for them. My boss doesn't know and thinks Cromwell is a poor, abandoned dog and all the time he is using her.

"This technology is far too dangerous in their hands. I fear getting hold of the Professor is only part of their devious plan, and the allocation to the Food Factory just a sideshow. They want control of the Eternity Project," I said, looking Cleopatra straight in her eyes. "We need to get below as soon as possible, and you need to tell me how to do it."

"That might prove difficult, as I no longer have contact with my handler. I still keep on passing messages so the sleeper system must still function, therefore there must be access points. I suggest you simply write a letter explaining what has been going on and I deliver it to a dead drop and wait to see if anyone replies."

"And, Cleopatra, what of Colonel Pickle?"

"He had nothing to do with the Eternity Project, despite being in the Special Operations Department. Only a special few are and above his or my level. The only reason he had the only remaining tablet is because I gave it to him. He is the one who would gain most from the President's downfall. Don't trust Colonel Pickle!"

***

The man, woman, and young son sat in their room, looking at the map hanging on the wall.

"This is most out of the ordinary, Edith. We have to refuse this request and report back up the chain."

"Edward, how can we ignore this information? It seems our sleeper system and the Eternity Project have been compromised. Mr Jackson delivered the letter directly to our dead drop and addressed it personally to us. How could he know about us? Even we don't know our handler or other sleepers."

"Yes, dear, but as you know, we can't break cover under any circumstances."

"But this is not any other circumstance. Mr Jackson has even named Gertrude Lawnsworthy as another one of us. There is a mole in the mole world, and we have been compromised."

"Look, Edith, we are humans and run by the Eternity Project. Our job is not to ask questions or know these strange people and animals who mysteriously come out of our greenhouse and other places. To consider Mr Jackson's plea for help is treason. It is our duty to report it."

"Report it! Do you only follow orders, regardless of the consequences? Mr Jackson obviously knows who we are and could have reported us to the police when he came back through our greenhouse. But no, he didn't, and he has never mentioned it again. He just politely goes his own way as if nothing ever happened."

"He couldn't exactly report it, could he, Edith? How should he inform Sergeant Dawson that he died, but only a little, and then came back to life again through our smoke-filled greenhouse? He had no choice, dear, just as we have no choice."

"But we do have a choice, Edward. The choice between what is right and what is wrong. Mr Jackson is asking for our help to go back below and clearly at great risk to himself. He asked us because he came out of our greenhouse when we were the allocated access point. He also wrote he found an Eternity Project email address and used that to get Colonel Pickle out, whoever he is, and even that was compromised as there was a trap waiting for him. And, what's more, whoever left the letter knew exactly it was our bench. Mr Jackson is not working alone. How much more evidence do you need the system is rotten?"

"I see your point. What would you do, my darling?"

"I would go directly to Gertrude and tell her what we know. We are not the current access point and maybe she is. All Mr Jackson is asking is how to get back down below. He is not asking any more of us."

"OK, I agree, and I just hope Gertrude will not turn us in."

"Gertrude. Turn us in? No, I know her too well. And anyhow, I have a feeling she is rather anti-establishment at the moment after losing her job as the Forsythe-Twyke's cook in such circumstances. Disgusting to be treated like that after so many years loyal service," added Edith angrily.

"Yes, dreadful family. Wasn't her brother, the lovely Gerald Lawnsworthy opposite us, also treated the same way?"

"I believe so. Thrown out after such a long time and on such a pittance of a wage. No wonder he doesn't have a family. How could anyone raise children on such an income and, thankfully for him, he inherited his parents' house."

"Just thank goodness the Forsythe-Twykes have nothing to do with our business," sighed Edward.

"Quite. So, what is your decision?" Edith asked pointedly.

Edward turned to face their son. "Earl, get your shoes on. We're going to visit Gertrude."

"Ah, great, I get to eat her scrummy cake."

***

More than one party was feeding me with information, but who were they and what was their purpose? It was with this in mind, I pondered what I so far had? A stalking monk, a mystery person on a photograph, a letter from my father and a note in an atlas. Then there was Colonel Pickle's arrival, Jemima Kingston's role, Cromwell and the mysteries of the Forsythe-Twykes. What about the Eternity Project and the random notes—*Kloss's*, *Town*, *Old*, *China* and *Field*? I felt rather uninclined to get involved in the hunt for the secret person or to involve myself in the plots of the Forsythe-Twyke family. But one thing was for sure – I had to go back below, the place I put so much effort into escaping from.

Chapter Eight
Blood is Thicker than Water

The crackling and spitting of the glowing fire mesmerised Felicity, Clementine and Bartholomew Forsythe-Twyke, all sitting in their soft chairs and holding whiskey glasses.

It would be fair to say you believed Felicity to be behind all of the devious plotting, but that is actually quite far from the truth. The brain behind the scheming was conniving Ormerod, who only kept the family members in the loop when needed. Bartholomew worked closely with his father, and even he wasn't privy to everything, but unfortunately Felicity actually knew very little. She was only motivated by greed, and Ormerod knew that. Bartholomew stoked the fire, escaping sparks shooting up the chimney in an explosion of light before he broke the silence.

"How is my dear Cromwell doing?"

"As good as a dog living in a handbag can be. Could be worse and in the Food Factory," Felicity replied, trying to be funny.

"Aunty, please don't talk about him like that. His well-being is close to my heart. I am merely enquiring about how our work is going?"

"Cromwell is our eyes and ears on Jemima Kingston and constantly reports back about her activities. It's so good to have a spy deep in that building. Some time ago, she received a file and a picture which seemed to have affected her emotionally."

"And I hope you are comforting your friend," added Clementine in a caring manner.

"All in good time. She's been mumbling and rambling the whole time about how sad she is and what she loves always being taken away. Something to do with her father and late husband, I believe. I am sure you and Ormerod are up to things and not telling me!"

Bartholomew smirked to himself, hiding his mouth behind his glass.

"Yes, such a shame when her husband died a few years ago. Have they ever found his body?" asked Clementine with genuine care and innocence.

"No, never," butted in Bartholomew. "The police never found it and recorded it as a death."

"And in this emotional state, she ordered Mr Jackson to investigate our family, and in particular me. I'm not sure this is a good thing; what if he uncovers some of our secrets?" asked Felicity with a concerned look on her face.

"Mr Jackson is doing exactly what we want him to do, my darling aunty. He will uncover only what we intend, and our real secrets will remain hidden. My father has everything under control."

"This all sounds rather complicated," chimed in Clementine. "A dog called Cromwell spying on Jemima Kingston and reporting to a secret minister. Wasn't your late brother called Cromwell? And wasn't he standing next to you, Bartholomew, when he accidentally tripped over in front of a London bus?"

"Yes, he was, Clementine, and please do not involve yourself in such matters. Just report the allocations as I instructed you to do. And for your information, yes, it is complicated and for good reason."

Clementine looked rather put out. "It seems everyone has a role to play. Can't I do more important tasks, like something secretive?"

"Allocations are vitally important, my darling sister," Felicity replied. "It is the bedrock of our business, and therefore the funds for Ormerod's operations. Just remember he enlisted you in his clandestine operations many years ago. You are handsomely paid for the work you do and taught never to question your orders. We just never knew we were sisters, but it doesn't change anything."

"If you say so," replied Clementine glumly. "But I have always found it strange what the moles are up to below the ground. I just wish I knew more!"

Felicity looked proudly at both of them. "And I am sure my darling Vanessa will soon fight for our cause, too. She has most certainly already informed Mr Jackson we are sisters, and then we will make her rat on him."

"Yes, all we have to do is monitor and follow him once we have fed him with enough information. He can do our work for us. That pesky man can investigate and lead us to the prize!" added Bartholomew cunningly.

***

Jemima Kingston sat at her desk, cradling a glass of whisky, her eyes mesmerised by the golden-brown liquid swilling gently in her hands. She sipped at it between loud sobs, tears streaming down her face.

"Why? Why always me?" coughing her sad words out.

Strewn across her desk were various documents, newspaper clippings, the purple file, the picture of her late husband in a picture frame and an invitation to the annual Upper Molehampton horse show. Cromwell peered out of the top of her handbag, carefully taking in the scene.

She picked up the purple file and flicked through its contents for the hundredth time.

"Cromwell," she blubbed. "Cromwell, my real father is still alive and living in the Molehamptons and under my very nose. I can't believe after all these years the truth is finally coming out. But I don't have his name. Why? And who should send me such a file and omit his name. It's just so cruel."

She threw the file back on her desk, her sobs echoing around the office, and then picked up her late husband's picture.

"And my darling husband, Robert, taken from me in the prime of his life."

She carefully stood the picture frame back on her desk, blowing a kiss in its direction before picking up a newspaper clipping.

"And my dearest stepbrother too, the renowned Professor Wingnut. How nice, kind and clever he was. He died too, Cromwell," she snivelled, wiping the tears from her eyes with a handkerchief. "I know Felicity is behind all of this. Why is she raking up my painful past?" She patted Cromwell on his head. "At least you have someone who loves you, unlike the nasty person who left you on my doorstep. Yes, you are my sweetest and cutest darling."

She surveyed all the material on her desk, swallowed a large gulp of whisky, stopped crying and looked ever so serious.

"The Forsythe-Twykes want me to know they are sending all of this stuff. Cromwell, to the last breath of my life, I vow to destroy this family."

She looked at the invitation, snorted in contempt, and with great ceremony ripped it up and put the pieces through a shredder.

"And that's what I'm going to do to Felicity just for starters."

Cromwell retreated into the darkness of her handbag and grinned.

***

Vanessa Forsythe-Twyke was born into a family steeped in tradition and secrecy. They had lived in their mansion in Upper Molehampton for many generations, were big landowners, controlled local politics, had always played key roles in the Secret Service and also owned the Food Factory. They were extremely rich, and she wanted for nothing.

Vanessa knocked on the door of her mother's study and immediately entered. She was dressed in a smart skirt and blouse, quite different from her normal attire.

"Aah, I thought I would see you soon, darling daughter."

"How so?"

"Two reasons. Firstly, Sergeant Dawson, a gossipmonger as he is, told me you had an argument with that Mr Jackson. Quite why you socialise with such riff raff from Lower Molehampton is a riddle to me. And secondly, my production manager at the company, Mr Walsh, told me you had accompanied him all day to see how everything works. At last, Vanessa, it seems you have accepted your responsibilities."

"Please don't be so smug. I fell out with Connor because of a difference of opinion, but you are correct about my responsibilities. I know about our family's history, and it would be a shame for the Food Factory to be inherited by someone else, namely that fool Bartholomew. It is my right and responsibility, and I intend to create a legacy nobody will forget," she finished self-assured and with a sly grin.

Her mother, normally someone who ignores what people say, heard this loud and clear, surprised at her daughter's confidence. "That's what

I like to hear and spoken like a true Forsythe-Twyke. Your grandfather, George, would be most proud of you. So, you are on my side now, Vanessa?" Felicity winked and smiled. "And, darling, I know everything."

Vanessa stared at her mother with large eyes and a blank look on her face.

"I know you were below the ground with that Jackson man and, thank goodness, escaped back up here with the help of that lovely little tablet. We are thankful you are on the surface with us," explained Felicity, matter-of-factly. "A ghastly affair, but all for our cause!"

Vanessa's mouth was wide open and it took a while for her to get over the shock. "Your cause? I had no idea what you were doing and still are doing. How was I to know I would die in a car crash, go below, find out I wasn't really dead, live with moles, do special operation missions and then come back like nothing had happened? Somebody should write a book about it one day."

Although Vanessa now knew a lot, she had no idea about how deeply her family was actually involved in the world of moles. But this was about to change. Part of Ormerod's plan was to involve Vanessa much more, thus Felicity was given the task of explaining how it all started.

Vanessa's great-grandfather, Beaumont, originally set up the world of moles and the Eternity Project with his best friend, Oldfield Thomas. They thought moles were better suited to administer memories and control the allocation of creatures on the surface. Unfortunately, Beaumont's father, and his son, George, both plotted against him, but he got the better of them. He arranged for his three elder daughters, Annabelle, Agnes and Beatrice, to disappear with all the secret technology, leaving George with only the Food Factory. And just in case you need to remind yourself who is who, here is the complicated family tree again!

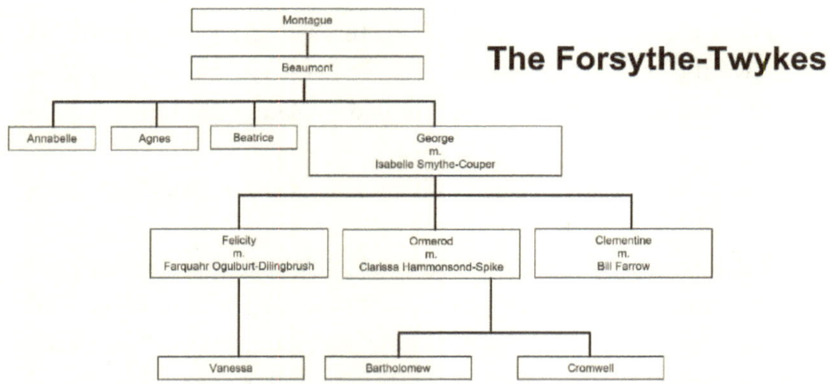

Don't worry if you find this hard to follow. There's much more to come about the history of the Forsythe-Twykes and how Beaumont and Oldfield Thomas set up the mole world!

Ormerod has made it his life's quest to track down the three sisters' relatives and even infiltrated the Eternity Project. Its leader, known as *the target*, went into hiding. This is where Professor Wingnut comes in, as he is the key to some secret technology and also the whereabouts of *the target*, hence the attempted theft of his memory. But let's come back to the setting up of the mole world. Beaumont also made other enemies as the voles were most put out at not being given the role the moles assumed. They have been looking for revenge ever since and Ormerod's secret organisation now has a pact with them.

"And what is the name of this secret organisation?" Vanessa quizzed her mother.

Felicity looked around the room and beckoned with her finger for Vanessa to come closer, and then whispered in her ear. "The Cult of Azoth."

"And thanks to Connor, I am now back here and not involved in all of this."

"Good," she added slowly, ignoring her daughter's comment. "Your feelings for him will undoubtably prove useful. Now, tell me what he knows."

Vanessa told her mother everything she knew, and Connor's suspicion he was receiving information from different parties.

Felicity now looked surprised. "He received notes. From whom? What do they say?"

"So, the notes are not from you? Oh yes, I nearly forgot. A Buddhist monk keeps on appearing in the Molehamptons and often observes Connor's house for a long time – in total silence."

"Yes, I've heard about this monk fellow. Could he be behind the notes? But then so could Bartholomew, as he's always up to secret things. But we now need something from you." Felicity smiled broadly at her daughter.

Vanessa looked at her mother with a distrusting look on her face. "And what may that be?"

"You should make up with Mr Jackson."

"Get back in his good books? Never. He can do the grovelling. He's from Lower Molehampton."

"That's the Forsythe-Twyke spirit, my dear. But there's more. I need a sign of loyalty from you. You see, I already know through my sources he's going back below, and I need to know how, when and where. If your information is correct, I will know you are on our side. But for him to believe you, Vanessa, tell him everything I just told you. Make him think you are loyal to him and betray me."

"But why all of this plotting, mother?"

"Because he should interrogate Professor Wingnut and come back to the surface. Then, armed with the information from us and other sources, he should find *the target*. And with you."

"And where should we go?"

"Bangkok!"

***

"There, there, come to Mummy now," said Jemima Kingston in a pampering tone. She took Cromwell out of her handbag and stroked him gently on his head. "You are such a well-behaved little boy and just adorable. All of my friends are ever so jealous I have you. Yes, fine, fine."

Cromwell silently gnarled his displeasure but knew he had to soldier on and finish his mission. He had already been in the handbag much longer than envisaged, owing to the failed theft of Professor Wingnut. Nevertheless, he had been assured his efforts were not in vain, and he should glean any information available for the good and benefit of the Forsythe-Twyke cause.

"Nice picture, Mrs Kingston. Your husband?"

She looked at me sadly for quite a while before returning her gaze to the picture. "Yes, Mr Jackson, and taken away from me at such a young age. Just like so many things in my life."

"I just wanted to update you on some information regarding the research job I am doing for you." I looked at Cromwell and added, "Even your poor dog can listen. I heard he was abandoned!"

My comments had the desired effect as Cromwell flashed his teeth in my direction.

"Now there, Cromwell, you know I love you," added Jemima caringly, "and I'm sure Mr Jackson does too."

"Yes, of course," I added slowly and sarcastically, looking directly at Cromwell, delighted I easily riled him.

Cromwell knew I knew, and I knew Cromwell knew. But what about my boss? How deep was she really involved in all of this plotting? Was she merely the innocent bystander, or was there something more sinister behind the scenes? Something about her didn't add up.

"What is it then, Mr Jackson? What have you got for me?"

"I have an interesting lead and have to go away for a few days for some more investigations."

"Of course, anything you need. You know you always have my support in this Forsythe-Twyke matter. And who will you investigate?"

"Oh, just a Professor I know. I am sure he can provide some missing links." Cromwell's ears pricked up.

"And where are you going if I may ask?"

"It's rather off the beaten track but I will use the underground!"

She looked rather bemused but not Cromwell as his ears pricked up again.

"I'm going on Wednesday and plan to arrive at six in the evening," I replied slowly and over-pronouncing the six.

***

The bar was quiet this evening, the counter propped up by four elderly men, cradling their beers and gazing into their amber liquids. The barkeeper was gawking blankly at the TV, oblivious to the world around her until a phone rang, breaking the silence like a gunshot. All five people turned around in a flash to look at me.

"Hello," I meekly replied.

"Connor Jackson! We need to talk!"

The call didn't leave much room for ambiguity I thought, smiling at the five people still staring at me. That's the Vanessa I knew when I first met her. She of course didn't arrive on time and eventually burst through the door of the bar like a television game show host coming on stage, causing those at the bar to spin around again in surprise.

"Well, Connor, what have you got to say for yourself?" she shouted through the bar before she had even sat down.

"Vanessa Forsythe-Twyke, I sincerely apologise for what I've done, and I really mean it. After all we have been through, I should have told you what I was doing." Even though I wasn't as loud as Vanessa, anyone in earshot would have heard what we were talking about.

"Yes, you should have, and I hope you feel guilty."

"I feel ever so guilty," smiling at her and dropping my voice. Her stern face also turned into a smile.

"Good. Well, that's out of the way then. I believe everyone is convinced we fell out, even Sergeant Dawson. He actually told my mother about it, and he hates her."

"I told him to do it. Even told him I was going on a journey. He seems to be enjoying all of this now the shock has settled in," I laughed.

"Oh, how clever of you. She really believes it. But now I am here, I have to tell you things straight away. I know why you were tasked to investigate my family and especially my mother. Well, to be blunt, she is absolutely crazy and has to be stopped, but it is not easy double-crossing my family. You know the saying; blood is thicker than water."

"Why? What do you know?" I whispered seriously.

"She and her relatives are behind all the unrest below and are purposefully increasing the Food Factory allocation to exert maximum pressure."

"I already know that."

"But there's much more. The man in the photograph you received is simply known as *the target*. He holds secret technology and Professor Wingnut could be the key in identifying who and where he is. My family sent you the picture and you are to find him."

"I suspected that too, and the picture was taken in Bangkok. But who is he?"

"I do not know, my mother neither. Ormerod knows, and he is the one sending the information. Bartholomew has also set up an office in Bangkok and I can only presume this is a cover for hunting *the target*."

"I agree. The notes, the picture, the monk and the office all point toward Thailand and your family has been feeding me with information. They want me to do their dirty work. But who is this monk? Whoever he represents wants me to do their work for them too."

Vanessa shuffled around, clearly keen to ask something. "Connor, when are you going below to interrogate the Professor?"

"We will arrive at six tomorrow evening and that, Vanessa, is the official story, but not entirely true. I purposefully made sure Cromwell heard the time, so a trap will be set for us. However, we will arrive at three in the afternoon. It will also give me time to repair the machine and interrogate the Professor before escaping again."

Vanessa got up and left, patting my shoulder on the way out. I sat there smiling to myself, sure everything was going according to plan. My plan. Vanessa also smiled as she left, sure everything was going according to plan. Her plan.

***

The annual equestrian centre riding show was in full swing, the restaurant area teeming with people sipping on champagne and snacking on exquisite canapés. A vast array of decorative hats, some resembling tropical rain forests, were on show and quite out of place in the Molehamptons. The sound of stamping hooves in the show jumping area merged with the haughty laughter coming from the spectators, clapping to appreciate a good jump and sighs when a horse clipped a fence. For the Forsythe-Twykes, this event was the highlight of their social calendar. Felicity personally oversaw the guest list, ensuring those she wanted something from were given VIP status. This was her opportunity to see and be seen. She was not alone, accompanied today by Clementine, Bartholomew and Vanessa proudly presented as the future Food Factory owner. Vanessa was visibly uncomfortable with the situation, not only by the attention but also her attire and the senseless small talk she had to engage in. This was quite out of character for her but, on orders of her mother, this was for the good and benefit of the Forsythe-Twykes. Bartholomew was dressed in a pin-striped suit and bowler hat, standing in a huddle of similarly dressed men. Clementine was running around like a headless chicken, trying to match people up, all on her sister's strict orders.

Vanessa and her mother went to the office so they could talk, as Felicity put it, *out of earshot of the social clingers.*

"Time to increase the allocation by two percent and really put some pressure on the system down below. And I have even had my controllers calculate that if we increase pork production by two percent, we can run a special offer in the supermarkets and sell even more at discounted prices. Even more money for us, Vanessa."

"But who should buy all these poor animals? Surely there's already enough meat on the market. It's absolutely saturated and a lot of it is thrown away because they can't sell that amount."

"Saturated, my darling. Please wise up! It's not my concern who buys it and their reasons for doing so. My business is to purely get the supermarkets to buy as much as they can. And anyhow, stop referring to them as animals. We have products, Vanessa dear."

Felicity opened the filing cabinet's door revealing a metal pipe, leading down through the floor. This was the same pipe Vanessa saw when she had infiltrated a cat called Fussy on a special operations mission.

"This is how we do it." She pressed the button, put the receiver to her ear and waited. But there was no reply at the other end. "Damn. Where's the President?"

"Maybe he's in hiding. Your bid for power below is running quite well, so well in fact that the President is now unavailable. You've shot yourself in the foot there." Felicity looked at her daughter with a puzzled expression. "And Colonel Pickle is up here trying to work out with Connor what to do to stop it. However, I must admit I haven't really heard of the Colonel doing too much. He's quite inactive if you ask me and everything is playing into his hands, or paws."

"Yes, well, nothing he can do against us anymore. It's too late and the wheels have been set in motion. But, Vanessa, what news have you got for me?"

Vanessa looked at her mother. "What time do you already have for Connor's arrival below?"

"Six o'clock today, Vanessa."

"That is what you should believe and what Cromwell told you. But they will go at three o'clock, so they have time to interrogate the Professor and get out before a trap is sprung."

"Well done, Vanessa. You have shown your loyalty. Does he believe you are loyal to him?"

"Oh yes, and he even believes our falling out was planned. He thinks I am totally loyal to him," said Vanessa smiling to herself as her mother turned around to leave.

"Come on, let's go back and inform Bartholomew. He and Ormerod will be most proud of you."

***

Bartholomew had been trained by his father and had a good network, above and below the ground. This included Mrs Grae de Vole who worked at the equestrian centre, constantly feeding him information on Clementine's activities and the gossip of the visitors. Bartholomew had his chauffeur take him back to the mansion immediately after Felicity informed him about Connor's arrival time. Professor Wingnut and his secrets would not be allowed to escape from his clutches this time. He went straight into the house and carefully ensured none of the staff saw him before going into the cellar. Convinced he was alone, he entered an office elegantly lined with wooden bookshelves, panelling and masterfully handcrafted furniture. He put his hand behind a book and pressed a button, automatically releasing a lock. It opened silently to uncover a passageway. Bartholomew stooped, went inside, closed the secret door behind him with a dull click before switching on a light. At the end of the passageway was a metal door with a golden emblem embossed on it—a staff with large wings with two snakes winding their way from the bottom to the top. This was the caduceus and the symbol of the Cult of Azoth. The operations room required a password for entry and only known to him and Ormerod. Montague had secret tunnels, passageways and this office built into the house many years ago, but he never revealed them to his son, Beaumont, not trusting him to carry on the Forsythe-Twyke's work. Instead, he revealed everything to George and taught him his dark ways. The room was elaborately decorated with colonial style paintings, thick fabric wallpaper and a plush red carpet to absorb any footsteps in the room.

"Colonel," barked Bartholomew into the receiver. "Now listen carefully. Mr Jackson, Colonel Pickle, Cleopatra and a dog called Ludwig will arrive at six o'clock this evening. Make sure you are well-prepared as these people have caused us trouble before. Mr Jackson is clever and cunning so don't underestimate him. They will have with them Professor Wingnut's memory and a part of the memory interrogation machine. Take everything off them and return Mr Jackson to the surface as I have need of him. Arrest the two dogs and put them into the Food Factory."

This may well now surprise you that Bartholomew purposefully passed on the wrong time, despite Vanessa telling something different. It was all part of a test of her loyalty. In reality, they wanted Connor to go below, interrogate the Professor and get out again armed with the information to hunt down *the target*. But nobody else needed to know this.

"And what of Colonel Pickle?"

"Let him return to the President."

***

The social event was in full swing with champagne freely flowing and the high-pitched chatter and laughter of the guests whistling through the marquee tent. Vanessa still looked uncomfortable, permanently adjusting the position of her hat.

"Why do we have to wear such silly hats?" she annoyingly exclaimed.

"They are not silly, my dear. They are ever so stylish and suitable for the occasion and clientele," chimed in Clementine, proudly fingering her lavishly decorated hat."

"Your hat is full of plastic fruit and leaves and looks like a walking fruit bowl. And my mother's is full of tropical feathers and could pass as a bird cage. You should both be on display at a natural history museum."

The clock chimed three o'clock and Felicity signalled they should follow Bartholomew to a quiet place behind the stables.

"Are you all ready to play your parts?" he asked earnestly.

They all nodded eagerly to show their agreement and recognise his authority.

"Good. Mr Jackson will be allowed to interrogate the Professor and then we will pounce. Once the Professor is safely in our hands, we will have him transferred for safekeeping. Then, we will complete the takeover below the ground and ensure the Eternity Project has no influence there. The Colonel can take over control and we will have no need for the Minister anymore. Are you prepared?" he said, looking at Felicity. "You will then have free rein over the allocation program."

"I've been prepared for this moment for ages."

"Vanessa, once Mr Jackson is back on the surface with his tail between his legs, you are to start arranging for your journey to Bangkok. You should base yourselves in Chinatown where all of this began many years ago and hunt down the real prize we are after. *The target*."

Chapter Nine
Going Back Below

Trout Lane was surprisingly active this morning with the residents going about their own business. The Kennedy brothers, dressed in their standard red tracksuits, were sitting amongst bags of rubbish and junk in front of their house, munching on bags of crisps and guzzling fizzy drinks. Earl Pike was busy skidding his bicycle up and down the driveway, gouging deep marks in the gravel. Mr Lawnsworthy was on all fours with a hand vacuum cleaner, sucking out any unwanted particles from his artificial grass and beautifully designed rockery. Each stone was also individually cleaned and replaced exactly where it was before. He was extremely proud of his new front garden, especially as it was now safe from any molehill attack. But he kept on looking up at my house with a suspicious look on his face. Lastly, a nod from Mr Khan in my direction as he and his family came out and packed their car for what looked like a day trip. But there was something annoying today—my slippers were missing, and this time Cleopatra claimed her innocence.

It was now half-past two, and the sound of an approaching siren indicated it was time for action. I went back inside just as Sergeant Dawson's police car screeched into Trout Lane and stopped outside the Kennedy brothers' house, the Khans and Mr Lawnsworthy looking over to see what the commotion was all about. It wasn't often that Sergeant Dawson was in such a rush and only the second time he had used his sirens. The last time was the eventful night when I was kidnapped.

"Let's go, everyone," I commanded, turning away from the window. "Our distraction has arrived."

"What? Now?" questioned Colonel Pickle. "But you said six o'clock."

"Yes, I did, and I've changed our plan for security reasons." I liked plans, especially when they were mine!

I picked up a bag containing Professor Wingnut's memory and part of a machine, then unceremoniously stuffed Colonel Pickle into it. A loose panel in the garden fence gave Cleopatra, Ludwig and I access to a field. We skirted around houses until eventually coming out not too far from the back of Gertrude Lawnsworthy's Pasty and Pie shop.

"Let me out of here! Now!" screeched Colonel Pickle, protesting from the bag.

"Quiet, you fool. You are not very secretive for someone apparently trained in being secret. You will be let out soon."

Gertrude Lawnsworthy greeted us. "You're early, Mr Jackson, but don't worry, I have set everything up. Come in. Quickly now and follow me into the kitchen," she said kindly.

I took Colonel Pickle out of the bag and placed him on the floor, the rest of us towing above him.

"My goodness," stammered Mrs Lawnsworthy. "I haven't seen a mole up here for ages, and an officer too. In fact, I haven't had many customers passing through my location for a long time. Do you know, I often wondered why we have no more contact with our handlers, but then only the other day, a duck came through here. He was acting rather strangely I must say. Well, not for me to worry about. I am best left to cook pies and pasties now."

Cleopatra growled to gain our attention. "In the old days, we used the access points much more often as the technology available allowed us to stay on the surface for only a short time. But then two things happened. The Eternity Project was compromised and reduced its activities and also Professor Wingnut designed the tablets we took, allowing us to stay here permanently, therefore there's little need for sleepers. Imagine the possibility of mass-producing these tablets! Professor Wingnut has the secrets locked in his jar and we're about to take them back below."

Colonel Pickle looked up at everyone. "I have heard about these sleepers but even I don't know who they are. That's why I had to contact Mr Jackson to get out. I couldn't use the special operation's exit point through Mr Tinker's store because I wanted to keep my arrival a secret, but nevertheless still compromised. There is obviously a mole!"

"Yes, there is a mole and maybe more than one," added Cleopatra seriously. "Personal contact with sleepers was never made before, only instructions on where the access points were. But things have changed."

Mrs Lawnsworthy opened her large oven door. "In you go now. Don't worry, this is my latest idea for a secret access point. Nothing to worry about. Good luck."

We all stared at the oven, and quite rightly a bit unsure about climbing in.

"I'm not going in there," exclaimed Colonel Pickle.

Before he could say anything, Cleopatra picked him up with her large teeth and tossed him through the open door. I then plucked up my courage and clumsily squeezed myself in going headfirst through the small opening and into a short duct. After squeezing my way along, I found myself in a small chamber, the only light coming from the kitchen. But, as soon as the oven door slammed shut, we just stood there in pitch darkness waiting for what would await us next. A hissing noise indicated the beginning of the transformation process as special gas was pumped into the room. I smelt fumes and suddenly became quite lightheaded, and a strange sensation gripped my body as I felt myself being somehow being pressurised and compacted, my bones clicking under the unseen forces as I was shrunk. Suddenly it was over, and I carefully patted myself to make sure everything was there and in the right place. A harsh light forced myself to shield my eyes and I felt a tickling feeling in my face. I slowly removed my hand to find myself looking directly into Colonel Pickle's eyes, his breath gently wafting over my face. Yes, I was now the size of a mole, an experience I never wanted to repeat, but here I was going back below into their world.

"Move out of the way!" shouted Cleopatra, as she grabbed a piece of rope and opened a hatch in the floor. Without hesitation, she poked her head through and then jumped. "Come on then, follow me and don't forget to close the hatch behind you," we heard as her voice disappeared down into the darkness below.

I awkwardly lowered myself into the hole holding onto the rope with one hand and my bag hanging in the other. The hatch banged shut above my head and I just dangled there, petrified of what awaited me. With a gulp and a groan of fear, I let go but the drop was thankfully short, and I landed on soft earth. It was not flat and, despite trying to hold on with my fingers, felt myself slipping until I lost my grip. I started to slide uncontrollably down a smooth tunnel and felt myself being spun around and shot downwards like in a swimming pool slide. My journey ended abruptly as I skidded to a halt on my back, legs and arms splayed around like an upside-down tortoise. I spat out dirt, shook the dust of my face and put out my hands in the blackness to feel the unmistakable damp mud of the tunnel wall, the earth loose in my hand as I rubbed over it. The stale air and musty smell brought back the memories of this place deep below the ground—the place I was so happy to escape from.

***

A few hours earlier in the Molehamptons, Mr Story from the Angler County News started hollering at the first person he saw.

"Scribbler! Here. Now."

Timothy Scribbler had just arrived in the office and begrudgingly approached the chief editor. "Yes, Mr Story, what have you lost now?"

"Less of your cheek, Scribbler. The internet is down again and you're going to sort it."

Timothy Scribbler took one quick glance at the back of the computer and started grinning. "It would help if you had a network cable attached. They are quite useful if you want to explore the mysterious online world."

Mr Story shot around his desk to look embarrassingly at the empty socket. "Get me another one!" he ordered.

But a quick look around the journalists' computers brought only bad news.

"All gone! They must have been stolen in the night! Who would come in and only steal the cables?"

***

Can you imagine a world deep below where you live? A tunnel world run by moles where each creature was the same size and could talk with each other. Shops, restaurants, salons, job centre, transport shuttles, and much more, with everything stolen from the surface by ingenious scavenging crews. A magical world mirroring life on the surface and far below the Molehamptons. The fresh air of my time back in the village had undoubtably blasted some memories away, but nothing could really prepare me for my return. The four of us walked along the gloom of a freshly dug tunnel towards a solitary light. Colonel Pickle remained strangely calm, with an unnervingly stern look on his face. On the lookout for danger, Ludwig took the rear. He was angry and for the first time I saw a steely menace in his eyes as we started his mission to free Basil. Cleopatra stopped at a wooden door barring our way, then pulled it slightly ajar.

"OK everyone, we are still quite close to the surface and in the special operations area of Red Five. First, we have to find the closest station and go much deeper. There are many creatures out there so just act normally and we shouldn't arouse any suspicion."

"How can one act normally breaking into the world of moles?" I sarcastically whispered.

Ludwig looked at Cleopatra seriously. "Don't you think we need some sort of disguise? Everyone else will be wearing overalls."

This was a Ludwig previously unknown to me. He always came across as a slow-speaking dopey dog, but not now. He was completely alert and thinking for the rest of us.

Cleopatra nodded in agreement and exited through the door.

"Straight to the memory interrogation room then?" I asked the Colonel.

"No! We're going to see the President in his hiding place first as I have to report back to him. Also, he will be shocked to see you as I told him you were decommissioned and does not know you escaped with the Professor's memory."

"And why would you let him think that?" I asked, my suspicion about Colonel Pickle rising even more. "Remember, my plan is to interrogate the Professor and get out swiftly."

"Mr Jackson, I'm not going to waste words now as the President is going to ask me the same question," he replied bluntly.

Cleopatra quickly returned with a trolley carrying a block of salt and a box.

"Right, you two into the box with the bag," she commanded. "Connor, you can push, and I'll go in front. Put these on," passing me a set of blue overalls and a cap. "Easy to get these from the scared workers," she added, flashing her teeth with a menacing look in her eyes.

The area we came into was a hive of activity, with many scavenging crews moving supplies around. Some dogs barged past, pulling a chain of socks all tied to each other. A rabbit bounced along with a cart of what looked like computer network cables. Light bulbs, tools, cutlery, you name it – everything needed down here had been stolen from the surface at night-time and was now being taken to storage areas.

"How are we going to find our way back?" I whispered. We had already taken so many turns and by now I was completely disoriented.

"I know where to go." whispered Ludwig from the box.

"But you can't see where we are going?"

"Dogs don't need to see. We can smell our way back."

Suddenly, Cleopatra stopped dead in her tracks and her ears pricked up as she sensed danger. An open-top toy car with two policemoles in the front seats came out of a side tunnel and drove straight towards us. They were cruising slowly and observing what everyone was doing. It was a remote-control toy car, adapted with electronic equipment and repainted in police colours with a light added to the top. They were not driving themselves so the car must have been operated by a control room. Without saying anything, Cleopatra immediately opened a door and we all followed suit, just managing to close it before they reached us. The car stopped directly outside the door and the two policemoles looked slowly around, got out and started checking things in the tunnel. My heart was racing, and the palms of my hands glistened in nervous sweat. I was astonished we had not already been ambushed; such was the risk we were taking. We all cowered behind the door waiting for the inevitable, but nothing happened. And after what seemed an age, the two policemoles eventually got back in their patrol car then spoke into a smartphone and slowly started driving away. I let out a sigh of relief as we sat there for a while, but the peace was rudely broken by a violent jolting sensation and the churning of drills somewhere near us.

"Ah, I hear the moleway construction crews are at it again," said Colonel Pickle from the bag. "The new transport system is quite advanced now."

"Why do you need a new system? Surely the shuttle transport is quick."

"It is, but the police need to move around quicker so a new superhighway, or moleway as we call it, was designed to connect the different levels down here. We supplied the police with new cars and a road network only for them, everything controlled remotely from an operations centre. It is all really quite ingenious with discarded smartphones, network cables and other electronic devices used to run the show. We can also dig much quicker with power tools supplied by the local construction company. Our research team devised a way to fix an electric drill to the front of a car and now we can bore our way through the earth at lightning speed."

"Your thieving skills really have no end, don't they?" I added, looking around to see where we were hiding.

We were in a sterile white corridor with what looked like an airtight door at the end with a sign – MOLEcule research.

"What is this place?

"This, Connor, is one of the many laboratories run by the moles. Professor Wingnut used to work in a place like this," Cleopatra said, looking at the box with his memory.

I tiptoed towards the door and peeked through the glass. Moles in white laboratory coats were heating some sort of fluid in test tubes whilst others were examining things under microscopes. At the far end of the room, a large glass jar was clamped into a device and a mole dropped into it. A fluid was then added and then the jar sealed. A researcher pressed a button, and the jar at once began to be violently vibrated then spun around at high speed. The poor mole's face was pulled in all directions by the centrifugal force and its whiskers stuck to the inside of the jar. I didn't want to know what they were doing and bid a hasty retreat.

Our pace picked up as we wanted to get away from all of these creatures. But then Cleopatra reacted again, this time sniffing in the air and wagging her tail. She had recognised something she liked. And there they were – sitting on a cart being pushed past us were my missing tartan slippers. The darn, thieving moles had managed to steal my slippers from under my nose. Unbelievable !

A few minutes later, and without further incident, we arrived at the station and nervously waited on the platform for a shuttle to arrive, trying to act inconspicuously amongst cats, sheep, cows, squirrels and other humans. My pulse was racing in anxious excitement. But the atmosphere was different to what I remembered. Before, the creatures went around their business in an orderly fashion, following sets of rules dictated by the moles. But now the creatures were openly discussing and angrily challenging the system. I overheard a horse strongly berating a cow for not protesting against the corrupt system. An angry pig shouted out his protests and a fox threw dirt towards a picture of the President. I sensed fear in the air.

I was jolted out of my thoughts by a vole, prodding me in my chest. "And you. Are you just going to stand there and pretend nothing is happening? Join the protests, my friend. This corrupt regime will end now and today. Follow me and let's release the political prisoners." He turned around and scampered off, followed by other creatures shouting out their demands.

I was utterly shocked and just stood there trying to take in what was going on around me. Going back into the depths of this world, halfway between life and death was not an easy decision to make. But I didn't expect this. Then came the moment I had been dreading. The first sensation was wind blasting down the tunnel, followed shortly after by two lights like beady eyes shaking their way towards me as it rattled down the tunnel. I saw a crazy looking mole wearing goggles and a flying cap, furiously pulling on a brake lever as the transparent shuttle with red caps thudded down into the station in a cloud of dust. The shuttle was originally intended for pneumatic post systems in buildings, but the cunning moles had long stolen them and cleverly converted them into modes of transport. The fuel at the back of the shuttle was still fizzing and hissing when the dust covered mole shouted out.

"On board, everyone. Quick now. I've got targets to meet," shouting above the din in the station as other creatures arrived.

I pushed the trolley into the cargo area at the back and sat next to Cleopatra.

"Buckle in. We're off," instructed the driver.

Before we even had the chance to do so, he released the brakes, the fuel system ignited into life, the shuttle started shaking and we shot off down a tunnel into the darkness. Last time I was here there was a safety brief but this time, nothing, with not even the time to fasten the belt and put on a helmet. I struggled for some time, hitting my head a few times on the roof before managing to secure myself.

"Where do you want to go?" barked the driver, craning his neck around in the strong headwind, the sides of his flying cap viciously flapping and dust swirling around his face.

"Salt warehouse obviously. What do you think we're carrying?" answered Cleopatra sternly.

"OK, keep calm. I'm just doing my job. We get fired and sent to the Food Factory in a jiffy if someone complains."

"No complaints from me, but if you don't get us there as quickly as this contraption can go, I will personally deliver you to the Food Factory."

The driver increased the speed, the fuel system bursting out more flames at the back and we rocketed forward at an even greater pace, the shuttle banging violently on the sides of the tunnel. The driver was hanging on to the levers with all his might as he was shaken fiercely around, his whole body vibrating in the effort. But he was experienced and knew where he was going in the dark tunnels, apparently anticipating every bend despite the high speed. We cannoned off the walls, shot around sharp bends and dropped down harrowingly steep drops as we made our way down into the deep depths of the mole world. Squeals of pain and shouts for help came from the box as Ludwig and Colonel Pickle were rattled around like dice in a beaker. I felt no better, the seat belt made of rope biting into my stomach and my teeth rattling uncontrollably together. We went deeper and deeper, flashing through stations at a ferocious speed as though the driver's life depended on it. Just as I could take it no longer, the driver yanked on the brake lever and switched off the engine. The shuttle's speed decreased immediately, and we ended up having the smoothest of landings in the soft earth directly stopping at the salt warehouse sign. It was a skilled piece of shuttle driving, even though absolutely terrifying. The driver sped away, a look of utter fear on his dust splattered face, leaving us alone at the dimly lit station.

"Now, get me out of here before I have you strung up!" shouted Colonel Pickle.

It was a funny sight. Both Colonel Pickle and Ludwig were wrapped around each other, with Ludwig's snout directly in front of the Colonel's mouth. Ludwig's fur was a complete mangled mess and the Colonel's normally immaculate uniform a crumpled and creased disaster. The two of them were so shaken and dizzy, completely unable to stand up without wobbling that they needed my help to get out of the box.

"That's not the last you hear about this, Cleopatra. Now, let me lead the way," commanded the Colonel and picked up a torch hanging on the wall.

The tunnels were professionally built with smooth walls, and only a few dull lightbulbs suspended from cables offering minimal light. We were the only ones in this deserted place, our movements echoing off the walls as we walked along drab tunnels. A white glow appeared in the distance, getting ever brighter as we carried on, until at last we turned a corner and were met by a huge white wall with crystals glinting in the Colonel's torchlight. On closer inspection, it was made of immaculate white blocks of salt symmetrically cut with amazing accuracy. It was a vast salt warehouse. I pondered about the reported thefts of salt from the local hunter and also the many trolleys with salt blocks down here. What did the moles do with all of it? The Colonel walked towards a hole in the wall, previously unseen in the white glare. His torch created an eerie light in front of us, like a car headlight shining off snow as he slowly guided his way through the inner web of the labyrinth. Every channel looked identical, with perfectly straight walls, no signs to show the way, and I wondered how he knew where to go. After some minutes, he stopped at a crossroads, slowly checked around, turned right, then started counting his paces and stopped.

"Do you know where we are?" I whispered.

He looked at me, rolled his eyes and then pushed a block of salt until it fell out on the other side with a thud. A few more were moved, making a hole in the tunnel large enough for us all to climb through into a room. An old mole in a pin-striped suit, supported by an umbrella, stood there glaring at us.

"I thought you wouldn't come back, Colonel Pickle. And you look a little worse for wear," the mole said. "And who might these be?" he asked, looking at us suspiciously, tapping his umbrella on the floor. The sound reminded me of something I had heard before, but I couldn't quite place it.

The Colonel stood straight as a dye and tried to straighten his dishevelled uniform. "Mr President, this is Connor Jackson and Ludwig."

"But Colonel, you assured me you had them decommissioned. You of all people lied to me and after everything I have done for you," he retorted angrily.

"I can explain, Mr President."

"It had better be good!"

"I did it for your own protection as there's still a secret minister betraying us, and I haven't worked out who he could be. It was best that Mr Jackson and his team stayed alive to look after the Professor under Cleopatra's protection. Here, we can no longer tell the difference between friend or foe, and I am the only one down here who knew about it. I fear, in the current climate, we would have already lost the Professor to the enemy. Even the molehill observers who watch number three Trout Lane don't know whose house it is."

"Colonel, your explanation is just plausible. However, why take such a risk and bring them all down here and, as you say, in the present climate? Others on the surface must know who he is and what he has."

"As I suspected, the Forsythe-Twykes are behind all of this—their plot much more advanced than we thought. They want to take over down here and steal Professor Wingnut's secrets, so we have to interrogate him first in order to reveal the identity of the treacherous minister."

"A compelling argument, Colonel, but I have my doubts. It's far too dangerous and if the Professor were to end up in enemy hands, then our system as we know it is over. We are on the precipice of a world dictated by greed and unbridled competition."

"I agree, but only by being one step ahead do we stand any change of turning this around."

The President sat down to take a rest, the excitement probably too much for him. "Mr Jackson, nice to make your acquaintance but I wish in different circumstances. However, may I now introduce you to Dusty here," he said, looking towards a previously unseen rabbit who came out from behind a cupboard. "He recently joined me here after I was left alone."

"We've already had the pleasure of meeting," responded Dusty with a wink. "Nice to see you again, Connor, and I hope my rabbit colleagues are proving useful!"

"Is this a conspiracy? Am I not told anything anymore?" exclaimed the President. A look of confusion then came over his face. "How can you interrogate the Professor anyhow? The machine is out of order."

"Actually not, I took a critical part when I left. I thought it best if I held all the cards."

The President looked slowly at everyone in the room. "And why is this dog here? Something else I should know about?"

Ludwig ignored the President and just walked straight up to the Colonel, staring him in the face. "Your loyal Colonel here has taken Basil, our dear friend, hostage to force us below. His plan worked and I'm here to make sure we get him back. I'm Ludwig by the way, Mr Rye's dog."

"I can't disagree with the Colonel's tactics if it meant getting Mr Jackson down here. I'm sure he wouldn't have come on his own accord. And who's Mr Rye? Is he also a conspirator?"

The President looked slowly around the room and then a look of authority came back. "Colonel, I need you to get out there now, assess the situation then meet Mr Jackson at the memory interrogation room. Ludwig, go and find out where your friend is and take Cleopatra—she knows where the prisoners are kept. Dusty, you can find something appropriate for Mr Jackson to be moved in, as we really don't want him discovered after getting this far. Mr Jackson and I need to talk."

***

Basil was alone in his cell, deep in thought about his family at the riverbank. He stared at the blank wall and dreamed about being back with them below the roots of the willow tree—his home. He had been infiltrated by a poo bombing mission and forced below the ground, a dreadful place he had hoped never to see again. For a duck, being below the ground in this dank and musty hole was just the worst possible situation to be in. The cell was like a small box with bare earth walls and just a sock on the floor for warmth and comfort. At least they knew what to feed him on and twice a day he received a small portion of river insects and water. But Basil had absolutely no idea why he had been taken and who was behind it, his captors remaining silent. Time passed slowly in this dimly lit pit, nobody to communicate with and no comprehension of time. Every now and then he shouted out, but a response never came, as he brooded in his cell.

But suddenly the silence was dramatically broken by the sound of some sort of fracas nearby. He had no idea what it was, but it was getting louder and closer. There were voices, many voices, and shouting like they were protesting. Loud crashes and bangs added to the commotion, some sort of objects being smashed together in an act of violence. Basil shouted as loud as possible, trying to gain their attention in the ever-rising din, and it seemed to have worked. Shortly after, voices were right outside his cell followed by loud beating on his door.

"Here I am," cried Basil. "Please get me out of here!"

A loud bang preceded the sound of a creaking door before it came crashing down in front of Basil.

"You're free," shouted a fox, standing in front of him. "Run. Get away now!"

"What's going on?" Basil asked.

"An uprising, my friend. An uprising. The whole place down here is in complete turmoil, and the police have now lost control. The President is in hiding and nobody is in charge. Flee now, whilst you have the chance."

Basil didn't wait to be told again and took his chance of freedom, waddling out of the cell. He was quickly sucked into the wave of protestors streaming along the tunnel and celebrating the end of the political system. Horses, cows, sheep, foxes, voles and many other animals loudly chanted their freedom, smashing objects along the way. But this was not an uncontrolled outburst of anger, as Basil saw the danger too late. Behind them, a group of dangerous looking moles egged them on. Something wasn't right here, Basil thought to himself, looking around for a way out of the crowd. But it was too late. He was pulled along and around a corner to find the way blocked by another group of moles brandishing sticks.

"It's a trap! Run back," screamed a cow. "It's the Food Factory press gang. Run for your lives!"

But the way back was also blocked, and it was indeed a trap. For Basil, this was out of the frying pan and into the fire.

***

Ludwig and Cleopatra left the salt warehouse and soon found themselves in a melee of different animals and humans, chanting about the downfall of the system. All around were moles encouraging them to protest. They heard shouting and singing coming from all directions, the crowds celebrating and ecstatic, but also out of control.

"Freedom from the system! Free markets! No regulation! Capitalism has won!"

"What are they shouting about?" asked Ludwig.

"Actually, I don't think they know themselves. And if they knew what they think they have just won, they wouldn't know what to do with it," replied Cleopatra. "Quick, let's go down here and get away from these crowds."

Ludwig sprinted after Cleopatra as they bounded purposefully along different tunnels, eventually coming to a skidding halt at the entrance of an area marked as restricted access.

"Slowly now, Ludwig. This is where Colonel Pickle keeps his special prisoners, and I don't know what we will now find here."

The two dogs carefully turned a corner into a small, dark alley with many cells.

"Strange. There are normally guards here, but they have all left their posts," whispered Cleopatra.

They cautiously went further, exploring the side tunnels, to find all the cell doors smashed down, but no prisoners.

Ludwig sniffed deeply, went down one dark tunnel, and stopped at a cell. "He was here, and I have his scent. Follow me now," as Ludwig slowly sniffed his way along some tunnels. But Basil was nowhere to be seen in this now deserted prison area.

"Stop! Listen," ordered Cleopatra. "I can hear something," craning her neck in the direction of the noise. "Down here," hissed Cleopatra, as she sped away.

Rounding another corner, they found what was causing the noise. A group of moles were harshly beating their sticks on a group of animals, herding them down the tunnel.

"Faster. Faster!" ordered one of the moles as he smashed down his stick on the back of a cow.

Ludwig tensioned himself, just about to leap into the group but was stopped at the last moment by Cleopatra.

"Not now. We have to wait. If you jump in there now, you will not get out again, and I alone cannot help," murmured Cleopatra, now standing in the way of Ludwig, still coiled for action.

"But Basil is in there. I can smell him, and I can't just leave him. Come on, Cleopatra, let's take them on. They will be scared of you!"

"No, Ludwig. It's brave, yes, but also foolish. There are just too many of them. We should follow but keep our distance which gives us a chance of weighing up our options. I fear we haven't got many though as I know where they are heading."

"And where's that?"

"The Food Factory, Ludwig. The Food Factory."

Cleopatra and Ludwig followed, using doorways and shadows for their cover. They were close enough to see what they were doing but far enough away so they couldn't be seen.

"I still haven't seen Basil," said Ludwig with disappointment.

"He's in there for sure. But we must wait, or we will end up in that crowd too and then we won't be of use to anyone if we end up in the Food Factory."

They turned one more corner and saw the group come to a stop in front of an entrance with a sign above it – *The Food Factory*. Inside, a conveyor belt with boxes full of animals slowly ground its way upwards at a steep angle and then through an opening into darkness. At the entrance, another group of moles ticked lists before pushing the animals into boxes to begin their journey up towards the surface.

Basil was in the group, powerless to do anything other than accept his fate. He turned around and saw Ludwig in the distance, staring at him in terror. But Basil chose not to shout out so not to give Ludwig away, instead being pushed into a box.

"There he is," Ludwig indicated excitedly, priming himself to leap ahead as he recognised Basil's distinctive colours.

But, yet again, he was stopped by Cleopatra. "Ludwig, you are brave and loyal to a tee, but it's too late."

Ludwig stood there and started to whine and whimper at the loss of his friend or his inability to help.

"He's gone and we can't save him here. We will have to get to the surface and rescue him from the Forsythe-Twyke's factory," added Cleopatra defiantly.

Ludwig stared on helplessly as Basil's box trundled up the conveyor belt and disappeared through the opening, his bright yellow beak the last thing to be seen.

Chapter Ten
Talking to Memories

Way back in history, people would often be buried with their possessions to accompany them into the afterlife. But what about our experiences, knowledge and dreams? Do they just disappear forever when we are no longer here? Quite a sad thought when you think about it. But this is certainly not the case, as the moles store our memories in stolen glass jam jars in vast warehouses deep below the ground. Did you know it is actually impossible to destroy a memory? And what do the moles do with all of this information? They can also interrogate the memories, an abhorrent thought for me, but that was exactly what I was now on my way to do.

Thankfully, the President's wish to talk to me privately had solved a problem—how to speak to my father's memory without Colonel Pickle in attendance. The opportunity now presented itself as I departed the salt warehouse, leaving behind the dejected President, looking somehow guilty as though he was hiding something. When the President told Dusty to find something appropriate, I never imagined he would return with a hollowed-out salt block. I had to practically fold myself in half to squeeze into the tight compartment along with the Professor's jar before it was firmly closed. My head repeatedly banged against the lid in time with Dusty's bouncing as he pushed me along the tunnels.

I now had the chance to contemplate my conversation with the President, the click-clack of his umbrella's metal tip on the salt floor still in my head. He knew a lot about the Forsythe-Twyke family and their involvement in the setting up of the mole world below the Molehamptons. I found out a lot more than Vanessa did from her mother.

Beaumont Forsythe-Twyke, Felicity's grandfather, was best friends with Oldfield Thomas, and they both studied zoology together at university. Oldfield Thomas spent many years in Siam and whilst there discovered a secret domain of moles administering the world above them. The two men were deeply angry about man's barbaric activities in the Great War and set up the same system below the Molehamptons in order to strip power away from humankind. The council of animal elders voted nearly unanimously for the moles to take over administration of the storing of memories and returning creatures to the surface correctly programmed for their tasks. I said nearly unanimous. The voles were the only ones to vote against as they wanted power for themselves and have been seeking revenge ever since. Beaumont Forsythe-Twyke and Oldfield Thomas created the Eternity Project in order to set allocations with the agreement of all other creatures on the surface. A system based on pure equality. The Eternity Project was not only the interface but also keeper of ancient technology.

I also asked the President why the moles forced everyone to believe the world was only the Molehamptons.

"Countries were created by man and forged by conflict. It is an unrealistic construct, Mr Jackson, but as a human maybe you don't understand. Animals don't need countries, no desire to create artificial borders and highlight ethnic differences between each other. A cow would never dream of thinking another cow inferior just because they come from a different area. For the animal world, an absurd thought. Humans are born innocent, but it does not take long for the bad behaviour, greed and competition to start taking over. At a more advanced stage, they are most destructive. Countries and ethnical differences were created by man alone and most definitely a programming error by someone a long time ago. That is why we tell everyone down here the world is the Molehamptons. They don't need anything else. We don't want bad thoughts from humans passed to others down here and the threat of the Food Factory usually works."

Despite Beaumont Forsythe-Twyke's good intentions, he was double-crossed by his father, Montague, and his son, George. The two of them wanted control over the Eternity Project but Beaumont sensed their plan and arranged for George's three sisters to disappear into hiding, taking control of the Eternity Project with them and more importantly, the secret technology. The eldest sister ran the Eternity Project and handed everything over to her first child, the identity of whom has remained a secret to this day. As we already know, Ormerod Forsythe-Twyke came close to uncovering this person who then went into deep hiding, taking a lot of technology and secrets.

And this is where Professor Wingnut came into play as he was an expert on ancient Siam and also a biologist specialising in genes and cloning technology. Ormerod Forsythe-Twyke arranged an accident and the Professor ended up doing research below the ground in an attempt to recreate the technology taken by the Head of the Eternity Project. The Professor was watched even closer when Cromwell was assigned to be his supervisor, so he decided to do something about it. He had himself decommissioned and put in a glass jar. And this was exactly what prompted Cromwell to have him stolen and my ultimate involvement.

The President was happy to tell me a lot but also tried to convince me not to interrogate the Professor. Although I was a good judge of character, there was something out of place about him, but I just couldn't put my finger on it. He also didn't want the Colonel to hear any of what he told me, further increasing my suspicions about Colonel Pickle's involvement.

The sound of smashing objects jolted me back into reality and, through some air holes in the block, I saw what was causing the noise. Groups of different creatures were marauding through the tunnels, looting shops and causing general mayhem. Quite often Dusty had to duck and swerve as objects were thrown out of shop windows, crashing down on the street. We passed the dog salon on the main high street and saw a group of foxes ransacking the place and making off with anything they could carry. Drinkers spilled out onto the street outside the Tunnellers' Arms, their thimbles of beer sloshing around. A drunk squirrel slightly nudged a tipsy cow, causing a fight to break out. A rabbit pushing a trolley went quite unnoticed in the chaos. Thankfully, Mr Tinker's store remained unharmed with a police presence outside and the protestors keeping well away from it.

Looking at all of the chaos and what the Forsythe-Twykes were doing, I felt the President's days were numbered and wondered who would benefit most. The answer was obvious—Colonel Pickle.

***

The memory warehouse was completely deserted, the workers either taking part in the ugly scenes or just hiding in their rooms.

Dusty, "I want you to find a memory for me—Kloss. I wouldn't imagine there are many of them and possibly just one."

Now alone, I entered the interrogation room and found it just as I remembered—a table in the middle of a circular room and some chairs. The electrical memory interrogation device hung above the table, and it was into this machine I now inserted the missing component. I have to admit it wasn't easy as I had removed it in a hurry, and it took me a few moments to find the correct place. Wondering if I had damaged it, I pressed the button. To my relief, the room was immediately plunged into darkness. But that was it, and I waited for a noise to come from the machine. Nothing! But after a few nervous seconds, a faint whirring noise came from within and ever so slowly a dull blue light from the lens shone on the table. I heaved a sigh of relief, followed immediately by the arrival of Dusty, pushing a glass jar in front of him.

"Good to see it still works," he smiled. "Oh yes, here you are, Kloss as ordered, " he said, and handed over my father's memory jar. "But shouldn't you wait for the others? Colonel Pickle must be on his way and Cleopatra promised to come and stand guard."

"No, I'll do this in complete privacy. Dusty, please keep watch as nobody must know that I am interrogating this memory. And when I am finished, please make sure it is well-hidden so only you know the location. Can I trust you?"

"Sure, you can. Loyalty is a word loosely used down here, but you can trust me."

I now sat alone in the room looking at my father's memory, nervous at the prospect of speaking to him as if he were still alive. When I was last here, I looked for my parents' jars but there was nothing to be found as they had stored them under a different name—Kloss. It was only when I rummaged through my house, did I realise my father had hidden it for me to find at a later time. But strangely I had also mysteriously received the same name on a note from an unknown source. I now carefully placed the glass jar under the lens's beam, sat down and anxiously waited for my father to be activated.

"And who's there? Who's woken me up?" I recognised my father's voice immediately and saw a miniature version of him begin to materialise in the jar. I fought back the tears as my eyes welled up and found myself unable to reply. "Who's there?" he demanded again.

I eventually plucked up enough courage and found some words. "Father, it's me. Connor."

"Connor, is that really you? At last, you have come for me," he replied emotionally. "So, my plan worked, you received the letter I left with Mr Pence and found the note in the house."

"Yes, Father, and now my house, your house, looks like a bombsite. You hid it well."

"I had to, son, I really had to. Hearing your voice again naturally makes me happy, but the fact you are down here is bad news, as the enemy must now be too strong and it is time for action."

"Yes, I believe it is, Father. Sorry, but we don't have much time. Nobody knows I'm with you and soon Colonel Pickle will be here so we can ask Professor Wingnut's memory some questions. Just as you instructed me to do."

"Quite right. Our memories alone are quite useless, but together we can unlock many other secrets."

"Yes, and maybe the mystery *him*."

"He's so well-hidden only someone like you with enough information can possibly work it out."

"Where do you fit in to all of this, Father?"

"I somehow fell into it all by mistake. Many years ago, when they were setting up the special ops and infiltration bombing missions, I myself was infiltrated by a bird poo hit. I can only remember bits, but I know I was sitting in the garden with you on a fine summer's day. You were young and in a swing. I can remember birds circling above us and you shouting out something."

"Bird poo!" That's what I said. I can remember it too."

"Yeah, that's right. Bird poo. That's what you said. I can then recall a weird sensation taking over my body and then I started acting strangely."

"Were you aware of what was going on?"

"Partially. I could see and think but had no control over my body or actions. Like being in a dream, I suppose. I started doing things I normally wouldn't do. I didn't know at the time, but Professor Wingnut was experimenting with the first infiltration mixtures. Your mother started to mention how strange I sometimes acted and then I suddenly returned to my old self. After a while, I started receiving messages left at the top of molehills in our garden, asking me for a meeting. Somebody called Brigadier Pickle. Funny, I wonder if he's related to this chap you just mentioned."

"Don't rule it out, Father!"

"Obviously for me it was strange to receive messages at the top of molehills, but I was already affected by my sudden changes of character because I was splatted on by these dive-bombing crazy pigeons more than once. I thought I was going crazy, and I couldn't talk to anyone about it. And who would have believed me? So, wanting an explanation for what was going on, I wrote a note back to the Brigadier agreeing to a meeting and stuffed it down a molehill. Deep down, I hoped I was just going through a bad patch, and nothing would come of it. But it did. The next day, I received a note instructing me to wait in our garden shed at a set time. I'll never forget nervously waiting for Brigadier Pickle. And then I had the shock of my life when a talking mole, dressed in military uniform appeared. After I had managed to compose myself, he told me about life below the ground and they were experimenting with special operations, scavenging and other different technologies so moles like the Brigadier could go to the surface. He said it was in a young phase and the technology was not yet mature. He then asked me if I would consider helping them and I agreed, and I still don't know why, even to this day. Maybe I was bored at my everyday job in the bank; understandable too because it was mundane. It excited me to take part in a world below us unknown to everyone around. It started off quite innocently, collecting thimbles and glass jam jars. And then I was ordered to gather more things and leave them in our garden shed to find it all gone the next day. I even broke into the glass jam jar factory and stole all their supplies. I can remember a young police sergeant was very angry as nothing criminal ever happened in the Molehamptons."

"I think you mean Sergeant Dawson."

"Yes, that's him," chuckled my father. "Lovely man and I felt ever so sorry for him as he never solved the case. I never knew what the things were for but was told it was extremely important and one day I would know why."

"I can vaguely remember you collecting things, and now I know why after coming down here."

Talking to my father's memory was a surreal situation, and I really should have been more emotional. But I had little time, so I needed to get to the point even though I wanted to sit here chatting for hours."

"How did you end up down here? I mean, everyone comes down here at some stage," I asked.

"I passed away of natural causes one evening in my sleep. They were expecting me, and I started working in the special operations program with my dear friend, the Brigadier. It was important work and also exciting. Thankfully, I had something to offer them, but not everyone was as lucky as me, you know."

"Better than being stored in a glass jar or in the Food Factory, I suppose?"

"Yes, but it was a small operation back then. Life down here was good, and I always believed what we were doing was correct. We had a life of equality and fairness, all of our needs catered for, and we wanted for nothing. Until one day when everything changed for me. A political officer called Cromwell turned up. I don't know who he was, but he was cunning. He ordered Professor Wingnut to work on secret projects—technology most dangerous I found out later. He also helped expand the Food Factory system down here and used his power to scare people. Things changed for the worse and the President was unable, or unwilling, to stop him. He must have had a powerful backer! At some stage the Professor, the Brigadier, and I all feared for the future, so we made arrangements through one of our close friends for some of the technology to be removed before it was too late. We knew what the consequences were, but we had to stop Cromwell."

"Well, he's still up to no good and with powerful backers. The Forsythe-Twyke family is behind it all."

"Just as I suspected. Once Cromwell found out, we all went into hiding, but made sure we only had parts of the information chain. I had myself decommissioned and stored under a false name—*Kloss*—because I heard the Professor use it at some stage but had no idea of its relevance. I don't know what happened to the Brigadier and the Professor."

A perfect miniature image of my father hovered just like a hologram in the misty fluid. And, even though I was only speaking to his memory, I saw him become angry as I explained how I came to be keeper of the Professor's jar. I just hoped when I turned the machine off, he wouldn't keep on thinking about our conversation.

"And now you are back down here because you need answers and the Forsythe-Twykes think they know where the secrets are. But they need you and that is good because it shows our plan worked. They have some information, however not enough it seems, and you must stop them from getting hold of more. Even better, defeat them and make sure the Eternity Project returns to what it was originally designed for."

"What secrets are you talking about?"

"Azoth. The secrets of Azoth."

"I've heard of if but no idea what is means."

"Son, Azoth is the universe. It is, if you believe it, the Elixir of Life. The secret potion for eternal life. This is why humans have been seeking this for thousands of years. The Cult of Azoth believes the Eternity Project holds this secret and will stop at nothing to get it."

"That sounds rather far-fetched. Surely it can't be true?"

"I am not saying it is true, but there are bad forces out there who have been on a quest for centuries to obtain the secret technology of Azoth. Son, we haven't got much time and you must ask me some questions whilst you are alone."

"Your letter said you would reveal important information. What is it, Father?"

"It is only a code number I was given. I have no idea what it means but told to pass it on when the time is right. Such is the security in our system to stop the Forsythe-Twykes getting all the pieces of the jigsaw."

"Go on, I'm listening."

"It is 5742469471. Have you got it"?

"Of course, I'm an analyst, and repeated the number back."

"Good, son, I hope you can find out what to do with it."

"One final question, Father. How did you leave the letter with Mr Pence at the bank and the note in the atlas? You were already down here."

"Easy, Connor. I helped set up special operations and I often visited you, but you just didn't know."

There was a knock on the door, indicating our time was up. We quickly bade our emotional farewells and I promised to speak to him again when all of this was over."

Dusty quickly took my father and disappeared out of another door.

***

The work crew were busy smoothing the walls of the new tunnel. They were paying particular attention to the junction where they had now stopped, more so than would normally be done, working on the same section over and over again. From their position, they had a perfect view towards a wooden door. Normally a work crew would just spend a few minutes at one spot, but they had been here for some time now. Passers-by might find their behaviour suspicious but anyone coming out of the wooden door wouldn't realise anything was out of place.

"They should have been through here by now, Colonel. Do you think something is wrong?"

Colonel Eccles, disguised as a tunnel cleaner, replied. "My gut feeling is something is wrong. We were told six o'clock and we arrived well before and it is now well after. I am not happy with this situation. I believe we've either been tricked or given wrong information."

Just at that moment, a vole came scampering down the tunnel at high speed. Normally voles were the arch enemy of the moles but the ones who defected were put to good use owing to their pace and cunningness.

With a husky voice, the vole passed its message. "Colonel, they are already here. I have only just acquired that information and was told to report to you immediately. You know we are not trusted to do more," added the vole slyly.

Colonel Eccles, visibly angry, turned around. "Pack up, everyone. Remove your disguises and follow me," he said, ripping off his overalls and uncovering his military uniform below.

"Where shall we go, Colonel?" asked a rabbit from his special operations team.

"Sergeant Springer, go straight to the memory warehouse, capture them and secure the Professor. Go now and you will be greatly rewarded if you are successful.

Sergeant Springer and another rabbit bounced off down the tunnel leaving Colonel Eccles and the others in their wake. Rabbits were very useful to have on a team.

***

Colonel Pickle entered the memory interrogation room to find me putting the final touches to the machine.

"There, that should do it. I think it should now work, Colonel," I said, looking in his direction.

"For your sake, and especially Basil's, you should hope it does work." Colonel Pickle was quite clearly agitated and kept on looking at his watch.

"Something wrong?"

"Yes, we've already wasted too much time, and the risk of getting caught ever higher. We should really get on with this."

"I couldn't agree more," quite wary of the Colonel's motives as he was acting strangely and had been since getting back down here.

We put the Professor's glass jar in the machine and started the process, waiting for the blue light to radiate and show his memory.

"Professor Wingnut. Professor, can you hear me?" shouted the Colonel impatiently as the small image slowly came into view.

"Hello," came a quiet reply. "Can't you lot leave me in peace?"

"Good evening, professor, this is Connor Jackson again. And Colonel, you just have to be patient and wait your turn," I added, frowning at him.

"You show an unusual amount of interest in me. Who are you anyhow?" The Professor looked at me, confused. "I can't recall ever working with you."

"Just someone looking after you for a while."

"Cut the small talk and start the questioning," spat out the annoyed colonel, glancing yet again at his watch.

"And you are?" asked the Professor.

"I am Colonel Pickle, and we have some important questions for you. The future of life down here depends on your answers."

"Fire away then. Anything I can do to help, I will. Not much else to do, really!"

"What exactly were you working on, Professor?" I asked.

"I was in fact working on many research projects, but my main task was to recreate technology which had been removed by someone. I was tasked to do it with Brigadier Pickle!" The President looked long and hard at the Colonel.

"Go on," ordered Colonel Pickle, trying to stay composed at the mention of his father.

"With Brigadier Pickle and his special ops team, we experimented with different tablet mixtures for infiltration. There were lots of mistakes and they didn't all work, but eventually we got there."

"You worked with my father?" asked the Colonel, not being able to keep it back any longer.

"Fine man. Yes, we worked together, and it was all very exciting until Mr Cromwell turned up. Horrible little man. He then changed the whole team to one of his own and we had to strictly work for him."

I sensed we were now getting close to the information needed.

"And who did Cromwell work for?" I asked, hoping he would know the name of the secret minister.

"No idea, and sorry to disappoint you. I once had free access to anyone and everyone down here, including the President. We were good friends, but Cromwell changed all of that. I was practically his prisoner and did everything he told me to do. He threatened to have so many of my dear colleagues decommissioned if I didn't do what I was told."

"And your research?" butted in the Colonel, trying to speed things up.

"Cromwell tasked me to work on many things. A new tablet allowing those who take it to remain as themselves and go freely between both worlds using the sleeper system. The tablets were close to perfection, and we only produced seven."

"But surely there must have been other projects? We already know about the tablets," stammered Colonel Pickle.

"Yes, but please give me time to explain. The most important and secretive projects were cloning, gene manipulation and behavioural programming. With this technology, we would have had the possibility to individually adjust and adapt creatures with the exact characteristics required. As you already know, the normal system has pre-set processors with which a certain breed of dog, for example a retriever, is programmed with the characteristics of a retriever. But the results of our research would have allowed us to manipulate and play with its abilities. We were attempting to copy technology received many years ago from Siam but was removed by the Eternity Project along with a lot of other high-level information. Well, at least that's what I was told. Cromwell had me work on it, but the research was extremely difficult without the documents."

"You keep on mentioning the Siam system. What is that?"

"Mr Jackson, that is the base system we were trying to copy. A perfectly balanced system of fairness and equality. Our technology was quite basic in comparison."

"Yes, but did you finish the work?" yelled the Colonel, leaning towards the jar.

"Mostly, yes, Colonel. It wasn't perfect and nearly functional. I was so scared of the technology and convinced it would only be used for bad intent. For evil purposes. For greed," the Professor replied slowly and seriously.

"You weren't wrong to think that," I added.

"But where is this technology now? Where are your documents? Where are the recipes?" demanded the Colonel, sweating with excitement.

"I had it removed before Cromwell could get it from me. I kept on delaying him, telling him I was still tweaking it. But my excuses were wearing thin, and I knew he was coming for me. Thankfully, I managed to get a message, a plea of help to the Eternity Project, asking for assistance."

"Yes," shouted the angry Colonel, "and where is the technology now?"

"It was taken away, Colonel. Removed from harm's way and hidden, hopefully far away."

"Who took it?" pressed Colonel Pickle, now livid with rage, and going straight for the kill. He really needed to know who had it.

"Don't ask me. All the communication was in complete secrecy, and I never knew who I spoke to. Always in darkness and my counterpart unrecognisable. The handover was the same, making it impossible for me to compromise who collected it."

"So, you have no idea who has it or where it is?" asked Colonel Pickle, slumping back into his chair.

"No, Colonel, I do not and that is a good thing."

"Why did you not tell me all of this when I asked you last time?" I asked.

"I only like to answer the questions posed to me."

"I could ask you who Cromwell worked with down here?"

"You could."

"He was working with a minister. Who was it?" I quizzed, craning forwards in eager anticipation.

His miniature mouth opened, just about to reveal the minister's identity, when there was a loud knock on the door and Cleopatra shouted a warning.

"Get out of there right now. You haven't got any time. Escape now."

Chapter Eleven
Escaping back to the Molehamptons

There was no stopping Ludwig, so great was his anger that he had failed Basil. But retrievers are a special breed of dog, and don't give up easily. Cleopatra couldn't convince him to leave and go with her, so he lay still in the shadows, quietly monitoring the entrance. Despite being loyal and protective, he wasn't reckless, and chose instead to gather as much information as possible rather than stupidly charging through the front gate. Maybe, just maybe, there was another way in. Ludwig saw press gangs force marching their booty into the system, and with so many protesting in the tunnels today, it was easy picking for them. Those being marched to the Food Factory were hemmed in by stick carrying moles, not scared to beat their catch. Not only moles, but there was also a fair smattering of voles to be seen handing out the beatings. There was no way out for the poor creatures, destined for the same fate as Basil.

Ludwig observed the work of one press gang, always looking for a way in, creeping silently on his stomach until he was as close to the entrance as possible. He witnessed each creature put individually into a box on the conveyor belt, before being promptly transported up and away out of sight. The creatures were pushed up a small ramp to the top of an empty box and simply shoved in. But Ludwig guessed the moles must use another entrance to get into their working area. Staying in the darkness and hugging the tunnel walls, he followed a group of moles and saw them approach a door, his assumption correct. He lay on the ground, prone for action, as the moles went through, waiting until the last one had disappeared before pouncing, just getting his snout in the opening before the door closed. There were voices coming from an office, so Ludwig stealthily slithered by unnoticed before going up a steep incline. He came out in an open area where the conveyor belt arrived, not at the surface as he previously thought. The distressed creatures were roughly pushed into large pens with names above—one for cows had a small board with *Allocation 45* written on it. The cows were forcibly pushed in until the pen was full to breaking point so that they couldn't even fall over. Their screams of anguish resounded throughout the whole hall. Another pen was for sheep, another for pigs, one for chickens and one further away for ducks. Ludwig watched whilst new intakes filled the pens, a mole counting until the set allocation had been reached. On the mole's order, a gate was opened, and the cows loaded on another conveyor belt which headed steeply up to the surface. Once the pen was empty, the mole wrote a new number on the board and waited for more cows to arrive. This was nothing more than a sorting area for the Forsythe-Twykes Food Factory above.

But not all were animals normally associated with human consumption. People themselves, squirrels, ferrets, foxes and many other creatures were herded into one huge pen signed as *Products for Conversion*. Ludwig guessed these were assigned to another area before being converted into animals for the food chain.

Where was his dear friend, Basil? This was his only chance to free him before he was transported to the surface. He slowly edged towards the duck pen, frantically looking for one duck amongst many. And find him he did, but not in the pen, as he saw Basil disappear in a cage towards the surface.

***

The escape from the memory room was easy, too easy actually, further raising my suspicions about Colonel Pickle. In fact, everything since our arrival was just too smooth. Had he planned it all and was really working for the Forsythe-Twykes? Cleopatra's warning gave us just enough time to get out of the room but not enough to take the Professor with us. Colonel Pickle was already away through a door, but I turned round to see two rabbits bounce directly into the room from another entrance, seize the Professor's jar and exit immediately.

We ran down tunnels as though our lives depended on it, barging through protesting crowds and avoiding objects flying through the air as protests turned to riots. We eventually got back to the relative safety of the salt warehouse—maybe the only safe place down here.

"We've lost, Colonel. The enemy has the Professor and a functioning machine, so they can now interrogate him and find out everything."

"There is not much he can tell them—he didn't really reveal anything to us either. But they can now protect the identity of their treacherous minister, and we might never know who it is. I've failed the President and it's all over!" added Colonel Pickle sadly.

I wasn't sure if he was putting it on because if he was the minister, then he had achieved exactly what he wanted.

"I can't believe how much this place is in disarray, Colonel. All control has been lost."

"Yes, I can hardly believe it myself. But the signs of discontent have been there to see for a while. As loyal as I am to the President, I have to say he failed to read them and thought the system would just carry on. Something has to give, and it now has. He blindly followed his allocation instructions without questioning and this has led to all the chaos. He never questioned the system."

"And have you questioned the system?"

"My job is not to question but to offer complete loyalty to the President. I am in charge of his personal security, not to question his instructions."

"Well, your security is not working at the moment. Thankfully for us, the rioting and protesting definitely helped us get away and the police must have found it impossible to follow us through the looting crowds."

"Protesting is not their right, and it won't lead to any good. But I fear change is on its way whether we like it or not and we must be ready for it. I just hope the President is."

"Stop," I whispered. "I can hear someone coming."

There was nowhere to hide in the smooth, white-walled complex as we stood there anxiously waiting for our possible capture. But we were able to heave a sigh of relief as Cleopatra came bounding around a corner and towards us.

"Thank goodness it's you. I thought it was the police."

"No, Connor, just me. I easily made a diversion and shook them off after leading them on a wild-goose chase."

"And what about Ludwig and Basil?" I asked.

Cleopatra then explained what had happened to Basil and she couldn't get Ludwig away from the entrance of the Food Factory. In the end, she had no choice but to leave loyal Ludwig behind.

"A disaster," I said sadly. "We've lost everything. Vanessa was right when she told me what I was doing was too risky and I would put everyone in danger."

"You lost the Professor?" Cleopatra questioned in disbelief.

"There was no time when you gave the warning. He was just about to reveal the identity of the secret minister, but we had to scarper at once with the Professor still sitting in the machine."

We all dejectedly trudged back to the secret hideaway to inform the President of the worst possible scenario.

"So, this is really the end," confirmed the President sadly and weakly. "After all we have set up for the good of our world. If only they knew what they were doing. Free market. Competition. It has never worked and never will. The only thing that works is the rich get richer through greed and power." The President looked sternly at the Colonel. "And there was nothing you could do? Not even find out the name of the sneaky mole amongst us?"

"No, Mr President. The situation was out of control before I came back and I'm afraid the enemy even has the Professor. They have what they always wanted and can now protect their own mole."

"Yes, I saw two police voles take the memory just as we managed to get out." I explained, purposefully lying. I wanted to see if this story would come back to me through Vanessa and see if either the President or the Colonel could be the secret minister.

The President slumped down on his chair and looked at the floor in defeat. He remained in this position for a long time, reflecting the situation before looking up slowly.

"Mr Jackson and Cleopatra, I can only tell you to get out and back to the surface just as soon as you can. Save yourselves and leave the rest of us to our fate."

He smacked the metal tip of his umbrella on the floor and stood up.

"I now have no choice but to resign my position and let someone else take over. I am the first President to do this. Our constitution stipulates my designated successor takes over as acting President until the ministers either confirm the role or elect a new President."

You could have heard a pin drop in the silence.

"Colonel, I formally give notice of my resignation. You will now be known as President Pickle."

***

Meanwhile above the ground, Sergeant Dawson was tidying up his office, a job he really didn't enjoy doing but had to be done occasionally. His small storeroom was a bit of a mess, and it was here he was now rummaging around, moving things from one shelf to another. On his hands and knees, he started pushing boxes around in the dim light of the lowest level when he noticed a previously unknown socket with a plug attached. Had he checked, he would have seen the cable went through a hole in the floor. But he didn't. He just pulled it out.

***

If the police couldn't stop the rioting, there was one thing which could— no power. The world of moles was suddenly plunged into darkness, stopping everyone in their tracks.

For Cleopatra and I, a timely occurrence as we were struggling to work out how to get back up to the upper levels of the tunnel system and to Gertrude's Pasty and Pie shop. The protests and rioting had all but disabled everyday life including the transport shuttles. The only way back up was to steal a police car and escape along one of the newly dug moleways. I had never stolen anything in my life. OK, I had Professor Wingnut's memory and a part of the interrogation machine but that was not technically stealing. That was safeguarding. And here I now was, sneaking around the police car workshop when the lights suddenly went out, plunging us into near darkness and all machinery stopping.

"What's going on here? shouted a voice. "Another power cut!"

Fortunately, there was still a little light being emitted from the smartphone screens attached to the cars' cockpits as they could run on their batteries. The cars had been scavenged from Mr Player's toy shop in Upper Molehampton and converted in this workshop into police patrol cars. Police signs, new paintwork, sirens and lights, leaving no trace of what they looked like before. We sat in one car to work out how to use it and I put my finger against the screen to see what would happen. It flickered and then a mole suddenly appeared, its face illuminated by the glare of its own phone. As soon as it saw me and realised I was not a policemole, it shut down the connection and a blocked my phone, a big red cross now showing on the screen.

"Darn. We've been found out. What now?"

"There are those wind-up ones over there," replied Cleopatra, pointing to the other side of the room.

Keeping as low as possible, we crept through the workshop and stopped behind one of the cars. Cleopatra sat in the driver's seat with her foot on the brake and, with all of my might, I started winding up the mechanism. The clicking noise was deafening in the stillness of the dark workshop as I frantically wound the key until it went no further. The car started rocking backwards and forwards under the pressure as it willed to be released and Cleopatra struggled to keep it from shooting off.

Suddenly, we were bathed in light as the power was switched back on again. Unknown to us, Sergeant Dawson had in fact finished what he was doing and returned power to the world of moles.

"Stop them," shouted a mechanic as he saw me jump into the passenger seat.

Cleopatra immediately released the brake and we lurched forward like a rocket. Two cars were smashed out of the way and the door of the workshop ripped off its hinges as we crashed through into a tunnel. Policemoles streamed out of a room and ran for their cars to give chase.

***

Ludwig was now alone and had to get back to the surface as quickly as possible to save Basil. With his excellent sense of smell, he had no difficulty finding his way back to the higher tunnels and to the wooden door they had exited from. But Ludwig's journey wasn't entirely incident free, as he had to navigate his way through great turmoil in the tunnels and many press gangs. Ludwig was angry, very angry indeed, and nothing was going to stop him from finding Basil as he aggressively shoved his way through the crowds, snapping at anyone who tried to stop him. Luck was also on his side as the power cut hit, leaving the policemoles guarding the wooden door blind. Ludwig easily slipped past them and made his way back to the exit and Gertrude Lawnsworthy's shop.

***

Our escape was somewhat more complicated. On one side, our wind-up police car was faster than the remote-controlled ones. But, on the other side, it quickly ran out of power and Cleopatra had never driven a car before. Why would she have?

It must have looked like a scene from a comedy film. A dog driving a toy car with me as a passenger and chased by police cars with blaring sirens, flashing lights and policemoles. Our car only had one speed—maximum—Cleopatra only just able to handle the steering as she fought to keep it under control. We smashed off tunnel walls, leaving parts of the car behind and frantic creatures jumping out of the way before they were hit.

"Connor!" shouted out a clearly petrified Cleopatra. I had, in fact, never seen her scared before. "We're slowing down."

Our car slowly came to a halt as the wind-up mechanism ran out of tension. Fortunately, our car was much faster than the others, as the operators in the control room had great difficulty driving the cars at such speed remotely. I wound up the car again as quickly as I could, the sound of sirens approaching.

"Come on. Faster, Connor. They are nearly here."

The police cars screeched around a bend just as I managed to jump back in, Cleopatra releasing the brakes immediately. We shot forward again, my hands holding onto the door and my hair sticking up in the wind as we easily outpaced our pursuers.

"Do you know how to get back to the surface? Surely, we must use the new moleways recently constructed," I shouted out.

"Just around the corner," cried Cleopatra as the car smashed sideways into a wall. We slid around, ripping off the door on my side before coming to a tunnel on the right with a police barricade.

"Hold on, Connor!"

With loud barking, Cleopatra pointed the car directly towards the policemoles and barrier, smashing her way through. The impact left us without lights as we entered a steep spiral incline. It was like going up a corkscrew as we shot higher up the mole world towards the surface. But the car slowed down, and this was not the best place to stop. Just as we used the last power, the car crested and came to a stop teetering on the edge. I jumped out to stabilise the car whilst Cleopatra fell out, exhausted through the exertion.

"Come on," said Cleopatra. "The wooden door is not far from here," she wheezed, mustering some energy.

"But we'll never make it." Flashing blue lights and sirens indicated they were not far behind.

Cleopatra and I then smiled at each other, knowing what had to be done. We pushed the car gently and saw the wreck slowly pick up speed as it went back down the tunnel. Shortly after, we heard a loud crash followed by another, and another.

***

Far away from the Molehamptons, Ormerod Forsythe-Twyke was sitting at an outside restaurant surrounded by bright red and orange Chinese signs. The sound of loud chatter, wailing music and the constant tooting of car horns blasted down his phone.

"Let me put my earpiece in. Can't hear a thing in this annoying noise," he shouted. "That's better. What news, Bartholomew?" he demanded quickly, not waiting for any pleasantries.

"Professor Wingnut's memory has been captured and part one of the operation is complete. Now, all we have to do is get that pesky man to where you are and find *the target*."

"Excellent news. Where is the Professor now? Hopefully under lock and key."

"Erm, not quite. He was captured by two voles, and we are currently locating them. It really is quite chaotic down there. Don't fret, Father. You can trust me."

"That's what I'm worried about. And where is this Jackson chap now?"

"We allowed him to escape."

"Good. Just as we wanted. And what about the other part of our plan?"

"Felicity has primed Jemima Kingston well and with the information we've sent her, we are quite sure she will not stand in Mr Jackson's way when he asks to go to Thailand to investigate."

"And Vanessa?"

"She's proven her loyalty to us by snitching on Mr Jackson. She gave us the real arrival time which we purposefully didn't act on. We just wanted to see if she told the truth."

"The Cult of Azoth is close to achieving what it always wanted. The final quest is about to begin. Bartholomew, get Felicity to annoy Mr Jackson's boss. Tip her over the edge! He must travel here with Vanessa as soon as possible. I'm waiting and my agents are ready."

"Yes, Father, and I will also send two people to watch over them. They are not the brightest, but enough for our needs. Vanessa will keep them informed, so they know where to go. All you have to do, Father, is follow the two men and you can then keep your distance."

"And how will I recognise them?" asked Ormerod annoyed.

"Don't worry," chuckled Bartholomew. "You won't miss them."

***

Felicity Forsythe-Twyke was disappointed her close friend, Jemima Kingston, hadn't come to the annual horse show event. In fact, she hadn't even replied to the invitation, which was out of character for her. So, Felicity, a caring person as she was, decided to pay her a visit.

"Jemima dearest. What is wrong with you? You look absolutely terrible. Are you sick?" Felicity didn't wait for a reply and just barged

142

past her and made herself comfortable in the living room. "There, there, Jemima. Let your closest friend help you. Have you been crying, my dear?" she asked in her direct and unthoughtful approach.

Jemima took a deep breath, looked at the ceiling, rolled her eyes and then at Felicity. "Yes. As a matter of fact, yes, I have."

"Talk to me then, darling. Felicity can fix everything."

"Felicity, I'm not sure if you can help me and I'm sure you know nothing about it," replied Jemima sarcastically but her comment went straight over Felicity's head.

"Try me, darling Jemima."

"But you already know about my sad story. My husband disappeared and was formally registered as dead. My darling stepbrother, Reginald, also died. I was adopted at a young age by the Wingnut family and then my adoptive mother also passed away in 1978 when I was just twelve years old. My adoptive father died ten years later, and in this time, Reginald devoted a lot of time to bring me up. Such a clever man and an expert on ancient Siam. But, alas, I have never known who my real parents were."

"Yes, dear, a very sad story. And what's your point?" she blurted out bluntly.

Jemima took another deep breath at Felicity's heartless comment and was really struggling to stay in control.

"I recently received information that my real father is actually still alive and living in the Molehamptons and I have absolutely no idea who sent it to me. Why do this to me? It's just so cruel and spiteful."

"But records must show who he is?" prodded Felicity.

"No. There's nothing there and I've researched the subject many times. My parents gave me away for adoption citing low income, remaining anonymous. I just wish I knew which devils employed him," she added angrily.

"Imagine that. He's alive and kicking and maybe even knows who you are. This is so exciting!" Felicity gleefully added.

"Exciting! You really are such a big help, Felicity," sighed Jemima, holding back her tears.

"Yes, thank you. I do know."

The two women looked at each other in an awkward silence until eventually Felicity started again.

"Jemima dear."

"Yes," cautiously replying.

"I know you have a sad and personal story to tell, and I really don't want to bring this up."

"Well, I'm sure you are going to anyhow!"

"Your husband. What was his name?"

"Robert. Why?" she said slowly, wary of Felicity's intentions.

"Isn't it correct they did not find his body?"

"Yes, you are correct. Why do you ask?"

"It's just so odd, dearest Jemima. Disappeared without a trace and reported dead."

"True, and it's normal procedure after such a long time and also if there's enough evidence to support death. And there certainly was."

"What if ..." but Felicity didn't finish her question.

"What if what?"

"Well, if he's still alive after all these years."

Jemima couldn't control herself anymore and burst into hysterical bouts of crying. Felicity just sat there awkwardly, not knowing where to look until standing up and made to leave.

"Jemima, I'm sure I've been of great help to you. You could also confide in Cromwell here, I suppose. You know people say dogs are just wonderful listening companions."

Jemima sobbed even louder.

"I'll let myself out then, shall I?"

Just as soon as Felicity left, Jemima stopped crying and looked serious. "I'm coming for you. Now it's over to Mr Jackson," she said sternly.

***

A high fence with razor sharp barbed wire enclosed the Food Factory along with cameras, lights and security staff walking its perimeter. It was a highly guarded place, either to stop the animals from escaping or, more likely, to stop people from looking at what happened inside. He saw Mr

Cross working at the gatehouse and the constant arrival of lorries with happy looking animals on the sides, the sounds of squealing escaping from inside. Only silent containers left. With no possibility to get in, Ludwig decided to ask for help and returned to his farm to wait.

Sometime later, the headlights of a car approached, then stopped on the road at the end of the farm's driveway. The lights flashed a few times, followed by the short flashing of a blue light.

He quickly checked to see if Mr Rye had seen the lights and then, sure he hadn't, bounded off towards the car. Getting closer, he saw two people: Sergeant Dawson and a woman. The Sergeant, not wanting to face the rain, stayed where he was and wound down the window.

"Ludwig, I can get you on a truck into the Food Factory and Mr Cross will let you out on the other side of the gate. I've already spoken to him, but he needed some convincing. I obviously didn't tell him you could talk but said I had secretly trained you to do some work against the Forsythe-Twykes—he readily agreed. If you find him, he knows to let you in and out. Also, Mrs Pike will be able to lend support. Jump in," ordered the Sergeant, twisting around to open the door.

He turned to the woman who was staring ahead, eyes wide open and mouth open. "Come on then, dear. Let's go."

But the woman remained completely motionless.

"What's wrong?"

The woman, undeniably under shock, slowly turned her head towards her husband. "You were just talking to a dog! Why?" she only just managed to splutter out.

"Oh that, sorry darling, but I forgot to tell you."

The woman now started screaming hysterically, "You spoke to the dog and it appeared to understand. And then it replied and in our language. What's going on? We have a talking dog in your patrol car, and I haven't even been drinking."

Sergeant Dawson had taken the unusual step of asking his wife to drive the patrol car as he had had a few drinks too many. It was naturally not allowed but nobody in the sleepy Molehamptons would ever mind. What he had failed to remember was Ludwig had the ability to communicate with humans after taking the tablet. And then he remembered his first experience like this when he found Colonel Pickle.

He now had no choice but to explain some extremely strange facts to his wife who remained quite unconvinced. Still in shock, she nevertheless did what she was asked and drove in the direction of the Food Factory.

Despite failing to prepare his wife for a talking dog, he was good to his word with Ludwig. Sergeant Dawson turned on the blue flashing lights to flag down the approaching lorry. His wife had stopped far enough away from the entrance so as not to arouse any suspicion and stayed in the car, her face totally blank, still not being able to take in what had just happened. She just kept on mumbling about a talking dog under her breath.

"Just a routine check. Can I see your paperwork please and open up the back of the truck? Thank you very much," Sergeant Dawson said quite forcibly.

The foreign speaking driver readily agreed, and the back of the truck was promptly opened without any questions. Sergeant Dawson then led the driver around the truck to inspect safety aspects whilst Ludwig jumped in the back without being noticed. He thanked the driver, apologised for taking up his valuable time, and off the lorry trundled towards the factory in the distance, without any suspicion being aroused.

Sergeant Dawson's wife now drove him back to their warm, cosy home, and without doubt, to severe questioning about talking dogs.

One of the pigs looked at Ludwig with glazed eyes and asked, "What is a dog doing in here?"

Ludwig stared sadly at the pig. "I need to get into the Food Factory."

"Listen to him," shouted the pig. "The dog here wants to get into the Food Factory!"

The pigs briefly forgot their fear and broke into raucous laughter.

"Swap with me," came a shout from somewhere in the melee.

"No, me. I'll swap!"

I have to go in to find a friend who is in there by mistake. I want to free him."

"Free him. By mistake," shouted back lots of pigs amid hoots of laughter. "Why not free us as well."

Ludwig just stood there, horrified at the macabre scene around him, not able to respond to the jibes.

"Whoever you are, Mr dog, you are foolish. Once you're in, there's no way out," squealed a pig next to him. "But I must say, you are so brave, and I wish I had a friend like you."

The lorry hissed to a stop with light blasting in through the slits.

"Right there, open up please. I need to check." Ludwig recognised Mr Cross's voice outside.

"Again?" questioned the driver. "I was checked only a few minutes ago."

Mr Cross was happy to hear this, knowing Ludwig must be on lorry. "Just do it, please!"

Ludwig retreated further into the darkness and waited for the door to be opened before taking his chance and leapt out. He took a quick glance around then headed into the darkness between two buildings.

"Go. Go. Get out of here. But come back and save us," some of the pigs squealed after Ludwig.

Ludwig had to be extremely careful, so he hid under a rubbish bin and waited a while before venturing out to get his bearings. The reality of his situation now sunk in, making him quite scared, but he had to ignore his fear and locate Basil as quickly as possible. The Food Factory was a huge complex, and he had no idea where to start. Security personnel permanently roamed the premises, using their torches to search every nook and cranny.

He waited at the first large building and observed a roller door being used by some of the staff. At an opportune moment, Ludwig left his cover and just managed to squeeze himself under before it slammed shut. He now found himself in an arrivals area and saw the truck he arrived on being unloaded. There was no conveyor belt here from below, so he left the building and headed for the adjacent one. He guessed he was now in the right place when he found a hole in the ground with a conveyor belt, churning around with empty cages. Ludwig's natural sense of smell soon detected the scent of duck and, after intensively breathing in the air, also Basil. However, there was now no activity here, the ducks probably having passed through a while ago. Where was Basil?

***

Cleopatra and I had now returned to my house. I was actually feeling quite smug with myself. But maybe you are wondering how I could feel like that when I had just lost Professor Wingnut's memory. Surely, I should be distraught as my plan had failed and the Forsythe-Twykes had what they always wanted.

"We've lost the Professor and I no longer have a role here," said Cleopatra sullenly.

"Quite the contrary," I replied, picking up a box from the kitchen table.

"Who put that there? It wasn't here when we left. And what's in there?"

"Who put it here? My rabbit friends, Cleopatra. I had my backup plan all along."

With a cunning smile, I opened the box and put a glass jar on the table.

Cleopatra's eyes opened widely. "Professor Wingnut!

Chapter Twelve
The Journey Begins

Did you really think I had lost Professor Wingnut? I wasn't going to let that happen so easily and was confident it would work out. Yes, my plan wasn't without risk, but I was sure my rabbit friends would pull it off. They had long since infiltrated the special operations teams and were highly trusted in the mole world. Please remember, I don't leave things to chance.

It was raining hard as I sat in my room observing Trout Lane. The monk was standing, completely motionless in my front garden, just staring up at me. Dressed in his orange robes, a brown satchel and barefoot; he was completely drenched but it appeared not to bother him, oblivious to the horrible weather conditions and the rabbits now standing next to him.

I now had some real thinking to do. Yes, I had secured Professor Wingnut, but there were still a lot of open questions. What I had, after my visit below, allowed me to puzzle together some of the information. I was obviously being played by more than one party. Two of the notes made Oldfield Thomas's name and two others were clearly China Town. A picture of 'the man' in Bangkok, a strange monk observing me, and revealing conversations with Cleopatra, the President, my father and the Professor. And behind all of this, the rivalry between the secretive Eternity Project and the Forsythe-Twyke family.

But something still didn't make sense, and that was the note *Kloss's* and the connection with my father. I got out my laptop and started searching. There were quite a few hits for the word, most of them for products or adverts, but not enough for me to go on. And then suddenly something stood out like a sore thumb—Kloss's mole—and on reading further found some starting information. A mole found in Southeast Asia and belongs to the Talipidae family. They are found in Laos, Malaysia and north Thailand, the babies called pups and a group is a labour company. They like living in sandy soils, especially near rivers. Interesting I thought, and Professor Wingnut had even mentioned a perfect mole world in Siam. Was this what he referred to? Was Kloss's mole the connection I was looking for? But then came the real hit. The person who did the academic research on the mole was none other than Oldfield Thomas. I couldn't believe what I was reading, so delved further into his name and came up with some astounding news. He had written many research papers, one of them jumping right out about his work on the mole, commonly called Kloss's mole in 1881. And what has Bangkok's Chinatown got to do with it? A former trading point for Chinese merchants, it's one of the oldest parts of the city and on the banks of the Chao Phraya River, close to the old city with its abundance of temples.

"And, Connor," I said out loud. "What do you find in temples? Monks!"

I knew the Forsythe-Twykes had recently set up office in Bangkok, sent me some of the notes and provided me a picture of a mystery man they wanted me to find. They were on to something but didn't know everything I now knew. My father told me to find *him*, so it was clear we were talking about the same person—the Head of the Eternity Project. The person hiding the Azoth secrets! But I alone had one more piece of information, the code number 5742469471, which might unlock the mystery. Looks like I will have to go there and find out, but first a call to my boss was needed.

***

"Are you on to something, Mr Jackson?"

"Well, yes, as a matter of fact I am. I have to go away again, but this time for longer. My investigation has uncovered a deep and sinister secret. Mrs Kingston, there's an organisation involved in the development of technology, which in the wrong hands could shift the balance of power. It is currently being protected by a person who went into hiding some years ago and I need to find him before the enemy does.

Before the Forsythe-Twykes do," I explained, like telling a story from a spy novel. "I have to go to Thailand."

"I am aware of the possible existence of a secret organisation, high up and above the level of government. I have always believed it, to tell you the truth. But the Forsythe-Twykes? Well, my suspicion to get you to look into them has proven quite fruitful and I thought I had only tasked you to help finding my father."

I was astounded. "Your father?"

"Yes, Mr Jackson. I received some information," she said, fingering the purple file. "Information claiming my real father is still alive and living right under my nose in the Molehamptons. I am sure this is from the Forsythe-Twykes, but I don't know why or what their motive could be. I, as you probably know, was adopted at birth and never knew the identity of my real parents. But there's more, Mr Jackson. Felicity Forsythe-Twyke has been pressing me about my late husband. His body was never found, and Felicity is showing undue interest in the matter," she explained, staring at the picture on her desk. "The only connection with her I can find is the chief investigating officer was Ormerod Forsythe-Twyke, her brother. Go on your mission, Mr Jackson, and finish off this family!"

***

Bartholomew Forsythe-Twyke entered the room with a triumphant look on his face. He had just spoken to Cromwell and knew all about Mr Jackson's pending trip to Thailand. Their plan had worked: they had captured Professor Wingnut and Connor Jackson had all the information available to hunt *the target*.

"Vanessa, are you ready?"

"Ready than ever before," replying with a steely face.

"That's my girl. I always knew you would do what's right," trumped up Felicity, proudly looking at her daughter.

"But, Vanessa, you need to carry on with our game. Tell him everything so he trusts you and get him to take you to Bangkok. Use his friend, Basil, as the bargaining chip. He's in the Food Factory now and the fattening process takes fifteen days," he added cruelly.

"Yes, of course. I know how to play on his weaknesses. As discussed, I'll sort out the flights and book a hotel in Chinatown."

"Great. You will also be followed by two agents of mine."

Vanessa looked questioningly at Bartholomew. "Is this not really an overkill? We don't want to bring undue attention to ourselves."

"No, you're wrong," countered Bartholomew. "We want them to be seen, so all eyes are on them. They will be our red herring."

"If you say so," added Vanessa, but sounding unconvinced. "I'm sure you have everything under control. And on that subject—when's the Professor's memory being delivered up here?"

"Slight problem there." he hesitated. "Our minister informed us two voles captured Professor Wingnut and we've heard nothing since. Rest assured, they are being looked for and, I am sure, just lost in the mayhem."

***

The call came shortly after I finished speaking to my boss, and as expected, she told me everything the Forsythe-Twykes were doing. Cromwell had immediately informed about my plan to go away, and they knew two voles had captured Professor Wingnut's memory – this could only have come from the ex-President or Colonel Pickle. Also, Basil was in the Food Factory, her family holding him as ransom so I would do what they wanted. I knew we had an agreement, but could I trust her? Whose side was Vanessa really on? Whatever the case may be, I needed her to accompany me to Bangkok as I couldn't do this alone. Shortly after, she came by.

"Have I forgotten anything?" I asked, looking at my suitcase.

"Forgotten? Connor, we're going to Thailand, not hiking in the Highlands. Why do you need all of this? Fleece jacket, boots, woolly socks. No, Connor. No, this won't do."

"You never know," I replied meekly.

"Well, you plainly don't know. We're not traipsing around Thailand with thirty kilogrammes in this suitcase. Go and make a cup of tea and leave the packing to me."

I returned only a few minutes later and found Vanessa already finished, proudly holding up a small holdall.

"There, about twelve kilogrammes by my reckoning."

"But don't I need …," I started pointing at my items on the floor.

"No, you don't," she butted in sharply. "A few T-shirts, shorts, a sweater for the flight and a wash bag. Anything else you need we can buy there. I see you don't have sandals."

"Sandals. Why do I need sandals in the Molehamptons? I was thinking of taking my walking boots."

"You may well have a fine analytical mind, but you are a complete duffer at travelling. Connor Jackson, just bring your large brain with you and leave the travel arrangements to me."

"Good, because I haven't been further than London before and I wouldn't know where to go. All I know is that Chinatown is important."

"Well, we are flying tomorrow, so I suggest you tell me what you know."

"The information leads me to believe we are looking for a connection between moles, temples and monks. We should start by looking at temples."

"Connor, do you know there are over four hundred temples in Bangkok alone?"

***

Nobody noticed the man in a pin-striped suit arrive in Trout Lane, not even the monk, standing motionless and looking up at a room with a light on. The man parked his car around the corner and walked the remaining distance, protecting himself from the heavy rain with an umbrella. He knocked on the door of number five and immediately heard the loud trampling of an overweight person moving sluggishly down the stairs.

"Who is it?" shouted a voice from inside and then slowly opened the opened the door, wary of who might be there.

The man didn't wait and pushed past the man in a red tracksuit. Gavin Kennedy just stood there dumfounded, not able to react.

"Gavin and Joe Kennedy?" the stranger asked, rudely shaking off his umbrella in the hallway.

"Yes, both of them answered slowly," Joe having just arrived to see who was there. "And who are you?" asked Gavin.

"I am Bartholomew Forsythe-Twyke, and I have a job for you. From immediate effect, you work for me, and only for me. You will be well-paid!" he said as the Kennedy brothers both stared at him in confusion. "Don't look so surprised. You've done jobs for my family before."

"What do you want us to steal?"

"Nothing!"

The brothers now looked even more confused, which actually wasn't so difficult, as they weren't the brightest.

"I want you to follow someone."

"And who should we follow?"

"Mr Jackson from number three!"

"That sounds easy," commented Gavin, smiling at what appeared to be a simple job and easy money. "When should we start?"

"He'll be collected at eight-thirty tomorrow morning and accompanied by my cousin, Vanessa. Shortly before, a taxi will come for you. Here are two passports, flight tickets and a phone. You will find my number saved and I expect constant updates on his activities and movements. I want to know everything Mr Jackson does, and if he coughs, I want to know about it."

"Flight tickets?" queried Joe.

"Passports?" asked Gavin.

The brothers looked at each other and frowned, not saying anything but clearly puzzled about this strange request.

"We'll need payment now," piped up Joe.

"Here's enough money for your expenses," added Bartholomew, handing over an envelope. "You'll receive the other half on your return, providing you complete the job to my liking."

"Take two wide-brimmed hats and wear them all the time to protect yourselves from pigeon droppings.

Bartholomew left the house, leaving both Gavin and Joe with their mouths open.

"Pigeon droppings!" exclaimed Joe.

"Where's Bangkok?" asked Gavin, looking at his flight ticket.

***

Trout Lane was usually quiet, but this morning it was a hive of activity. Mr Lawnsworthy was meticulously tending his rockery, like an engineer cleaning an aircraft turbine, but kept on looking at me with suspicion. Mr and Mrs Khan were dressed in stylish salwar kameezzes and their children carrying cool boxes, preparing for what looked like a day out. Earl Pike was putting his bike through its paces, skidding around and pulling wheelies in his driveway. He then shot across the road and did spins in front of Mr Lawnsworthy, sending small stones over the rockery before being angrily chased away. Shortly after, I saw white blobs splatting on Mr Lawnsworthy's beautiful garden decoration, causing us to look up in the air for pigeons. There were none. And every few seconds, a new white bomb would explode somewhere on the rockery, sending Mr Lawnsworthy into an utter rage. These white splats didn't come from above as I saw one fly horizontally across the road and hit him right on his backside. It wasn't difficult to work out the direction they were coming from; Earl Pike every now and then standing up from behind a fence to fire a salvo of mushy white paper with his catapult. I smiled, as most adults would, remembering what we did as children.

But what stood out were the Kennedy brothers—dressed in their tracksuits, as you might expect, wearing wide-brimmed straw hats and standing next to two suitcases. The cans of fizzy drinks they were guzzling quickly ended up on the ground next to the piles of rubbish already there. Quite an eyesore in our lovely Trout Lane. I wondered where they might be going. Surprisingly, the monk wasn't here anymore, and I wondered what he might now be doing.

All of sudden, some dogs ran into Trout Lane, stopped next to Mr Lawnsworthy, and left their wet marks on his rockery. Now extremely angry, he tried to shoo them away, but they remained rooted to the spot. It was obvious they were on a special operations mission sent to observe me. However, it didn't take long for the cavalry to arrive as Cleopatra bound out of my house along with two rabbits and, after a brief fight, chased the dogs straight out of the Lane. Mr Lawnsworthy's pride and joy was now a complete mess as he stood there cursing after the animals.

This was a bad moment, but I had no choice, walking across to Mr Lawnsworthy to ask him to take my key and check on my mail.

"I hope nothing happens like last time," he angrily added before slamming his door shut.

Just as I was handing over the key to him, a taxi pulled into Trout Lane and stopped exactly where the Kennedy brothers were waiting, quickly followed by a Rolls Royce with Bartholomew in the front passenger seat next to his chauffeur.

"Come on, Connor, get your bag and let's go," shouted Vanessa excitedly through the open rear window. "What's wrong? You look like you haven't slept. Nervous?"

I tried to sleep last night but my mind was just too active, trying hard to think about what it would be like flying for the first time. After tossing around in bed, I gave up and spent some time reading travel reports about Bangkok, finding it difficult to imagine as I was sure to expect an explosion of new experiences. Vanessa was so calm, as though going away to this city was like going to the supermarket.

"The journey begins," I replied anxiously.

The chauffeur drove slowly through the windy country lanes, the Kennedy brothers' taxi strangely never far behind.

"Bangkok then, Mr Jackson? I've heard it's your first time," said Bartholomew, attempting to strike up a conversation.

"Yes, it is. Not much of a traveller really."

"Where do you intend to go?" clumsily fishing for information.

"I think you should ask your cousin that, but Chinatown sounds like an interesting place and close by the old city and many temples."

"Any place in particular?"

This being an obvious game of you know that I know, and I know that you know; I decided to play along.

"There are just so many to choose from but maybe Wat Pro. It particularly interests me," I replied, randomly choosing a temple I could remember from the tourist guides.

"And after Bangkok? Surely, you've got some plans."

"Actually not. I'm following Vanessa as she is the travel guru. But I'm sure we'll stay in touch," sarcastically finishing the conversation.

"Yes, do that," After a short pause he continued. "It's nice to see normal workers can afford to go on such journeys today."

I rolled my eyes over his snobbery and put my head back into the comfortable leather, hoping he would just shut up.

***

Whilst I was jetting high in the sky, Ludwig was getting ready for his night-time activities. He was thirsty and hungry but put his own needs aside whilst Basil was suffering. He started looking for his friend and, as most people had finished work, this gave him time to look at the whole facility. At the end of the hall where he last smelt Basil, three different doors led to different outcomes for the ducks. Direct slaughter for those deemed fit and plump enough, one for fattening for those with potential and one for shredding for those classified as not good enough. Ludwig was able to jump up and press a button, which opened an airtight door with a hiss. He was met by a wall of noise as hundreds of ducks were tightly packed into rows upon rows of cages, quacking loudly in discomfort.

Ludwig quickly scanned the room for workers and, happy he was alone, took a closer look at the first row. The cages had trays full of a mushy liquid at head height, allowing them to feed the whole time. Despite their quacking, the ducks appeared to be strangely subdued with slightly gazed eyes. Unlike the pigs in the truck, the ducks failed to notice Ludwig's arrival, as if they were drugged. He trudged up the aisles between the many cages, looking for Basil in this awful place, constantly calling out his name, but it was impossible to be heard in the noise. After passing many cages, he eventually saw a distinctive yellow beak and knew he had found him at last.

"Basil, is that you?" There was no reaction from his friend. "Basil," he asked forcefully again.

This time he looked up, and a small spark of light appeared in his eyes.

"Ludwig, is that really you?"

"Yes, it's your friend Ludwig, and I've come to save you. Come to get you out of here."

"Don't do it. Just get out of this hell and save yourself," came a slow and sad voice from the cage.

"You don't look good, Basil."

"No. I feel sick. This feed is made of chemicals, and we are being slowly drugged and fattened. Go, Ludwig. Get out. There's nothing you can do for me."

A noise of a door opening forced Ludwig to quickly get away from the cages. "I'll return," he exclaimed. "I promise."

"Make sure my family are OK," Ludwig heard Basil say as he carefully retreated away, keeping out of the roaming security guard's sight.

***

"Wake me up when the food is served, please," and she put her head to one side and closed her eyes.

You do realise I have never flown before, and I was getting more agitated by the second as we taxied and prepared for take-off. Looking around the plane, I saw relaxed faces, and some amazingly already sleeping. My heart was beating and stomach churning at the thought of being propelled up into the sky in a metal cigar tube. The Kennedy brothers were sitting a few rows behind, excitedly pushing every button available and giggling like immature school children. Since leaving Trout Lane some hours ago, they had tailed our every movement.

My thoughts were quickly distracted as the roar of the engines shook the plane, the force pushing me back into the seat. With white knuckles, I clutched my armrests and tensioned my body as we shot down the runway, accelerating and bumping along. Beads of cold sweat appeared on my forehead and then suddenly a strange sensation as I felt the plane lose contact with the ground and we angled steeply upwards. Until now, I had been looking straight ahead, too scared to look out of the window, but, summoning up my courage, I took a peek outside to see the buildings getting smaller as we soared up into the sky. There was suddenly a loud thud directly below my feet, making me look nervously around in panic at this unexpected noise.

"Don't worry," said the person to my right. "It's just the wheels being retracted."

A transport shuttle with a reckless mole driver was easily my preferred mode of transport compared to being suspended in the sky, no control over my destiny. The plane tilted sharply to the left and, holding my breath as though my heart had missed a beat, ended up looking directly down on a river far below. An alarm sound made me jump out of my skin, but it turned out to be nothing more than the seat belt sign being turned off. Everyone else seemed to be much more relaxed. Some started to walk around, and the cabin crew were busily preparing drinks and food. The next ten hours would be long.

"You look a little white, Connor, and your forehead wet. Please don't tell me you are sick already!" she said, laughing at my concerned face when I woke her up as requested.

Just as soon as she had finished eating, she put her head into her cushion. "See you in Bangkok," and promptly fell asleep like someone had switched her off.

The lights were dimmed, and I looked around the plane to see everyone settling down to sleep for the rest of the flight, the Kennedy brothers snoring loudly. I just sat there with large, open eyes wondering what I should do for the next eight hours. Why was I the only one who couldn't sleep? The only interesting thing I found to do was following the flight path as we cruised high in the sky somewhere above the Black Sea. Sometimes the plane jolted and shook in patches of turbulence, my heart landing in my mouth each time. Eventually, I took out my documents and Bangkok guidebook to see if I could find any more clues as everything was all still too abstract. Maybe I was still overlooking the obvious. I had already checked everything for any possible connections with the code number—phone numbers, post codes, coordinates. But there was nothing at all in front of me as I frustratingly decided I had to start blindly in Chinatown. We were now over India and four hours to go.

***

After what seemed like the night would never end, the cabin lights went on and the other passengers slowly woke up from their slumber. We were now just south of Bangladesh over the Bay of Bengal, as the busy cabin crew served breakfast in a slick and well-practised procedure. I felt a different sensation as my ears started to pop and the engine noise changed, then saw on the display we had started out descent towards Bangkok. It was early morning in this part of the world and the deep blue sea far below gave way to a lush green jungle. I now felt somehow more comfortable in the knowledge the ground was getting ever closer, with rural villages soon making way for a massive, sprawling city. We banked sharply and descended even quicker, allowing me to even see cars moving below. This time I was expecting it as an alarm signalled us to put on our seat belts, and a short while later a thump as the wheels came out.

Frustratingly for me, Vanessa stirred, yawned, rubbed her eyes and simply asked, "Are we nearly there?"

A short while later, the wheels hit the ground once, bounced and hit again before the engines burst into reverse thrust as we braked sharply along the runway.

"Phew, back on the ground," I declared, smiling at Vanessa for the first time since getting in the plane and relaxed my grip on the arm rests.

Now able to calm down, I started to get excited about the prospect of experiencing another culture and country. The climate-controlled airport was a hive of efficient activity, as we were processed through immigration and baggage retrieval in a jiffy. My head was constantly darting all over the place, picking up on everything I could. Foreign faces from the many different travellers arriving from all over the world, a loud mixture of different languages and signs written in a different alphabet, the circular writing meaning nothing to me.

"Connor, we're not on the moon, you know!" Vanessa poked fun at me, as I stood gawking at the lively scenes around me. "Let's go and change some money."

I was greeted by a long and drawn out *sàwàddee ká* by a woman behind the counter, her hands clasped together in a prayer like symbol. It means hello in Thai, and I had at least learnt that before I left.

Keen to learn the local culture, I copied the gesture and said *sàwàddee ka* back to her, only to be met by a tut from Vanessa.

"It's *sàwàddee kráb* for you. Women say '*ká*' and men say *kráb*," and then looked at the woman as she handed the money over and said '*khob khun ka*'. "That's thank you, by the way," she replied, looking back at me.

"Then I should say *khob khun kráb*. Correct?"

"Exactly."

"And now, Vanessa?" I asked, looking around the vast terminal, teeming with people in the many shops available. The Kennedy brothers were sitting on their cases not too far away, pretending they were not watching us. They looked just as bemused at their new experience as I did.

"We'll take a taxi to the hotel. It might take a while as the Bangkok traffic is horrendous and it's also early morning rush hour. I think you might also appreciate some air conditioning!"

"Don't worry about me, this is absolutely fine."

Vanessa raised her eyebrows and signalled for me to follow. The terminal's glass doors opened, and I was met by a wall of heat, stopping me in my tracks. The intense heat, the thick humidity and the closeness of the air immediately made me break out into a sweat. Vanessa looked at me and smiled seeing how I was already struggling in the suffocating climate.

"Are you OK?"

I said nothing, as rivulets of sweat started running down my red face.

"We are still in the shade and it's only eight o'clock. There's more to come, Connor!"

I nodded ever so slowly to avoid any unnecessary movement, now also incapable of speaking. It was like a sticky bathroom where a hot shower had been running for a long time. The taxi offered me an escape from the oven, but I was met with another shock to the system as it was like a refrigerator, the warm sweat on my body now turning into a cold shiver. I looked out of the rear window to see the Kennedy brothers also struggling in this harsh environment. Their faces were now the same red as their tracksuits as they feverishly tried to fan themselves by flapping magazines in front of their faces. But it was to no avail.

Bangkok's Suvarnabhumi airport is about twenty kilometres from the city centre, and it was a journey quite unlike one I had ever experienced. As you already know, I've spent the whole of my life in the rural Molehamptons, and a traffic jam is being stuck behind a tractor for a short while. Even my experience of London was nothing compared to this. The four-lane highway was just one fusion of near stationary traffic moving ahead at snail's pace. The highway was elevated above the city, offering me a view of the different buildings shrouded in the grey smog below. Amongst the haze, modern skyscrapers darted up towards the sky, surrounded by what looked to me like a lot of hastily constructed buildings, some held together by bamboo and plastic sheets, others only half- finished. Amongst all of this, golden temples stood out like bright candles in a dark room. I should really have been tired after not sleeping a wink during the flight, but the contrasting sights were so amazing it kept my eyes from closing, unlike Vanessa who was yet again snoozing gently away. My head turned in all directions not wanting to miss out on anything, like an excited child at Christmas not knowing which present to open first. It must have taken us at least two hours to snake our way slowly above the city until, at last, we dropped down into the world below where the traffic jam above seemed like a picnic. Trucks, cars, different type of tuk-tuks, mopeds and people pushing an array of carts created a frenzied mass of traffic, slowly inching forward at what seemed the speed of a glacier amidst a hail of horns and black belching fumes. Any open space was cunningly abused by mopeds, zig-zagging their way through the frenetic moving mass of mayhem, just avoiding certain death under the wheels of a truck. Finally, we arrived in, what I assumed was, Chinatown, owing to the Chinese style shops and writing. An amazingly dense area of the city with small alleys joining the main thoroughfare we were driving along. The pavements were used for market stalls, most of them spilling out from shops. Amid a crescendo of horns and revving engines, we stopped outside a hotel on Yaowarat Road. Another blast of heat hit me as I got out of the taxi, only to be dunked into a frozen bath of cool air in the hotel lobby. The Kennedy brothers burst through the hotel entrance whilst we were checking in, looking visibly disoriented and uncomfortable in this new environment. I just hoped I didn't look the same.

***

"Bartholomew speaking," he said, answering the phone in his secret study.

"They are in their hotel," added Ormerod bluntly. "And you're right about the brothers. They are particularly stupid, but at least doing their job of following and not inconspicuously. It will be easy to observe and follow them at a distance without Mr Jackson seeing me."

"Good, Father. Call me if you need anything."

"I don't need anything from you as the show is now here. Mr Jackson undoubtedly has information we do not have so he can investigate, put it all together and lead us to our *target*."

Chapter Thirteen
Burglars on the fourteenth Floor

Dressed appropriately for the oppressive heat of Bangkok, we were ready for our first excursion.

"Where to now, Mr Analyst?"

"Don't be so eager and expect immediate results. I've got little to go on, but am convinced at least a clue, or some answers are somewhere near here. I'm afraid we'll just have to look around and see what comes up."

"Do you mean you haven't got a plan?"

I deflected the question, only wanting her to know what she needed to know. "I can tell you what I have and that's an empty belly, and it needs filling. So, what's your plan, Vanessa Forsythe-Twyke?"

"That can easily be arranged," she said, smiling at me.

As if pre-programmed, the Kennedy brothers appeared out of the lift whilst we were walking towards the hotel door and gateway to the furnace. And this time they were wearing different clothes—their tracksuits were now green! Even though I had prepared myself for the wall of heat, it was still a shock when it came, as I immediately broke out into a sweat. My sunglasses and smartphone also misted up in the humidity, rendering them quite useless.

If I thought the weather was a shock to the system, well, that was nothing to what now met me—Chinatown. Yaowarat Road is the main avenue through this part of Bangkok and made up of a complex warren of extremely narrow alleys coming off the main road. Vanessa elected not to cross the crazy traffic bedlam of Yaowarat Road and stayed on our side, passing by a small supermarket, the ice-cold air pumping out of the open door. A beggar sat on the ground next to a Chinese store selling what looked like magic potions. She then turned right into a smaller side street with shops, market stalls, and street food stands. The footpath was tight, sharing the space with chairs and tables covered with assorted sticks and pieces of material draped across to create shade from the powerful sun. A spaghetti mesh of hundreds of electricity cables was suspended above the makeshift structures, all seemingly tapped into the same junction box. The kerbs were high compared to the ones at home, probably because of the large amount of rainfall in the monsoon season. Everything had been swept clean, the store owners keeping their own areas neat and tidy, but we had to take care where to walk with some paving slabs broken and large drain covers oozing with dirty water. The shops we saw looked more like garages, with shutters on the front, the goods displayed on tables in front and sometimes encroaching onto the road. I stepped off the pavement to walk around a stall, only to be swiftly pulled back by Vanessa as a moped came screaming down the road, expertly swerving between cars, people and stands.

Vanessa stopped at a strange place selling food, opposite a beautifully decorated temple nestling in between shoddy buildings and street vendors. The front of the kitchen had a glass case, which took up half of the footpath, numerous cooked ducks and hanging vegetables on display. Behind the case, a rather rotund woman sat on a stool surrounded by gas cookers, large pots of soup exhaling steam, a huge wok with sizzling fat, large piles of noodles and a fan to blow the hot air around.

"This will do," exclaimed Vanessa and went inside.

I wouldn't go as far as to call it a restaurant. It consisted of a single room, the walls half-tiled, and plastic tables and stools, pretty much like I would use for camping. On one wall was a wobbly-looking shelf unit stacked precariously with plates, bowls, cooking utensils, and many different sauces. There was a sink and cleaning area at the back with a little shrine next to it, a golden Buddha and incense sticks sitting on a small table. Cables hung loosely and connected to wall sockets in weird and wonderful ways, and I doubted if this place would pass any health and safety inspection. The menu was shown on the wall with numbered pictures, the woman specialising in duck or vegetable soups served with a choice of different noodles.

"Have you seen anything you like, or recognise?" Vanessa asked chuckling.

"That one," I said, stabbing at a picture.

"And imagine that was Basil! How could you?"

"I really didn't consider that. Yes, I suppose eating duck whilst Basil is in the Food Factory wouldn't be so appropriate."

I changed my mind and ordered a vegetable dish instead.

Soup, assorted vegetables and noodles were ladled into bowls and served directly. A basket on the table had different condiments available for adding to the soup: sugar, chillies, chillies and even more chillies. The only thing which differentiated them was the size. I had built up a healthy appetite after the excitement of travelling and the soup smelled absolutely delicious, even though the strange room was not attractive. This immersion into a world of exotic smells was a far cry from the local food I so loved. A light breeze in my back from a tabletop fan offered some relief from the intense heat, but the soup was just about to add a few degrees as I put the spoon into my mouth. The first sensation was the explosion of different flavours, followed by an outbreak of sweat on my forehead. Then the chillies hit, and I hadn't even added any extra from the table. My lips and tongue first caught fire and then I started hiccupping as the burning sensation arrived at the back of my throat. I grabbed for the ice-cold bottle of water in a bid to quench the fire, but it was to no avail, as my head turned even redder and the sweat poured down my face, arms and fingers before dripping on the floor.

The woman saw my reaction and burst out laughing and shouted, "Farang like ped ped!" She then slapped a duck on her well-used chopping board and proceeded to expertly chop it up at great speed using a large meat cleaver.

Gasping for breath, I was unable to ask what she said, so Vanessa clued me in. "She told you foreigner likes spicy," and started laughing at me too. "They call foreigners *farang* here."

"It's not funny," I managed to gasp, fanning my burning mouth with my hand.

"That green thing you just ate wasn't a bean, Connor, it was a chilli," she added now in hysterics. "Take another spoon but be careful."

Not surprisingly, I wasn't the only one having difficulty with the spicy food. The Kennedy brothers had also stopped for something to eat at the street food stand opposite and were now running up and down the road gesturing to their mouths and shouting for ice. They were bright red, like beetroots, soaked to the skin in sweat and now yelping like puppies. The sight of these two men making such a fuss in the street was too much for local people as they all roared in laughter at the sight. My reaction to the fiery food was, in comparison, somehow subdued as my mouth slowly returned to normal.

"Eat up, Connor. You'll get used to it, believe me!"

"I want to believe you but find it quite difficult in my current situation. And look at them," pointing to the Kennedy brothers, still trying to extinguish the fire in their mouths. "They definitely won't believe you."

Upon finishing our meal, we bade farewell to the woman who was busy laughing at the Kennedy brothers along with the other vendors. Vanessa turned down a narrow alley, covered by a collection of awnings, pieces of plastic sheet and boards, just like the structure of a den in a children's bedroom. We were now in an intricate set of small walkways comprising of market stands, hidden from the world above by their improvised roofs. I never would have ventured down here but Vanessa was confident and keen to show me the area around this part of the city. My mouth had experienced an explosion of flavours and it was now for my other senses to take over. I have never sucked in so many different smells in a short space of time coming from the exotic wares on offer. There were a vast selection of different sea food, fresh herbs, colourful spices, aromatic teas and flowery incense sticks just to name a few. But there were also some unsavoury smells of rotten rubbish and drain water bursting up from the ground only to be immediately replaced by another odour. The noise was like a loud delirium of nearby vehicles, honking horns, blaring music and the loud chattering of the local language by the hundreds of people moving around the confined maze. It was difficult for me to concentrate with so many new things thrown at me in a small space and in a short time. We snaked our way around the tight mass of people, sometimes ducking into a stall to get out of the way of mopeds stacked high with goods, carelessly shooting down the alleys. The dishevelled and confused looking Kennedy brothers were not far behind, pushing their way past people in an attempt to keep us in sight, which was quite difficult in the mass of moving bodies. They really didn't look like they were enjoying this place and their job. I was sure Vanessa was purposefully making them work hard as she kept on turning into side alleys, ducking out of the way, and then looking behind to see their reaction. They didn't look amused.

But I wasn't here on holiday and had an important task to do. I tried to slow down to focus on the many different shops and stalls, searching for anything resembling a link between the code number, moles, monks and Oldfield Thomas. But this proved nearly impossible in the kaleidoscope of scenes confronting me. Nearly all signs were in Thai or Chinese, both languages having no meaning to me, and the ones in English contained nothing at all interesting. Although mainly concentrating on signs and numbers, I was surprised at the goods on show, a lot of them selling only one product, for example coat hangers or handbags and even a gaudy collection of cuddly toys. Some stores were so tightly packed with goods it was necessary to climb over unstable piles, some reaching as high as the ceiling. I stopped at one store selling assorted sacks of dried fish and inspected them, intrigued by the many various types previously unknown to me.

"Interesting, isn't it?" commented Vanessa, also impressed by the selection.

"You could say that. I've never seen anything like this," I replied, mopping my sweaty brow. "But I think I've seen enough for today and my batteries are pretty run down now."

"Yeah, the climate can really take it out of you."

"And no sleep last night. Just look at me. I'm completely soaked through."

"Did you see anything interesting?" she enquired, fishing for information.

"Interesting, of course, but nothing to do with why I'm here. I need to shower, rest my brain from these new scenes and have a good night's sleep. Maybe I will see things from a different angle when I'm fresh."

"Good idea. And you aren't the only one in need of a shower," she added, nodding in the direction of the Kennedy brothers, trying to look inconspicuous behind a stall.

Chinatown was now being transformed into one big outside kitchen as the night market got underway under the glow of the setting sun. The food stalls, already overflowing onto the streets, spread out even further and now added to their areas with big gas cookers spouting flames and large racks of ice with fresh seafood, meat sticks, small pancakes and many other exotic delicacies. Street kitchens were now joined by a colourful range of homemade carts and mopeds with sidecars, equipped with barbeques shoddily attached to the side, spewing flames from hot coals. Gas bottles tied to the side fired large metal woks with hot spitting oil for deep frying. Small canopies provided another place to hang vegetables and kitchen equipment; with large wooden chopping boards, bowls, and bottles vying for space on the small work surfaces. If it wasn't already hot enough, the cooking equipment added even more to the temperature gauge, distinctly felt by a wave of heat when walking past.

With these amazing experiences churning through my head, I turned in for the night and wondered how my dear friends, Ludwig and Basil, were doing back in the Molehamptons.

***

Ludwig spent the day lying low and came out when most had left, to visit Basil, who was already showing signs of becoming larger in the fattening process. Ducks are clean animals and use their beaks and water to groom themselves, but it was not possible in these conditions, and even Basil after a day here looked in a sorry state. Further up the chain, Ludwig saw what happened when the end came as they were packaged into plastic bags, any resemblance of once being an animal lost. There were only thirteen cages in front of Basil and time was running out. Ludwig walked to another area where he watched pieces of what was once a chicken being whitened with bleach and then injected with water to make it juicy. If the treatment of animals was bad enough, what they did to the meat for their own consumption was just idiotic, tricking themselves to make it look good. Any food remnants and innards were swept up, put into boxes and sent to another area.

Ludwig had to do something, even if he didn't have the means to free Basil but as a show of defiance. He rummaged around the complex and returned with a small metal bar clenched in his jaws. His target was the electric bath used for finishing off the ducks after fattening. He then lay in wait before creeping stealthily forward to the motor which drove the chain. Inserting the bar into one of the metal links was easier said than done, especially without hands. He stood next to the chain, the bar protruding out of his mouth, and tried to poke it through a hole by moving his head and body. He failed again and again but Ludwig wasn't one to give up and, after slightly adjusting his position, managed at last to insert it. Sensing success, Ludwig wagged his tail in glee as the bar moved towards an upright support. It first banged against the support, causing the chain to shudder, rattle violently and then come to a crunching halt. The electric motor, however, didn't stop and kept on applying pressure until something had to give, and thankfully it wasn't the metal bar. Funny creaking noises and smoke started emitting from the motor and then it suddenly went bang accompanied by a flash of flames. Alarm bells and red flashing lights went off and pandemonium soon broke out. Ludwig was enjoying the spectacle so much he nearly forgot to hide. The sound of approaching voices made him jump and he only just managed to get out of sight as the first people arrived, running into the hall in panic.

"It's completely destroyed. Nothing I can do here, I'm afraid. Sorry, but we'll have to order a new motor and it might take a few days to arrive," said a confused technician.

"But we need it quicker," came the supervisor's reply. "Why haven't we got one in stock?"

"Because you told me not to, as it is too expensive having money sitting on a shelf."

Ludwig wagged his tail again, impressed at his work, and started to put plans together for what he might sabotage tomorrow.

***

It was a long day, and I was absolutely exhausted, not only from travelling and the climate but, above all, the thinking. I returned to my hotel room and looked out of the window to a wonderful view over the sights of Bangkok. Below me were the neon lights in Chinatown and beyond modern high-rise buildings shared space with beautifully lit-up golden temples. The most impressive of which was the main landmark of the city, Wat Arun, superbly illuminated next to the river. An impressive golden spire, thrusting towards the sky along with four smaller ones at each corner, which couldn't fail to impress in the skyline.

My head hit the pillow and I was out for the count, as the experiences of the day churned around in my head. Do you know the sensation of being in a dream which is so real you really believe you are there? And, in the random swirls of strange thoughts, that was exactly what I was experiencing. A noise entered my dream, a kind of knocking sound disturbing whatever I was trying to do, and it was in my room. I thrashed around in bed, trying to escape, but there was no escape and the noise kept on coming. The rhythmic tapping on something hard became louder until my eyes suddenly flashed wide open, and I sat bolt upright, drenched in a cold sweat. I shook my head, but the noise was still there. Tap, tap, tap. What was it? A burglar? A kidnapper? Shaking with fear, I nervously padded across to the window and, terrified what awaited me, warily pulled back the curtains. With a sharp squeal, I froze to the spot, mouth wide open in shock.

Suspended on a rope in the middle of my window at the dizzy heights of the fourteenth floor—a mole! Dressed like a burglar in a black jumpsuit, balaclava and goggles, it just stared back at me. A quick tug on a carabiner and the mole slid down, stopped on the narrow ledge, and spoke into a radio. More ropes immediately dropped, and three black creatures slid smoothly down and landed to form a team of special operation moles. One of them beckoned me to come with its paw and then pointed to the street below. All of a sudden, they all stepped backwards, dropped off the ledge and, with a zipping sound, abseiled into the darkness below.

I had experienced many weird events over the last years but this one was the icing on the cake as I stood there in complete shock. But, quickly understanding what they wanted, I shook my head to bring me back to reality. A few minutes later, I left the hotel into the tropical night. There were a few people sweeping the otherwise deserted pavements but no sign of the moles. An eery silence hung over the street, Chinatown looking different in the middle of the night without the people, traffic and stands. I slowly looked around, hunting for any sign of these small creatures and then I saw them standing at the corner of the next street. Without batting an eyelid, I followed them, not even paying attention to where I was going. The moles kept a good distance in front, scampering along between the bags of rubbish and broken paving stones. High above, the sky flashed as lightning streaked across the night sky accompanied by the deep rumbling and loud claps of thunder. Completely disoriented, I followed for what felt like a long time, criss-crossing through the narrow alleys, quite possibly passing the same place more than once. It was difficult to say as it all looked the same to me, especially at night-time with the shutters down.

I was sure they were trying to show me something as they were now much slower and, on taking a closer look, found everything so much different. Gone were the sprawling market stands, stacked goods and bright lights, replaced instead by the names of shops and numbers. Most had names, which I presumed were in Chinese and Thai, and some in English. My analytical mind clicked in, and I started processing names and numbers to see if I could find a clue. Maybe, just maybe, the number was hidden in a sign. But the dense area of Chinatown ended, and in front of me I saw a park and a beautifully lit temple complex, the ornate structure shimmering in the distance. I was now at Rommaninat Park and also close to a metro station. Looking around, I realised the moles were now nowhere to be seen. They were gone and I had no idea where I was, the name of the park not really helping me.

***

Meanwhile back in the Molehamptons, a tree's low canopy hid someone standing as close to the trunk as possible. This part of the village green was only dimly lit, allowing him to merge into the darkness, not seen by the approaching woman.

"Mrs Pike," the man spoke in a whisper.

She slowed and looked around, trying to see who called her, but the man remained hidden. Not feeling quite comfortable, she quickened her pace.

"Mrs Pike," he said a little louder.

Now stopping, she called out, "Who's there. Show yourself." Mrs Pike then relaxed as the sound of rustling in the branches revealed someone she knew. "Oh, it's you. What are you doing there?"

"We need to talk," he replied, whispering again.

"You look different when you are not in uniform."

"And I want to look different. Mrs Pike, we need to talk."

"Here? Now?" she replied, rather surprised at what was now happening.

"Yes, here and now. We shouldn't be seen," declared Sergeant Dawson.

"It all sounds very secretive."

"Because it is. Mrs Pike, I know what you and your husband do."

Mrs Pike looked unnerved at his comment. "I work in the Food Factory. It's nothing special."

"Yes, I know that. I'm talking about the other things. Your work with the moles."

"Moles? No idea what you're talking about!" she replied, looking at the noise coming from the pub. "Have you been drinking?"

"Yes. No. Well, maybe one, but that's not the point. I know you can't talk about what you do, but I have a message for you. Two of Mr Jackson's friends are in the Food Factory. Basil, a duck, is in the fattening program and Ludwig, Mr Rye's dog, is inside trying to free Basil. They have all been below and know about the world of moles."

Mrs Pike remained completely expressionless during Sergeant Dawson's explanation.

"Ludwig might well need some help, and you may be able to assist. I will do everything I can from the outside and ask you to turn a blind eye should you see anything happen. Oh yes, Mr Cross knows Ludwig is in there too."

She nodded in a possible silent agreement then turned, hiding a smile, indicating to the Sergeant the conversation was over. "I must get along now. My husband will wonder where I am."

***

I wandered around Chinatown, trying frantically to find my way back through the myriad of passageways. Hopelessly lost, I didn't recognise anything to help me on my way and even the few people I came across couldn't speak any English to point me in the right direction. I was beginning to panic when the moles suddenly appeared in front of me again. What was their game, I asked myself, and started following? Before I knew it, I was back on the same road as my hotel and then the moles disappeared again, leaving me to ponder the purpose of the last few hours. The first rays of light were just beginning to show their presence.

Vanessa, fit as a fiddle, called me quite early and suggested we meet for breakfast and discuss a plan of action. Armed with some notes and a map of the city, I started my day.

"Connor, what's happened to you? You look awful. Haven't you slept?"

It was true, I did look awful, and I must only have slept for three hours before being rudely awoken.

"Yes, I slept but not as long as I needed. I think I dreamt about moles at my window," but then decided to leave out the bit about my night-time walk and new furry friends. We looked at the map and decided the best plan of action was to visit the nearby temples first to find our monk friend from the Molehamptons. There were lots of monks here but the burn mark on his face was a distinctive feature which might prove to be a help. He must have visited me for reason, and it was the best lead we had. And still, I didn't divulge the code number to Vanessa, instead keeping this vital piece of information for myself. Vanessa, having visited Bangkok a few times before, planned a tour and, armed with a map, we set off. The Kennedy brothers were already waiting in the lobby but looking the worse for wear, appearing not to have slept much and rubbing their stomachs, the food definitely not being to their liking. We walked through the street obstacles and headed towards the river where we took a river taxi upstream from Ratchawong Pier. Chao Phraya is the main river in Bangkok with a diverse range of different ships plying its trade along the route, from long boats to ferries, barges, taxis and speed boats. Our first stop was the majestic Wat Arun, its spire visible from my hotel room. Were I here for tourism, I would spend hours exploring this particular temple and surrounding buildings. An absolutely beautiful site, as I stared upwards in awe towards the top of the spire, marvelling at the intricate craftsmanship which had gone into building it. The Kennedy brothers didn't share my enthusiasm and, with long faces, sat on a bench just keeping us in sight. There were no monks here at the main spire but there was an adjacent temple guarded by two fearsome statues, wielding giant staffs. They stood at least four metres high, dressed in colourful warrior clothes, garish faces, and death curdling mouths with small horns above the top lips. One guard was made of amazing white and gold and the other of blue, green, and gold. Taking off our shoes, we entered the richly decorated temple with a huge, golden Buddha some metres high, sitting on a platform and surrounded by a flower-laden alter. There were some monks chanting from religious texts and helping visitors to understand readings. But our monk was nowhere in sight.

The next stop on our list was a vast temple complex on the other side of the river. Wat Phra Kaeo comprising a huge temple with an accompaniment of towers, statues, pillars, and thousands of tourists with the Royal Palace directly next to it. It was by far the most impressive architecture I had seen. Elaborately designed buildings with golden roofs, rich colours, and a large abundance of gold impressed the huge number of visitors snapping away with their cameras. The temple in the centre still did not give up the monk I was looking for; it was like looking for a needle in a haystack.

The old city was densely packed with temples and the next on the list was really not too far away. Wat Pho was apparently home of a giant lying Buddha. For this small journey, we decided to take a tuk-tuk which was my first experience in this three-wheeled motorcycle with an open passenger compartment on the back. Colourfully decorated with a shrill sound of its two-stroke engine, we darted through the busy Bangkok traffic, sliding around on its plastic seat as the driver crazily veered left and right, accelerating into any gap he could find. This experience is a must for anyone visiting the city but has its drawbacks, as you sit at exactly the same height as the exhaust pipe of trucks and buses, meaning every now and then a black puff of fumes envelopes the passengers. The Kennedy brothers now had smiles on their faces for the first time as this new adventure in a tuk-tuk was probably like a ride at the fun fair. They really did look a funny sight, their tracksuit jackets stripped off to reveal string vests, bright red traffic light faces soaked in sweat and their large bodies squeezed into the tight, confined space. I heard their howls of delight as their tuk-tuk raced through the traffic, erratically following us.

It may sound like a high-speed car chase seen in films, but in reality, quite slow as the Bangkok traffic does not really allow for a great deal of speed and tuk-tuks actually sound louder than their fast appearance may give away.

There were many more monks at Wat Pho, making it quite difficult to differentiate them, as they all looked nearly the same. The only distinction I was looking for was the burn mark on his face. Taking off our shoes, we entered a long building with a snake of tourists walking along the length of a huge lying Buddha measuring a massive forty-six metres and coated with gold leaf. A guide I picked up showed the name in English—the Temple of the Reclining Buddha. The many tourists were jostling for position to get a better view of this impressive sight and to take the best selfie. But this was not our purpose, and we left the temple dejected and quite tired as the heat and humidity were taking their toll, even for a seasoned traveller as Vanessa. Outside Wat Pho, we found shelter in a row of quaint cafés, awnings shading us from the sun and refreshing fans to move the otherwise still air. Fresh coconuts on ice provided a welcoming, thirst-quenching refreshment as we charged our batteries.

"Still no monk," I said, cradling my coconut, "despite all the temples."

"We've only seen three, and that's hardly a lot. But at least we have the brothers to keep us company."

The Kennedy brothers, never too far away, seemed to have learnt their lesson from yesterday and now only sipped water.

"We've been out for some hours and, apart from a sweaty T-shirt, nothing to show for it. I think we should walk back to the hotel and go through Chinatown. Maybe we will see something from a different angle."

"Good idea," replied Vanessa, looking at the map. "The edge of Chinatown is actually quite close."

"I'm not sure they'll appreciate it," I added, standing up and nodding toward the brothers.

We walked along Charoen Krung Road until coming to Sam Yot metro station. I suddenly recognised it from my walk last night and also saw Rommaninat Park just down the road. This was the place the moles had left me alone. We entered Chinatown, and I began recognising some shop signs, confirming this was the way I walked. I was now concentrating hard as the view at daytime differed greatly from that at night-time. We walked past a small store stacked high with books outside on the pavement, only a small gap allowing access to the entrance. An old man was sitting on a stool, drinking tea in a cloud of smoke from aromatic incense sticks. Above him was a sign, in what I presumed was Thai and Chinese writing, and also something in English which had become quite faded over the years. And there it was, the clue I had hoped to find was staring straight at me—*Oldfield EncycloPaedias and Ancient Books*—the letters E and P both in capital letters. And a telephone number +66-02-5742-469-471. By taking away the first four digits, the code number from my father was now clear to see. I had found the clue I so much needed and perfectly camouflaged amongst other bookshops and stores selling amulets, hand-crafted jewellery and small antiques. All the clues led here, and it wasn't by chance I found it, the moles last night lending a helping hand. The books outside were old and covered in dust, and I could well imagine the old man had had no visitors in quite a time.

"What is it, Connor? Why are you looking so intently here?"

"I think I have something. Look, hidden in the sign is a clue."

"But you can't read it!"

"No, not that writing. Look at the small part in English."

"Oh yes," exclaimed Vanessa surprised and squinting towards the sign. "The name Oldfield and also EP. Very observant of you."

"But something is different," I added, turning around. "The Kennedy brothers are nowhere to be seen."

Vanessa and I approached the old man, who was gazing at the floor and calmly dozing. I coughed to get his attention.

"His head flicked up in surprise. "Visitors," he said, breaking into a grin.

"May we come in?" I asked.

"Well, of course. Come, come," indicating excitedly and allowing me to squeeze between the books into his dusty world of encyclopaedias. Vanessa paused for a while and then stayed outside. Between a gap in some books, I saw her take out a phone and speak."

The Kennedy brothers, not inconspicuous at the best of times, were now at the centre of attention and unfortunately for a bad reason. Bored of temples and tracking Connor, they decided to travel by tuk-tuk instead of walking. But then their criminal background got the better of them as they forcibly stuffed a tuk-tuk driver into the back seat next to Joe, Gavin now sitting in the front and in control. In a short moment, they were surrounded by angry locals and other tuk-tuk drivers, protesting at their unwanted and unwarranted behaviour. The brothers were laughing their heads off and indicating they wanted to drive, which made the local people even angrier. Everything just seemed a bit of fun for them, and they were oblivious to their unwelcome presence. Just as it looked as though the situation could turn violent, a foreign man appeared on the scene. He had a sun-beaten leathery face, was wearing a wide-brimmed hat and then calmly spoke to the protestors in their own language. He must have carried an aura of respect as the crowd immediately started to disperse, leaving him alone with Gavin and Joe. The two brothers, just realising the predicament they had put themselves in, now sat there in subdued embarrassment.

"And you two, get out and come with me!" he harshly spoke in a commanding tone.

Gavin and Joe immediately complied with the instructions from this stranger, releasing the tuk-tuk driver from the back of his own vehicle. He shouted something in Thai at the brothers, which probably wasn't complimentary, then drove his tuk-tuk away.

"What do you think you are doing?" shouted the man at the brothers.

"And who are you?" asked Gavin.

"It's not for you to know. You are being paid quite handsomely to follow and that is all you need to do. Where's Mr Jackson?"

Gavin looked meekly at the man. "We lost them in these small streets. They are on foot and impossible to follow but I did get a phone call saying they were in a bookshop somewhere in Chinatown, but she couldn't say exactly where. So, we thought we would commandeer a tuk-tuk and find them. Quicker than walking, and probably good fun too."

"You are not being paid for having fun," pointing angrily at the brothers. "Get into these little alleys and scour them for a bookshop. I suggest for your own sakes you do it now and quickly. Go!" he loudly ordered.

Chapter Fourteen
One Hundred and Fifty-Six Golden Buddhas

"Can I help you? I have had no visitors for a while now and you appear to be interested in something," the old man asked, grinning at me, the hint of a fine English accent behind his Asian dialect.

I didn't have many clues to go on. "Have you got anything on Kloss's mole, by chance?" I blurted out.

The old man stopped and looked at me, his face free of any expression. But then it changed to one of understanding and maybe surprise he had a visitor at all, but a visitor who even asked for something he might have.

"I think I can be of service."

He then spun around and scooted through a pile of books, threw some out of the way, climbed over others and then ducked down onto the floor. I wouldn't exactly call this a shop; it was more like a room with a life-long collection or various works which hadn't been sorted in years. As if suddenly transformed, he started darting around and bumped into a stack of books, sending them flying, before disappearing into a back room. I heard him rummaging around, the sound of objects crashing around.

"Be back soon," he shouted out, the sound of joy evident in his voice.

I used the time to glance around and immediately noticed a sizeable amount of his books were in fact atlases and loose maps, some of them extremely old. I randomly picked up a book just lying around, wiping away the thick layer of dust and cobwebs. "What's this?" I said aloud. "A Study into Bird Migration from Europe 1876." I opened other books, completely engrossed in the old titles, then noticed a leather-bound folder containing loose maps. For some reason, it automatically caught my attention and on closer inspection realised they were hand drawn, but had no legends, town names or location. Why would someone go to the effort of drawing a map with no indication of where it could be? Maybe a kind of treasure map. I quickly put the leather folder under a pile of paper, subconsciously thinking it best to hide what I had just looked at, then started looking at a book about penguins. The old man saw what I did and smiled.

I was so preoccupied; I didn't even notice Vanessa appear at my side. Poking me in the side, she said, "Hi there, Mr Analyst. Anything interesting?"

"I think so," I replied, holding a book in my hand.

"The Behaviour of Penguins 1887," she quizzed, glancing over my shoulder. "Connor, why does that interest you? We didn't come all this way to research penguins."

"No, of course not. The nice old man is just looking for something in the back room. And here he is now."

The shopkeeper wiped sweat from his forehead then blew dust off an old manuscript, made up of paper and bound with string.

"Here we are," he proudly exclaimed, handing it over to me. "Sit down and take your time," clearing some books from two stools and a rickety table.

"So, what's this?" talking to myself as I sat down. Research into the Himalayan Mole (Kloss's Mole), Oldfield Thomas, June 1881, Series 5,7(42):469-471. Unbelievable, I was looking at the exact number my father gave me.

"Oldfield Thomas," exclaimed Vanessa. "Two of the words on the notes you received. And Kloss also."

Out of the corner of my eye, I saw one of the Kennedy brothers frantically running around in the road outside, presumably searching for us, but thankfully we were well-hidden behind many piles of books. The old man quickly threw a sheet over the table outside, put the shutter down, obscuring us from their view, and then sat on his stool just inside the entrance. This shop and the man were definitely hiding something, and I had a strong suspicion it could have something to do with the maps. Better I keep that thought to myself.

***

The Kennedy brothers were shocked into action by the foreign man, and they were now taking their task seriously, both of them having split up. They raced down the alleys before returning and choosing different directions, meeting up sometimes to describe what they had seen. But they couldn't read the signs, there were lots of bookshops and they were tired, making their task extremely difficult. Ormerod followed at a safe distance, watching their every step, and shook his head as they often looked in the same place twice. A flight of pigeons circled overhead above the roofs of the buildings, not uncommon in Bangkok and went unnoticed to the people walking in the street, the Kennedy brothers included. The birds seemed to be on some sort of mission, formed into a V-formation then diving towards the narrow alleys. Splitting into three groups, they homed in on Gavin, Joe and Ormerod, went into a steep dive and then dropped their loads of droppings. The birds masterfully performed their flying duties but, thankfully for the three targets, they all had wide-brimmed hats on. Bird poo began splatting on the ground around the three men, some droppings even hitting their hats. But none landed on their bare skin and the infiltration mission therefore failed. The pigeons, now much lighter with their loads ejected, soared back up into the sky and away. However, one of the stray blobs did find a target. As some of the local people looked up in the sky to see where the white bombs were coming from, someone was hit by a smeary splat right in the middle of his forehead. He was pushing a cart of drinks, stopped what he was doing and just ran off down the alley, past Joe Kennedy, Gavin Kennedy and Ormerod before disappearing into the distance. Joe helped himself to a well-needed drink from the now unattended cart.

***

It was plain to see the manuscript was extremely old, and care had to be taken as I brushed off a good layer of dust, now ready to open the cover in eager anticipation to see what we would find. The first few pages were typed and seemed to be a draft document as it had manual crossings out and handwritten annotations, presumably from Oldfield Thomas himself. It really was his research work and most likely the original and only copy.

Not having the time to read in detail from the beginning, I turned some pages, picking up on the titles and reading some sections about moles. Originally thought to live in the mountains of China, Laos and north Siam, Oldfield Thomas found evidence of their habitat being much further south than widely believed. As far south as Bangkok in fact and therefore an exciting discovery for the zoologist. His research work went on, as one might expect, to describe size, fur, eating habits and so on. Although interesting, it didn't instantly reveal any information which could be considered useful to my task at hand.

The old man returned from his guard post. "Is this the correct book?"

"I believe it is, thank you. We would like to stay a while longer to study it if we may."

"Of course, feel free to stay as long as you like."

I leafed through the pages to get a better feeling of the contents and then found what I was looking for at the back of the manuscript. The last twenty pages or so were additional material added at a later stage after the official academic work had been completed. It was handwritten and had self-drawn sketches. Jackpot, I thought to myself.

"Where did you get this from?" I asked the old man, who was hovering nearby and seemed to be taking a keen interest in what I was looking at.

"From a good friend many years ago."

"Do you know all the books here?" asked Vanessa in amazement, scanning the collection.

"Of course, every single one. But this manuscript," wagging his finger in our direction, "is most interesting because you are not the first person to have asked about it."

"Really!" My interest peaked. "Go on."

"About two years ago, a monk came to visit and asked to see exactly the same book. When I returned with it, he had gone."

"Did he have a burn mark in his face?"

"Yes, funny you should say that. But yes, he did."

"And do you know where I could find him now?"

"Sorry, never seen him again."

I was disappointed but it was to be expected, especially as there were so many monks here. I returned to the manuscript and started reading his handwritten notes. It wasn't all written in full sentences, rather a mixture of random notes, in no particular order and interspersed with illustrations. He described something so crazy he could never write it in an academic journal. Whilst observing molehill and tunnel patterns in the parks in and around Chinatown, he witnessed some very strange things. Close to the molehills, he sometimes noticed items on the ground, which were quite out of place, and they often moved when he wasn't looking. Single socks and blocks of salt he recorded in his notes. Oldfield Thomas found out these molehills and tunnels followed a pattern, and all led back to one place. A temple in the old city not too far away. The next pages consisted of notes and sketches recording his findings, including drawings of molehills with socks next to them and a log with dates and times.

The next page was about his findings at the temple where the molehills led. Unfortunately, he did not write a name but did describe the temple in some detail. It was here that he made a startling discovery. Whilst secretly observing the monks, he witnessed moles coming out of a wooden chest and then the monks and moles talking to each other. To prove he wasn't crazy and seeing things, he carried on monitoring and saw the same weird occurrences on more than one occasion. He even visited other temples in the city and saw the same strange activity. Again, his sightings were all meticulously logged.

He wrote about a beautiful temple complex, however failed to realise at this point in his writing that all of them were actually quite amazing to look at. But this one in particular had a white wall around the outer perimeter with red doors giving access to a vast temple, white pillars supporting a green and red pagoda style roof. A narrow garden with lovely trees and bushes surrounded the main building, the lawn pepper-potted with molehills rather spoiling the immaculately tended area. A second and smaller temple was adjacent to the larger one, also with white pillars and a golden and red roof. It sat in the middle of a cloistered courtyard surrounded by many golden Buddhas, all sitting under the roof and pointing inwards. Oldfield Thomas recorded one hundred and fifty-six golden Buddhas. A large field was next to the temple complex, and it was here all the mole tunnels led.

Oldfield Thomas wrote there was clearly more to the world of moles than mere tunnels and molehills. Something unexplainable was going on here, and it was outside the realm of academia. He had to get even closer. The next pages were a rambling collection of his experiences and difficult to decipher here. I understood Oldfield Thomas became a monk, being the only way to uncover the secrets of moles. He also prepared his official research work, submitting it in 1881, leading me to believe the copy I now had in my hands to be the original but now with post-manuscript annotations. Hence, any copies in university archives would not contain these unbelievable notes. This was the only copy.

After some years of being a monk, they indoctrinated him into the secret world of moles under Bangkok and found out their true role in the world. Their interface to our world above was through a secret cadre of humans acting as monks. He now pointed out that regular monks knew nothing about what was going on and completed their magnificent work whilst the secret cadre hid amongst their ranks. The moles could talk, one of his notes stated, written in uppercase and ringed with exclamation marks. But he could never report this, as he would be immediately discredited. They regulated this part of the world, keeping everything in its natural balance and, he observed, were advanced creatures possessing technology far ahead of what humans had. Similar to the moles under the Molehamptons, they administered memories, but the major difference was their quest for secret technology—Azoth.

I put the manuscript down and whistled in amazement. "Unbelievable this has been sitting here for so many years."

Vanessa, in the meantime, had used her phone to search for any information she could find about Oldfield Thomas. "And, Connor, do you know where he lived?" she excitedly asked.

"No, but I'm sure it's most interesting."

"More than that. He lived in the Molehamptons with my great-grandfather, Beaumont, in our mansion."

I sat there with my mouth open. "I suspected there was a connection. Wow, that's unbelievable."

"Yes. He disappeared for many years but appeared again in 1916 suffering from shell shock and amnesia as a result of World War One. He was classified as mad and his old friend, Beaumont, brought him to the mansion to care for him where he lived out his last years as a recluse."

"I can't wait to see what else he wrote," as I turned over the next page. I signed in disappointment.

"What's wrong, Connor?"

"There's nothing more here and the last pages ripped out. Shame, but at least we have something to go on. We need to find a temple and I have a plan."

"Why does that not surprise me!"

"I would like to buy this manuscript. How much is it?" I asked.

"Oh, no need for that. It is quite worthless to me, but feel free to bring it back when it is of no more use."

"Thank you so much. That is extremely kind of you," I genuinely exclaimed, surprised at his offer and taken aback by his generosity and trust.

"And now, Vanessa, you use your phone and see if you can match the description here," showing her Oldfield's writing. "In the meantime, let's take the Kennedy brothers on a ride around the old city and at the same time see if I can find the temple. If you are quicker, Vanessa, then tell me where to go."

I went to leave by the front door, but the old man stopped me. "You can't go through here now, there will be people watching. The others—the Cult of Azoth," he whispered as though someone could be listening. "Leave by the back door."

But we all froze on hearing faint sliding sounds from an upstairs room, like someone was moving a chair roughly across the room. We stood in complete silence.

"That would be my wife," he said, as if thinking of an excuse. "Follow me, out of the back door. Come on."

We found ourselves in a small backyard stacked full of pots and pans, then left through a gate into a narrow alley and quickly walked to a junction at the end. Presuming the Kennedy brothers, Ormerod and his agents would be scouring the market, we decided it would be a good idea to quickly visit as many shops as possible to draw the attention away from the old man.

***

The Kennedy brothers had used up all their reserves in their frantic search and now sat back-to-back supporting each other in the middle of a small junction.

"Gavin, did you see that?"

"See what, Joe? I haven't got the energy to do anything, let alone look."

"That monk over there. He's been staring at us for some time," Joe said, pointing in that direction.

"I'm not surprised. I think a lot of people are."

"Yes, I know that, but I'm sure he's been following us. I recognise the burn mark on his face. Oh, now he's turned around and is walking away."

"He can't be that interested in us anymore then, Gavin."

"But, Joe, now you must put your head up and look. Mr Jackson and that Forsythe-Twyke girl are over there. They're coming out of the shop selling metal kitchen goods."

"Where? There's more than one selling kitchen goods."

"You're so dense, Joe. Over there with the red sign and green front. There are loads of silver pots and chairs stacked high in front. It's number fifteen. Oh, and now they are pointing at us and waving."

"Do you think they know we are following them?" asked Joe stupidly.

"I'm not sure but we should follow them. They're getting in a tuk-tuk. After them!"

The two brothers, with a huge effort, hauled each other up and waddled as quickly as they could towards a waiting tuk-tuk. With another burst of effort, the two sweaty brothers squeezed themselves into the back.

"Follow them!" screamed Gavin, indicating to a tuk-tuk disappearing around a corner.

The driver, probably thinking it was like a film, immediately did what he was told and with a screech of tyres, shot off down the alley, horn beeping to warn the passers-by to get out of the way. Joe and Gavin were not laughing like they were the last time they were in a tuk-tuk, this time their faces white with fear as the small three-wheeled vehicle skidded around corners, revved between cars and crossed junctions, with no regard for other traffic. Their driver was having immense fun and doing exactly what they asked of him. With a sly grin, the driver turned around and showed with the tips of his fingers that this service was going to cost them. The brothers both wildly nodded in agreement, their lives now in his hands.

The driver would have realised it, but not Joe and Gavin, as the wild chase criss-crossed the busy alleys of Chinatown, not going in any particular direction. Had they been attentive, they might have noticed they had passed the same shops on more than one occasion.

***

The old man sat on his stool, slowly sipping his tea with a contented look on his face, probably because he had had some visitors for the first time in a while, but they were also foreigners. The mid-afternoon sun had dropped, leaving him in the shade, long shadows dancing in the alley in front of him. His day of surprises wasn't yet over as another foreigner stopped in front of him.

Astonished, he looked up and said, "Good day. And how may I be of assistance to my third foreigner of the day?"

"I want to come in," demanded the man curtly.

The old man didn't reply to this short answer and just stood up, leading the way inside, meandering through his prized books.

"I don't want to buy anything if that's what you think," the man carried on in his abrupt tone.

"Then, what can I do for you?"

"Did you have two visitors today? A white man and woman."

"Now, let me think."

"Think harder man. I'm tired and visited lots of shops today asking the same question. My patience is wearing thin," snapped Ormerod, snipping with his lighter and menacingly eying the books. Some of his men were outside and preparing to close the door in an obvious threat.

"Well, yes. Come to think of it, I did," he stuttered back, knowing he was defenceless.

188

"That's better, old man," said Ormerod, sitting down and throwing some books on the floor. It had the desired effect, as the old man was now rattled. "And now you may tell me what they wanted."

The old man gulped and looked at his book collection.

"I have more than one book, you know," he replied, trying to play for time.

"As I can see. For the moment at least," replied Ormerod, flicking open his lighter again. "Quite impressive."

"They wanted a research book from an academic called Oldfield Thomas. It was about moles in what was Siam at the time of writing. Now let me think. Yes, Kloss's mole."

"Kloss's mole, you say. Interesting. When was it written?"

"In 1881, I believe. It's causing quite a stir as a monk also asked after it some time back."

"A monk?" asked Ormerod, surprised.

"Do you know why he was interested in it?"

"Absolutely no idea, because when I came back with the manuscript, he was gone. Quite strange."

"And where is this valuable manuscript now?"

"I gave it to the two visitors."

"Damn," shouted Ormerod, standing up and throwing his chair back into a pile of books, which crashed down in a dusty pile. He quickly pulled out his phone.

"Bartholomew. We have an important lead. Find out anything you can on a research book on Kloss's mole from Eighteen eighty-one written by an academic called Oldfield Thomas."

"Eighteen eighty-one," came the surprised reply from Bartholomew.

"Yes, you heard correctly. Mr Jackson has the book and is one step ahead, just as we wanted. But I don't want him to be more than one step ahead. There is obviously something of great value contained in this book and we need to find out what."

The old man smirked behind Ormerod's back.

***

Vanessa was trying as best as she could to read about the different temples in the old city to see if any resembled the rough description left by Oldfield Thomas. It wasn't easy as our tuk-tuk was scooting around the streets, like a formula one race. Vanessa clung on to a rail with one hand as we swerved around people and traffic, expertly using her smartphone with her other hand. We broke out of the dense maze of streets in Chinatown and entered the old city with its abundance of temples. I instructed the driver where to go, all the time observing the buildings around me and found that many temples could have matched Oldfield Thomas's description, a white wall not much to go on.

"Connor! Can't we slow down? It's impossible to read anything," she cried, slamming into me as we lurched around the corner.

"Yes, soon. We want to disorientate the brothers then lose them, giving us time to find the temple."

A straight road with the majestic Royal Palace on the left gave us the opportunity to accelerate and pull away from the Kennedy brothers, in hot pursuit around two hundred metres behind. Owing to their heavy weight, their driver was at a distinct disadvantage in this race, in particular around the corners where the risk of tipping over was high.

"I might have something, Connor. How many Buddhas were mentioned in the courtyard?"

"One hundred and fifty-six," I screamed above the din of the squealing motor.

"Bingo! I've just read Wat Suthat has one hundred and fifty-six Buddha images along the outside walls of the temple, just like Oldfield Thomas wrote. It must be it."

"Wat Suthat," I shouted to the tuk-tuk driver.

An immediate right turn along Lak Muong Road followed by a left turn on Rachini Alley left us driving parallel to a river to our right. Tyres screeching, we skidded sharp right over a bridge and headed back down the other side on Alsadong Road, waving at the Kennedy brothers now opposite and losing more and more ground to us. We carried on until reaching a large junction and careered left on Bamrung Mueang Road, then accelerated out of the turn and went straight directly towards a giant red swing.

"Wat Suthat," shouted the driver as we approached, a large smile on his face as he was easily winning the race.

"Don't stop," I bawled. "Now do what you want and lose the tuk-tuk behind!"

Grinning like a Cheshire cat, he opened the throttle even further and yelled, "Hold on!"

About one hundred metres further and the Kennedy brothers only just in sight, our driver slammed on the brakes, the back wheel locking up as we skidded left into a narrow alley. Permanent use of his loud horn forced angry pedestrians to jump out of the way, shouting obscenities behind us. The tuk-tuk flew over junctions and the driver, with the skilful precision of a fighter pilot, navigated his way left and right through dense market areas, ensuring the Kennedy brothers had absolutely no chance of following. We shot out from behind a market stall, bounced into an alley and skidded to a halt directly inside a repair company for tuk-tuks, tyres now smoking in protest. The workers at once put down the shutters, leaving us in the safe confines of the workshop and the Kennedy brothers nowhere in sight.

"My brother," indicated the tuk-tuk driver to an approaching man in blue overalls and grease smeared in his face. "You're safe here."

Chapter Fifteen
Crazy Pigeons at Wat Suthat

"Felicity! Felicity!" cried out Bartholomew as he ran up the stairs.

"What's all the commotion about?" she screeched back.

"Come down straight away. I need your help."

Felicity came stomping down the stairs. "What the devil can be so important for all of your noise?"

"We have a lead from Bangkok, and I need more information. Does the name Oldfield Thomas ring a bell?"

"No. Should it?"

"Maybe. He was a zoologist and wrote many research papers."

"And?"

"Well, he was great friends with your grandfather. Apparently, Beaumont started caring for him in 1916 and he lived his final years here until his death in 1929 and was then buried in the Molehamptons. In fact, Beaumont also died in the same year."

"How interesting, Bartholomew, but I fail to see what it's got to do with me."

"My dearest Felicity, Ormerod has just called me from Bangkok. Apparently, Mr Jackson has found a manuscript written by Oldfield Thomas in 1881 about moles in Siam. Mr Jackson has disappeared with this document, and it must hold important information. Ormerod will have him tracked so see where the information leads but we can also do something from here."

"But what can I do?"

"You know where the family archives are kept. We need to read everything we can about Beaumont and see if we can uncover anything more. Maybe we have information Mr Jackson doesn't have. The clue might be sitting right under our very noses, and that, Felicity, is where you come in."

"That I can do. Follow me, Nephew Bartholomew."

It wasn't only Bartholomew who had a secret office in the vast mansion riddled with tunnels and hidden rooms. Felicity led the way upstairs and passed portraits of family members, old and new, before entering the library and approached a bookshelf. With both hands, she pressed firmly on a wooden candlestick until it clicked, then pulled the shelf towards her, revealing a small door set inside the bookshelf and a hidden room behind. They had to duck down to enter, turned on a light and closed the door behind them, leaving no evidence of where they were. The small room was stacked high with archive cardboard boxes.

"I've heard about this room before but never been in."

"Only Ormerod and I have access, and for good reason. In here are generations of family records, pictures, diaries and personal notes. And, Bartholomew, not for the public eye. We have painstakingly collected and hidden family information here. In fact, even the family members themselves don't know what is held on them."

"Is there information on me too?" he asked, surprised.

Felicity frowned and chose not to reply.

Bartholomew walked around the room, brushing dust off old government folders and boxes. "And where is the information on Beaumont?"

"Oh, that's easy. It's all organised alphabetically," replied Felicity, fetching a small ladder. "Should be right here," as she climbed up stopping at the second shelf. "Here we go. Beaumont Forsythe-Twyke, 1858 to 1929. Take this, will you," dropping the old box into his hands.

Bartholomew sneezed as a layer of dust exploded in his face and then placed it on a table. The box had government markings with *Top Secret* stamped on all sides.

"Looks important," commented Felicity, as he started rummaging around inside.

"What have we got here? Files, envelopes, university papers and private diaries. Hmm, where should we start?

"I'll take the files and you his diaries," exclaimed Felicity. "What exactly are we looking for?"

"Anything which might contain information pertaining to Oldfield Thomas."

They spent the next thirty minutes randomly flicking through the material, scanning for important information but not finding anything remotely interesting. Felicity found, amongst other things, private letters, bank statements, club membership information and Secret Service reports but not what they were looking for.

"Oh, look here. Beaumont was listed as a dangerous political activist and put under surveillance. They believed he was a communist and followed the readings of Karl Marx. How interesting," exclaimed Felicity, quite astonished at this information.

"Hang on. I have something here," Bartholomew said, holding up a battered diary. "It's a sort of memoire and seems to be just about Oldfield Thomas and his relationship with Beaumont. These are notes about the years after his friend's arrival in 1916."

Bartholomew was rivetted, his mouth opening wider and wider the further he ran over the pages. "Unbelievable. Really unbelievable," he muttered out loud.

"Go on then, don't keep it to yourself."

"What I can gather is this; Beaumont and Oldfield Thomas studied zoology together in London. During this time, they became engrossed with the political theory of Karl Marx and were strongly against colonialism, coming to the attention of the authorities. When Beaumont inherited the Forsythe-Twyke mansion and Food Factory, the two of them returned to the Molehamptons to lie low. Oldfield Thomas did not come from a wealthy family, so Beaumont funded his research projects whilst he ran the family business. One such project took Oldfield Thomas to the Kingdom of Siam in 1878, a journey which profoundly affected his life, and he only came back many years later. He returned to live as a recluse with Beaumont in 1916, shunned by the academic world and labelled mad. Beaumont writes here about a research paper his friend wrote on a species of an Asian mole published in 1881. But he knew Oldfield Thomas did much more, leaving most of his papers and research work behind in Siam."

Felicity was listening with great concentration. "What a staggering story. And this information has been here the whole time. Go on please, Bartholomew."

"Beaumont never gave up on his lifelong friend, allowing him to live out his years in this mansion and pen all his stories and experiences. Beaumont writes here the four children would often sit around the fireplace late into the night listening to Oldfield Thomas's adventures. After he completed his research work, he stumbled on a world so unbelievable he could never officially record his story. He discovered a secretive world of moles deep below the surface and found out they administered all life forms above and below the ground. And there's more. The contact with life on the surface was through a secret cadre of Buddhist monks at various temples. The only way for him to find out more about this amazing world was to become a monk himself, and that's exactly what he did. There was no contact with Oldfield Thomas for many years, with many believing him to be dead. But out of the blue, he suddenly returned suffering from amnesia and shell shock. He somehow left Asia and ended up involved in World War One and returned home to a hospital. He only uttered mad ramblings about moles and always mentioned one name. Beaumont Forsythe-Twyke. He was contacted and had his friend transferred to this house to care for him. Oldfield Thomas was officially declared mad and, had he told his story to others, they naturally never would have believed him. But Beaumont did, and for many years listened to his stories and deciphered them."

"And what were these stories? Did Beaumont write about them?"

"Yes, it appears so, but not in great detail here. He has only written basic information and recounts stories of the perfect world of moles. It was an equal system and perfected beyond measure. Pure equality just as the two of them had envisaged in their university days with capitalism, competition and greed non-existent in this world. Beaumont also mentions about advanced medicines, remedies and other technologies the moles possessed, far surpassing what humans had at that time. Their technology was for good, while in the human world, it was used to create machines of war and death. The moles had the ability to store memories, program processors for newborn creatures and even manipulate them if necessary."

"Not so unlike what goes on below the ground here. And now we have Professor Wingnut, just maybe we will be able to manipulate processors too and create even better meat products," Felicity added with a sinister expression.

"Quite, Aunty Felicity," Bartholomew replied rather suspicious of her greedy motives. "Let me read on; Oldfield Thomas knew the western world was at the abyss of total destruction and wanted to save humankind from their own self-constructed fate. He secretly hid the most sensitive technical research work, which he learnt from the moles, intending to use it at the right time and then returned to Europe. However, he did bring with him notes about the basic technology to set up a new world modelled on Siam. And Beaumont also wrote about their long evenings trying to reconstruct what Oldfield Thomas could remember. It was difficult because of his amnesia but his memory slowly returned, and they were able to record recipes for various tablets, some blueprints and other technical descriptions. Oldfield Thomas's ideal was to use what he learnt and set up a mole system here, centred on the Molehamptons with his friend Beaumont. Humans couldn't be trusted to run the world so the moles would have to take over. And together, the two of them worked long and hard doing just that, achieving their aim then living out their remaining years ensuring the system worked as they planned."

"And where is all of this information now?" quizzed Felicity. "Surely it must be somewhere here."

"I'm sure if it was, we wouldn't have had to steal Professor Wingnut."

"Well, read on, Bartholomew. There's more there!"

"Don't be impatient, I can only read so fast. Now, what else do we have here. Oh dear, that's not nice. Look, Felicity, he wrote here; George was a bad egg and could not be trusted, therefore he had no choice but to put other plans in place. Beaumont found out George and his father, Montague, had schemed together so that George would inherit the estate, despite him being the youngest. Montague despised women and didn't want one taking over the Forsythe-Twyke fortunes so had the Secret Service discredit the three sisters: Annabelle, Agnes and Beatrice. His plan was to have them declared subversive and mad, thereby forfeiting their inheritance. Beaumont got wind of this and planned for the three sisters to immediately disappear, taking on new identities after his death.

This is exactly what happened and your father, George, only took over the Food Factory and some technology."

"But not the secret information. That disappeared with his three sisters," added Felicity glumly. "My father, George, told me his three sisters left the family, married and relinquished all of their rights including their names, never to be seen again."

"That's correct. You, as the eldest, inherited the family estate and your brother, Ormerod, was given the task of hunting down the secret information. He presumes, Annabelle, the eldest had it and her new family is now the Head of the Eternity Project. You know it's been his life-long quest to find them and the secrets?"

"I must admit all of this is new to me despite the information being under my very nose for ages. But Ormerod would know all of this already so I am not sure that what you have just read will help him. He wants to find out where the location of *the target* is and, even though this is interesting, there is nothing here to point him in the right direction."

"He not only wants the location of *the target*, but the location of the secret material Oldfield Thomas left in Thailand. We can only presume both locations are the same place. And that is why Connor Jackson is needed."

"Yes, to piece everything together. And he now has another document, this so-called manuscript which must contain the other information."

"Yes, he quite probably has a lead and Ormerod needs to be hot on his tails. The problem is the Kennedy brothers have lost Mr Jackson, and Vanessa has not yet made contact. He shook them off amongst lots of temples and market areas in the old city."

"Temples. Didn't you say Oldfield Thomas became a monk whilst in Bangkok? Is there anything in my grandfather's diary about where he did that? There must be something here."

"Wait one moment, let me take a look," replied Bartholomew, leafing through the pages again. "Yes, in fact it does, but does not name the temple. He writes, the mole headquarters is below a temple with one hundred and fifty-six Buddhas looking inwards to protect the secret. He also writes about an amazing second temple, intricately made of carved wood, and known as the repository for all information and technology. That's all, I'm afraid."

"One hundred and fifty-six Buddhas," exclaimed Felicity, already checking her phone."

"Let's hope you find something."

"And here I have it," beamed Felicity. "At the top of the list is a site with one hundred and fifty-six reviews about Wat Pho, but that has nothing to do with Buddhas. And the next one is a report about another temple," she said, clicking on the link. "Voilà! This one has a courtyard, surrounding a temple. It's called Wat Suthat."

***

Jemima Kingston cut a sad figure, sitting at her desk and dabbing the corner of her eyes with a handkerchief.

"There, there, Cromwell," she said lovingly, stroking his head. "At least I love you and you will always have me to look after you. Just be happy you don't have to be me."

Cromwell yawned and repositioned himself in her lap, bored to tears listening to her sob stories. He was not a sympathetic dog.

"My stepbrother died, I don't know my father and my darling husband also passed away. To cap it all off, Felicity is raking up my past, and I want to know why."

Cromwell yawned yet again as Jemima leafed through the file and looked at the picture for the umpteenth time. She was jolted out of her sad thoughts by the ringing of her telephone, but not her office phone. This time her private smartphone rang, a number only reserved for a few special people. She shoved Cromwell out of the way and jumbled around in the bottom of her bag.

"Yes," she answered after successfully retrieving it from between the pile of handkerchiefs, tissues, and make up items. Craning forward and squinting her eyes, it looked as though she was having difficulty hearing the other person. "It's a bad line. I can barely hear you. There's an awful din in the background and sounds like hundreds of loud lawnmowers. Please speak slowly," she yelled at the top of her voice into the phone. "OK. OK. OK," she kept on repeating. "You have a lead on the Forsythe-Twyke investigation. Out of comms for a few days," she shouted back, confirming the conversation. "Hello. Are you still there? Hello!"

Jemima tutted loudly, cut the call, stuffed her phone back in her handbag and carried on stroking Cromwell. He gnarled and flashed his teeth.

"Now, now, Cromwell. There's no need for that. One could believe you are a Forsythe-Twyke with that sort of reaction. But that can't be true."

***

After taking refuge in the garage for enough time to read the manuscript, we set off in the tuk-tuk to Wat Suthat, and this time at a more leisurely pace through the streets. However, not everything always goes according to plan, and when we approached the temple grounds, a tuk-tuk skidded to a halt in front of us. And who should get out? Yes, the Kennedy brothers. Either Vanessa had tipped them off, or they had a different source of information. The old man in the shop couldn't have known where we were going either, should he have been visited by Ormerod or one of his cronies. I also discounted Vanessa as the source as she sat next to me the whole time, reading the manuscript in the workshop, her phone tucked away in her bag. This time the Kennedy brothers were one step ahead, and I had no idea what information they had. I told the driver to go once around the complex, finding four red doors in the white walls. Magnificent pagoda roofs of the two temples rose high above the walls, one golden and red, the other green and golden, just like the description in Oldfield Thomas's manuscript. The entrance furthest away offered the best access, and at the opposite end to the brothers. The first temple we saw, the highest of the two with a golden and red roof, was in a pristine courtyard with glistening marble paving stones shining in the sunlight. A low-roofed cloister with many golden Buddhas all facing inwards enclosed the temple. This was undoubtedly the place described by Oldfield Thomas all those years ago. Vanessa and I picked up a brochure, took pictures and made selfies to pass as tourists, but all the time looking for some sort of clue. The brochure described Wat Suthat as a royal

199

temple of the first grade, twenty-three of which are in Thailand and ten in Bangkok alone. Between the two temples was a beautifully tended garden, decorated with bushes and plants. And guess what else? Yes, I am sure you already know. Molehills! There weren't just one or two, but many, and they formed a funnel shape, the narrowest part pointing towards the largest temple. All the tunnels headed in that direction, which was also mentioned in the manuscript. The temple complex was eerily empty, with only a few people walking around, some of them carrying baskets. This was in stark contrast to the ones we visited yesterday with the stampede of mass tourism.

We walked around, keeping out an eye for the Kennedy brothers; it wouldn't be difficult to spot them. But something didn't feel right, and my senses were correct as I suddenly heard the beating of wings and the shadow of birds on the shiny marble.

"Quick, Vanessa. Under the cloister roof now!" I ordered, pulling her with me.

We were just in time as a wave of white bird droppings splattered on the ground exactly where we were standing a moment before.

"That was close," whispered Vanessa. "And now look over there," she added, pointing to the other side of the courtyard.

The Kennedy brothers were frantically running in the open, chased by a low-level bombing squadron of pigeons, emptying their loads all around them. The only thing saving them from the bird poo was their large sun hats, but this protection was short lived. In a wonderful aerobatic manoeuvre, the birds swooped down in a steep dive, levelling out just below head height and flew straight past the Kennedy brothers close enough that their wing tips hit the brim of their hats. They scrambled to pick them up, but this short time was enough for the pigeons to come back on another bombing run, this time finding their targets with ease. Both Joe and Gavin were hit by bird plop slap in the middle of their foreheads as they looked up in the sky to see what had just knocked off their hats. For a brief instance, they stood straight and looked at each other in disgust with their normal dopey expressions. But then something changed, suddenly looking alert and started speaking together earnestly. They pointed to a monk walking across the courtyard, nodded in agreement and then ran towards one of the red doors in the outer wall and away.

I stood there watching the crazy scene from under the safety of the cloister roof, mesmerised by the pigeons' amazing flying skills. I thought we would be safe here, but how wrong I was when the same pigeons reappeared just above the surface of the courtyard, heading at speed directly towards us.

"These birds are damn good, Vanessa," I blurted out with panic on my voice. "Stand next to the pillars and move around them to make ourselves difficult targets."

The pigeons remained on their deadly course then abruptly veered left, flying between two of the cloister's pillars before turning sharply right, now under the roof. Extremely skilled in this confined space, the birds were now flying parallel to the Buddhas only one metre from the ground and approached us at great speed. We moved slightly around our pillars, attempting to move out of their line, but the birds managed somehow to bank sharply, just brushing past us and even let off a salvo of poo as they flew off back into the courtyards. It was an extremely close call and the droppings landed harmlessly on our shoes. I was absolutely shocked at their amazing flying expertise; they were much more advanced than Mr Tinker's bombing pigeons back in the Molehamptons. They flew with uncanny accuracy and were not hampered at all by their bamboo harness swinging underneath their bellies. They actually flew so close that I saw crazy grins on the range-finding mice as they tried to complete their missions with zeal. I was wrong to think the birds had stopped the attack, as they came in again, the sound of their beating wings reverberating in the cloister as they flew another mission of death-defying manoeuvres. Thankfully, after a few more attacks and probably running out of bird poo, they flew away, leaving us shaken and the ground around us peppered with white slime.

"Do you think it's over?" Vanessa asked, looking around in nervous panic.

"I doubt it, but we shouldn't stay here. We should go into the temple. I sure hope it's safe there from these madcap birds."

We checked the way was clear of pigeons and sprinted across the courtyard, bounding up the steep steps into the cover of the temple, leaving our shoes at the entrance. I marvelled at the sight now in front of me, briefly forgetting the lunatic pigeons, as I found myself looking straight at a huge Buddha elevated on an exquisitely adorned podium. The room was called an ordination hall and completely covered in superb murals, depicting the earlier lives of Buddha, and a rich red carpet covering the whole floor. At the base of the Buddha, were tables with objects which people had left here. In fact, I had seen a few people at the temple complex, and they were all carrying baskets containing various wares, such as pots with food, socks, salt and I even saw a light bulb. I understood this gift giving was called making merit, and although I had only read a little about Buddhism, I did understand that people bring items needed by the monks in an act of doing a good deed. A short while later, a monk appeared from behind the giant Buddha and started picking up some of the items. I also read Buddhist monks are only allowed to own eight items and are reliant on the acts of merit at the temples.

But this monk I now recognised. "It's him, Vanessa. It's him!" I said quite loudly and excitedly.

"It's who?" she replied, not entirely concentrating as she tried to take in the wonderful hall.

"The monk from the Molehamptons. Look, he has a scar on his face. It must be the same person."

The monk then glanced over, maybe annoyed by us speaking, offering no recognition, before turning away and going into a room at the back.

"Then let's follow him. This is not a chance encounter; he wants us to go after him."

Vanessa and I checked nobody saw what we were doing and walked across the hall to where the monk had just gone. Behind the Buddha was another room, lavishly decorated with thick material in red, orange and gold, hanging from the ceiling. One side of the room had a large opening with a view to the second temple, it's green and golden roof glinting in the sun's rays. Right in the centre of this room was a low chair with red material and cushions and, in front of this, a wooden chest. The monk was nowhere to be seen but some items he collected were now directly in front of the chest: a container smelling of petrol and a model tuk-tuk made of metal.

As the monk had disappeared, we started looking for exit points, pulling the drapes to the side and even looking under the cushions on the chair, but we found nothing.

"Quiet!" Vanessa whispered, putting her finger to her lips. "Did you hear that?"

At first, I heard nothing but then noises started coming from the wooden chest. First, a light knocking sound and then hissing. I went closer, bending over to hear better. The noises now became much more audible.

"There's definitely something down there, Vanessa."

I rubbed my hands slowly over the chest, looking for some moving parts. Under the cover, I found two small indents and pulled it ever so gently upwards. To my surprise it moved easily and opened up to reveal a narrow opening with stairs going deep down into the darkness.

"This is where he has gone. Come on."

I squeezed myself in and blindly climbed down the steps, the walls of the passageway brushing against my shoulders. It was pitch black and I had no idea how far down we would go but, after counting twenty steps, found the bottom as my feet touched on a level surface. And now, I only wished we had not left our shoes at the entrance.

"Come on," I whispered up towards the light at the top of the shaft. "I'm at the bottom now."

Vanessa followed, closing the chest as she came, but not before she managed to quickly fire away a message on her phone. The cover clicked shut and a light automatically switched on. The room we were now standing in was damp and smelt of fresh earth, similar to the mole world back in the Molehamptons, the air thick and stale. A large shelf unit stood against one wall and was full of various supplies including items like the monk disappeared with.

Apart from the stairs we had just come down, there was no other exit, leaving us mystified as to the whereabouts of the monk.

"This is a strange room," Vanessa said. "But this must do something," pointing to a cord hanging from the ceiling.

Without another word she just pulled it and, almost immediately, a hissing sound began, and the room slowly began filling with gas. I waited for the strange sensation I knew was about to start. This was undoubtedly the entrance to the mole world below Bangkok.

"Are you ready for a journey? I believe we are now going to enter another world of moles, following in the footsteps of Oldfield Thomas over one hundred years ago."

Chapter Sixteen
A Call to Action

The red post box stood resolute in the village green, as it had done for over one hundred years. It was about the only thing not moving in today's autumn storm battering the Molehamptons with big gusts of wind, rudely barging their way through the streets. Leaves and twigs flew in big swirls in the blustery air and smashed against any object in their way. Nobody in their right mind would think about venturing out today, and even the village dogs quietly brooded in their homes, making no effort to move. But one person did indeed brave the storm, walking past the village pub and towards the green. He wore a large yellow raincoat going down over his knees and the hood completely masking his face. Whoever it was, was walking slowly, his head facing downwards to either protect himself from the weather or not wanting to be seen. Occasionally, he turned around to check behind, taking quite a long time and being extra careful. He didn't want to be recognised and the foul weather was the perfect cover, as the whole village was completely deserted.

The person crossed the road and made the last steps towards the bright red post box, carefully avoiding the many molehills. One last glance around him and then he unzipped the front of his jacket, stooping forwards to protect five envelopes. He looked carefully at the first one, addressed to Jessica Walsh, and pushed it through the slot with a sense of purpose. The next was for Sergeant Dawson, followed by one for Timothy Scribbler. Two envelopes remained in his hand, one for Mr Cross and the other for Mr Kowalczyk. The man closed his jacket and peered through the post box's slot, making sure his precious letters had really fallen to the bottom. He clapped his hands in delight, turned around and retraced his steps back through the village. Two molehills suddenly sprouted up in Sergeant Dawson's pristinely kept front garden at the police station as the man passed by. He stopped, looked at them and then carried on along the street, the molehills drenched in the torrential rain.

***

Somebody was sabotaging equipment and Felicity Forsythe-Twyke was livid about the loss of production and the fact somebody had even dared to do it, especially after everything she has done for the good and benefit of the community. A technician had just successfully finished repair work to the chain after a piece of metal mysteriously became wedged in a machine. All members of staff were warned to be on the lookout.

"Come on, Mr Kowalczyk, no slacking now."

"Coming, Mr Walsh. Fast as I can," piped up Mr Kowalczyk, walking fast with a large bucket.

"Have you put the correct dosage in the feed?"

"Yes, Mr Walsh. Just like you said me," replied Mr Kowalczyk, looking at the cages in horror.

"Squirmy, are you?" asked Mr Walsh, smirking at his new worker. "First time for you here in this part of the factory?"

"I'm good. Please not worry about me. But these ducks, they are in not good condition."

"Don't be soft. They will all end up in a pot, so it doesn't matter if they look a bit dirty, and besides, you don't cook their feathers. According to Mrs Forsythe-Twyke, cleaning slows down production and adds unnecessary costs. That's why we strictly check processes to ensure the highest level of productivity and quality. Every second counts, Mr Kowalczyk."

"I understand," Mr Kowalczyk replied slowly and rather unconvinced.

"Now, feed the ducks before anyone notices us wasting valuable time!"

Mr Kowalczyk looked sadly at the ducks and spooned the foul-smelling feed into the trays with a loud splat. He turned up his nose at the awful smell and moved up the chain going past Basil and eventually left the hall.

"Basil. It's me," came a whisper.

"Ludwig. Is that you?"

"Yes," he replied, coming out from behind a pile of boxes. "Oh my, you don't look well."

"Of course not," retorted Basil slowly. "I have no idea what they put in the feed but it's not good."

Ludwig looked glumly around, especially towards the end of the chain. "We've got a few more days, Basil, and I'm doing my level best. I've even got a plan for this evening which will keep them all busy in the morning."

"I know, my dear friend, and I'm grateful but am slowly giving up hope of getting out of here. The factory has increased security after what you've been doing. It's very courageous of you but even the brave and loyal Ludwig has his limits."

"I can't just give up," Ludwig replied angrily. "I have to do something. But what?"

Both of them looked at each other dejectedly knowing time was quickly running out despite Ludwig's heroic efforts.

"I've got an idea. A last chance."

"Let's hear it then," Basil responded slowly and listened to Ludwig.

"I'll be back soon, Basil," he said turning to leave but will need help from either Mr Cross or Mrs Pike to get out."

Basil looked at his friend with large, sad eyes as Ludwig walked away.

"I will come back with an army," exclaimed Ludwig.

***

She was sitting on her bed, headphones on, frantically typing on her smartphone with an angry and rebellious expression on her face. Her room was decorated with graffiti and posters of her favourite music stars, quite similar to many other teenagers like her.

"Jessica! Jessica!" screamed a woman's voice somewhere in the house. "Jessica!" Then the noise of stamping feet as the person came up the stairs, clearly angry at no response. The door to the girl's bedroom flew open and her mother strutted in and yelled at the top of her voice, "Turn your darn music down!"

"What?" shouted Jessica loudly, not realising how loud she was.

Her mother indicated for her to take off her headphones, Jessica reluctantly complying with a loud tut.

"What do you want in my room?"

"You have post?"

Jessica looked at her phone. "No, nothing here."

"You have post, I said. Real post made of paper."

Jessica looked at her, confused at her mother's statement. "Paper post?"

"Yes, here it is," turning it in her hand. "It has been typed and looks kind of official. What have you been up to, Jessica?"

"Nothing. Give it to me," and snatched it out of her hand and then looked at her name on the front. Her mother remained standing in front of her. "Why are you still here?" came a curt remark, not looking up.

"Aren't you going to open it?"

"Yes, but when you've gone. It's private. That's why it's got my name on it and not yours."

With a stroppy look, her mother turned around and left the room, slamming the door behind her. "What am I going to do with her?" she mumbled to herself stamping back down the stairs.

Jessica waited for her mother's loud trampling to disappear before carefully looking at the envelope.

"Jessica Walsh," she whispered to herself. "Why should anyone write to me? I'm only fourteen. And no official markings either," turning the envelope around to inspect it.

She ripped it open, pulled out a letter and some pictures then sat there for a long time reading it over and over again, looking at the images with a distressed expression. Whatever it was; it was having the effect the sender obviously intended. Jessica exhaled and stared long and hard in deep thought at the ceiling. The pictures were looked at again and the letter read ever so slowly. She turned up her mouth in a show of disgust.

The look of a stroppy teenager, high on the pressures of puberty, drained from her face in an instant. Standing up purposefully, she walked across the room to her messy desk, and with one great sweep of her arm, shoved everything off, papers and objects flying through the air and landing with a crash on the floor. She slapped a piece of paper down on her desk and started writing down names and the schools they attended. Nodding to herself to show the job was done, she said aloud, "Let's open the doors!"

This now appeared to be a different Jessica Walsh perceived by her parents, teachers and, in fact, all adults who knew her. She was labelled a troublemaker but sometimes the reality of life can be so different and what we might show on the surface is not what is hiding inside. Like many other people, and especially teenagers, she spent most of her time glued to her phone, communicating with anyone and everyone. Despite her stroppy and rebellious exterior, she was going through the strains of puberty like we have all experienced. Jessica was angry with the world, felt misunderstood and not taken seriously. Whoever wrote the letter to her, knew this and saw another Jessica Walsh on the inside. This Jessica was just about to explode in a way that would not only affect the Molehamptons, but a much wider audience. Her friends in the local community were loyal, caring and stuck together. She was just about to fire up her vast army of contacts, and if they were looking for a cause to vent their teenage anger, then she was going to give it to them. Her parents were in for a shock they could never prepare for, especially her father who was the production manager at the Food Factory. Some might say it was a privileged position as it ensured meat on the table three times a day, seven days a week.

Jessica had never liked it!

***

The garden was diligently tended by the hands of a loving and passionate person. Although not large, it was a perfect combination of different natural elements: a carefully crafted rockery containing a small pond, the calming noise of trickling water, and the grassed area decorated with beautiful flower beds, comprising a mixture of plants, flowers and bushes. But there was something here, quite new actually, and entirely out of place. Molehills! Of course, these annoying mounds of earth were not out of place in the Molehamptons, which will not surprise you, knowing what really goes on below the ground. In the past, this gardener would have flattened them and at once sowed grass seeds, however, he had lately appeared to have given up this course of action and changed his tactics. The hills were left as they were, the gardener electing not to squash them with his spade, but decorate them instead with broken pieces of porcelain, designing artistic patterns. One molehill even sported a face and had an old hat on top. Something had changed the gardener's mind.

"Good morning, Sergeant Dawson."

"Good morning, Mr Singh."

"I see you've finished cleaning up after the storm. Such a lot of damage and there was debris lying all over the place."

"Yes, just finished clearing the leaves and twigs away. At least I don't have to water anything for a while after the deluge of rain. How about your efforts at the community centre?"

"Mrs Khan was particularly active mobilising everyone, and in no time, we had a small army going through the village, including Mr Kowalczyk. He's fairly new here and I think he works at the Food Factory. Very helpful man."

"That's nice to hear."

"I have a question, Sergeant. Why have you started decorating the molehills?" he asked inquisitively, looking at the garden in front of the village police station.

"Oh, you know, Mr Singh, it's like this. These little chaps below the ground also need their space, and us humans cannot use everything up here. They must do a lot of building work, whatever that may be, and I suppose they have to deposit their excavated soil somewhere. So, I decided if you can't beat them, join them!"

"Oh yes, I have some post for you, by the way. Completely forgot about why I was here," chuckled Mr Singh. "I've also got a letter for that company in a garage near the village green—VoleWeb. I've actually never seen anyone there. Looks strange to me."

"Yes, come to think of it, neither have I."

"Better be on my way as I'm sure the local police have better things to do."

"Thank you and always a pleasure to speak to you. And don't worry about me." He put his head closer to Mr Singh and whispered, "Between you and me, not much happens here anyhow."

Sergeant Dawson took his mail, bade farewell to Mr Singh, returned to his office and sat down at his desk. The drawer was wide open and in panic he started rummaging around inside.

"Blast. All the biscuits are gone. Damn moles!" he added and threw his hands up in the air in despair. He brushed some biscuit crumbs away from the desk and looked at his post.

"Bill. Bill. Another bill. And what's this?" he asked himself, holding an envelope, his name and address typed but no indication of who it was from. He pulled out a single sheet of paper, sat back and started to read, his interest and eyes growing ever bigger. He read it again then put it down, blowing out in surprise, looked up at the ceiling and read once more but this time slowly and concentrating. His round face turned redder and redder the further he progressed, clear to see the contents were making the normally placid man extremely angry. His chair crashed back as he jumped up and started walking angrily around the office, eyes always fixed on the letter lying on his desk.

"I'll show that darned family," he said, clenching his teeth in fury. "I've had enough and it's time to make a stand. And I'm not alone!"

"No, you are not," came a quiet voice from somewhere in the room.

Sergeant Dawson spun around towards the noise, took one pace forward and slipped on a previously unseen sock. Thankfully, he was just able to keep his balance but then stubbed his foot on something hard. This time it was enough for the bulk of a man to go flying and he landed with a big thud in the corner of the room.

"What's this stupid thing?" he barked, looking at the floor. A block of salt was the guilty culprit. "And where are you?" asked the Sergeant, wanting to know where the mystery voice came from.

The door to his small storeroom squeaked as someone pushed against it.

"Who's there?" bawled Sergeant Dawson, ripping the door open. His eyes opened wide in shock at what he now saw. The storeroom had been totally rearranged, his items now in a pile on the floor and the shelves full of items which did not belong to him.

"You!" he declared. "I should have guessed," looking down at Colonel Pickle.

"Yes, it's me. Back I'm afraid," he replied, brushing biscuit crumbs from his uniform.

"And what's all this stuff here?" the Sergeant spat out, pointing to the items.

"This is not stuff. These items have been carefully selected and scavenged. I will keep them here for safekeeping."

"Scavenged! You mean stolen! I've got stolen goods in here!" The Sergeant's face had now turned white in shock.

"I didn't say stolen. I said they were scavenged and there's a legal difference, I believe."

"I'm a policeman, Colonel Pickle. I can't deal in stolen goods, or scavenged things."

"And I'm a Colonel and I say you can. And what's more, I need your help."

"To do what exactly? To get more stolen goods?"

"Yes, Sergeant. Exactly that. You can do it, and nobody would suspect a thing. I've thought it all through rather carefully. A moletight plan."

"And why can't you do it?" asking with deep mistrust.

"We have a few problems below," explained the Colonel, pointing at the floor. "It's nearly impossible to tell friend from foe and we need to fight back. But, Sergeant, I need a place to store things. A safe place. And I also need things."

"But why me?"

"Because everyone likes Sergeant Dawson, and you will never be suspected. You also know about what we really do. Oh yes, expect to see other moles here too."

"Do they also talk?"

"Of course, they can talk but you won't understand them."

"So, why can I understand you?"

"Because I've taken a special tablet enabling me to communicate with everyone, especially humans."

"You mean just like Connor, Vanessa, Ludwig and Basil?"

"Yes, Sergeant, just like them. Cleopatra and Cromwell too."

"Who are they?" the Sergeant asked, scratching his head.

Colonel Pickle didn't have time to reply as the sound of a car door slamming and someone shouting the Sergeant's name at the top of her voice interrupted their conversation.

"More of that later, Colonel. I have to go now. Visitors."

"Sergeant Dawson!" screeched a high-pitched voice from outside.

"Oh no, not her. What does she want now?"

Sergeant Dawson closed the storeroom and before he could do anything else, the office door flew open, nearly flying off its hinges, revealing a livid Felicity Forsythe-Twyke standing in the doorway.

"Good morning, Mrs …!"

But before he could finish, she was already in full flow.

"Doing something. Doing what? You said you would do something!" she snarled at him.

"Do what?" replied the Sergeant, with new confidence in his voice.

"Exactly that. Nothing. You've done nothing. Whilst you've been greedily stuffing your face with biscuits, I've been suffering from industrial sabotage."

"Well, I'm sure there's a good explanation for that. Just come over here, take a seat and calm down," he replied, mischievously eying the sock and block of salt on the floor.

'Calm down' was not an expression to use on Mrs Forsythe-Twyke, as she aggressively approached Sergeant Dawson, snorting like an angry bull. He wanted to say something, warn her maybe, but then thought better of it. She first slipped on the sock, arms flailing around attempting to regain balance. Then she stubbed her foot straight into the block of salt and left the ground, looking like a bird about to crash land, which is exactly what she did, right on the floor with a loud bang.

Sergeant Dawson smiled, unseen by Mrs Forsythe-Twyke, and then stooped down to help, his kind gesture repaid with a loud wail.

"I think I've broken my arm!"

***

Another scrunched up piece of paper flew unceremoniously at the waste bin, bounced on the rim and fell to the floor, joining many others. In fact, the floor was full of paper, chocolate wrappers, files and newspapers.

The desk was no better, with just a small gap in the middle giving access to a grimy computer screen covered in yellow stickers. A man, head in hands, was looking depressively at the monitor.

Timothy Scribbler was a young journalist at the Angler County News. Scruffy, unshaven, dirty shoes, smeary glasses and his appearance matched the surroundings. He prodded his glasses back into position, moved some papers out of the way and started typing, speaking the words aloud as he went along.

"Flower show in Upper Molehampton draws the crowds." He stopped and let out a sigh of frustration. "How boring. Doesn't anything exciting happen here? The last thing I can remember were the strange events at the County Cup football match some years ago."

"Scribbler!" shouted a voice from the corridor. "Moaning again?"

"Just commenting on how amazingly interesting it is to write about the flower show."

"Are you still dreaming of writing about your activist friends? No chance here, Scribbler. Don't want to upset Mrs Forsythe-Twyke," the man added, now standing behind him.

"Oh, surely not. Never. How could I think of such a thing? The family is just, well, so respectable," he sarcastically quipped back.

The man didn't recognise the sarcasm. "Well, Doug Gardener from the news channel certainly agrees with you."

"Doug Gardener is a nincompoop!"

"Steady on, Scribbler, he's my brother-in-law," retorted Mr Story. "I need your article by lunchtime, and you've got post," throwing an envelope up into the air.

Timothy caught it to find his name and address typed but no sender's address. Some photographs and a single sheet of paper fell onto his desk as he ripped open the envelope. He started reading, gasped in shock, smiled and started reading again.

"Wow!" he exclaimed. "Wow! This is explosive. Great." He then looked at the photographs and his expression changed from delight to sadness. "Oh no," he muttered.

The sender had created the desired response and Timothy's face had changed from boredom to inquisitive excitedness since reading the letter. "Got you!" he said triumphantly.

His head moved sharply to the window on hearing the sirens. The office overlooked the small hospital and he saw an ambulance followed by a police car arrive, with Sergeant Dawson squeezing himself out then approaching the back of the ambulance. Who else but Felicity Forsythe-Twyke was assisted out and into a wheelchair, clutching her arm and her face scrunched up in agony? She was yelling at the top of her voice, a stream of expletives audibly heard from the office. Sergeant Dawson was taking the full brunt of the abuse and Timothy was quite sure he saw the Sergeant smiling.

"Yes, I've really got you," Timothy Scribbler exclaimed, beaming from ear to ear.

***

"Good evening, dear," called out his loving wife as Mr Cross arrived home. She came into the hallway to find a sad looking husband. "Not a good day then, I see?"

"How can these days be good? Working for this monstrous family is pure torture for me, especially after the freedom of running the ferry for so many years."

"Come, my dear, let's have a cup of tea."

"Something stronger would be better, but tea is a good idea."

"You must be hungry after such a long day, and you did overtime too."

"Hungry? No. Any appetite I may have had is always lost in that industrial machine of death. The smell and sounds are just awful."

"I didn't think you had to enter the production. You do the security."

"Yes, I do, but in the last days there have been a few suspicious machine breakdowns and that crazy Mrs Forsythe-Twyke is convinced it's industrial sabotage. And, to cap it off, she's blaming me for it."

"You?" she said flabbergasted.

"But she might not be entirely wrong about industrial sabotage," he added.

"Is that a smirk I can see on your face?"

"I know nothing about it," he added, now smiling mischievously. "Why would I wish ill on this family? Not only did I lose my wonderful job as the ferryman, but they've completely spoilt the river environment. There's hardly an animal left to be seen when I walk along the riverbank. The sound of ducks has been replaced by the rumbling of lorries and squealing animals."

"You're quite right to be angry. If only there was something we could do."

"Yes, if only."

"Oh, nearly forgot. A letter arrived for you this morning. At least Mr Singh is still cheerful these days," added Mrs Cross.

"Let's see who wants something from me," he enquired, taking the envelope. "Hmm, typed but no sender's information. Who's this from?" pulling out a single sheet of paper from an anonymous sender. He shifted his position and started to read, his face showing more and more interest the further he got. He read it again but this time much slower. "Well, darling, we're not alone now."

"What do you mean?"

"This letter is a call to action from an unknown person. It gives me a name and I should help her. Jessica Walsh. And the aim is to defeat the Forsythe-Twykes."

"Jessica Walsh. I've heard of her. Oh yes, she's the local troublemaker."

"I'm afraid so, and I'm really not sure how she can help. It's actually most strange because only a few days ago Sergeant Dawson asked me to help in a matter regarding the Food Factory, which I did."

"That is interesting. What did he ask you to do?"

"Try out a new security dog called Ludwig," he lied to his wife. "In fact, I was working with him just before I left work." What Mr Cross meant was he helped Ludwig out of the Food Factory a short while ago, but his wife needn't know that. "And now this letter. Who's behind all of this?"

"Does it say what you should do?"

"Yes, turn a blind eye and help Jessica Walsh. I will know when it happens. I should also assist a local journalist called Timothy Scribbler and give the utmost assistance to Mr Kowalczyk."

"And my dear, will you help?"

"Help? Damn right I will!" he proudly exclaimed.

They were interrupted by the ringing of their phone.

"Mrs Cross speaking."

Mr Cross heard the shrill voice of Felicity Forsythe-Twyke on the other end. His wife held the receiver away from her ear and then passed it to her husband.

"Mr Cross here," he answered, keeping the phone far from his ear. "Oh, that is most unfortunate," he said grinning. After a short burst of screaming from the other end, he put the phone down.

"What does she want?"

"She's broken her arm in an accident and is convinced there's a plot against her."

***

The small room was sparsely furnished with two beds, a rickety wardrobe, a small table, two chairs and one hotplate for cooking. It was an old room, a lick of paint badly required and the furniture urgently in need of replacing.

A man opened the door and shuffled in to sit at the table next to his roommate.

"How was your day, Jakob? You look tired today," he asked with a thick eastern European accent.

"Exhausting and horrible. Can't think of other words in English to describe."

"I'm quite lucky, I suppose. I work in despatch and only have to package the frozen goods for shipping to Thailand."

"I not have it good like you, and I started in new area today. My job is to prepare disgusting feed and spoon it into trays. They call it fattening and we measure everything. No waste, Luca. No waste. I never see anything like this before. The poor animals scream and sit in small cages. This is not correct."

"Now we know why everything behind the fences is a secret. Nobody should find out what's going on," replied Luca to his friend, Jakob Kowalczyk. "Oh, I nearly forgot. A letter came for you today," said Luca, handing it over.

Jakob was surprised. "Oh, a letter for me. Not expecting anything. Oh, no markings and typed. It looks official."

Jakob Kowalczyk started reading and slowly, as his command of English was not perfect, unlike his friend Luca who had worked here longer. Once he finished, he sat upright, flattened the letter on the table and started reading again, his finger running over the words. He had a serious face.

"Yes, I will help," he whispered.

"Help who, Jakob?"

"Oh, nothing. A friend asked me to do something."

Luca turned around to make a drink whilst Jakob read the letter again, a look of steely determination on his face. The writer had awoken a fire inside him, a fire of protest and action. Jakob looked angry and ready to fight.

***

Mr Cross and Mr Walsh were in one of the warehouses, surveying the scene of some overnight damage. Strangely, lots of boxes had tipped over, causing hundreds of thousands of polystyrene chips to spill out over the floor. The workers from the production were reassigned to clear up the monumental mess, finding it rather challenging as the chips kept on flying through the air.

"Quicker now. Come on. She'll be here soon and best she doesn't see this mess," shouted out Mr Walsh.

"Too late, I fear," added Mr Cross, just as Felicity Forsythe-Twyke's screeching voice was heard coming their way. They turned towards the shrill sound and saw her stomping towards them, her arm in a cast supported by a sling.

"What's going on here?" she barked at them. "And you," she ordered, turning around to Mr Kowalczyk, "keep up."

"Yes, coming," he replied, carrying her bags.

"Good morning, Mrs Forsythe-Twyke," said Mr Walsh.

"How can this be a good morning? I've broken my arm, there's even more sabotage here, I'm losing a lot of money and surrounded by idiots."

The three men just stood there, none of them daring to say anything as she worked herself up into an absolute hysterical state.

"Don't just stand there, Mr …"

"Mr Kowalczyk."

"Yes, well, whatever you're called. Haven't you got a job to do?"

"You told me to carry your bags, Mrs Forsythe-Twyke."

Everyone closed their eyes in anticipation for the explosion of anger which came immediately.

"Don't answer back," she screamed, spit flying out of her mouth. "Give the bags to Mr Walsh and do some work. You're losing me money!" She wheeled around to face everyone working and tidying up the mess. "Doesn't anyone understand me? Just think of the poor people who will be affected by a slow-down in production. This company stands for helping the community and we should be compared to a charitable foundation."

Mr Kowalczyk was just left rooted to the spot, baffled at her outburst.

"Now!" she bellowed.

Mr Kowalczyk handed over the bags to Mr Walsh and started cleaning up the mess with the other workers.

Her rage intensified and her face became a dark red colour as she now turned on Mr Cross and Mr Walsh, yelling at them, "Explain this to me. Now."

"Well, erm, it's like this," Mr Cross stuttered back at her.

"I haven't got all day and your stuttering is also costing me more money."

"It appears the bottom boxes were ripped open, weakening their structure, and causing the upper boxes to tip over."

"And what caused the boxes to be ripped open?"

"That is rather curious as we've found large teeth marks."

"Teeth marks. Large. Are you implying we have a monster in here, you imbecile?"

"No, of course not. We haven't quite worked out what animal caused this but we're working on it with great priority."

"And Mr Walsh. Why are you standing there just doing nothing?"

"I'm holding your bags, Mrs Forsythe-Twyke. You told Mr Kowalczyk to give them to me."

"You fool! Give them to Mr Cross and help clear up this mess. Sabotage, delays and idiots. What should I do?"

Mr Walsh handed over the bags quickly, leaving poor Mr Cross alone with the enraged Mrs Forsythe-Twyke.

She looked at Mr Cross, defenceless against her fury. "Don't just stand there. Do something."

"But I'm holding your bags."

This was now the worst thing he could have said as she let out a long and loud scream lasting several seconds. "You dunce. You're my security man and should have never let this happen. Why are you not trying to find those responsible? Instead, you talk about an animal with large teeth. I've heard it all now. The best and only place to keep animals is in cages in my production hall. Follow me to my office, Mr Cross, then go and do your job if you still have one by the time we get there."

She spun around and stomped away, holding her arm gingerly and whining about her pain. "Mr Cross, get my phone from my handbag and dial Mrs Kingston. She's saved as Jemima. I can't dial in my poor state. Oh yes, hold it against my ear whilst we walk," she ordered.

Mr Cross duly did as ordered and did his best to walk next to his boss, trying to keep the phone next to her ear.

"Jemima darling. It's been just awful. Headache? You've got a headache? Stop complaining, woman, and listen to me. There's a plot against me, that I am quite sure of. The factory is being sabotaged and, what's more, Sergeant Dawson attacked me and now I have a broken arm. Yes, Jemima, I've got real problems. And I think you should help me get to the bottom of it. That's what loyal friends are for."

Mrs Forsythe-Twyke made a sudden change of direction, not giving Mr Cross the chance to react and bumped straight into her broken arm. The rest I think you can guess!

Chapter Seventeen
Bookshop Secrets and Unexpected Monks

The side streets in Chinatown were relatively quiet for such a busy part of Bangkok. But this was quite normal in the oppressive afternoon heat, most shopkeepers and vendors choosing to take it slowly and retreat from the blasting rays of sun to pass the time under umbrellas or shop entrances. One vendor braved the heat, pushing his street food wagon and casually ringing the bell. He was sitting on a small motorbike, pushing a bright blue trolley attached to the front of the bike. It carried many bottles containing an array of colourful liquids, presumably used as some sort of mix for a refreshing drink.

An elderly white man stood out like a sore thumb, everyone else moving as slowly as possible to avoid sweating, but not him. He was walking briskly down the street, constantly looking left and right to survey the shops, seemingly looking for someone. He wore a wide-brimmed hat and tried in vain to stem the sweat running down his leathery face with a handkerchief. His phone rang, making him stop outside a store selling kitchen goods with a red sign and green frame. Outside on the pavement, metal goods were stacked high on both sides of the narrow doorway with stools, large pots and utensils hanging from string. A quick glimpse inside showed the same chaotic stacking system.

"Yes," the man panted into his phone. "What is it, Bartholomew?"

"Vanessa sent a short message a while ago—*Brothers infiltrated. Going underground.* And that was it, but I'm sure you can make use of this."

"Yes, I can. I was wondering where they all are. Haven't heard from the stupid brothers for a while and also no sight of Vanessa and that pesky Mr Jackson. I've been scouring the streets and was just going to check the hotel, but it would be taking a risk."

"Where are you exactly?"

"Just around the corner from the hotel. It's a small side street just off Yaowarat Road and it's called, wait, let me take a look." He turned to the metal goods shop. "It's Plaeng Nam Road, number fifteen to be exact."

The man set off again, walking out of the quiet side street and towards a junction of a busy road. Buses, trucks, cars and tuk-tuks flowed by in a maelstrom of noise, the old man having to shout for Bartholomew to hear clearly. He turned left and straight past the hotel, weaving through the food stalls on the pavement.

"I'm going back to the office to await news from my agents. Maybe the Kennedy brothers will turn up too."

The office was set up by Bartholomew not too long ago to handle the container imports from the Food Factory in the Molehamptons. He had recently expanded the office to include a plant to process the animal waste left over from the production which nobody wanted. It was packed into boxes, frozen and shipped in containers to Laem Chabang Port, then transferred to smaller vessels for transport along the Chao Phraya River into central Bangkok. The last part of the journey was by truck. The food waste was pulverised and sold, nothing going to waste from what originally began at the Food Factory in the Molehamptons.

"Strange things have been going on, father. Felicity is paranoid and believes she is being targeted. Apparently, some production lines were damaged, leading to delays and a reduction in output. She's convinced it's industrial espionage."

"I hope she's not losing it at a critical time of our operation. Industrial espionage you say. I can well believe Mr Jackson has something to do with it, but he's here. No, she must be imagining it. Get in there, Bartholomew, and put her back on the straight and narrow. Make sure our production stays high as you know it's our main revenue flow to fund our operations here."

"There's more, father. She's broken her arm and is now telling everyone in the village that Sergeant Dawson did it. I'm afraid she can't be taken seriously. Sergeant Dawson wouldn't hurt a fly."

"Damn. Damn. Why now?" a normally controlled Ormerod demanded, showing signs of losing control himself.

"What now, father?"

"Mr Jackson must have something more than the book and I also know he went into lots of shops in this small area. He is keeping important information from Vanessa, but I just don't know what. I have the feeling there is more hiding here, so I'll activate my agents and get them to turn this area over. Somebody must know something, and I need to know. The agents have been once, but they can pay visits again. It's time to turn up the heat!"

"Turn up the heat. I thought it was hot there?"

"Fool," said Ormerod, putting away his phone.

***

The room was old, and the furniture looked as though it was from a film set from over one hundred years ago. A thick layer of dust was caked over all surfaces and the slightest breeze created a haze of minute particles dancing in the air. The room had at one stage been lived in, evident by the old books and manuscripts on the writing desk and in the shelves. The desk itself could have been a museum exhibition piece, finished off with a now-faded green leather surface. An old typewriter, ink pot and a paraffin lamp had been untouched for years, now decorated by the many spiders' webs forming ever so complex patterns across the vintage keys. The room, made entirely of wood, was dark and musty, the smell of unused years hanging like a blanket. The only light to enter the room came through a crack in the thick curtains. One could imagine an academic person once worked here.

But the room was not unused, signalled by the creaking of the adjoining door and then the entrance of a man in the shadows. Stepping carefully across the carpet, he avoided touching anything as if he did not want any trace of his presence left. He stopped a short distance from the curtains and angled himself so he could see through the crack but not be seen from the outside. The sound of heavy traffic, vehicle horns, a small motorbike in the street outside and the ring of a bicycle bell filtered into the room. The man used a handkerchief to wipe the sweat from his forehead, sweating profusely in the humid heat.

Through the crack in the curtains, he saw a typical Chinatown day. Street vendors were preparing and cooking their food over hot coals and gas cookers, at times bursts of flames soaring upwards as large woks were tossed over the fire. The smell of barbequed meat, hot fat and fish wafted upwards towards his window. It was late afternoon now and not as busy as it would be in a few hours when the night market was underway, some vendors still hiding from the heat under pieces of material strung up over their stalls. But not everyone was hiding from the heat. A group of men entered the street, walking fast and aggressively before they split up and entered shops. They looked like a local gang going after their protection money. The man in the upstairs room heard the shop bell ring as one small group of thuggish looking men entered the shop directly below him, holding what looked like a picture in their hands. The shop owner was heard welcoming the men, polite as he was, and then loud and aggressive sounding voices pressing for information. He could not understand the language being spoken below him, but it was quite clear the visitors wanted something, and he knew what. Only yesterday, a *farang* man and woman entered the shop, spoke kindly with the owner, stayed quite a while and then left out the back entrance. He later saw the same people going in and out of different shops on this narrow street before disappearing down one of the many side alleys. The men below carried on asking questions, but the shopkeeper remained calm, never raising his voice. Eventually, the rude visitors left, joined up with other gang members on the street, all holding pictures and pointing to other shops, maybe all confirming the presence of the *farangs* in different places yesterday. They plainly wanted to know who they were and exactly what they were looking for. Frustrated and angry, they threw their hands up in the air and promptly left the street, probably to carry on their search elsewhere.

The man retreated from the shadows and left the room, leaving no trace he had been there.

***

Surrounded by his piles of prized books, the shopkeeper sat in the semi-darkness, cradling a picture in his hands. The din of a constant river of vehicles from a nearby street was audible with the piercing honking of horns like a badly directed orchestra. He got up, stood under the entrance where the light was better and looked closely at the picture. It was black and white, quite grainy and had become faded over the years. The corners had dog ears and the back a name written on it: Oldfield Thomas ca. 1915. Two men were on the picture—one a white man about sixty years old and the other an oriental man, who had an uncanny resemblance to the old man now looking at the picture. He sat down again, guarding the narrow entrance to his shop, the stacks of books towering above him.

"My dear friend, what lovely times we had together. Whatever happened to you, and why is everyone now looking for you? What did you discover?" he whispered to himself with a look of sad remembrance on his face. "Whatever they are looking for, I won't help them. Those crooks who just visited are up to no good, but I will help the young man. He's good and he knows the code which only you and I shared." He looked up at the shop sign. *Oldfield EncycloPaedias and Ancient Books +66-02-5742-469-471.* Only special people have this number.

The noise of a piece of furniture being moved came from above the shop, causing the man to look up and smile, his old face shining in the harsh early evening sunlight. He then looked to his left at the neighbouring shop, number fifteen, selling metal kitchen wares. The owner waved at the old man and said, just loud enough to be heard, "I didn't give anything away."

"Neither did I," the old man smiled back.

Both of them nodded, appearing to confirm a prior agreement, and retracted back into their respective stores, their secrets going with them.

***

They all bowed their heads and clasped their paws together as a mark of respect when the President scurried in. An aura of grandeur was projected, with rich tapestries hanging on the walls and gloriously crafted furniture. The President took her place, looking intently but with respect at her fellow ministers, the atmosphere radiating mutual respect as the ministers waited politely for the proceedings to begin.

"Ministers, I welcome you today and thank you for coming to this quickly convened meeting," said the President calmly, all ears turned in her direction. "It is not often such high-powered meetings with all ministers are called and has only happened a few times in the thousands of years moles have administered the world above us."

"Rarely, I agree, but now the third time in about one hundred years," commented a minister.

"Yes, Minister for History, quite correct, and we are here for exactly the same reason as both before. Another foreigner, a *farang*, has arrived down here yet again. A man from Europe and the third in just over one hundred years."

"And can we presume he is here for the same purpose, namely, to steal from us?"

"Minister for History, you are quite right to be sceptical, and so am I. We don't want visitors down here and, to be exact, there are two of them. Connor Jackson and Vanessa Forsythe-Twyke."

The Minister for Security stood up and interjected, "Our special operations were unfortunately unsuccessful in stopping these visitors, despite releasing many infiltration bombs in challenging conditions. The two who made it down here proved skilled in avoiding the white blobs, unlike the two stupid men following them who proved to be easy targets. They were infiltrated and will wake up with a surprise."

The Minister for History then carried on, "Madam President, did I hear correctly? A member of that frightful family is down here right now. How did we let our guard drop?" There was a sharp intake of breath from the other ministers.

The President stood up and didn't speak for a while, allowing the room to become silent. "Because I permitted it," she replied firmly, staring at them all in their eyes as she panned around the room.

A murmuring of disapproval followed before she spoke again. "There is good reason for it, and I will now explain. As you all know, Oldfield Thomas worked with the monks and with us for many years. He was taught in our ways and instructed in our technology, but then disappeared for a long time, only to resurface back in his homeland armed with much more than he should have and could ever have learnt from us. Quite what he did in the years thereafter, we never found out, but we do know he expressed a deep and meaningful interest in moleology and ancient secrets. Some believe he found what we have always searched for – the Sanctuary of Epidaurus and the secrets of Azoth held within."

A gasp of shock erupted from everyone in the room.

"Of course, the Sanctuary may only be a myth but we, and many others, have been researching ancient manuscripts for many centuries now, trying to find out if there is any truth in the stories. As we know, myths are normally based on some sort of truth, especially when the same myth appears in the fables of different cultures in a slightly different form. If only humans knew the pyramids are really molehills," she chuckled, trying to lighten up the mood in the room.

"Yes, if only," the Minister for History giggled. "They still haven't worked out how they were built. And then there was the story of King William of Orange who died back in 1702 when his horse tripped over a molehill at the battle of Culloden. Our Scottish brothers deny all allegations but the moles there are strongly revered by the Jacobite society today who profited from his death. Yes, a rather embarrassing event!"

"Back to Oldfield Thomas," she added, now sounding serious. "But this was exactly the reason we allowed him to work with us as we wanted to tap into his amazing academic and research skills. We needed him to help us find the universal medication, the Elixir of Life, known to us as Azoth. He had a real burning motivation to discover ancient stories and quite how, where or who roused his interest in these matters is unknown to us, but we do know he already had a lot of information when he turned up here. And then one day, in the middle of his research, he just disappeared into thin air. The next we heard about him was about twenty years later when he started to set up his own mole administration system in the villages of Lower and Upper Molehampton and with none other than a gentleman called Beaumont Forsythe-Twyke."

"This is an unbelievable story," piped up a minster. "We knew a fledging state was set up over there, but not about the rest."

"Quite, Minister for Foreign Affairs, and few know about it. However, it is now time for the truth."

"And what about the second visitor who was here some years ago?"

"Minister, the second visitor was the Head of the Eternity Project, an organisation originally set up as an interface between the mole world and humans above and finally entrusted to safeguard the secret technology gleaned from here. But the organisation has been severely weakened and the secrets at risk of falling into the wrong hands."

"Protect from whom exactly?" demanded the Minister for Foreign Affairs.

"The Forsythe-Twykes work for the Cult of Azoth," answered the President.

The shocked minster gasped back, "And one of them is now down here?"

"Yes, and for a good reason. It's a trap," she answered slowly and powerfully. "We're trying to lure the Forsythe-Twyke family out of their lair and defeat them."

"Do you not consider this a dangerous course of action?" the minister carried on, sparring with the President.

"I understand your concern, but it is the only course of action to take, with the decision not taken lightly. Three visitors found us in the last one hundred years, and we must put a stop to it. Somewhere out there is a clue about us and our secrets, allowing us to be compromised, and we've had our moles burrowing and scouring the country for clues but have found nothing. If Oldfield Thomas, the Head of the Eternity Project, and Connor Jackson could find us, then so can the Cult of Azoth."

"But a Forsythe-Twyke has found us!" shouted out a few minsters at the same time.

"I need her to prove our existence so her family can be lured into our trap. The part of her memory about how to get here will be deleted using one of our potions, leaving our borders secure."

"How can you be sure they will fall for your trap? The Forsythe-Twykes will smell a rat," asked the Minister for Merit.

"Because, dear Minister, greed is their weakness and will also be their downfall. I am sure our existence alone will prove to be good bait."

"And what of Mr Jackson?" quizzed the Minster for History.

"He will be kept here for a similar purpose as Oldfield Thomas. It is obvious he has something about us, which we do not possess, and we have other pieces he is looking for. Somewhere between these manuscripts and the mystical Sanctuary of Epidaurus is the key to the puzzle, and Mr Jackson could be the one to unlock it. But there is another problem."

"Please clarify, Madam President," prodded the Minister for History.

"A research list was kept by Oldfield Thomas which we unsuccessfully tried to understand. We intended to use the Head of the Eternity Project to do this for us, but he had other ideas. He destroyed it and then disappeared."

"Why would he destroy such important information?" exclaimed the Minister for History.

"To protect the links between us and the secrets. You see, we believe Oldfield Thomas really did find the Sanctuary of Epidaurus and the secrets of Azoth. Presumably the Head of the Eternity Project did too. The information hidden here, is too dangerous to fall into the wrong hands and the Forsythe-Twykes are unrelenting in their search. But then something strange happened a few years ago when the Head of the Eternity Project came out of hiding and was seen. He was sending a message to everyone, including us, that he wanted to be found. He is the bait, the Forsythe-Twykes are the fish and we are the anglers. Mr Jackson's arrival is no coincidence, and it comes at a time when the Forsythe-Twykes are most powerful and dangerous, using their Food Factory to influence the allocation system in their favour. Also, the mole world in the Molehamptons is in open revolt and the President in hiding. We know from our sources that it is only a matter of time before the Forsythe-Twyke family has total control and it will be them who administer the memories and allocations. Additionally, they also have agents everywhere and it will not take them long to find us. We must defeat them before it is too late. Mr Jackson will therefore be afforded all assistance and I will personally speak to him about putting a plan together."

"And what exactly should Mr Jackson do?" asked the Minister for Security.

"He should go to the Repository and study the ancient manuscripts like those before him. He must already hold a piece of the jigsaw we do not have, and once he has found what he needs, he will want to leave and probably secretly. We will allow him to do that but have him followed, hopefully leading us to the Head of the Eternity Project and the prize. At the same time, Mr Jackson will be followed by the Forsythe-Twykes, and the trap sprung."

"I will do everything to assist and I'm sure my fellow ministers will also," approved the Minister for Security. "We have developed our system and culture for thousands of years and also had peace with our neighbours. I feel this could now be at risk and we cannot allow it to happen. Contact with the western world can only end bad."

"Mr Minister, I am sure we all agree with your fears, and so do I. It is true they have stolen our technology and copied our system, albeit in a basic form. We know what true equality really is, but you must all remember it did not come overnight and we also had our problems in the past. They are weak in the west with their desires based on greed, but they are nevertheless a real danger to us. I can tell you all here today that we have two choices; Shutter our borders and turn a blind eye, maybe destroying ourselves in the process. Or we help Mr Jackson defeat the devious family, allowing their mole world to be brought back on track. I believe we should help. And you?" she demanded, her voice shaking with emotion. "Are we in agreement? Do I have your support?"

Slowly each minister nodded in approval.

***

Gavin woke up with a start, feeling really quite drowsy and the last he remembered was following Mr Jackson to a temple, then nothing more. He now found himself sitting on a small stool, so he couldn't have been asleep, which added to his confusion. Looking down, he noticed he had nothing on his feet but that wasn't the most obvious thing he saw. He was dressed in a bright orange robe. Joe roused shortly after and experienced the same puzzled feeling, rubbing his eyes and slowly looking at himself, also dumbfounded to realise he was barefoot and wearing an orange robe. The two of them looked at each other, realising they both looked the same, their eyes becoming ever wider.

"Joe. Joe. Why is your head shaved? You are totally bald?"

Joe's hands shot to his head and with panic tried to ruffle the non-existent hair, rubbing his smooth head instead. Joe looked at Gavin and his face turned ashen.

"You too, Gavin, but there's more. You have no eyebrows."

Gavin's hands darted to his face and the top of his head to confirm his brother's comment. "You haven't got any eyebrows either!"

Both Joe and Gavin stared at each other in utter shock, not able to take in what had happened to them and then let out a slow shriek.

"Psst," came a voice from somewhere nearby, and then a whisper in an unknown language.

Gavin and Joe didn't understand but automatically knew they should be quiet. They stood up to see where they were. It was indeed true, they were bald, had no eyebrows, were wearing orange robes, had nothing on their feet and had no other possessions with them. Worst of all, no phone and no money. To complete their bewilderment, they turned around in a circle, finding themselves in a richly decorated temple, a huge golden Buddha at one end of a high hall. There were monks sitting on the floor, praying in complete silence.

"Joe, what's happened? Why are we here and dressed like this? How could this happen?"

"I've no idea, Gavin, I was asking myself the same question," he replied quietly, capping his hand over his mouth. "The last thing I can remember was following Mr Jackson at the temple. Then pigeons. Yes, many pigeons."

"Why are we Buddhist monks?" both of them whispered to each other at the same time, their voices and faces distressed.

"And I'm starving," added Joe, rubbing his large stomach. "I wonder if there's any grub around here?"

"No," came a harshly whispered reply from an elderly monk. "It's the afternoon and no food until the morning now. Meditate then sleep. Your training will begin tomorrow morning," he added, pointing to an open shed.

"Training?" both of them shot back.

No other choice available to them, Joe and Gavin Kennedy retreated into the silence of their strange and unexpected surroundings where they had a restless night indeed. Not only did their stomachs constantly gnaw with hunger, but it was impossible for them to get comfortable on the wooden floor with only a blanket to cover themselves. They had no creature comforts with them, it was oppressively hot, they had their heads and eyebrows shaved and to cap it all off, they were now apparently trainee monks. The most worrying thing about their situation was they had no memory of how it had happened.

Early morning eventually arrived, and the sun was just poking its hot rays from behind the temple tops, the bright light reflecting off the golden surface like an explosion. Both of them sat there, observing their strange surroundings, trying to fathom out what was going on and what they should do.

"Look, a monk is coming towards us. Maybe he can get us out of here," Gavin said excitedly.

The monk approached slowly and, just as Gavin was about to speak, put his finger to his lips for him to be silent.

"Welcome", he whispered. "This is your first full day so some basics for you. Monks eat only once or twice a day, the last meal taken before midday. You may not eat elephants, leopards, snakes, dogs, some other animals and humans."

"Humans! That's a relief," replied Gavin, followed by the monk looking at him harshly, clearly disapproving of him speaking.

"As I was saying," the monk continued, "you may now eat. There is breakfast prepared consisting of turnips, bread and porridge."

Both Gavin and Joe just stared at the monk as though it was their last day on earth and, before they said anything, he turned and walked slowly away, the brothers trudging unhappily after him. The breakfast was just as described and difficult for them to swallow. This was really not their type of food, but their acute hunger got the better of them and they reluctantly ate.

Following breakfast, the monk, who seemed to have been chosen as their trainer, gave them cleaning chores, and armed with large mops, the two distraught brothers cleaned the vast marble floors, making sure any dirt was carefully removed. They were not used to manual work as they had never had a job in their lives and being out of shape made them sweat profusely and pant heavily.

The brothers knew nothing about Buddhist ways, not that it particularly interested them, but their next job gave them their first insight. They had to accept and store items from visitors to the temple and it was explained Buddhists give offerings for gratitude and inspiration. They believe in karma and can also accumulate merit through these offerings, which hopefully result in a better rebirth and release from any suffering. The visitors bring useful items such as candles, flowers, food and drinks, but there were also some more unusual things such as electrical cables, small light bulbs, toy tuk-tuks, salt blocks and miniature toy furniture. All the offerings were carefully stored on shelves in a large room. The monk explained he could not really say why these items were offered but they were happy to accept anything so long as it helped Buddhists gain merit. Strangely, the monk told them a lot of the items disappeared in the night.

Villains at heart, the brothers started looking for smartphones to steal, desperate to communicate to the outside world. But their plan was thwarted as the clock struck midday and then they settled into their afternoon of meditation and hunger. Their situation could not have been any worse.

Chapter Eighteen
Upsetting the Apple Cart

You may well have your opinion about the use of smartphones, but one thing is for sure, just a few clicks can be enough to mobilise people and that is exactly what Jessica Walsh did. She was not particularly accomplished at school but lurking below the surface were other talents just waiting to be discovered. The letter's arrival was enough to awaken a burning passion for right and wrong, and in this instance; she was quite sure she knew what was wrong. It was about time the truth was revealed and people couldn't turn a blind eye anymore. And now she was going to do something about it.

Jessica put down her phone after a wave of pings and buzzes, all messages confirming the senders' agreement to her suggestion. She got up, put her jacket on and went downstairs.

"Jessica, off out are you?"

"Yes, mum, might be a bit late."

"But I've got dinner ready soon. Some lovely pork."

"Yes, but I'm a vegetarian, mum," and off she went, leaving her mother perplexed.

"A vegetarian. You weren't this morning!" shouting after her daughter as she slammed the door.

Jessica walked the short distance to the youth club, a small building next to the village green and right next door to a garage showing *VoleWeb*. She waited patiently, and as requested, a steady stream of young friends started joining her, their teenage voices aching to be heard, eager to protest for the cause successfully mobilised by Jessica. It was a pity organisational skills were not part of the school curriculum, because Jessica would have scored top marks. In a short space of time, she had hatched a plan in quite minute detail, all the people bringing something with them. Paval had a drum, Danika a banner, Vilma a trumpet, Katie a megaphone and many other people with assorted items required for the plan to work. Jessica stood there like a sergeant major marshalling people, instructing them what to do, and ensuring everyone was reaching out to their contacts. Once the last people arrived on the number seven bus from Anglerton and were briefed, they all set off.

The group of young people, numbering around fifty, left the building and on Jessica's signal, erupted into a mass of noise. Drums, trumpets, rattles, whistles and anything else which made annoying sounds were now effectively utilised as they marched once around the village green, passed Sergeant Dawson's police station and straight up the road towards the Food Factory. The disturbing protest had the desired effect, the village residents running out to see what the fuss was all about.

Sergeant Dawson jumped out of his chair and plodded outside as quickly as his size would permit. Standing there in awe, the young people marched past banging, beating, shouting and whistling with Jessica Walsh at the head. He did nothing to intervene, just standing there with his arms crossed, watching the scene with pride.

"Are you not going to do anything?" shouted Mr Rye, as he ran up towards the station.

"Do anything? Do what exactly?"

"Well, stop these troublemakers."

"Troublemakers. I can't see any troublemakers. I thought they were musicians and, besides, they're not breaking the law."

"But they're marching to the Food Factory. Just look at their banners, Sergeant Dawson. They're demanding access and want transparency."

"That is also not a crime, Mr Rye. Musical processions and also protests have to be registered according to the law, and this they have done. Just look here at the notification form submitted by Jessica Walsh. Everything is perfectly in order," said the Sergeant, shoving the form in front of Mr Rye's face.

"Well then, it must be correct if you say so, but mighty strange if you ask me. Mrs Forsythe-Twyke will be most angry."

"Yes, Mr Rye, I am quite sure of that," he replied, returning to his office with a huge grin on his face. "I'm sure she will. Jessica Walsh is just about to upset the apple cart."

***

Felicity Forsythe-Twyke sat in her office, cradling her broken arm, but she was in quite good spirits despite the pain as everything was going according to plan. Or so she thought. Vanessa was underground with Mr Jackson, Bartholomew was supporting her and, more importantly, the increase in security had done the trick with no new acts of sabotage reported in the last twenty-four hours. All she had to do now was sit back and wait for Ormerod to report with the good news. What could go wrong?

The noise at first was distant, far enough away that Felicity didn't even register it, but then it became gradually louder until eventually she couldn't fail to notice. She started looking around in her office to find out where the strange noise came from. It became louder still, so she went to the window to survey the surroundings. She definitely heard something but could not see anything and assumed it was some awful Lower Molehampton musical event she hadn't thankfully been invited to. She started to turn around when a noise erupted like a volcano. Spinning around again, she saw a mass of people appear over the brow of a low hill and march purposefully towards the Food Factory entrance. They were enthusiastically banging and blowing on an assortment of instruments and also held up banners showing *Let us in*! A young woman led the entourage, but Felicity didn't recognise her. She would soon!

"A protest. A protest. How dare they and after everything I've done for the good and benefit of the community. Scoundrels," she spat out, froth dribbling down her chin. "I'll have a stop to this devilish work," she carried on yelling with venom and eyes bulging wide as she grabbed for her phone.

"Sergeant Dawson speaking. How may I help you?" he asked over politely, already knowing who was calling.

"I know it's you, you blithering idiot."

"Mrs Forsythe-Twyke, so nice to hear your voice and it's always a pleasure. What can you be concerned about on such a lovely day?"

"Concerning me, you dare to ask, you nincompoop. There's a noisy protest going on right outside the Food Factory. Disperse it at once, imprison the ring leaders and throw the keys in the River Angler."

"I'm sure there's a good explanation for it. In fact, the newly formed marching band were practicing today and maybe you've mistaken a protest for a band."

"Mistaken! Then why are they holding up signs demanding entry? Sergeant, get here now!"

"Well, I suppose I can find the time to look into the matter. I'll make a call to Anglerton and then come by myself. After I've finished what I am doing of course," he said, brushing the biscuit crumbs off his lap.

"And these ghastly people have no respect for animal welfare. My poor animals will be distressed and won't be able to sleep. This situation is absolutely ghastly, and I can't believe the locals are in open revolt against me."

"I can understand your compassion for your products. I'll be in touch soon."

Felicity wanted to answer but Sergeant Dawson had already put down the phone and was roaring with laughter. He needed a while to compose himself, tears running down his chubby cheeks, then looked at the letter again and made a call.

"Timothy Scribbler," answered the voice on the other end.

***

A chain reaction of protest against the Forsythe-Twykes had been ignited above and below the ground.

Firstly, Ludwig had successfully exited the Food Factory and immediately went back below at great danger to himself. Here, he found Colonel, now President Pickle, and challenged his loyalty— it was after all his fault Basil was now in his predicament. Despite my suspicions about the Colonel's intentions, Ludwig saw something else in him. The Colonel's plan to force me below the ground worked, but then it backfired leaving Ludwig an easy task of making him feel guilty. And it worked.

"Yes, you can count on me," replied Colonel Pickle.

Meanwhile, Sergeant Dawson certainly did not look to help Felicity Forsythe-Twyke, quite the opposite in fact, as he sought Mr Cross and Mr Kowalczyk, knowing they had also received letters. A small camera was handed over for them to film what really went on in the Food Factory.

"Yes, you can count on me," they both replied.

Sergeant Dawson then returned to his station, stopping briefly to adjust some decoration on a molehill. He was as proud as mustard now having a new purpose in his bland job. He was revelling in his new role as the organiser of clandestine activities against the Forsythe-Twykes, and never again would Felicity Forsythe-Twyke talk down to him.

Suspicious about what the moles might have been up to in his absence, he gingerly opened the storeroom door. His worst fears were confirmed as he gasped in amazement. It was full of new items and plainly not his. Wire cutters, metal bars, hacksaws, screwdrivers and a good assortment of other tools. And there was still this plug socket with the power cord leading into a hole and, scratching his head, wondered what it was for. He would have great difficulty explaining this if his superiors decided on a spot inspection.

The ringing of his phone startled him out of his shock, forcing him to plod across to the desk and plump down into his chair. "Sergeant Dawson speaking."

"Got you at last, and I've already called a few times. It's Dawn Boltcropper from the DIY store. You wouldn't believe it, Sergeant Dawson, but there's been a burglary but oddly no sign of a forced entry."

"Are you quite sure?"

"Yes, of course, but it is weird as none of the expensive items are missing, instead the small items used for cutting are gone. Not just a few, but all of them. Everything taken. I really can't understand who should need, or even steal such things."

Sergeant Dawson looked at the storeroom door and then back to the phone. "Yes, I agree, most odd. I'll come by and make a report as soon as I am free." He put down the phone and checked the storeroom, finding the items here exactly fitted Dawn Boltcropper's description.

"What are these moles up to?" he spoke out loud and started smiling. He could sense change in the wind and, with an air of confidence, sat down again and dialled a number, stabbing the keys in glee.

"Yes, hello, Mrs Forsythe-Twyke. I hope your arm is not causing you too much pain?" he asked, prodding for a reaction, and he got it. He held the receiver away from his ear in anticipation of the torrent of abuse coming his way. He just sat there chuckling to himself, his cheeks wobbling uncontrollably. "Laughing. No, Mrs Forsythe-Twyke, I'm not laughing. Just shaking off a little cough. Anyway, I'm calling about the protests as I promised to investigate the matter. I can gladly report all is in order and the protest was correctly registered. As mayoress, I am sure you understand there is nothing illegal about it."

He again held the phone away but there was only silence. She had put down the phone and was probably on her way to his office right now.

****

The noisy protestors parted peacefully as the gates of the Food Factory opened, remaining respectful and non-violent as they promised from the outset. Their numbers had now swelled to well over one hundred as new friends joined and more were on their way, a snowball effect as young people were heading for the Molehamptons in their droves. Mrs Forsythe-Twyke's Rolls Royce, shining brightly in the sun, left the Food Factory as the protestors upped their volume under the direction of Jessica Walsh. Felicity didn't dare to look at them, staring ahead with her face crunched up in hysterical anger.

"Get out of here now," shouting angrily at Mr Creswell, "and take me to the police station sharpish."

It was only a short distance to the village but enough for word to spread and, believe me, word spreads quickly in the Molehamptons. The first thing Mr Creswell noticed when passing the first houses was a fine spray of water appearing on the windscreen and bonnet, surprising him as it was not raining. The next thing was a dull thud as soft objects hit the car. Whatever this was soon became apparent, exploding in a puff of white powder, turning the shiny car into something resembling a moving sack of flour. He stopped the car to inspect the situation.

"I would stay in the car if I were you," he advised Mrs Forsythe-Twyke, but there was no stopping the livid woman as she stomped off in the direction of the police station. Mr Creswell stood in the middle of the road watching what happened next. Suddenly, from a few front gardens masked by hedges and bushes, jets of water arched up into the air before falling back to the ground, landing directly on Mrs Forsythe-Twyke and drenching her in just a few seconds. She stood motionless, soaked to the skin and looked up at the sky. She was just able to make out the movement of small objects, not easy for her, as her face and eyes were wet, and also unclear what these things were. It soon became evident as soft packages started raining down, finding their mark on her and bursting open in a big white cloud of fine white powder. Looking like a ghost, she remained completely static, too shocked to move. But the attack, by whoever it was, had not finished and the eggs which now followed accurately hit her, breaking open with their gooey contents slipping down her hair and face. Her head now looked like a cake mixture ready for beating.

Mr Creswell remained untouched as he looked on, a smirk on his face. Mrs Forsythe-Twyke just stood there and let out a long painful scream, her cry reverberating through the village streets. The silent residents returned to their houses, away from their unseen hiding places behind the hedges. Sergeant Dawson was now approaching, waddling up the street with a huge smile on his face, Mrs Forsythe-Twyke too immersed in her own situation to notice. And he wasn't the only person smiling in the village.

***

Sergeant Dawson did what he promised and visited the DIY store, confirming his suspicion the stolen goods were now in his storeroom. Wary about what would happen next, he returned to the station, but nothing could prepare him for the scene which now met him.

"Attention!" came a shout and then a loud bang as row upon row of moles stood straight. The Sergeant was utterly speechless as he looked down to see the whole office floor covered with platoons of moles, all bolt upright and dressed in camouflage uniforms. He had experienced a lot lately, but this was too much as he attempted to speak, but nothing came out of his mouth.

"Reporting for duty," cried Colonel Pickle, appearing from under the desk.

"Reporting for duty. What duty?" Sergeant Dawson just managed to stammer back.

"We attack tonight."

"Attack where?"

"The Food Factory of course. Under Ludwig's guidance, we will stop the production and create, how should I put it, some problems. Now, Sergeant, please be so kind and leave us. We need your office for briefings and preparing our weapons. And thank you for looking after them, by the way," added the Colonel.

"I didn't remember being asked. And what's more, this is my office, and you can't just tell me to leave."

"The last time I looked, you were a sergeant and I a colonel, and now President. Return with your car at twenty-three hundred hours and make sure it's empty. Oh yes, bring blankets too," he ordered.

Sergeant Dawson obediently turned around and left his office, closing the door quietly behind him. "Attack tonight. Oh dear, I think we're in for trouble," he said to himself.

"Troops," shouted Colonel Pickle. "Get your weapons now."

***

The car had seen better days Once it had been bright red, but now it was more of a dull reddish-brown colour, and it also once had smooth bodywork but now resembled the surface of the moon. The dilapidated car hissed and squeaked its way up the slight incline like an old steam train as it came over the brow of the hill, stopping right in front of the protestors with a big bang and cloud of black smoke. The tall man had difficulty getting out of the cramped seat, needing three heaves with his hands holding on to the frame. He eventually forced his way out, stooping until he could extend his long body, crisp bags and food scraps falling to the ground. He brushed off some crumbs and pulled out a notebook from his inside pocket.

The protestors had created a permanent wall of noise since their arrival, never interrupted until the arrival of this car. A young teenager signalled for everyone to start again before walking over to greet the man.

"Timothy Scribbler," he said, extending his arm.

"Jessica Walsh," she replied, shaking his greasy hand and then wiping it on her trousers.

"Jessica, I'm from the Angler County News. Probably read it, I think."

"Actually not," she replied.

"Well, it's the best regional newspaper you might read. I would like to ask you some questions about what you are doing here. Is that OK?"

"Sure, any publicity we get would be great."

Timothy immediately whipped out his camera and started taking pictures of Jessica, the protestors and the imposing entrance of the Food Factory. Just at that moment, some other vehicles approached over the brow of the hill. Five minibuses full of protestors and a coach bristling with journalists armed with cameras.

"Ah good, more protestors, as arranged," Jessica smiled triumphantly.

"And the journalists I arranged," quipped Timothy back. "But I was here first, so the story is mine."

Jessica nodded her agreement and then took a selfie with the hoard of new arrivals in the background and promptly shared it with her army of followers. A few seconds later, the message pinged on phones all over the world.

"Jessica, if I may begin. What are you actually protesting about?"

"Against the Food Factory. We want to know what is going on behind this security. How can it be a secret when it ends up in our stomachs? We demand transparency."

"But why now, Jessica?"

"I was woken up to the meat industry when someone sent me a description and pictures. It was horrific. I should have already guessed it, but I probably didn't want to know."

"Are you a vegetarian?"

"Since yesterday, yes."

"Is it your intention to turn others into vegetarians?"

"No, absolutely not."

"Then what is your aim, Jessica Walsh?"

"We just want to make people aware of what is going on so they can make their own informed decisions. It's impossible that this amount of meat can be processed in decent conditions. Just impossible. We accept animals die so we can eat them but not on this barbaric scale. They are also living beings and we do not have the right to eat everything we want on this planet. We have to share our home."

"Strong words, Jessica and thought-provoking. I'm sure our readers will find it interesting. Thank you very much for the interview."

"And there's more."

"Go on, please."

"I've heard secrets are hidden behind the walls. Secrets about the Forsythe-Twyke family. They are hiding something."

Before Timothy Scribbler could press her further on the subject, a mass of journalists and film crews scrambled towards them to interview Jessica. He was rudely shoved out of the way, but he now had his story and made his way back to his office to be the first to print. Jessica was suddenly illuminated by glaring camera lights and the full scale of what she had started slowly dawned on her.

Mrs Walsh was standing in her kitchen, enjoying a cup of tea and watching her favourite television show. It was suddenly interrupted by breaking news. Her teacup fell to the floor, smashing loudly into hundreds of pieces as her daughter was beamed into the screen.

It will not surprise you that there's more to Jessica Walsh than meets the eye. She had effectively mobilised protestors at short notice, using social media platforms to make the issue go viral. It didn't take long for people to start turning up from all over the country, Jessica chaperoning new arrivals and organising them into protest groups. The next stage in her plan was arranging people into shifts, allowing them to take rests and keep the protest going around the clock. She called Gertrude Lawnsworthy, who also mobilised friends, and asked her to help out with a kitchen to feed the young people. Jessica had everything well under control.

But the letter Jessica received contained more information and she now decided to act on it. News of the protest was now on global television, and she used that to send a stirring message to the Forsythe-Twyke Food Factory workers in Thailand. She told them they only received the food waste and their pay and conditions were not up to what should be expected of a global company. She called on the workers to come out on strike and join her protest movement. The workers readily agreed, stopping production in Bangkok immediately. The Forsythe-Twykes were now under attack from more than one angle, the pressure definitely getting to Felicity. But things were about to get a whole lot worse for them!

Chapter Nineteen
Monks, Moles and Moleism

It was as if I had been transported to another dimension without even noticing it; no sensation of being shrunk to the size of a mole and by a much more technically advanced process. The room slowly came into view as the mist cleared, and it certainly wasn't the one we had entered. Exquisite textiles and fine wooden panels decorated the walls, but there were no doors. We stroked the surfaces, looking for a way out but found nothing, however the sensation of a light breeze and the smell of fresh air indicated an entrance must be somewhere here. Moreover, where was the monk we followed?

"And now?"

"Quiet," I whispered, cupping my hand to my ear. "Can you hear that? A tapping noise, right here."

Suddenly, a crack of light appeared, and a panel slid silently open, proving advanced artisanship skills. A mole entered, dressed in an immaculately tailored pin-striped suit and bowler hat. He stopped right in front of me and peered straight into my face, so close his whiskers tickled my nose. Despite having been below the ground, the strange sensation of being the same size as moles and other creatures never ceased to amaze me. He said nothing, just stared at me before turning abruptly to the right and circled us, carrying out a thorough visual check. The mole looked us up and down again, inspecting us closely, and then slowly started sniffing us before circling us a few more times. Eventually, after his inspection seemed to be finished, he spoke for the first time.

With a slow voice, he declared, "We know who you are seeking."

"And who exactly?" I countered confidently.

When I first entered the mole world, I was naturally shocked and nervous, but not now. I felt fairly experienced in their ways, and the show of pomp wasn't going to intimidate me.

"The person visited us in the footsteps of another European who lived with us over one hundred years ago—Oldfield Thomas. We rarely have visitors, so we are extremely cautious about who we let in."

"Cautious? The monk led us directly down here."

"Which monk? I can't see anyone," he replied, surprised. "You are not alone in your search, Mr Jackson. Many have hunted the person you seek for a long time. He has information."

"What information?"

"That, Mr Jackson, is for you to find out."

He paused, then approached my ear and whispered, "I may tell you more but without her," now looking disapprovingly at Vanessa. "We don't like visitors at the best of times, but a Forsythe-Twyke down here—never. They are dangerous, and Mr Jackson, you should not trust her. She's been sending messages to her family behind your back and has double-crossed you. We've been observing both of you since your arrival and also successfully got rid of the two idiots following you. But her," he added harshly. "She must go."

Another unseen entrance opened and two moles in brown police uniforms marched in, unceremoniously lifted Vanessa up by her arms and carried her out of the room before she could even protest.

"Vanessa," I called out, but it was in vain as the door closed them.

"And now, Mr Jackson, you may come with me."

***

This place was much different to the Molehamptons where it was politically controlled, the moles using their power to great effect along with the fear of ending up in the Food Factory. Here, there were no political signs, no visible police and everything seemed so much more relaxed with larger tunnels and proper roads mirroring what was happening above the ground in Bangkok. Flat tunnel walls allowed buildings to be constructed two storeys high unlike the rounded and smaller tunnels below the Molehamptons. Every few metres street food stands cooked Thai food, the lovely smell wafting into my nose. Here the air was also fresh and well-ventilated, a far cry from the dank and musty climate beneath my village.

It was still an awe-inspiring experience and my eyes darted everywhere, taking in all the different scenes. A tuk-tuk full of blocks of salt sped by, then there were some monks collecting offerings in the street and listening to what people wanted to get off their chests. If people and animals didn't believe about going back as a different life form, they sure did now. Everyone was desperate to give offerings to the monks in a last chance of increasing their merit points they might have missed out on above the ground. The scent of incense and barbeque smoke blew through the tunnels, sometimes rudely replaced by tuk-tuk exhaust fumes. I had seen toy tuk-tuks being delivered to Wat Suthat and wondered why the monks needed them. The answer was the monks did not, but they were needed down here instead and then adapted for use. I now wondered what the normal monks made of the strange offerings they received and where the items disappeared to.

I was rudely jolted out of my thoughts by a screeching horn as a tuk-tuk hurtled past me, the trunk of an elephant poking out of the side and nearly knocking me over.

"Careful, Mr Jackson," said my guide, picking up his pace. "Follow me. Things to do."

"What things?" I shouted after him as another tuk-tuk rocketed past with three monkeys clambering around on the frame, making the whole vehicle rather unstable. The innovation of the moles seemed to have no end.

"You'll find out. I have to take you to my office and explain everything you need for your mission," the mole yelled out above the noise of the traffic.

"Mission?"

"Yes, Mr Jackson. You are not here by coincidence, and I already know you don't believe in them."

"Usually not, no," as I dodged different animals, trying to keep up with him. "You seem to know all about me."

The street we were on kind of looked familiar and then I saw a sign for Yaowarat Road, the same as the one my hotel was on. I wondered if we were directly underneath now. The mole turned right down a narrow road, and we went past a shop selling metal kitchen goods and also a bookshop. Unbelievable, I thought to myself. It was an exact mirror image of the streets above in Chinatown and I asked myself what was first, the version above or below the ground. In any case, this place must have been really old.

"So, you recognise this place?" he questioned, stopping and grinning.

"Yes, sure I do," I confirmed, looking around.

"Let's go to my office," he said, and he scurried back towards the shop selling metal goods, number fifteen Plaeng Nam Road. It looked like a replica of the one above, even the same metal pots and chairs stacked up high outside the entrance. We weaved our way through the piles of goods leaning precariously in all directions and headed towards a door at the back of the shop. Above was a shelf with candles and burning incense sticks along with the rhythmic chanting of a Buddhist prayer coming from a loudspeaker.

"Here we are," he added, entering his office. "My name is Ricky Rulob and I'm a liaison officer between the world down here and up there," he added, pointing a paw upwards. He sat down at his desk and ushered me to do the same, then pulled out a file which he started reading before looking up.

"Connor Jackson, we've been monitoring you for a while now. A talented analyst and your rescue of Professor Wingnut quite impressive. Escape from the mole world below the Molehamptons along with your friends. Well planned. Mr Jackson, impressive reading, really. You were flagged up back then and will prove most useful to us."

"Useful. Now Mr Rurob, I'm sick and tired of everyone using and abusing me. I'm not down here to do your work. I have to find somebody, defeat the Forsythe-Twykes and release my good friend, Basil."

"Yes, we know all about that and we can mutually support each other. We have the same aims, and the utmost importance is the defeat of the Forsythe-Twykes. A big mistake that was, I tell you."

"What was a big mistake?"

"Later, Mr Jackson. This might take a while for you to digest so let me give you some basic facts about our underground world, and you may find it quite different to what you know. I've already told you I'm a liaison officer with the world above and directly with monks. But not ordinary monks because they do their real job of enlightening people, and they are truly wonderful people I have to say. I liaise with a secret order of monks who live amongst, but unknown to the ordinary monks, and assist us in our interests."

"Can it be that one of them has been observing me in the Molehamptons?" I asked looking at him seriously.

"A monk observing you? I can assure you he has nothing to do with us. We are aware of other secret monks who are also here hiding in our very ranks. But nobody knows who they are or what they do," he whispered, coming right up next to me. "They are extremely secretive," he added in a hushed voice.

"Until now I have only known about the moles under the Molehamptons. Do moles do this type of activity all over the world?"

"According to ancient manuscripts, the role of administering the world and controlling allocations was indeed entrusted to moles. We have always been responsible for keeping the natural order in balance and the storage of memories once creatures have been passed to us. The Gods entrusted us with this task and well before humans became so powerful, eventually taking over the world. If you believe the myths, that is."

"The Gods gave you this task?" I frowned at him, not able to take him seriously.

"Yes, many thousands of years ago."

"But that does not explain how the Molehamptons were set up fairly recently, especially as you say the moles have always done this."

"Very astute of you, Mr Jackson. The manuscripts also state the moles slowly lost control of the world, losing it piece by piece, and what now remains of this ancient system are a few mole systems dotted all over the world. We have left our mark and many of your stories, fables and cultures are actually based on ours. Have you ever wondered what the separation of the physical body and the spirit was all about? Physical bodies indeed disappear but not the spirit with its memory, which is impossible to destroy. It is our job to preserve memories in a dignified manner. Unfortunately, Mr Jackson, the system in the Molehamptons has been abused."

"That I can believe. What happened to the rest of the world?"

"Like all systems and cultures, greed even got the best of us moles and things started to fall apart, anarchy taking over. Greed, Mr Jackson, is the root cause of all evil. Fortunately, it never took hold here and we still adhere to the pure form of moleism."

"Moleism?" I said with a questioning expression.

"Yes, moleism is the purest form of equality where greed does not exist. The monks play a large role in this above the surface, spreading enlightenment and highlighting the dangers of greed."

"Your system must be so old."

"Yes, and we are proud to be the oldest and purist mole world existing."

"Are there many remaining?"

"Some, yes, but sadly for the planet, only a few pockets. Where we do not control the natural order, anarchy reigns and usually to the benefit of the humans. Hence our suspicion of foreign visitors and, including you, we have now had three. The first two didn't end well for us."

"I believe Oldfield Thomas was one of them?" I probed.

"He was a real academic and useful to us. He, like you, found his way in and that is not easy. Once here, his skills were recognised and his interest in Buddhism and Moleism developed, eventually being ordained as a monk in our order to learn about our technology and secrets. He moved between the world of monks and moles, which was quite unheard of as a foreigner, but he possessed talents which nobody else had. He was extremely good at analysing data. Despite my criticism of humans, they can be quite good at that, much better than us actually, and Oldfield Thomas was particularly good. Just as you are, Mr Jackson."

"I've read a little about him. Apparently, he came to Siam, as it was known then, to study moles," I asked, genuinely inquisitive about what he was telling me.

"Yes, exactly, eventually leading him to us. But you, Mr Jackson, are even more interesting because you found us in days, not years."

"Forget about me because I want to know more about Oldfield Thomas."

"I know you do. And I also know there is a missing link, and you need to find it. Did you know Oldfield Thomas studied our system for some years, inspired and awed by our perfect equality? He called it utopia. He feared for humankind, especially as World War One was fast approaching, and wanted to copy our system and introduce it in his homeland in the vain effort to save humanity."

"And you let this happen?" I was surprised as they seemed so careful to keep their secrets.

"Yes. You have to remember our world was in decline with only a few homelands remaining. We saw a chance to reintroduce a mole world in an area long since controlled by humans."

"But something must have happened as he didn't entirely copy your system."

"He just disappeared into thin air as he was coming to the end of his training. One day he was researching academic manuscripts and the next he was gone. I must say he became obsessed with the myth of a secret garden, a garden containing potions, pills and secret ingredients. His academic mind was racing, and he wanted to prove its existence, much to our joy because we had been doing the same for an age, but unsuccessfully. He was on the cusp of the discovery, and we along with others are still searching for the Sanctuary of Epidaurus."

"Who are the others?" I asked, becoming rather suspicious.

"Everyone who believes the myths. Researchers, monks, moles and the Forsythe-Twykes under the command of the Cult of Azoth."

"The Forsythe-Twykes!" I replied bemused. "I knew they were up to some strange things but didn't connect them with the hunt for a mythical garden."

"Yes, they are most interested. Why do you think they are here? Why did they try to steal Professor Wingnut? And what's more, why are they using you? The answer is easy. They want the secret."

"This is a lot to digest."

"I told you. And there's more. We, and everyone else, are still studying hoards of ancient manuscripts, trying to decipher whether this so-called secret garden is myth or reality. We believe Oldfield Thomas found a clue which led him to the garden and unfortunately chose to go alone, not sharing it with us. He disappeared for twenty years, resurfaced in Bangkok then the Molehamptons, and with none other than the Forsythe-Twyke family. His version of our mole world was set up but watered down. He left with some of our secrets and technology but learnt enough to create what you now know. Our system here is much more advanced and we only taught him what we wanted him to know. But what he did in the missing twenty years remains a mystery."

"Such an interesting story. You say you are still searching today but how exactly? I mean, you've been searching for so many years and yet uncovered nothing." I had my doubts to his story and thought he was only drip-feeding me what I needed to know.

"We do it from three sources of information. The first by interrogating memories in our warehouses which technology you've seen before in the Molehamptons. This is technology Oldfield Thomas took with him. The other method is by studying the vast amounts of ancient manuscripts stored in the Repository."

"What is this Repository? Where is it?"

"In good time, Mr Jackson. That is your next port of call."

"Great, thanks for sharing your plan," I added sarcastically. "And the third?"

"This is a source of information we have tapped into for many thousands of years. Basically, devout people go to the temple for enlightenment and explain a lot to the monks. We listen by using our molehills, record with our specialist equipment and analyse the data."

"So, you steal people's private thoughts?"

"Kind of, I suppose. I wouldn't go as far as calling it stealing, as they openly say it, and anyone could be listening. It's open source, Mr Jackson."

"No, it's not. It's unethical and plainly wrong. You moles just twist the rules and laws to suit your own purposes," I angrily exclaimed, "and the moles in the Molehamptons are no different."

"In the old days, people would go to ancient temples in Greece, temples resembling giant molehills. They would have their ills cured by priests. Did you know this? Maybe from story books but it is true. People would go into a chamber and lie on a stone slab, snakes slithering in a pit below, then fall into another sphere, possibly induced by drugs, and tell the priest everything. The moles would sit below the pit and then sell the information to the highest bidders. Thankfully, such practices are not allowed today."

"And thank goodness for that," thinking this practice is not too dissimilar to our information being sold on the Internet today! "And what happens at this Repository?"

"Easy. The monks on the surface research during the day and we copy their information at night."

"Stealing again, I would say."

"And what did Oldfield Thomas do? He stole our information and used it to set up his own system with the Forsythe-Twykes. Very irresponsible of us to let it happen without us being in control of the process. And that is why they must now be defeated before they can get more technology. They must have information we do not have, leading them part-way to the secret but, as I said, part-way. We believe you can help us solve the mystery."

"Why me?" I openly showed my frustration. "Can't you sort this out yourselves?"

"No, Mr Jackson, we can't. You, Oldfield Thomas and the other person who visited have information we do not, and thankfully neither do the Forsythe-Twykes. But it is just a matter of time. You've found the chink in our armour."

"The other person. Who do you mean exactly?"

"The Head of the Eternity Project, known by some as *the target*. You don't know who he is, and in fact, nobody knows his real identity. He came here with only one intention, and that was to destroy the record of what Oldfield Thomas was researching. He must have found it, and with the destruction of the records, we lost any link between this man and Oldfield Thomas. We believe you have the key."

"You really don't think that. And even if I had the key, which I don't, I wouldn't tell you."

"Maybe, but we can come to a deal. You reconstruct what Oldfield Thomas was looking for, give us the information and we will help you defeat the Forsythe-Twykes. And your friend, Basil, can be released."

"I see you have more to gain from this than me. However, Basil is dear to me, and we need to act now. Also, the Forsythe-Twykes are hot on my heels, so it is only a matter of time before they discover the secret for themselves. But I have one demand.”

“Go ahead.”

“I plan everything myself and you allow me to go to the Repository before I make my decision. And finally, I can leave your mole world at will to prepare for my mission.”

“I think we can work with that. Mr Jackson, we have a deal.”

“But back to the Head of the Eternity Project. Tell me more about him.”

“Yes, him. A terrible experience and he completely duped us, claiming he was related to Oldfield Thomas and therefore had the ability to find us. We certainly believed he had knowledge of many things, and he even mentioned the Sanctuary of Epidaurus by name. There were things only someone with direct access to Oldfield Thomas’s memoirs and manuscripts could know. We therefore let him carry on with the research hoping he would finish what we were not able to and lead us to the mythical prize. However, he had a different agenda and, after fully gaining our trust, set about destroying all of Oldfield Thomas’s notes and research material, but not the ancient manuscripts. He then disappeared and left us pretty much at square one again.”

“But surely you must know who he is or at least where to find him?”

“That is the problem. He is an expert in disguise, constantly taking on new identities. He certainly does not operate under his real name, and nobody really knows what that is. He is the ultimate expert in clandestine operations and closely matched by his arch-rival, Ormerod Forsythe-Twyke. We knew our visitor was the Head of the Eternity Project, in hiding from the Forsythe-Twyke family. Immediately after his act of destruction, he secretly left here, maybe to the sought-after secret Sanctuary of Epidaurus. But a few years ago, he made a move and was seen publicly, some believing him to have made a mistake. We think he did it purposefully and wants to lure the Forsythe-Twykes here and into a trap. He knows they would have been watching and was also sending a message to us. It has worked, because you would otherwise not be here. And it’s your job to finish them off.

***

The first thing I did was return to the hotel to find Vanessa. I was too late. She had already checked out, leaving a message about helping her mother, sabotage in the production, an assault by Sergeant Dawson and an attack on the Food Factory. A quite surprising turn of events, and nothing to do with me if you had thought that.

My mind was now racing with all of the information I had heard. But despite the presentation of a perfect life below the streets of Bangkok, they were motivated by greed like everyone else, their real aim to find the secret garden. But they weren't alone in this quest as it was also the aim of the Forsyth-Twykes and the mysterious Cult of Azoth. They all needed me to find and unlock the secrets, so I decided to play along, or at least appear to do just that. A plan began to formulate.

After getting my thoughts together, I headed back to Wat Suthat. Apparently, there were also other access points at various temples around the city including the famous Wat Arun. Mr Rurob's escorts had me quickly transformed, quite a routine event for me now, and back into the mole world.

"Mr Rurob, nice to see you again," I said, walking into his office. He was dressed in another pin-striped suit, perfectly pressed and not a piece of fluff or mole hair on it.

"I need to get to the Repository as soon as possible. Could you show me the way?"

"Show you the way. My dear Mr Jackson," he answered, chuckling, "It is not around the corner, and we will have to organise transport to get you there."

"I thought it was close by," I asked genuinely. "Time is not on our side."

"I agree and delighted you want to get there so quickly."

He immediately dialled a number. "Get me a tuk-tuk. The fastest we've got and a reckless driver. And now."

The sound of a tuk-tuk skidding to a halt signalled my journey was to begin.

"You will be accompanied by Mr Renangrong. This way please, Mr Jackson," he said, gesturing for me to follow him.

The tuk-tuk was just like those on the surface, made of shiny metal and a kaleidoscope of bright colours. The passenger seat was covered in plastic foil, not the best material for staying in position. The driver gave us a cheeky and roguish grin, winked and gunned his tiny engine, making a high-pitched squeal.

"Hold on tight," he shouted, and off we sped down the street, passers by jumping out of the way and shouting complaints after us. A short time later, we entered a tunnel—low, narrow, straight as a dart, and disappearing into the darkness ahead. There were only a few lights to show us the way and it looked like some highway just for tuk-tuks. The driver put his head down low over his handlebars and wound the throttle back to maximum, the tuk-tuk shaking and vibrating with the turn of speed. We shot down the tunnel, the lights of the tuk-tuk blurring the walls which I could touch if I put my hand out.

"It will take two hours to get to the Repository," he shouted, laughing as he rocketed along.

Crazy shuttles. Insane tuk-tuk drivers. I would never get used to the fear as my hands grasped the frame tightly and my teeth rattled together as I was shaken like rice in a tin can.

***

The gruelling journey to the Repository seemed to last an age and wasn't entirely without risk, the tuk-tuk driver performing the most dangerous overtaking manoeuvres when the tunnel became wider. I hadn't quite decided which was worse: the transport shuttle under the Molehamptons or tuk-tuks under Thailand. As I got closer, I started to imagine what the Repository actually was or looked like. Of course, the name gave it away as a repository or a collection of documents, but it must have been huge according to what I was told, and I understood it to be above and below the surface. What awaited me nearly blew my socks off and was by far larger than anything I had experienced in my first adventure: namely the arrivals area and the memory warehouse. This was in a different league.

Mr Renangrong showed me through the vast underground tunnel system connecting the largest offices imaginable where, mainly moles, but also different animals and humans, sifted through heaps of paper and entered the information into smartphones used as computers. Now I knew what happened to smartphones we discard! There were rows upon rows of creatures studiously reading vast quantities of data: books, newspapers, manuscripts, reports, letters and any other source you could imagine.

Mr Renangrong explained to me as we went through the rows of desks that all the data was gathered on the surface from any source available, sifted through down here and then entered into huge databases. The system in the Molehamptons was far more rudimentary and information only gathered through interrogation in the transition phase, or if necessary, by questioning memories. They did this too but were far more technically advanced. I asked what they did with this colossal amount of data, but he cleverly deflected, never giving me a straight answer. I thought back to my conversation with the mole liaison officer who told me in ancient times moles sold information to the highest bidder and I wondered if they still did that. The next room was unbelievably large and only moles were permitted to work here. It was a vast office solely for the research of ancient manuscripts, most of them religious documents and stories of ancient legends, where teams of moles carefully picked their way through these old books, writing down anything of interest. Interestingly enough, they also seemed to be copying notes made by other people. Mr Renangrong explained a sourcing team acquired documents on the surface and made sure the unsuspecting monks got them, then let them do the research. The moles copied their notes and papers, in other words – they stole it. And somewhere amongst this vast amount of stolen data must be the key to unlocking the secrets.

The last surprise awaited me now as Mr Renangrong wanted me to go above the ground to observe the monk's work. After standing in another smoke-filled chamber and being transformed back to my original size, I came out in a jungle area behind a sign. Tourists filed by on a track, and I was soon able to join them until we exited the jungle onto a rocky outcrop. I was met by a huge temple made entirely from wood sitting precariously next to the cliff, waves smashing violently against rocks far below. The sea breeze ruffled my hair as I breathed in deeply, savouring the fresh air after the oppressive humidity of Bangkok. Storm clouds circled menacingly overhead with rolling thunder beating away in the sky. But then a thud on the ground caused me to look around in panic as I presumed pigeons were attacking. Thankfully, it was not a white blob but a huge raindrop and the first of a severe shower, forcing me to find shelter in the majestic building.

This temple was unlike those I had seen in Bangkok. It was made entirely of wood, dark brown and covered in intricately carved sculptures. A central spire reached high up into the sky, smaller ones surrounding it at its base where it met the main structure. This was made of four halls forming a cross, supported by pillars with over-lapping layers of pagoda style roofs resting on top. Grand statues sat on the tip of each of the many roofs with smaller ones along the eaves. The inside was absolutely breath-taking, all surfaces including the supporting columns, walls and ceiling, decorated with masterfully carved figures. I stood for a long time just staring at the sheer size of the place and marvelling at the skill and beauty of the ornate craftsmanship before entering a large hall. Row upon row of monks in complete silence diligently studied old papers, their research written down and stored along with the manuscripts in cabinets. I pictured the moles swarming through here at night-time collecting all of the material, taking it away only to return them some hours later with the monks none the wiser.

The walk around the temple gave me the opportunity to think and it was now clear what I had to do. On my return to the world below the Repository, I initiated my plan. Ormerod Forsythe-Twyke's agents in Bangkok had to be dealt with firstly.

"Wait, there's more, Mr Renangrong" I said.

"And that is?" suspiciously looking at me.

"Can you arrange for your special forces to sabotage something for me?"

Chapter Twenty
Smoke and Sparks

The pieces of porcelain glistened on the molehills under the full moon illuminating the Molehamptons as Sergeant Dawson pulled his patrol car up in front of his office. He had completely emptied it as instructed by Colonel Pickle and now walked towards his office, dreading what he would now find. The moles were all formed up in perfectly straight platoons, but this time armed with an assortment of tools from the storeroom. Colonel Pickle now stood proudly in front of the parade of his soldiers. The army required by Ludwig.

"Sergeant Dawson, we are ready for action. Please turn off the light in front of your police station and open all the doors including the boot of your car."

Sergeant Dawson had not been so energised in such a long time and sprang into action on the Colonel's command, tapping on the window to indicate he was finished.

Turning around and puffing out his chest, the Colonel addressed his troops. "Soldiers! This is our opportunity to defeat the horrors of the Food Factory system, a thorn in our side for many years. Victory will end anarchy and return us to normality and our valued freedoms. Never again will humans have power over allocations. You've all been briefed and know what to do. Let's go!"

Platoon after platoon of moles, armed to the teeth with cutting tools, followed the proud Colonel out of the station. Sergeant Dawson watched in amazement as the moles marched past in perfectly straight ranks, climbed up the wheels of his car and poured into anywhere they could find. When all moles had disappeared from the pavement, he carefully peered in to find every single possible space occupied. A few layers of moles were on the seats, the footwells full, also the glove compartment and the boot crowded to the top. He looked at the hundreds of shining eyes, putting blankets over them before closing the doors.

"Careful now," whispered the Colonel.

Sergeant Dawson pressed himself into his seat, trying not to tread on any of the moles, even the ones squeezed between the pedals. With utmost care, he set off to the Food Factory and their mission. He drove a secluded route, using a narrow lane for his approach, his lights off so not to be seen approaching the fence. On opening the car doors, the moles immediately prised themselves out, streamed out of the car and formed up in their platoons again.

"Psst. Hello, Sergeant," came a voice from behind a tree.

The Sergeant looked ever so nervous, scared of being caught by the security. "Who's there?"

"It's me," and Ludwig bounded out in front of the platoons, scaring the Sergeant even more.

"Don't do that, Ludwig. I'm jittery enough as it is."

"Punctual as arranged. Well done, Ludwig," said the Colonel.

Colonel Pickle took one last check, then signalled to one of the platoons. A section of moles scampered towards the fence and in no time had expertly used wire cutters to snip a hole in the mesh, the piece of metal silently landing on the ground. Another signal followed and all the platoons filed through the hole and away into battle. Sergeant Dawson couldn't believe his eyes, as this professional entry had only taken two minutes before the last mole had disappeared through the fence. He then drove to the main gate and greeted people as if nothing had happened.

"Good evening, Sergeant Dawson," said Jessica Walsh.

"My dear, Ms Walsh. How nice to see you again. Lovely night, isn't it?" he shouted above the din of the protestors' instruments.

"What are you doing here at this time?" she asked suspiciously.

"Oh, no reason. Just watching the factory in case something should happen," he replied, winking at her.

Meanwhile, Ludwig led the way into the main production building and directed the platoons in various directions. They had meticulously prepared their mission, based on descriptions of the layout from Ludwig, and were able to disperse to their designated areas with great speed. Within minutes, the platoons had swarmed around nearly the whole of the Food Factory and their spree of destruction began. They picked padlocks, cut cages open, sawed through electrical cables, removed fuses, jammed machines with pieces of metal, short-circuited the power supply and made holes in water pipes. In no less than ten minutes, the Food Factory spluttered to a hissing, creaking halt, sparks flying into the night sky and smoke rising from the roof. Ludwig was there, urging the animals in the cages to escape and follow him which they did without question.

"What's happening in there, Sergeant Dawson?" Jessica asked, her eyes fixed on the main building. Sparks flashed through the windows, the sound of screeching metal as machinery ground to a crunching stop and finally the lights went out with a loud bang. The protestors, now speechless, stared on in amazement and one by one stopped making noise until there was peace outside. The whole area was suddenly blanketed by an eery silence, journalists, protestors and Sergeant Dawson fixed on the building waiting to see what would happen next, and they didn't have to wait long. First there was a groaning sound, then creaking followed by the wall of the main factory shaking violently until, with a loud crash, it fell down in a cloud of flying bricks and dust. An industrious platoon had successfully burrowed under the foundations causing it to quickly collapse. Once the dust had started to settle, another strange sight met the onlookers. A dog covered in dust ran out first, followed by an endless line of animals all whooping in joy at their freedom. Chickens, ducks, cows, sheep and pigs poured through the hole, dancing over the bricks and stampeded across the grass towards the perimeter in a mass bolt for freedom. The operation was planned to perfection as a large section of the fence suddenly fell down, cut at exactly the right moment by a platoon of fighting moles, for the animals to have an escape route into the fields.

Felicity Forsythe-Twyke, obviously alerted to the trouble, now arrived in her car and skidded to a halt amongst the protestors and journalists. It was a sight not to be missed as the hordes of animals trampled noisily through the hole straight past the protestors, who were now loudly cheering, into the fields and away in the moon-lit sky.

Felicity stood there, hysterically crying, "Stop my animals. That's my property! Doesn't anyone have a care for animal welfare?" and then started running across the fields after her precious products. The front pages of most international newspapers made for interesting reading the next day.

Ludwig, his job done, waited next to the hole in the fence with some of the soldiers, proudly looking at their accomplishment, fumes and steam rising from a dark factory behind him. He was joined by Sergeant Dawson, who was proudly looking at the smoking mess, and now able to talk freely as all eyes were on the disappearing animals and the crazy Felicity Forsythe-Twyke.

"Did you manage to release all the animals?" Sergeant Dawson asked.

"Nearly. There was one room we couldn't get into and that happens to be where Basil is. And now the place is swarming with security so we can't get back in," Ludwig answered sadly.

"Ludwig, I promise we will finish the job, but we might need her help," Sergeant Dawson confidently replied, pointing at Jessica Walsh.

The sound of sirens wailed in the distance as police and fire crews from Anglerton raced to the scene of destruction.

"Best I get away," said Sergeant Dawson, beaming from ear to ear, and quickly drove off before he was seen.

***

It was impossible for anyone in Lower Molehampton not to be awoken by the commotion at the Food Factory. Bartholomew Forsythe-Twyke was no exception, and he immediately got into his car a few minutes after Felicity had left and drove in the direction of the disturbance. He approached the factory to find a shocking scene, with hundreds of animals stomping their way past him in the fields. His mouth dropped and his car came to a slow stop. If that wasn't enough to stun him, then the next scene was the icing on the cake. Felicity ran past, her broken arm bouncing in its sling, the other arm waving whilst she was shouting at the top of her voice for the animals to stop. She and the animals then vanished through a hedge into another field and disappeared in the darkness of the night.

Bartholomew stared out of the side window, his hands still gripped firmly to the steering wheel, then turned his gaze to the Food Factory to see smoke rising from the roof. He couldn't believe what he was witnessing. Who could have done this? He was suddenly jolted back into reality as his car phone rang, his irate father on the line.

"What's going on? Vanessa has just left Bangkok to go back and help her crazy mother. Has everyone lost their minds at your end? I'm trying to run an operation and I'm now on my own," Ormerod spat into the phone, quite livid at what was going on.

Bartholomew tried to compose himself and then explained what he was just witnessing, but it did nothing to placate his father.

"Look, I don't care. I haven't got time for your petty problems," Ormerod screamed back, clearly not understanding what was currently happening. "Bartholomew, get on a flight at once and come and help me. And your workers here in Bangkok are striking too, so get it sorted!"

"Yes, Father. Right away. I'll drive straight to the airport," Bartholomew replied, his voice shaking in shock.

"And some good news. We have sighted Mr Jackson at his hotel, so at least I know he's still around. He seems to be the only person capable of doing a job correctly."

***

Most would describe Mr Lawnsworthy as a lonesome old man, never seen with any family members or friends. Tending his garden was his passion in life, making sure every blade of grass stood perfectly to attention and leaves were banished from his property. He was now taking a stroll through Lower Molehampton, the protestors' din at the Food Factory clearly heard as the sound was carried on the light breeze. He had already seen the news on the television reporting that the protestors' ranks had swelled to well over two hundred and the action had also gone global, notably in Thailand where the Forsythe-Twykes also had a plant. He found it quite amusing to watch the latest scenes of the Food Factory with smoke and sparks rising from the building, followed by escaping animals and Felicity Forsythe-Twyke running crazily after them.

He walked past Sergeant Dawson's immaculately kept front garden and stopped briefly to view the amusingly decorated molehills. His face remained expressionless but nodded in clear approval then carried on. The convenience store was packed full of people queuing to buy the local newspaper reporting last night's events and intrigue in the Forsythe-Twyke household. Timothy Scribbler had written an excellent article and could well make a name for himself one day. The article ended in a simple question. *"What are the Forsythe-Twykes hiding?"*

A newspaper tucked under his arm, Mr Lawnsworthy carried on his walk, nodding to a woman wearing a blue coat on the other side of the street. They smiled courteously at each other and went on their way.

***

"So, Ms Walsh, how delighted are you at your success here?"

"Very! It's beyond my wildest dreams," she replied, beaming at the journalist. "I only activated some close friends, and the rest has just snowballed."

"Surely, it's more than a snowball. You have them highly organised and doing exactly as you say."

"Yes, I suppose I do. I must have found something I'm quite good at, I think. Better than school," she added, laughing at her own joke.

"Your protest has now caught on all over the world with people gathering outside meat production plants. What message do you have for them?" shouted out another journalist.

"Keep the good work up and, above all, be respectful and non-violent."

The journalists, until now allowing each other to speak in turn, all started putting their hands up and shouting questions at the same time, surprising Jessica at their sudden aggressiveness.

"Very admirable," cried one journalist louder than the others. "But some people say you want to have factories like this banned. Is there any truth in that?"

"No! Absolutely not," she quickly retorted. "We only want to raise awareness of the food industry in general, so consumers understand animals are not just products on a conveyor belt. We also want to challenge why such businesses are behind such high security. What are they doing? What are they hiding? We open our mouths and stomachs to eat the food they produce, but they do not open their doors to us.”

“You say you run a non-violent movement, but only last night there was a mass attack on the Food Factory, crippling its production. Just look at the scene of destruction behind you. Were you behind it?” yelled out another journalist, clambering to be heard over the racket. “Certainly not a peaceful protest.”

“No,” she shot back defensively. “We had nothing to do with it and none of our protestors have gone past the perimeter fence.”

“So, how can you explain the attack? The holes in the fence, the smoking debris and the collapsed wall didn’t happen alone.”

“I can’t,” replied Jessica, her voice cracking as the journalists attacked her.

“Nobody believes that Ms Walsh. Everyone will hold you directly responsible. Also, what have you got to do with the strike at the Forsythe-Twyke’s plant in Bangkok. Have you got a personal vendetta against the family? Isn’t your father head of production here?”

The questions rained down on her from this particularly aggressive reporter, maybe keen to make a name for himself, and not allowing her the opportunity to answer.

“This is Greg Anchor transmitting live from the Molehamptons. And now back to a copy anchor,” he said, laughing at himself, referring to Doug Gardener back at the newsroom. The camera lights went off and Jessica was left alone in the dim morning light holding a placard with the words *#openthedoors*. The first tears beginning to run down her face as she lost her composure.

***

“Have you heard about what happened?” gossiped the two people sitting in the coffee shop. They carried on eating their cake and slurping on their coffee whilst reading the news about the Food Factory. “Unbelievable what’s happened. And it’s all Jessica Walsh’s fault.”

Jemima Kingston sat alone, drinking her tea and reading the news on her smartphone. She was amused about what was going on and smiled inwardly whilst listening to the gossip. The events hadn't quite happened how she had envisaged when she tasked Mr Jackson with investigating the Forsythe-Twyke family. And now he was in Bangkok, quite far away from all of this. She couldn't bring herself to believe this quiet and unassuming analyst had arranged all of this. All he did was analyse data. So, if it wasn't him, then who? And they were certainly doing a good job.

She left the coffee shop and walked across the bridge into Lower Molehampton. An old man was walking on the other side of the street, a newspaper folded under his arm. He politely nodded and smiled at her, Jemima naturally returning the gesture. She had seen him many times before, which wasn't a surprise here in the Molehamptons, but didn't know his name.

***

The departure lounge was crammed full of travellers waiting to board their flight to London. Television screens were broadcasting the global news with a constant steam of repeated stories when suddenly a live report from the Molehamptons interrupted the channel. Vanessa, who up until now was exhausted and had been trying to snooze, sat bolt upright, surprised at her village being shown here. The departure lounge erupted in hoots of laughter as scenes of farm animals escaping though a hole in the fence and then bolting across the fields were broadcast. The laughter increased as a woman hysterically ran after them, attempting to stop the mayhem. Vanessa just sat there, her head in her hands, trying to comprehend what she had just seen. The news then changed to scenes of protest at the Forsythe-Twyke factory in Bangkok and then linked back to the Molehamptons with a brief report of Jessica Walsh's movement – *#openthedoors*. Relief arrived for Vanessa as the passengers were called to board the plane, saving her from any more embarrassing news about her family. A good job nobody here knew who she was, or so she thought.

As she presented her boarding pass, the airport worker looked at her card for much longer than usual before loudly saying, "Miss Forsythe-Twyke, you may now board the flight," pronouncing her name with great emphasis.

266

The man obviously intended to use the opportunity when he recognised her name and successfully managed as everyone started looking at her. Vanessa spent the rest of the flight with people walking past her smiling, others unashamedly pointing at her, clearly the brunt of gossip.

***

Bartholomew had just disembarked his flight from London to Bangkok and was walking though the terminal, past a sign showing *Welcome to Suvarnabhumi Airport*. He stopped in mid-stride as a breaking news report caught his attention. He stood there watching the same news story Vanessa had just seen, shook his head and left the airport delighted nobody knew who he was. But his brief pleasure was short-lived as he was bathed in bright light, spat at by the clicking and whirring of cameras and then a barrage of questions.

"What secrets are the Forsythe-Twykes hiding?"

"Who attacked the Food Factory?"

"What do you think of the protest demands in Bangkok?"

Bartholomew quickly managed to regain his composure and pushed his way through the mass of journalists, jostling to get a better position and sticking microphones in his face. A driver from his company was waiting here, foolishly holding up a sign with his name on it. Bartholomew was sure he saw some of the journalists give him money as he settled in the backseat. It took an absolute age to battle through the notoriously bad Bangkok traffic but they eventually made it to the office some hours later. His mood wasn't made any better as he was confronted by angry protestors demanding better pay and conditions and, for the second time in the last hours, had to fight his way through an attacking band of journalists. As soon as he locked himself in the relative calm of his office, he called his father, and detected panic in his voice for the first time in his life. Ormerod Forsythe-Twyke was rattled.

***

Felicity Forsythe-Twyke, a person who thrived on being seen, was now doing exactly the opposite. She was walking in the village, wearing a large baggy coat and a huge hat to cover her face, hoping nobody would recognise her. She was losing control of things so decided to go for a walk and clear her head after last night's events. Bartholomew had flown to Bangkok, Vanessa was currently in the air in the opposite direction, leaving Felicity pretty much alone.

A strong coffee was now needed so she entered a café owned by one of her staunchest supporters. Thinking she was safe in a secluded corner; she had just started to tuck into a piece of cake when the door opened, and a group of journalists burst in. They immediately confronted her, throwing combative questions and taking her completely off guard. She was normally confident in such situations but not today. Felicity Forsythe-Twyke was losing it.

"What are you hiding, Mrs Forsythe-Twyke?"

"What secrets are in the Food Factory?"

"Why don't you let the people in?"

Felicity was incapable of forming a reply and just glared at them in shocked silence. She hastily gathered her things, pushed the cake to one side and prepared to leave when Clementine rushed through the door. Felicity wanted to tell her sister not to say anything, but it was too late and before she uttered a word, Clementine started to talk with a huge smile on her face.

"Oh, isn't this just so exciting. My darling sister and all the press wanting to see you. You must be basking in the attention."

The journalists spun around in surprise, turning their attention now to Clementine.

"Did you just call Mrs Forsythe-Twyke your sister?" blurted out one of the reporters.

"Yes, of course. Isn't it just lovely? It was kept a secret for so many years but now we're telling people. Only a few though." She stood there in an embarrassing silence as it slowly dawned on her what she had just said. "Ooops," but it was too late. The journalists had their bite and their story. Timothy Scribbler stood there grinning at Felicity Forsythe-Twyke who just sat there with a dismayed expression on her face.

Chapter Twenty-One
The Cult of Azoth and the Elixir of Life

Do you know the truth about life and death? Well, I believe I found it below the streets of the Molehamptons. Once we finish our lives, moles administer our next step by assigning jobs below the ground or allocate us as another creature back on the surface. In case of the latter, our memories are removed and stored in glass jars in vast warehouses.

But the world of moles under the ground in Thailand was quite different. The sound of a squealing troop of monkeys passing in a nearby tunnel grabbed my attention and, after following them, found myself in a most unexpected place. A jungle as far as the eye could see. It was in was in an enormous cavern with giant palm trees reaching high towards the roof carrying hundreds of green coconuts.

"Impressive!" stated a mole, which had just appeared at my side.

"That's an understatement. It's unbelievable. I presume your source of food."

"No, not at all. We acquire that from above. This is our warehouse. In exactly these coconuts," he said, pointing, "we store memories. And we use monkeys to do the work." Look, watch them," he added as a troop of monkeys ran past us and shot up into some trees.

In no time at all, they reached branches laden with coconuts, pulled some off and tossed them to other monkeys waiting below to put them in carts.

"They take them to a room, fill them with memories using our Memming technology and then hang the coconuts back up again.

Unlike the politically controlled mole world under the Molehamptons, here I could walk around freely and discover many new things. There were also some scavenging missions, but this was considered an old-fashioned and clumsy method of acquiring goods. Instead, it was left for people to provide for the moles by giving offerings to monks. In the dead of night, special units of moles would disperse around the country, leaving notes in people's homes. These notes were carefully prepared by the logisticians below the ground and listed exactly what they required. They were called merit notes. People waking up the next morning would read their note and then trot off dutifully to the temple, bringing with them whatever they were instructed to. Everyone was happy: the people increased their merit ratings, and the moles got what they needed without the risk or bother of scavenging. The monks were somewhat confused as they received items really not needed, but strangely disappeared shortly after from their storerooms.

I also visited some molehill observation posts, the moles keeping a beady eye on those above the ground, but this was a rather antiquated form of intelligence gathering down here. It was just the tip of the iceberg. They had also burrowed into many other places using rather ingenious ideas. For example, at the Sanctuary of Truth they had tunnelled into the wooden pillars and sculptures, setting up listening stations using the latest mini-camera and microphone technology. People above the ground would never have known they were being spied on. All of this technology was linked back to a control centre, a vast room with many moles sitting in front of monitors, observing, listening and recording information. All the equipment had been acquired from above. Other teams of moles analysed the data, created reports, and stored everything in a huge database. The crafty moles stole any information they could get their paws on.

Their special operation missions were trained at a high level. Another huge cavern housed the pigeon bombing flight with a replica street built with shops, street food, obstacles and mannequins. Here, the pigeons were put through their paces in challenging conditions to train them for low-level missions in built-up areas. I had first-hand experience of their skills at Wat Suthat when we were attacked by pigeons. The Kennedy brothers were hit and successfully infiltrated here. I wondered what they were doing now.

***

They were struggling in their environment as the Kennedy brothers were not born to be Buddhist trainee monks and this fact was visible to all around them at the temple. Staying here without any possessions and eating the food on offer was killing them. They had to escape but without money, possessions and no idea where they were, this would prove difficult. However, Gavin had seen monks returning to the temple with items and had an idea. On asking, he found out that trainee monks would go to the local villages and accept offerings from those bidding to improve their merit, so Gavin discussed this with Joe and decided if they could do this task, they might be able to get some money and away from here. They asked their supervisor if they might learn something more about being a monk, trying to show they were interested, and suggested getting offerings from the local village. The monk was naturally reluctant but, in the end, agreed, seeing the good in all people. Therefore, Gavin and Joe were instructed what to do and set off on foot for the local market. They were told to be quiet, peaceful and were not allowed to accept money, but this would prove a problem because they were naturally loud, and it was exactly money that they were after. So off they went, wearing their orange robes, barefoot, and both carrying a large urn for any offerings they might receive. Heads bowed slightly and hands grasped in front, they showed respect when receiving items, the local people not suspecting anything foul. And, yes, they actually started quite well, observing correctly what they should do, and soon started to receive offerings of food and drink. But they soon became bored of this pious activity, and it was then things started to get difficult. Gavin was the first to ask for money, arguing he needed it to call his sick mother and they were poor monks. The person, who couldn't speak English but understood the demand for money, became annoyed and left. Both Gavin and Joe carried on asking for money and it didn't take long before a crowd of local people gathered, angrily shouting at them. The brothers, not being able to understand Thai, nevertheless comprehended the villagers were not happy. The villagers, quickly seeing they were imposters, were only too happy to provide a tuk-tuk and sent them packing to the next large town. Here, they carried on with their scam tactics and did actually manage to get just a little money but not enough to get out of the area and back to Bangkok. Then Joe had the idea of asking a bus driver if they could travel for free as monks were not allowed money or possessions. Gavin agreed and they walked around trying to act like pious monks again until they found the bus station. Their plan worked and shortly after were sitting on a bus to Bangkok.

The journey took some hours, and they solved their hunger problem by eating everything in their urns which was really meant for the temple. They drew discerning looks from other passengers as they tucked into their goodies, especially since it was after midday. Eventually, they arrived back in the city and, fortunately, the little money they had collected was enough for a tuk-tuk to their hotel on Yaowarat Road. The hotel staff were extremely surprised but remained polite, helping them with new key cards. Two days ago, they left in tracksuits and full heads of hair only to return wearing orange robes, barefoot, heads and eyebrows shaven. They were the centre of attraction in the hotel lobby, not only for the staff but also for the tourists who waited to have selfies taken with these curious men. In their room, they rummaged through their bags, trying to find contact details for their handler. Not being the brightest, they had no idea where he worked, only he was a Forsythe-Twyke. But luck was on their side. Openly attracting attention, it did not take too long for a livid Ormerod to find out through his agents and make contact.

***

Monks, moles and the Cult of Azoth were still chasing shadows, desperate to be the first to find the Sanctuary of Epidaurus. That was the name so sought after and based on a myth shared by many cultures. There were many stories about a mystical garden, just like the story of the Garden of Eden. Could they really be true? Oldfield Thomas had apparently succeeded in finding it, but the Head of the Eternity Project had destroyed his research notes.

And I should find the secrets in a few days! I painstakingly leafed through the vast pile of material about mystical gardens I had asked for. A manuscript described the most amazing and lush garden one could ever imagine, located next to the pools of a high waterfall, completely surrounded by jungle and closed off from the outside world. The garden was lovingly tended with all kinds of plants, vegetables, herbs, flowers and trees growing there. Despite the beautiful description, it could have referred to many similar locations around the world, but there was something else interesting here. According to what I was reading, the garden was tended by a person expert in using and growing what was produced to create medicines and potions. Similar stories were found in other documents, all with the same description of a garden next to high pools of a jungle waterfall. All of this information was completely useless without a map or location and thus remained only a myth. Not wanting to give anything away to the moles, I studied many diverse documents often annoyed but sometimes positive about what I was looking at. My only intention was to leave a confusing set of notes behind which nobody could understand.

My analytical mind was racing, clear to me the key must lie not only here but a place which only connected me, Oldfield Thomas and the Head of the Eternity Project—the bookshop. Protected by a code number, it had gone undiscovered for so long and right under everyone's noses in Chinatown. The shop had ancient maps without any location, just like obscure treasure maps, but maybe I could work out the location by connecting the descriptions in the manuscripts to these maps. Is this what Oldfield Thomas had done? I had the advantage of modern technology and the internet so perhaps the answer was actually quite easy. The Forsythe-Twykes now knew about the shop but not about the maps and as long as that stayed a secret, then I had the advantage. Now I understood why my father and the Eternity Project had gone to such lengths to hide the location of the shop.

But have you not asked yourself a question? The moles who led me through Chinatown obviously intended for me to find the shop. Who were they working for? If not the moles, the monks or the Forsythe-Twykes, then maybe the Head of the Eternity Project. I was sure finding the secret garden and the Head of the Eternity project were intricately linked.

***

"Mr Renangrong, when can you get me back to Bangkok? I need to do some research and contact with my workplace. Hopefully, that might lead us to the prize."

"Mr Jackson, I will arrange for a tuk-tuk immediately."

"No, I don't want to go back by tuk-tuk. I want to be seen and attract maximum attention to myself. Can you arrange for me to go by train?"

He paused slightly, thinking hard before he replied, "Yes," he carried on slowly. "Yes, if that is what you wish, and I can understand your thinking. If Ormerod's agents are watching everywhere, then they will be sucked in like bees to pollen. Good idea." He shouted for an assistant to come in. "Train ticket for Mr Jackson. Bangkok. As quick as possible."

Half an hour later, his assistant was back, ticket in hand.

"Where did you get this from so quickly?" I asked, surprised at the speed.

Mr Renangrong chuckled, finding it all quite amusing. "We built a tunnel into the ticket office right next to the printer. All we have to do is wait for a ticket to come out and, when not seen, take it for ourselves."

"Stolen goods yet again."

"Yes, as a matter of fact, it is. And now have a safe journey," and he ordered another assistant to take me to the railway station.

It was just a short tuk-tuk journey to an access point leading straight to the surface. When the transition to my full size was over, I pushed ajar a door and looked through the crack to see where I was; the heat bursting through similar to opening a hot oven door. I saw daylight and people passing by, so slowly exited and joined the crowd unnoticed. I had come out of a circular advertising column, no trace of a door remaining once it had closed behind me. These moles were really ingenious. I looked at my ticket and found they had even doctored it with my name typed on – *Mr Jackson – Carriage 11 – Seat 31 – Bangkok*. A perfect forgery. Whilst waiting for my train, I looked around the railway station with great interest. It was rather quaint and reminded me of railway stations in films from the nineteen-fifties, made entirely of wood and painted in red and yellow. The train pulled into the station with a squeal of brakes clanking as the wheels came to a slow stop on the tracks and a burst of black diesel fumes puffing into the air. Many layers of shiny paint covered the old wooden panelled carriages. The seats were made of dark red leather, with switches on the wall to turn on the ceiling fans, which were welcoming in the humid heat. The experienced travellers opened the windows straight away, pulling them down in their frames to allow a constant draft of fresh air to blow through the carriage. A big shunt signalled we were ready to go, and the train slowly rolled out of the station, clattering and rattling its way ever so slowly towards Bangkok. We were all treated to a permanent stream of vendors selling a large choice of food and drinks, chicken curry, sandwiches, pork sticks and much more. It was the first time since my arrival that I could sit back and really relax and take in the beautiful countryside. Until now, my time here had been a rollercoaster journey, mainly through the bustling metropolis of Bangkok, and I now enjoyed a completely different view of the country as we slowly trundled our way through rural rice fields and villages. After about four hours, the countryside gave way to the vast sprawling city of the capital, rolling along slowly right next to houses, apartment blocks, shacks and office buildings. The speed decreased to almost walking pace as we chugged along through many market stalls, so close I could almost touch them when I stuck my hand out of the window. Eventually, with a grinding and squealing of brakes, we pulled into Hua Lamphong railway station.

I stayed on the station's concourse for a while, pretending to read an international newspaper, whilst all the time wanting to make myself a target for those following me. The final journey back to my hotel in Chinatown was just a short ten minutes in a tuk-tuk. However, I didn't go in at once, giving Ormerod's agents more chances to see me as I ate some street food directly outside the hotel entrance. I couldn't have made my presence more obvious.

***

Ormerod was in a foul mood, but there was nothing new about that. He had good reason to be so because everything that could go wrong, had gone wrong. He had seen the television report of the escaping animals and Felicity foolishly running after them. His sister was an utter embarrassment to the family, and his other sister, Clementine, plastered all over the newspapers proudly exclaiming she was a secret sister. She was meant only to be bait for Connor Jackson, not a local gossip story. And now his son, Bartholomew, was here. A failed banker and completely useless at running the government's Food Standards Ministry. Ormerod arranged for him to get the job and, if it wasn't for its importance to the profits of the Food Factory, now regretted his decision. Bartholomew had never achieved anything and now he was here trying aimlessly to stop the strike and protests.

"Yes," he shouted harshly into his phone. "Oh, good. At last Mr Jackson shows his face again. Where is he now? In the hotel. Excellent. Double, no triple the watch on the place. Completely surround it and if he moves, I want to know about it."

Ormerod had worked in intelligence for all of his career and was very experienced, especially after being nurtured by his father, George. My return naturally interested him, but he had just made the first in a series of fatal mistakes. In his greed, he failed to ask himself the question why I was being so open about my return, something which in normal circumstances would have been second nature to him. However, he was absolutely paranoid about what information I had learnt. He was a person who wanted to control the narrative, but he was now blind, knowing nothing about where I had been or what I had done, and that infuriated him. Unfortunately, Vanessa's feedback about my time below was rather patchy as parts of her memory had disappeared, convinced she had been drugged by the moles. She remembered nothing about the shop, what was in it or how she went below the ground at Wat Suthat. The Kennedy brothers were put out of action, and this could only have been done with the help of others, making him even more paranoid. Ormerod was now blind to all these facts and completely frantic. It just goes to show what greed can do to people.

***

If I was part of the Head of the Eternity Project's plan, then he must have some way of monitoring me. Therefore, I believed he was not in the secret garden and must be nearby, and I suspected where—the bookshop. I removed Oldfield Thomas's manuscript from my hotel safe and read about a boat journey in his hunt for the secret garden. He described it in great detail He could only have travelled in the Gulf of Thailand, therefore allowing me to considerably narrow my search field. I had to get back to the shop to confirm my theory, but, this time, without being seen.

A peak through the curtains revealed Ormerod's agents hiding amongst the street food stands. But it was now late and time for action. I had already seen an unlocked staff room on my floor from where I took a purple hotel uniform and hat . Disguised as a cleaner, I exited the hotel through the basement and thankfully attracted zero attention. I now criss-crossed different alleys, always checking I hadn't been followed. Once I was sure it was safe, I walked to the bookshop and waited in the shadows for a while, carefully observing the street and shop. After a short time, I knocked on the door until eventually a light went on and the door opened. The owner, quite understandably annoyed, spoke to me quite harshly in Thai before he recognised me and gestured for me to come inside. Time was important as I had to get back to the hotel fairly quickly, but I knew exactly what I wanted.

"I'm so sorry for the intrusion at this hour," I apologised to the old man.

"You are most welcome at any time. What help do you need? I presume you need help judging by the hour and your disguise."

"Exactly. When I was here last time, I noticed you had many maps. I need to see them."

"All the maps?" he started laughing. "That will take you some years but come this way."

He led me into his back room and closed the thick heavy curtains, the dim light he now put on not visible from the outside. The room was stacked high with thousands of maps, but the old man immediately produced the leather folder I saw last time.

"Here you go. This is what you hid!" He winked at me, then left me in peace amongst an enormous pile of manuscripts and documents.

I had the description of the coastline and secret garden firmly engraved in my head and believed if the map depicted exactly that, I might recognise it. Everything was now down to luck as I slowly leafed through hundreds of old pieces of paper, taking great care as the paper was fragile. I stopped at a few maps, similar to what I was looking for but decided they were not close enough. But then, one map suddenly caught my attention. Had I just found what I was looking for—an inconspicuous map of a coastline which could have been anywhere in the world? There was no writing or settlement, just a rough sketch of a waterfall. But it was the three pools which caught my eye and on further inspection, the description of the coastline was extremely similar. This must be it! Had I really just found the link so many had been hunting for many years? But this map was no use without the other information which had remained hidden all of this time. I took a picture then sat there wondering what I should do with it as it contained the only link between the manuscript and the prize. Someone else would eventually find it.

"Let me take care of that," said the old man. "Its safekeeping is my job alone, entrusted to me personally by Oldfield Thomas."

"But that would make you over one hundred years old," I stammered.

"Gorgon blood," he replied, smiling at me. "Let's be off with you," and ushered me to the door.

"Gorgon blood?" I whispered back, but he only responded with a smile as I left.

I remained in the shadows for a while to make sure I was not seen before returning to the hotel. But I was seen! The curtains of the room above the shop moved ever so slightly as I walked back down the street.

Back in my room, I set my alarm for three hours later, then called a mole to set the next part of my plan rolling. It was now time to turn the tables on the Forsythe-Twykes.

***

They were located all around the hotel, hiding behind early morning street food stalls and trying to be inconspicuous. For me they were easy to spot, and I made it even easier for them to see me. At a pre-arranged time, I exited the hotel, stood in front for a while, and then strolled through the streets. Using the reflection in my smartphone and shop windows, I recognised I was being followed. At the same time, high above the rooftops, pigeon spotters began identifying targets for the main wave of bombers to follow on. There was no proper plan to my actions as I started going into various shops, out again, doubled back and went in circles, but my purpose was to flush out as many of Ormerod's agents as possible. Confident I had achieved this aim, I donned a wide-brimmed hat, stood under an umbrella, and waited for the fun to begin.

My hat was the signal for the attack to commence and a few seconds later, spotter pigeons started arriving above the roof tops to identify their targets. Squadrons of pigeons followed, coconut shells hanging under their bellies as they dived towards the tight streets and alleys. The people of Chinatown had no idea what was about to hit them—literally. Ormerod's agents without hats were targeted first and the first indication was the sound of many birds beating their wings, flying directly down the street a few metres above the ground. These pigeons were the best of the best and had already practiced close-quarter bombing raids over the last hours. They were so skilful that range finding blobs were not needed to find their targets, relying only on the spotter birds to indicate their prey. People now started to realise something was amiss as the thunderous sound of attacking birds flapped down the street, swerving by cables, ducking under awnings and shooting past people's heads. Some started screaming and ran away and this is exactly what the pigeons wanted as the agents remained in position but looked up to see what was causing the fuss, presenting their faces as perfect aiming points. The expert bombers couldn't miss these easy targets, the first bomb smacking straight into the middle of an agent's forehead. Disgusted, he wiped it away with his sleeve, but it was too late as the blob made contact with his skin thereby allowing the special forces soldier to infiltrate him. His body was immediately requisitioned by the agent and ran away down the street out of Chinatown. All the agents without hats were hit in the first wave, diminishing their ranks considerably and I was sure the same was happening in the other streets around the hotel judging by the screams I heard. The next to be taken out were the agents with hats, posing a more difficult target. But this was no problem for these expert fighters as they flew at extremely low-level, deftly swerving in and out, up and down and even through people's legs, arriving just below their targets, then shooting up and knocking off the hats on their way. Other bombers were waiting above and came in to finish off the job, their loads smashing down on Ormerod's shocked agents. The whole attack couldn't have lasted more than a few minutes and all the agents I had identified were now gone. Some pigeons carried on low-level flying to check if they had missed anyone, much to the consternation of the locals, but none remained. I waited a short while before taking off my hat, signalling the end of the mission, and then witnessed the pigeons beating their way up into the sky and away out of the tight streets. Once I was back in my room, I watched the local news already reporting a mass attack of pigeons in Chinatown.

***

A good trick in the book is to cause confusion and that is what I now did, starting by lighting a big bunch of incense sticks in the corridor well away from my room. It didn't take long for the hotel's fire alarm to go off with a high-pitched ringing, followed immediately by doors bursting open and guests pouring out of their rooms. Dressed again in a hotel uniform, I mingled with the crowd and filed out of the hotel, making sure my face was covered. Sirens wailing, the fire engines arrived, and the crowd grew as onlookers gathered to see what the fuss was all about. I saw the Kennedy brothers and wondered why they had shaved heads, as they stood confused in the throng of people.

Ten minutes later, I was sitting in an Internet café, obviously not wanting anyone to know what I was searching for. Two hours, by my estimation, was all I had to find a piece of coastline with only the picture I took in the bookshop to help me. I started at the south-west point of the Gulf of Thailand, guessing this was the area Oldfield Thomas could only have been in. He would have used the same map but did not have the advantage of the Internet, having to sail the route instead. No wonder it took him two years! The part I was looking for was quite distinct, so I zoomed in and started following the coastline northwards towards Bangkok. I took in each island but found absolutely nothing remotely resembling my map. The firefighters might by now have worked out what had happened as I passed south of Bangkok. Time was running out and I still had the coast towards Cambodia to cover. Passing Rayong, I started to feel I would never find it and then I reached the last island in Thai territory. Just as I was about to pack up and leave, my eye was drawn towards a part of the coast looking quite similar. Could this be it? I quickly compared it with the map on my smartphone and found this part of the coast to be almost identical. The Internet version showed a pier which obviously wasn't on the original map, and I also had to remember whoever had drawn it would have done from the perspective of the sea so the original couldn't be perfect. Despite appearing to find the correct part of the coast, I was irritated as there was no sign of three waterfalls and a garden in the dense jungle. However, it was the best I had. The island was called Koh Chang and the village at the pier Bang Bao.

My time was up and, after deleting the search results, made my way to the hotel just in time to find the guests trudging back in. My absence had been noticed because on my bed was a piece of paper with a room number written on it.

***

Room 1508 was exactly above mine. The door was slightly ajar, and after checking the corridor was free of people, gently pushed it open to find it completely dark.

"Come in and close the door," a voice came from somewhere. "I've been waiting for you, Mr Jackson."

"And who are you?" I replied to the mystery voice, gingerly making my way through the darkness, feeling in front of me with my hands and feet.

"You've been looking for me but don't know who I am. In fact, nobody knows what my real name is." A dull torch beam briefly illuminated a chair in the darkness. "Sit down, please."

"I suspected you were somewhere near here, not in the Sanctuary of Epidaurus."

"Yes, I actually sent for you and am delighted you're up to the challenge. You have successfully followed in my footsteps, and those of Oldfield Thomas."

"But why send for me?"

"You inadvertently became involved in this plot when you came across Professor Wingnut. Not only did you escape from the mole world, a commendable feat, but you have also kept his memory safe."

"I really don't want to become involved in this any further than I already am. I just want to investigate the Forsythe-Twykes and save a good friend of mine."

"Yes, I know all about Basil in the Food Factory. Your aims are the same as mine, the defeat of this family, but for different reasons. The Forsythe-Twykes are using the wealth of the Food Factory to fund their ambition of taking over the mole world, defeating me and finding the hidden prize. I tried my best to hinder them, but their rise was not to be stopped. It was only a matter of time until Ormerod tracked me down, so I devised a plan to bait him here by showing myself. But they are not as clever as they thought, having to use you to find me. I also sent you some clues via other sources to push you in the right direction."

"Yes, I received a photograph of you at Bangkok Airport."

"It was one of my disguises and part of my plan."

"And the monk observing me works for you too?"

"Yes, and the moles who led you through Bangkok also work for me but completely unknown to their colleagues down there."

"What about the different notes I received?"

"Notes. No, they are not from me. Must have been part of Ormerod's work?"

"He sent some, but not all."

"That is surprising and means someone else is in play." The mystery man sounded alarmed.

"I also received a letter from my late father, which eventually led me to the bookshop. It wasn't easy though."

"This was a test for you. Only Oldfield Thomas, you and I know of the importance of this place and its link to the information held in the Repository. Not only did you find that, but you've also successfully drawn Ormerod out and left him completely alone and exposed. Good work, Mr Jackson. The family in the Molehamptons is in disarray, so now it is time to finish them off."

"I must ask you something. Did you find the Sanctuary of Epidaurus?"

"No, I didn't even try, as it would have been far too risky. My purpose was to retrace Oldfield Thomas's steps up to the Repository and destroy any links between the manuscripts and bookshop. I presume the moles were less than amused at my actions."

"You could say that, and they've been trying to reconstruct it ever since."

"But it was only a matter of time before someone worked it out and you turning up shows it is possible. The net is closing in, and the cult of Azoth has a long reach."

"What is the Cult of Azoth? I have heard about them a few times now?"

The man in the darkness then filled in the gaps to make sense of everything.

Oldfield Thomas really went to the Sanctuary of Epidaurus and found a person tending the garden, creating magic medicines and potions just as described in legends. But the real prize sought after by many was also there—the Elixir of Life. The ancient myths were indeed true. He returned to the Molehamptons and, armed with what he learnt, set up a mole world with his best friend, Beaumont Forsythe-Twyke. However, the secrets in the garden and its location remained hidden away and protected by an organisation they set up—the Eternity Project. The Cult of Azoth, an ancient organisation dedicated to finding the secrets of the Sanctuary of Epidaurus, set about stealing what Oldfield Thomas found and recruited none other than Montague Forsythe-Twyke, Beaumont's father. I already knew Beaumont had four children and the eldest child, Annabelle, was secretly given the role of becoming Head of the Eternity Project after Beaumont. But George, his youngest son, was dangerous and, on his father's passing, had his three eldest sisters declared mad so he could legally take over the family estate. He was in fact supported by the Cult of Azoth through the Secret Service. However, his sisters were one step ahead and they all disappeared taking the secrets into hiding. The Forsythe-Twykes have relentlessly been searching for all three sisters and their children ever since.

"So, as Head of the Eternity Project, you must be a Forsythe-Twyke."

"Yes, my mother was Annabelle Forsythe-Twyke. And now, Mr Jackson, this must come to an end. It's up to us now."

"What do you want me to do?" I replied showing a steely determination.

In the darkness, we discussed a strategy and made our plan. A plan to instigate the demise of the Forsythe-Twykes.

Chapter Twenty-Two
The Demise of the Forsythe-Twykes

Sergeant Dawson was holding a memory stick in one hand, a biscuit in the other and looking at a town council motion on his desk with a mischievous look on his face.

Splosh! One half of the biscuit fell into his tea after being dunked just a little too long.

"What do you think we should do now?" asked Colonel Pickle, who was standing on the desk, nibbling on some biscuit crumbs.

Sergeant Dawson was in his favourite position, relaxing in his chair whilst slurping on tea, and munching his beloved biscuits. He was usually a rather lazy person and didn't like to rush around, but today he had things to do and put the memory stick in his pocket. The demise of the Forsythe-Twykes would now be set in motion.

"Oh, I think you've done enough for the moment. You've certainly made sufficient damage to stop most of the production operations, although they have people in there urgently repairing things. I've heard the power has been restored."

"We can take it out again!" the Colonel barked back excitedly.

"Noooooo," replied Sergeant Dawson, glaring at him. "I would prefer it if you went back home." he said, hoping to go back to normal.

Since the army of moles had moved in, they had turned his normally tidy office upside down, the mole soldiers using all spaces to live, sleep and train in.

"Go back? No, Sergeant. We're here to stay until this show is over."

"What?" he stammered. "Staying here? In my office?"

"Down there is far too dangerous, and besides, defeating the Forsythe-Twykes should stop the unrest below."

"Oh no!" exclaimed Sergeant Dawson loudly, dropping a new biscuit in his tea and splashing Colonel Pickle.

"What is it?" he asked, wiping his furry face.

"She's here!"

"Hide yourselves, and sharpish!" ordered Colonel Pickle.

There was a loud rustling movement as the moles scampered for cover, disappearing as the door opened. Sergeant Dawson just managed to cover Colonel Pickle with his police hat before Felicity Forsythe-Twyke came in, Vanessa just behind.

"And a splendid morning to you," beamed Sergeant Dawson.

"Everything is far from splendid!" she screamed back.

Felicity was usually elegantly dressed and wore copious amounts of make-up, but not today. She was now a shadow of her former self, standing there with a broken arm, looking tired, her hair a mess and her clothes creased as if she had slept in them. Vanessa stood behind her, remaining aloof and neutral.

"This place is a real mess, Sergeant. And get rid of that too," she angrily said, pointing to a block of salt.

"Yes, sure thing," replied Sergeant Dawson, getting up and kicking it to the side of the office. "There you go. No trip hazards now," he added sarcastically.

Felicity's head shot towards the sound of laughter coming from the storeroom.

"Who's laughing at me?" she scowled, already moving towards the door.

It was then Vanessa, until now quite withdrawn, became involved. "It was nothing and you're stressed. Let's speak to the Sergeant as we agreed before."

"If you wish," replied Felicity, turning around. "Sergeant, we demand protection and you're incapable of giving it, therefore I want you to call your superiors straight away. And I intend to stay whilst you do it so you can't fob me off again. I don't trust you anymore because you always promise to do things but never do. Go on, do it now," she ordered aggressively, jabbing with her finger to the phone.

Sergeant Dawson did as instructed and called the Anglerton Police Station for support.

"See, that wasn't too difficult, was it?" she said smugly to him. But her attention was suddenly diverted towards his police hat on his desk. "What was that?"

"What was what?"

"Your hat. It moved."

"No. That's not possible," he replied, now turning red as he blushed.

"Don't play games with me. You must have seen it move too. You were looking directly at it. It was as clear as day."

"I didn't see anything," beads of sweat now forming on his brow.

Vanessa jumped to his support. "Me neither and I was looking straight at it."

"There's something mighty strange going on here," exclaimed Felicity suspiciously.

"Why not go home and lie low for the day. Hopefully, nothing else will happen," added Sergeant Dawson with a sly grin as Vanessa started leading her towards the door.

***

Jessica Walsh stood proudly and confidently, hands on hips, perusing the sight in front of her. A tented camp had sprung up in the last days, a field kitchen, an arrivals centre and a press tent. All of this in such a short space of time had put the Molehamptons centre stage of the world map. Little did she know when she sent her first messages that this would have had such a global appeal, her hashtag attracting millions of followers. The protestors here alone amounted to well over a thousand, consisting of many age groups from all over the world. Moreover, similar protests had sprung up globally, all marching under the banner of *#openthedoors*.

She had managed to pick herself up following the aggressive press interview. Enough people had seen it and rushed to support her including Timothy Scribbler, embarrassed by his colleagues' behaviour and someone she didn't expect—her mother. She had seen it on the television and went straight to the camp to comfort her daughter. Now, she stood by her side, beaming in pride for her accomplishments. The message and aims from the supporters had now matured, from not only demanding access but to complete transparency in the food industry from source to the table. They were demanding the government take an active interest, in particular the Food Standards Ministry. Things were just about to become even more uncomfortable for the Forsythe-Twykes.

As I said before, Sergeant Dawson had things planned for the day and the first of which included handing Jessica a memory stick.

"What is it?" she asked, intrigued.

"You will know what to do with it," and he left to plan other things.

***

"Order! Order!" shouted the woman at the front of the seated gathering in the town hall. "I hereby declare the opening of this extraordinary meeting of the Town Council. Unfortunately, the mayoress is indisposed so we will have to carry on without her. Ladies and gentlemen, we have received an anonymous motion to discuss the conduct of the mayoress, Mrs Felicity Forsythe-Twyke. The motion received the required signatures, as stipulated in the bylaws, legally obliging us to hold this meeting."

Shouting and cheering immediately erupted as those attending made an open show of supporting this move. Sergeant Dawson, who was everywhere today, sat at the back, observing the proceedings.

"Are you OK in there, Colonel?" he whispered to his hat on the table in front of him.

"Yes, a bit cramped but I can hear everything," a muffled response came from within.

The boisterous meeting lasted about an hour with only a handful of people supporting the mayoress, praising her services to the community. In normal times everyone would have done this, but times were now so different, most people angry about the changes in the village and the expansion of the Food Factory. Abuse of power could not be categorically proven, but a vote was nevertheless taken, a clear majority electing in favour for her to resign her office.

Sergeant Dawson grinned from ear to ear at the expected result.

***

"I can't believe it; all my agents have just disappeared off the face of the earth. Not one left remaining," lamented Ormerod to Bartholomew.

They were in his office at the plant in Bangkok, the chanting of loud protests heard outside.

"It's not the only problem we have, Father," Bartholomew said. "I've just received a message from Vanessa about a news story we should see on television."

Ormerod and Bartholomew just sat there in horror, watching the secretly taken footage from the Food Factory. They were not horrified because of the disgusting images, rather they knew what it meant for them.

"Blast," shouted Ormerod. "Who the hell is behind all of this? Mr Jackson is here and there's no way he possibly could have organised such dreadful acts. We are under attack from a new and unknown perpetrator."

They were disturbed by a phone ringing. "Oh, it's the Prime Minister's office," Bartholomew added in surprise, looking at his display.

"Then answer it, you fool," ordered his father harshly.

"Bartholomew Forsythe-Twyke speaking." His face was sullen as he listened to the other person, nodding his head in silent agreement at what was a one-way conversation. "Yes, Prime Minister. I understand your reasons. Yes. Good day."

"Well, what is it, man?" added Ormerod impatiently.

"I've been dismissed from the Food Standards Ministry—a direct result of the video. They don't want a Forsythe-Twyke connected to the Agency. Not good PR, they say."

"Damn and blast. Why are they so jumpy? It's only a video about some useless animals."

"Yes, I agree, but I believe the Prime Minister is being forced to do something in anticipation of a public backlash. It's all aesthetics."

"You've been sacked yet again. Useless, that's what you are."

"Not really sacked, Father, just being moved sideways and maybe just down a little. A diagonal downwards move would be a good way of putting it."

"Diagonal downwards? This is why I don't work in politics. And where will this slanted journey now take you?"

"The Prime Minister has rewarded me for my good work by giving me the position of Minster for Data Protection."

"And are you experienced in data protection?"

"No, I know nothing about it."

"Perfectly qualified then," Ormerod sarcastically quipped. "And which super-qualified person will take over your now vacant post?"

"They're going to move the Minister for Welfare into the post, a perfect candidate for the task at hand. I'm sure he comes with the ideal skill set for the job. And, Father, I have to return to London at once."

"Can this get any worse?"

"Yes," replied Bartholomew, looking at his phone. "Felicity has just been asked to resign by the Town Council."

***

Vanessa was trying unsuccessfully to comfort her mother, who just sat there rocking backwards and forwards, cradling her arm.

"Ouch, the pain, it's absolutely unbearable. Ouch. Ouch," screaming in big sobs to her daughter.

"Now there. You've had the maximum number of painkillers today. I'm sure it's not too bad now."

"Ouch. Ouch," she carried on, and then completely changed her face to one of surprise, quickly forgetting her pain. "And they asked me to resign. The cheek of it and after everything I've done for them." Her face turned back to one of pain. "Ouch. Ouch, my arm!"

"I thought you could ride out the storm but this video, well, it's too much."

"But they had already called for my resignation before the release of the video. The ungrateful fools," she spat out.

"I can see they don't recognise your gracious contribution to society," added Vanessa sarcastically.

"And don't forget my work supporting animal welfare too!"

"It seems like the others have a different opinion."

"Nothing else could go wrong now, could it, darling daughter?"

"Actually, it can," Vanessa said, looking down at her phone. "Bartholomew has been sacked and is on his way back now, leaving Ormerod alone."

"Sacked!" Felicity yelled in anguish. "Sacked! How could the Prime Minister do this to our family, and after all we've done."

"Damage limitation. The Prime Minister has to do something and is keen to distance herself from our name."

"Ouch! Ouch!" Felicity wailed further, then became serious again. "And what of the Food Factory?"

"It's partially back up and running after the attack, with quite a bit of the damage repaired."

"But, who's behind all of this ghastly behaviour? You left Mr Jackson below the ground in Bangkok, and even he can't be so effective from there."

"No, it's not him and I have no idea who it could be," replied Vanessa truthfully.

"And now? What should we do now?"

Vanessa looked at her mother with a cunning look. "I think you should consider your position as mayoress and also as Chief Executive Officer of the Food Factory."

"You mean resign both positions?"

"Yes, that's exactly what I mean."

"Ouch! Ouch!" and Felicity carried on holding her arm and wailing.

***

The newspapers on Jemima's desk did not contain any good news: protests at the Food Factory, a call for Felicity Forsythe-Twyke to resign and the release of a video from within the factory. To top it all off, contact with the minister had dried up and he had no way of communicating with the mole world. There were other characters in play here and he was blind. Cromwell sat in the darkness of the handbag and the reality slowly started to hit him—he was about to be defeated yet again. Whoever was pulling the strings really puzzled Cromwell. Mr Jackson was being kept busy in Thailand and there was no way he could have orchestrated all of this. If not him, then who?

***

It was with a heavy heart Felicity Forsythe-Twyke wrote the two letters. The first was to the Town Council informing them of her immediate resignation as the mayoress. The other was to the Board of Directors of the Food Factory informing them she was standing down as Chief Executive Officer, her daughter, Vanessa, to take over.

The family and business were in tatters, attacks coming from all directions. Bartholomew was on a plane, Ormerod not contactable and her sister, Clementine, no use at all. Vanessa was the only person who stood by her side offering valuable advice. She had become so mature and would do a grand job in charge of the family business.

It didn't take long before Timothy Scribbler received copies of the letters, his boss wondering why he had access to this information before anyone else. Maybe, just maybe, he would move Mr Scribbler to a new role at the newspaper. Timothy Scribbler's article prompted immediate debate about who could run for the office of mayor. The popular choices were all from Lower Molehampton including Mr Tinker, Mr Rye, Mr Cross, Gertrude Lawnsworthy and Sergeant Dawson. No candidates from Upper Molehampton were being discussed at all, the other side of the river keeping fairly quiet about the whole Forsythe-Twyke affair. And more noteworthy, nobody came to her rescue.

***

Loyalty is a virtue and Ludwig had lots of it. Before Vanessa even had the chance to do it herself, Ludwig was jumping at Sergeant Dawson's window urging him to come out in a last-ditch attempt to save Basil. Soon after, they were at the gates of the Food Factory and, along with Jessica Walsh, entered the premises. Vanessa joined them and off they all marched to the only remaining hall still in production.

But Ludwig wasn't the only person who was loyal, as Mr Walsh had kept production just about running under extremely challenging conditions. At the end of a long conveyor belt her father was opening the last cage, just about to send the ducks to their end. Basil's beak clearly showed among them.

"Stop right there!" she shouted, as her father looked up.

Ludwig, following just behind, didn't wait to be told and ran straight up to Mr Walsh, gnarling and flashing his teeth. Mr Walsh hesitated, clearly scared and confused, with Ludwig champing next to him, giving Mr Kowalczyk the opportunity to calmly lead him away from the now open cage.

Vanessa's first decision as manager was to call the animal welfare authorities, asking them to immediately come and care for the animals. Basil, now in Sergeant Dawson's arms, was taken away first with Ludwig wagging his tail in delight at the successful rescue of his friend right at the last moment.

***

Bartholomew's dismissal made the national news, the government keen to act following the outpouring of disgust at the video. Jessica's protest had achieved success more than she could ever have dreamt of. People wanted to know exactly what they were eating. They wanted more transparency, their message being heard loud and clear, and not only in the Molehamptons. It wasn't enough for the government to just proclaim a new Food Standards Minister, who only paid lip service to people's concerns and hoping the fuss would blow over. The government had no choice in the face of massive public pressure but to listen to the people.

Jessica put the wheels in motion, Sergeant Dawson pulled the strings, Mr Cross provided support, Mr Kowalczyk bravely took a video, Timothy Scribbler reported on real facts and Ludwig never gave up on his friend. The culmination of brave acts by a few, not only triggered the demise of the Forsythe-Twykes, but also forced the government to act.

However, someone else prompted them to do it. Someone secret, and it wasn't me!

Chapter Twenty-Three
Talking to a God

"You!" I exclaimed.

The monk with the scar on his face didn't say a word and breezed into my hotel room and made himself comfortable. A few minutes later, dressed in a hotel uniform, I hung the *do not disturb* on the door and left a satisfied-looking monk with the room service menu, trusting he would keep the hotel staff busy with orders. My laptop, notes and books were on the desk to show I was working, and the monk told to hide in the bathroom when room service came. He nodded in agreement.

I sent a message to Mr Renangrong informing him I was close to unlocking the mystery, but now needed three undisturbed days in my hotel room. The moles, their greed now fully awakened, readily agreed to my proposal. However, I needed someone pretending to be me, and this I left to the monk in my room.

Only discarding my disguise once it was safe, I hailed a taxi and even changed three times on my way to the airport. With so many tourists taking taxis to their holiday destinations, getting lost in the crowd was easy. Ten minutes later, I was in a taxi to the island of Koh Chang. The night-time journey took five hours, passing by Rayong, Chanthaburi, Trat and, eventually, reaching a small harbour near the border with Cambodia. I looked at my watch and smiled, imagining what had just happened in Bangkok. Don't worry, you will find out about that soon. A ferry docked in the harbour when the sun started to rise, its ramp clanking down, ready for boarding and the thirty-minute crossing to the island. Fruit and vegetable laden trucks filled the vehicle deck whilst mopeds squeezed into any space available. Vendors sold food and drinks on the passenger deck as refreshing sea breeze streamed through the open windows for the short crossing.

The next, and final part, of my journey was to Bang Bao Pier in the south of the island. I stood at the entrance of the harbour and relished the slow life, particularly after Bangkok. A line of open-sided taxi vans waited for the rush of visitors to be taken to the many resorts on the island, the drivers slouched asleep over their steering wheels whilst others huddled in small groups smoking cigarettes. Not only was this place rather sedentary but also the noises completely different as my ears tuned in to the orchestra of bird noises screeching from the jungle. A pleasant change to the tooting of horns and revving of engines. The drive took about forty-five minutes and was absolutely spectacular, passing amazing coastal scenery, quaint villages, tropical beeches, steep cliffs and enough hairpin bends to keep myself alert. It was still quite early in the morning and the coastal villages I went through were mainly empty, with only a few people sweeping their shop fronts and stray dogs patrolling the streets. The villages stretched out along the coast, hemmed in by the dense jungle hills on the left and the beach on the right, passing by many hotel resorts, tourist restaurants, shops and bamboo shacks. The early morning sun was already beating down with great ferocity when I arrived at Bang Bao pier, the temperature and humidity rising every minute. I checked the picture of the map I had from the shop and compared the coastline, considering the pier wouldn't have been here when it was drawn. It was unmistakably the same place and even more accurate from this angle; the person who had drawn it probably standing not too far from where I was now. What I now needed was a place to stay and where I would pass as a tourist. A young lady at a travel office pointed across the bay, advising me to take a taxi for the short distance to Klong Kloi beach, then look for a lady who owned the green huts. Only a few minutes later I was there, my journey finally over, and I quickly found the owner enjoying her breakfast at the beach restaurant. As a lone tourist, I wouldn't arouse any suspicion to my true purpose. I thought about Oldfield Thomas standing here over one hundred years ago and wondered if he would recognise the place, his two-year boat journey also quite different to mine. Maybe one day I could speak to his memory, but something told me it would be extremely well-hidden, and a good thing too.

Can you remember there were some ripped out pages from the back of Oldfield Thomas's manuscript? Well, the Head of the Eternity Project had really done a good job removing links to the island. Instructed not to open the envelope until I had arrived at my destination, I now sat on my bed holding the missing pages in my hands. They were notes in Oldfield Thomas's handwriting and described his arrival by boat at Bang Bao and the subsequent discovery of the secret garden. I was close to discovering the mystery which had entertained different people and cultures since the dawn of time.

***

Some years ago, several Thai people also received notes informing them it would be beneficial for their merit ratings if they took large toy boats with motors to the temple as an offering. The notes were quite specific and even supplied exact details of the boats, brand name, model and a picture. The people obediently followed the instructions, leaving the boats with the monks, surprised at these rather strange offerings. The moles were delighted their plan had worked, stole the boats from the temples and their Special Operations Water Fleet was founded.

The special operations moles, dressed in camouflaged uniforms, waited until deep in the night, before loading their boats with cutting equipment. Their mission—attack a container ship in the Port of Bangkok. The Chao Phraya River was choppy but proved no problem for these specialist soldiers, trained to operate on the waterways of Thailand. Twenty boats, two moles in each, sprang into life and splashed across the water in the direction of a vessel at anchor in the river, waiting to be allowed to dock in the port. The operation was not without risk as these small boats were thrown up and down in the waves like matchboxes, but they eventually managed to arrive and tied up on the anchor's thick chain. Immediately, forty moles climbed up the metal links, onto the ship deck, and headed straight towards one particular part of the ship, already knowing where the Forsythe-Twyke containers were. The leader of the secret mission whispered orders and the mole soldiers scurried in small sections towards their designated targets. The refrigerated containers held animal waste from the Food Factory in the Molehamptons on their way to their factory in Bangkok for further processing. Their orders were really quite simple—destroy the refrigerated units keeping the frozen waste at a constant temperature. Armed with their cutting tools, they expertly cut cables, slashed hoses, destroyed electrical circuitry and drilled a few small holes in the container walls until the units were completely destroyed. With so many thousands of containers carried on this ship, nobody would ever see the damage caused by the moles. Successfully completing their mission, the moles sped away again in their boats, the sun just rising in the early morning sky with its red carpet slowly spreading out over the vast city. It didn't take long for the penetrating sun to heat up the containers and their loads like a pressure cooker.

Six hours later, the unloading of the containers began, and it was only when the four Forsythe-Twyke containers were stacked together on the quay, did the harbour workers notice something was wrong. First it was the awful stench and then the red liquid leaking out which forced the workers to raise the alarm, causing the port authorities to seize the containers. Upon inspection, the disgusting load was identified as rotting meat waste from the Food Factory in the Molehamptons. Port workers not only informed the government officials but also the local press. One hour later, the news story was broadcast on the news, adding another nail to the Forsythe-Twyke family coffin.

***

Ormerod was sitting alone in his office, head in hands after watching the news story about the seized containers in Bangkok. It was more bad news for their crumbling business empire, and also more ammunition for the government against the Forsythe-Twykes. Bartholomew was going to get the full brunt of it when he reported back.

Completely isolated as not a single agent had reported back for a while now, Ormerod was unable to contact any of them. Felicity was completely hysterical and there was absolutely no point in talking to her. Vanessa was strangely not answering her phone, but she probably had enough on her plate looking after her mother. The only others he could turn to for support were the Kennedy brothers, but they had turned out to be completely useless. Nevertheless, they were all he had so he called them at the hotel and ordered them to his office.

In the meantime, a now completely frantic Ormerod left and decided to stake out the hotel himself. What was Mr Jackson up to? This was an unusual and risky course of action for such a highly trained intelligence officer. But greed can get the better of most people and force irrational decisions. For Ormerod to publicly do the active work himself was unheard of. Blindly obsessed, he even asked at the reception about Mr Jackson's whereabouts to be told he was working in his room and couldn't be disturbed. Ormerod then sat in a café opposite the hotel and waited, getting more nervous, more frantic, and more irrational as each minute ticked past.

***

Bang Bao fishing village was much different to the place Oldfield Thomas landed at in 1903. The pier was now not really used so much for fishing but as a tourist attraction with trendy souvenir shops, chic restaurants, beautiful guesthouses and a departure point for boats full of tourists wanting to visit some of the nearby idyllic islands. Even Klong Kloi would have been unrecognisable to him, just a small, secluded beach back then. Today, it boasted small beach restaurants and huts, nestling on the beautiful coastline and jungle interior, thankfully not being attacked by concrete hotels as seen further north on the island.

My hut was only twenty metres from the beach, the glorious sound of waves slopping against the sand easily heard from here. It was a basic hut with air conditioning and fridge, but I needed no more. I used the first day to study the literature I received, namely a handwritten detailed description on how Oldfield Thomas found the garden over one hundred years ago, and the map. Oldfield Thomas had landed at Bang Bao, back then a small fishing settlement, and moored his boat at, what is today, Klong Kloi, before venturing into the dense jungle starting behind the beach. His description was extremely detailed, writing about the weeks he needed to slowly work and cut his way through the jungle just to find the waterfall. He frequently returned to his boat to rest and get supplies and even thought of giving up many times, thinking it was not possible for a garden on the scale described in the ancient manuscripts to exist in this harsh environment. But the descriptions he read described exactly this place, so he persevered, every day advancing a little further, until finding, not only the waterfall, but three pools as described in all the literature. He had read at the Repository of three pools on the right hand-side of the waterfall and a beautiful view over the bay from the top pool. It was exactly this view he found after weeks of cutting his way through the undergrowth.

This was really a tropical paradise and easy to understand why people visited here. I understood a waterfall close to us in the jungle was a popular tourist attraction for those wanting some activity. My chance to visit arose and I tagged along with a small group of tourists, then waited for an opportune moment to slip away.

We took a jeep along a bumpy jungle track, slowly winding steeply uphill until eventually arriving in a clearing. The guide led us on foot along a slippery pathway, the exertion causing me to sweat heavily in the humid heat. Ensuring I was at the back of the group, I waited until we were far enough away from the jeep, ducked into the undergrowth and squatted down whilst the rest of the group plodded on. Nobody even noticed my disappearance and, after waiting a short time, stood up and looked again at the map and notes. Oldfield Thomas didn't have the luxury of the track to the waterfall and spent several weeks painstakingly cutting his way through the jungle, every day taking new routes through the dense green wall. But he never gave up and his perseverance paid off when he eventually heard the sound of crashing water. Getting closer to his aim, he clambered over treacherous rocks and cut away overhanging branches to get to where I now hid amongst the coconut trees whilst the tourist group bathed in the water, waiting for them to go back down to the vehicle. Once they had gone, I was left alone and read Oldfield Thomas's description yet again and followed exactly what he did. I started exploring the right side of the waterfall, but it was nearly impossible to get through the extremely slippery ground and thick undergrowth. I spent the next few hours slowly advancing up the side of the waterfall, finding a path in the undergrowth until at last reaching the top and the third of three pools with a fantastic view over the bay, exactly described by Oldfield Thomas and the manuscripts. I was perfectly sure

I had found the correct place. It had taken Oldfield Thomas some weeks to cut his way up here but, fortunately for me, I knew exactly where to go and could follow new and old footpaths through the jungle.

However, I now came to the same quandary as Oldfield Thomas—there was no clearing nor garden to be found, especially in the size described. The whole area was completely overgrown and impossible for such a large open area to exist as described in the writings. So, where was it? I read the notes again and realised he eventually found a wooden door near the second pool. It wasn't easy to get there, and tourists were only led to the largest pool at the top of the waterfall where I was now standing. The other two pools were only just visible and further away from the path, meaning I had to fight through dense undergrowth. Extremely slowly, I clambered through the steep jungle and slip my way downwards over slippery rocks and branches until finally reaching the second pool. It was dark here, the pool encased by the jungle canopy throwing its arms over the water. There was absolutely no space available to walk around the pool, so I was forced to climb over roots and then into the water itself. Waist deep, I slowly waded around the edges holding onto vines for support, all the time careful not to lose my footing on the slippery obstacles. I then came to part of the jungle which was slightly less dense and spotted a narrow opening, at first glance nearly impossible to see. It looked like it had been cut open many years ago and had since grown over but not as thick as the rest of the jungle. I climbed out of the water and started pulling branches and vines out of the way, advancing slowly and deeper into the dark jungle. At one point it became so thick, I had to grapple my way through a dark tunnel on my hands and knees until I could go no further and, pushing my hands in front of me, found a hard object stopping my way. Frantically pulling the undergrowth, I suddenly found myself looking at a solid wooden door.

***

The two shaven-headed men left the hotel and took a taxi to the address Ormerod had given them. As they had lost their prized tracksuits, and had nothing else to wear, the two men still wore their orange robes. Not acting as Buddhist monks should, the brothers caused a stir wherever they went because they were loud, had money and ate whatever and whenever they liked. Of course, they always became the centre of attraction, often shouted at and accused of being imposters.

On their arrival at the Food Factory, they found a peaceful protest at the gates and, although they could not understand them, they presumed it was about better pay. They forced their way through the crowd and found Bartholomew's empty office, so they just sat down to await further instructions. Not long after, they heard sirens which was not an uncommon event in Bangkok. The wailing got ever louder and ever closer until police cars screeched to a halt outside the factory. The protestors, presuming the police had come to break up their strike, shouted and chanted even louder. But the police were not there for the protestors and entered the building, showing their search warrants to the surprised security guards. The reason for the search was as a result of the containers' seizure and the discovery of what was inside, evidently not legal. As Bartholomew and Ormerod were not to be found, the police's attention turned straight away to the two men, falsely acting as Buddhist monks. This made the police extremely angry as it was an insult to their religion and culture. The bemused Kennedy brothers were led away in handcuffs, met by the Bangkok press on their way out of the factory. Yet again, the Forsythe-Twykes Food Factory was in the news for all the wrong reasons.

Ormerod sat in the café, one eye on the hotel entrance, and the other on the news. He put his hat on and left when his picture was shown on the television along with Bartholomew's, both wanted by the police for tax fraud. Ormerod had lost complete control over the situation, and driven by obsessed greed, would now do anything at all to get to the prize. The opportunity would shortly arise.

***

The door was ancient, a layer of green moss covering a lot of the wood and set between two massive trees. Should anyone ever venture into the thick jungle, and I don't know why they would, it would be impossible to see this door, unless of course you knew it was here as I did. I heard voices of another group of tourists arriving at the pool but, safe in the knowledge they couldn't see me, started pulling away the vines and branches covering the door. Once it was free of foliage, I realised it was only about two-thirds of my height and had some sort of symbol embossed on the surface but not clear to see, as it was covered by the moss. Scraping away with my fingers, I soon found a staff with a snake wound around it and a mound at the bottom resembling a molehill. I had seen such staffs before, usually used to show some sort of medical facility.

"And now for the truth," I said to myself, possibly standing at the entrance to a garden existing only in myths and legends.

The door didn't budge one bit as I pressed against it with my hands. Harder still but nothing, so used my shoulder for extra force, difficult in the confined space as I had to stoop down and found it difficult to stop slipping on the slimy jungle floor. On the fourth attempt of barging against the wood, a creaking noise signalled some movement, and, after a few more hefty shoves, the door slowly groaned open just enough for me to squeeze through. I left the dark jungle undergrowth and now found myself standing completely upright in the bright light of a clearing. Adjusting my eyes to the sunlight, I was now looking at another world. I was in a huge open area comprising beautifully tended gardens, flower beds, and vegetable patches as far as the eye could see. Gone was the dank, humid climate of the jungle, to be replaced by a freshness never experienced before. Turning around, I found the door I had just come through was not there anymore, instead a thick tree trunk. I know you've heard me say it was the most amazing thing I have ever seen, and I'm afraid I have to say it again, as I stood shell-shocked in the garden, gawping at the wonderful sight in front of me. The clearing was enormous, stretching far into the distance and surrounded by the tallest trees imaginable. Strangely, this large open space did not show on satellite imagery, making me believe I was indeed in a magical place. A stone path weaved its way between lush plants and, walking quite slowly, I started to look at everything here in more detail. The first impression was the beautifully fresh smell of the various plants and flowers, a fragrance so intense, as if someone was spraying an air freshener directly at my face. Every time I sniffed in the air, I found exciting unfamiliar scents tingling in my nose. It was somehow hypnotising as I breathed in tremendous amounts of air, eyes closed and lost in the magical perfume of the garden. Shaking my head, I tried to concentrate, astounded at the rich colours presented to me as though I was now a character in a glossy oil painting, the artist using the richest and deepest colours available. In just a few metres I saw plants, herbs, flowers, fruit, and vegetables until now completely unknown to me, and also huge leaves with the most interesting patterns and textures. I really had entered a different world. The sound of rainfall and gushing water now distracted my gaze. To my left a mini-rain cloud hovered over a vegetable patch, held in place by a rope as it ejected its water exactly where it was needed. A fresh breeze indicated another sensation and to my right saw a huge fan made of jungle leaves beating up and down and operated by some sort of wooden contraption.

Rounding a bend in the garden, I came upon a huge mound in front of me which looked cannily like a molehill. It was surrounded by a few other similar mounds but much smaller in size. A loud whooshing noise made me duck for cover as a bird beat its wings over my head followed by the buzz of a chasing bee. I stood up again to look at the strange sight, the bee being about the size of my hand. Flapping graciously behind the bird and bee, a dragonfly as large as my lower arm followed, and the three creatures flew towards one of the smaller molehills and disappeared into a hole at the top. This was truly a mystical garden and now I can understand why most cultures have a story of such a place in their myths. It was a natural balance of all the elements creating the perfect biosphere.

But somebody must be here, I thought to myself. Somebody must have created all of this and so carefully tended the gardens. But who? The manuscripts had only mentioned a mystical garden and others had spoken of secrets, but there was no mention of a person, or a creature maybe, living here. All of a sudden, I saw something move, although I could not yet make out what it was. Part of the air seemed to be a little darker and moving around. I moved a little closer and was sure I saw the outline of a transparent human-shaped form. And then in a flash it was gone. Walking the few metres to where it had been, I brushed my hand through the air but there was nothing. It must have been the light playing on my eyes. The outer ring of molehills was a little larger than me and only a short distance away and I now audibly heard noises coming from within, maybe some sort of tools being used.

"Hello," I whispered quickly and nervously, not knowing what to expect.

The noise abruptly stopped and then a huge head of a mole appeared through the opening at the top. The mole, maybe as large as me, opened its eyes in shock and darted back down the hole. The biggest molehill in the centre had some steps leading up to a doorway in the side. Now knowing I was definitely not alone, I plucked up my courage and walked up the steps, a cold sweat of anxiety building up on my body, as I approached the door. My knocks on the wood were quiet, almost as if I didn't want anyone to hear them, apprehensive about what I might find inside. No answer came so I gently pushed against the door and entered into the darkness of this huge molehill.

"Mr Jackson, I've been waiting for you," a voice said out of the dark interior.

"Who are you? Show yourself!" I stuttered a nervous reply.

The room slowly became brighter, and I saw light slowly emitting form what like a massive glow-worm. Half of a giant coconut shell was in the centre of the room and from this a man, using it as a chair, stood up. He was extremely old, wore a grey robe and supported himself with a wooden staff, a snake entwined around it.

"Who are you?" I asked him again.

"My name is Asclepius. And you are Connor Jackson," he answered slowly and with a croaky voice showing his immense age.

We stared at each other until I broke the silence. "Asclepius, you say. Strange name if you ask me. What's your surname then?"

"Gods do not have surnames," he retorted sharply.

Again, I stood there and paused, not really knowing how to react to such a statement. "Gods," I eventually said, emphasising the plural meaning of the word. "I was always told there was only one God, and I'm not even convinced of that."

"You young people know nothing today. Of course, there are gods, and I am one of them. Asclepius!"

I decided this conversation was really going nowhere and thought all my effort to get was wasted by meeting a crazy old man. He was quite convincing though!

"So, Mr Asclepius, please tell me who you really are."

He looked at me absolutely amazed at my question. "Who I really am? Only one God? Oh dear, Mr Jackson, this really wasn't what I was expecting of you. Most disappointing," he added sadly, turning around to sit down again.

I walked around the coconut shell chair to face him. "Disappointing. What do you expect me to say when someone says he's a god? And when you say gods, I presume there are others?"

"Of course, there are many gods, and I am just one of them," he answered, slouched in his chair and looking quite disinterested.

It took a lot of effort to find this place, so a show of interest was necessary. "Well, what type of god are you?"

"This conversation is really pointless. You burst into my home then question my status and even the very existence of gods. I am the God of healing and medicine, and my name is Asclepius. Have you never heard of me?" he asked now beginning to believe I had really never come across his name or role.

"I apologise, and I don't mean to offend you, but I've never heard of you. However, I recognise your staff." We remained in eery silence, not really knowing how to continue from here. "I'm an analyst, you know, and deal in facts. I've never really interested myself in religion."

"Hmmn," he groaned, looking at me with suspicion.

"But assuming you are a god, why are you here hidden away in this beautiful garden?"

Asclepius had now calmed down slightly and noticed I was making an effort. He beckoned for me to sit down in another coconut shell seat, and I hoped he was now prepared to tell me more.

"This beautiful garden, as you call it, is really called the Sanctuary of Epidaurus. But, Mr Jackson, you are nearly correct about one God," he started to explain. "Many thousands of years ago there were many gods, and there still are actually, but a restructuring process was carried out by the management, and we all lost our jobs. It was decided only one God was to remain."

"Restructuring?" So, you are an unemployed god?" I added bemused at his explanation.

Asclepius moved uncomfortably in his seat, embarrassed at me presenting the facts like this. "Yes, I suppose I am," he eventually replied.

I pressed him again. "I didn't know gods could be unemployed."

"A few minutes ago, you didn't believe in gods and now you appear to question my information, thereby I assume you now believe I'm a god," he smiled, sparring with me.

I realised he was now enjoying our lively discussion, so played along. "What happened to all of you then?"

"Look, Mr Jackson. Gods can't die – we are immortal beings and now split up around the world. The new God, or the one God as you refer to him, banished me here to practice my trade for eternity."

"I'm sorry to seem uneducated, but I've really never heard of a god called Asclepius." I was telling the truth, never having invested much time in Greek mythology.

"Have you heard of Apollo?"

"Yes, sure, everyone knows him."

"Hmm, OK. Well, he's my father," he added, still disappointed I'd never heard of him.

I was slowly beginning to believe him, owing to his age and where he lived. "And why were you expecting me? It seems everyone wants to see me and needs me to do something. Even gods maybe!"

"So many questions from you, Mr Jackson, and it's a long story. Did you know I hadn't had any visitors for thousands of years and then suddenly, in a brief space of time, two of you turn up. Firstly, a lovely gentleman approximately one hundred years ago. Yes, Oldfield Thomas. I did enjoy his company. And now you, Mr Jackson."

"Thousands of years?"

"Yes. I was once mortal, you know. One of Zeus's thunderbolts actually killed me because I was good at my job and saved too many lives. Hades, God of the underworld, was most angry because I was stopping people from coming to him, hence he complained to Zeus. The problem was I was born mortal because my father had a fling with my mortal mother, Koronis, and I'm the result. However, Apollo brought me up and left me in the care of a centaur called Chiron. He taught me absolutely everything."

"But if you are mortal, how come you are still alive? You died. I really don't understand," I asked, my interest now quite genuine. There was something real and deeply interesting in everything he said.

"Apparently my skills were sorely missed, so they brought me back to life and made me a god. People flocked to me willingly, which was rare back in those days. It was mere mortals who made temples of worship to me and gave me cult-like status. You can see me in the sky too if you look carefully for the constellation Ophiuchus."

"Sounds like a resurrection story if you ask me. It's all a bit far-fetched."

"Maybe for you, but it's all true, even if you find it hard to believe. How do you imagine gods to look anyhow?"

"Usually depicted as a man with a beard."

"Such a shame you've never heard of me. I'm actually quite good at my job," he exclaimed, sounding a little frustrated.

"I have no doubt, Mr Asclepius. Just look at this impressive place."

"Chiron trained me well in the anatomy of humans and animals, and the information was key to everything. Information is knowledge, Mr Jackson, but I am sure you of all people already know that. And knowledge can only be gained by the meticulous keeping of records."

"But why me. Why are you interested in me?"

"That's why we sent for you."

"We. Who's we? And why is everyone sending for me? I'm just a boring analyst."

"The Head of the Eternity Project and me. You initially thought he was hiding in the garden and that is one of the reasons why you are here."

"You've met him?"

"Not exactly. We have contact through an intermediary, but I would like to meet him one day though. You see, you are all connected to Oldfield Thomas, a person dear to me. I also know the Head of the Eternity Project is protecting my location from those whose greed is their primary motivation. And I am most grateful for that. I know everything that is going on and I also appreciate your efforts," he added kindly. He then lent forwards and started to whisper to me. "It's quite nice talking to a human again. Only talking to moles can be a bit tedious at times."

"Yes, I believe that. But what do you want me to do?" I quizzed him, getting rather annoyed that he never really answered the question as to why I was here.

"More of that later. First, let me show you something interesting," he said, leading me to a bookshelf.

Pointing to a bottle on the shelf, I asked, "What's that?"

"That, Mr Jackson, is Gorgon blood."

"Gorgon blood?"

"Sure, and that's what landed me here. A mere mortal using godly tools and upsetting the balance of the world. I wasn't allowed to use it, but I did. A single drop keeps a mortal being alive or brings them back from the dead. This is the Elixir of Life."

"An amazing story. And what else have you got hidden here?"

"I grow plants, fruits and vegetables—all for medical purposes. My workers mix them into various potions and medicines in our workshops here. The technology you've seen below the ground also stems from here. Potions for the manipulation of creatures' inner control systems were also my work, but dangerous in the wrong hands I must say."

I looked at him, astonished at his revelations. "You said you can't leave the garden, so how do you get your potions out."

"Pigeons. I give everything to the pigeons who distribute my work and messages. That's how I communicate with my intermediary too, as he is not allowed to know this location. Security you know!" he added, winking at me.

"Pigeons! I could have guessed." Then a thought came to me as I contemplated what he explained. "The intermediary. Do I know him?"

"Yes. He's sitting in your hotel room now, posing as you."

"Of course, the monk."

"And my technology, or bits of it, is passed through channels to the moles without them even knowing it's from me. Their task is to administer the world—or was thousands of years ago at least."

"Tell me," I said, looking at him, "do you live here alone? I'm sure I saw something resembling a human form in the garden."

"Oh, you saw her. That was Mnemosyne. She's the Goddess of memory and remembrance and also responsible for inventing language and words. A useful god to share this place with. It's because of her myths, stories and sagas are passed on. But unfortunately, not well enough," he said, looking at me sternly. "Moles too. I share this garden with moles. They are my workers and made everything here. Quite industrious little creatures actually."

"But why moles?"

"I don't think you know, but I am also known as Asclepius, the mole hero. Some people have written about this fact, and it is quite true. I gave them their job on this planet, their primary task originally was medicine, healing and the storage of memories and knowledge. If you know nothing about me, what about moles?"

I thought quite hard about his question and then replied, "Well, before I met them below the ground, I thought they were just blind tunnel burrowers. Now, of course, I know more and understand they try, or are trying, to administer memories and the part of the world they live under."

"Not bad, but do you know how they came into existence?"

"Actually not."

"Phaeton, he was a Triton, cursed King Phineus by turning him into a blind mole, thereby creating the species. There is also a magic element about them, even folklore in different cultures believed mole parts could heal diseases. Some say you can gain the powers of divination, the ability to look into the future, by eating the fresh, beating heart of a live mole."

"This all sounds quite disgusting and more like a fairy tale."

"Oh, maybe stories are twisted over time, but it is all based on truth. The moles are my guild of doctors," he added, chuckling.

Now why is that not a surprise, I thought to myself. Then Asclepius suddenly became serious.

"Do you know anything about the Cult of Azoth?"

"A little, yes."

"It is because of the Cult of Azoth you are here. Your services are needed."

"My services! I didn't realise I offered any services and certainly not to Gods." I was now becoming more and more surprised the further this conversation went on.

"Yes, Mr Jackson, your task is to hunt down the Cult of Azoth and destroy it."

"Surely you have godlike powers and can use thunderbolts," replying rather sarcastically.

"Not all gods have weapons," he shot back. "Finish off the Forsythe-Twykes first and then you will have to turn your attention to the Cult of Azoth itself."

"Tell me more about the Cult."

"Let me explain in more detail. There was once a Cult of Asclepius which offered places of healing, or simply put, temples to revere me. The Cult was made up of a guild of doctors following my teachings and the most important place was the Sanctuary of Epidaurus. That's how Oldfield Thomas created the name *Eternity Project*, using the E and P from Epidaurus."

"There are temples named after you?"

"Yes, and there's more. You must have seen symbols around the word depicting my staff and snake here," he replied, holding it in front of me. "Yes, I am shown everywhere but it seems nobody knows me and my snake. Shame."

"Who is your snake? A god too?" I asked, now prepared to believe nearly anything he said.

"No, not a god. Once, I rescued an injured snake and it whispered all its secrets in my ear. That's how I learnt a lot of my skills."

"I've seen the symbol many times before but didn't realise it's importance. What about temples? Would I have seen any?"

"Maybe. There is one particular temple of great importance. The Thymele, which is a round marble looking building with a huge underground labyrinth. People used to believe snakes to be there, but they are not—the moles are! Both I and Mnemosyne are revered there."

"Sorry, but I've never heard of it. Does it still exist?"

"I am not sure if it exists, but you might have heard of it as the Sanctuary of Asclepius at a place called Epidaurus in modern Greece. There was a tholos next to my temple, a round building, called Thymele. People would go there for healing and explain all their woes to priests, a great pit of withering snakes below them. Maybe there were snakes there, but also moles. Unfortunately, they went slightly astray and started selling what people told the priests as information to the highest bidder. It was not what I intended them to do."

"This modern-day Cult. Where is it?"

"That is the mystery. The Cult of Asclepius was taken over by those wanting my information and in particular the Elixir of Life. Today, they call themselves the Cult of Azoth, its emblem two snakes wound around a winged staff—the caduceus. And Ormerod Forsythe-Twyke is under their command.

"The Forsythe-Twykes again. It never ends."

"This is a fight of possession. I, Asclepius, want to ensure medical information is freely distributed around the world, and the Cult of Azoth wants if all for themselves. That, Mr Jackson, can never change."

Asclepius clapped his hands. "Mr Jackson, we've spoken enough, and you should leave now. By the time you get back, your plan to dispose of Ormerod Forsythe-Twyke will be over but Ormerod must not be totally destroyed as you will need to follow him to discover the true conspirators. Your plan with the Head of the Eternity Project is similar in a way to what happened at Thymele. Ormerod, with his bottomless pit of greed, will most certainly fall for the bait."

Chapter Twenty-Four
Ormerod's Bottomless Pit of Greed

Ormerod Forsythe-Twyke was a high-ranking officer in the British secret service. In reality, he was a mere foot soldier and member of the Cult of Azoth, the organisation's long tentacles transcending governments, international organisations and global businesses. The Cult's aims were global possession of medical cures and memories protected by the Eternity Project. Ormerod was tasked with finding its leader and bringing back the secrets they so desired. He was hungry to succeed in the task given to him, actively seeking promotion, but this hunger turned into blind greed and would ultimately prove to be his downfall. He was completely alone in Bangkok and hunted by the Thai police. The time was now ripe to bring him down.

I knew Ormerod was so greedy, snaring him would be easy, but the plan I forged actually didn't involve me. How could it? I was with Asclepius!

Ormerod was now sitting in the back of a taxi, directly opposite the hotel, waiting for any sign of me. But a man walking along the street suddenly caught his attention and what stood out was his secretive behaviour. He wasn't just strolling along; he was taking great care not to be seen. Although very good, he was not better than Ormerod, who had the briefest of chances to see his face. It was the same face on the airport photograph.

"Got you at last," whispered Ormerod, hardly able to control his excitement. "I knew you would have to break cover at some stage. Patience pays off!"

The man walked past the hotel entrance, and after a quick check, walked down a ramp into the carpark.

"Taking another route in then," said Ormerod, now ecstatic at his discovery. "Everyone eventually makes a mistake. Going to see Mr Jackson, no doubt. Don't worry, I've got all the time in the world."

Ormerod waited and waited, his impatience and anxiety growing with his every breath. He even started imagining seeing *the target's* face in different windows, staring back at him. His ringing phone startled him out of his thoughts.

"Yes, ma'am," answering seriously.

"We are concerned about your operation. I have entrusted you to bring *the target* back, but all around you is chaos."

"We've been under constant attack from external sources, and I fear more than one enemy is involved. I've seen *the target* and I'm close. Very close indeed."

"Get closer still and complete the mission. The Cult only accepts success. I expect you to capture him within the next hours, by whatever means you have at your disposal."

"Yes, ma'am. I will not fail you. I will not fail the Cult."

Ormerod looked nervously at the hotel and knew it was time to take a big risk. He had no choice but to go on the attack. In the basement shadows, he held his knife to the neck of a hotel worker and forced him to call for Mr Jackson's room number. Once he had the information, he disabled him with chloroform before putting on his uniform. Ormerod was a slick and professional operator and now waited near room 1408, showing a *do not disturb sign*. This was now a huge risk, as he did not know what to expect, but one thing was undeniable to him, *the target* must be with Mr Jackson. Silently, he stood next to the room, his ear against the door and heard voices coming from within. Using the hotel worker's key card, he opened the door and braced for action, charged into the room awaiting the worst. But something quite unexpected awaited him. He stood dumbfounded next to the bed; the tension now gone in a flash. A monk was lying on the bed, surrounded by empty crisp packets, bottles of drink and watching television. The monk didn't even acknowledge Ormerod's presence and carried on watching the show with great concentration on his face. Ormerod, slightly regaining his composure, quickly searched the room and found Mr Jackson's clothing and laptop, but no sign of him or *the target*.

Hi senses sharpened again at the sound of a person whistling. He rushed to the door and saw *the target* at the end of the corridor, walking in the direction of the lift. Ormerod sprinted after him, turned left and saw the lift display showing a downwards arrow. It seemed an age until a lift eventually stopped, as he frantically stabbed at the button. Sweating and furious, he entered the lift full of people, aggressively pushing his way in. They stopped at nearly every floor making the already agitated Ormerod even more livid. The guests looked suspiciously at this foreigner dressed in a purple hotel uniform jacket, but he didn't care anymore as he was focused on his prize. The lobby was full of hotel guests and, in his panic of losing *the target*, violently threw people out of his way, looking left, right, backwards and straight on for the face firmly imprinted in his mind. Nothing. Bumping through the crowd, he exited the hotel, looking frenziedly on the busy street. And then he saw him, but only a glimpse, his face in a departing taxi. Ormerod sprang into action and jumped into the road forcing a taxi to brake hard with a toot of its horn. He pulled open the door, forcibly ejected the driver, leaving him crumped on the street, got behind the wheel and took up the chase himself in the last rays of the day's sunlight. He knew *the target* was good, as he followed the taxi at a safe distance, making many different turns and stopping on a few occasions, the sign of an experienced operative watching if he was being followed. But Ormerod possessed more skills and secretly kept his distance. What Ormerod had not considered was *the target* was even better than him as he wanted to be followed. He had been successfully baited and was now driving into a trap.

But Ormerod wasn't the only one to see *the target's* face. The moles also observed him at the hotel, though this was actually part of the plan I had discussed. Above the streets, observation pigeons tracked both the men through the tightly woven streets of Bangkok as they left Chinatown and crossed the river heading northwards and out of the centre. After quite a while, the front taxi stopped at a small shack on the side of the street, the driver exiting to buy a drink. They were now in a narrow residential street near one of the many side arms of the main river, called klongs here. Ormerod killed his lights and left his taxi, waiting in the shadows to see what his prey was up to. *The target* waited quite some time before leaving his taxi, paid the driver at the kiosk, and walked up the street. It was now dark, not much light available from the few lamp posts and the sound of water from the klong heard sloshing against buildings, the moonlight glinting on its surface. It was quite the opposite to the bustle of downtown Bangkok, trees dotted along the edge and branches offering perfect cover. Despite still being in Bangkok, this waterway area had some sort of rural feel about it as Ormerod carefully followed him. Eventually the street came to an end and the man opened a gate, entering a garden protected from view by large bushes. The pigeons, permanently reporting back on their movements, now lost sight of *the target* and shortly thereafter Ormerod too.

Keeping well out of sight, Ormerod crept along the street, careful to remain silent and unseen until at least he reached to the garden. He stopped at a tree for a brief moment, checked around him and went through the gate, placing each step carefully on the gravel path, only making the faintest of noises as he approached a wooden bungalow. A single candle illuminated a window. He had him at long last and Ormerod felt triumphant his search was now coming to a climax. *The target* in the bungalow was trapped between him and the water with no way out. This must be his secret lair, Ormerod thought to himself, and his feelings were confirmed when he saw a sign on the door—a staff with a snake entwined around it and a molehill at the bottom, the emblem of the Eternity Project. The smell of incense wafted towards him and as though drugged by the fragrance, he opened the door to the bungalow, entering a small hallway. Incense sticks giving off a sweet and somehow mesmerising scent wafting in his direction. The fragrance entering his nostrils seemed to have an effect on him, but he failed to notice his defence systems shutting down, driven by his greed and desire to get to his prize. The smoke circled around him as dizziness took hold and he gave up all sense of awareness.

"If you want the prize, come and get it," a voice hissed from a doorway, *the target's* face briefly appearing through the smoke. Then he was gone.

"Yes," whispered Ormerod obediently, as he stumbled forward in a kind of trance, holding onto the door frame for support. He entered a darkened room and just made out a bed in front of him. Vaguely aware of his drugged state, he stumbled across the short distance and aimed for the bed, collapsing immediately on the soft mattress. He heard a noise of metal against metal as the door closed behind him. Ormerod lay on his back as the sound of hissing snakes and the chanting of a priest came from below. Ormerod was now in a temple to Asclepius, where patients told everything to the priests, and that is exactly what he now did, the drugs having completely taken control. He told them all he knew.

***

The Head of the Eternity Project had completed his task as he closed the metal door behind him, securing it with a heavy-duty padlock. But it was now time for him to take a different path, and a very reluctant one.

He had been successful in preserving the true form of the Eternity Project, despite coming under sustained attack from the Cult of Azoth using Ormerod Forsythe-Twyke as its pawn. They had come close, dangerously close, to uncovering him and his true identity, so an elaborate plan lasting some years was conceived. Unknowingly, I became part of this. The plan to bait Ormerod had to be genuine, as it was the only way he would fall for it, but it wasn't without risk. Therefore, he was allowed to know about Oldfield Thomas's manuscript in the bookshop. Of course, the purpose of the bookshop in Bangkok had now served its purpose after remaining a secret for many years. It was now time for it to turn over a new chapter.

The Head of the Eternity Project now knew a lot more about the Cult of Azoth through a drugged Ormerod. The Forsythe-Twyke family had been defeated, losing all the credibility they had amassed over the years, but they still remained an extremely wealthy family and should never be underestimated. The moles had assisted him in his plan but, like everyone else, they were also still greedy for the prize. He was sure Connor had found the garden and hopefully had left by now, the moles unaware he had ever been there, still believing him to be sitting in his hotel room. But the Head of the Eternity Project now had the unsavoury task of informing the moles that Connor had been unsuccessful and could not prove the existence of the secret garden, the myth therefore remaining a mystery. Moreover, he would tell them Connor had been recalled back to his job in the Molehamptons at short notice.

The Head of the Eternity Project first entered the mole world again and returned to the Repository after giving them the bad news but promised to carry on the quest himself. He also had to justify why he destroyed the information some years ago. The moles, clearly disappointed in the news, were nevertheless content they had the Head of the Eternity Project back under their control. Their greed, like that of everyone else, the driving factor behind their decisions. But it was never his intention to stay too long and, after being there some weeks, waited for the moles to drop their guard and slipped away unnoticed. He disguised himself, something he was particularly good at, and made a journey to Koh Chang. He was accompanied by the old man from the bookshop carrying a bag full of maps and manuscripts.

***

Ormerod slowly woke from his drugged sleep, extremely drowsy, confused and unaware of his surroundings. The first things he recognised on waking up in the darkness were being rocked gently from side to side, the strong smell of sea water and the sound of an electric motor. Ormerod climbed off the bed and then fell on the floor as, wherever he was, lurched violently like crashing through a large wave. Scrambling with his hands on the wooden floor, he reached out for the walls and found they were made of metal.

"Where am I? Let me out!" he shouted in panic.

He had absolutely no recollection what had happened after entering the garden the night before and it now began to dawn on him that he had been drugged. Starting off on his knees, he felt his way around and slowly stood up, eventually finding a switch. The bright light forced him to shield his eyes, squinting until he had got used to the glare. He was in a red room made of metal; a bed secured to the floor in the middle with a loudspeaker underneath. The container was supplied with electricity providing only light and fresh air. In one corner were boxes of water and dry food and in another corner a chemical toilet. Next to the door was a red button which he now pressed to see what happened. The sound of hissing snakes, the chanting of a priest and his voice played in his metal cell. Ormerod slumped down on the floor, head in hands and accepted his defeat.

***

The huge container ship was completely alone in the vast blue ocean stretching as far as the eye could see, a single plume of smoke snaking up to the sky. High above, a large flock of pigeons hunted it down and started circling directly above it. Right in the middle, a red container was marked with a large white emblem—a snake entwined around a staff with a molehill at the bottom.

Chapter Twenty-Five
Intrigue and Slippers

Mr Lawnsworthy rested against his broom, looking around Trout Lane. He politely nodded at the Khan family, just returning home from doing their weekly shopping. The Kennedy brothers' house remained empty, and he had heard a rumour in the village they were being held in a Thai prison. Apparently, they had been working for the Forsythe-Twykes who had put all the blame on them regarding tax fraud and a seizure of animal waste. Nobody believed this as the brothers were too stupid to run a company and even commit tax fraud. Another rumour was they had become Buddhist monks. He also had a parcel for me and left a note in my pile of post. Mr Lawnsworthy carried on brushing his garden, frequently looking up at my house, blissfully unaware of the many molehills sprouting up in his back garden. But this was Lower Molehampton!

***

I returned to a gigantic pile of post on the floor of my hallway, which I now spread out all over my dining room table. Not being the person who received much in the post and usually bills, I reluctantly started to open them. A piece of paper stuck between two letters fluttered down to the floor and I found it to be a handwritten note from Mr Lawnsworthy informing he had a parcel for me. A few minutes later, I knocked on his door and, to my surprise, he invited me in for a cup of tea. We had never really spoken much before, despite being neighbours for all these years. Even less so since the events in Trout Lane over the last years, and I was sure Mr Lawnsworthy was still in shock. He left me in the living room whilst he went to the kitchen, and then my naturally suspicious mind started to kick in as I looked around. A black-and-white picture of a younger Mr Lawnsworthy cradling a newborn baby was on the top of the mantlepiece. Next to that, a picture of him dressed as a gardener, the Forsythe-Twyke mansion in the background. But taking centre stage was a beautifully carved box made of dark wood and contained three compartments, all with key holes. I stroked the box then tried to pull out one of the compartments only to find it locked, as well as the other two. I stretched up to have a look at the top and what I then found really surprised me—the name *Beaumont Forsythe-Twyke* skilfully engraved in the wood. What connection could Mr Lawnsworthy have with the Forsythe-Twykes, I asked myself? And who was the baby in the picture? But these weren't the only questions I had for him, as I decided there was more to the man than met the eye.

Mr Lawnsworthy returned with two steaming cups of tea and saw me glance at the mantelpiece.

Sitting down, he said, "I was once the chief gardener at the Forsythe-Twyke mansion. Did you know that?"

"I think I've heard about that before. Did you do it for long?" I replied.

"Yes, my whole working life, and my father too. My family and the Forsythe-Twykes go back a long way, until they went bad that is."

"You surely must know a lot about them?" I pressed, now finding another source of information about the family I had never even suspected.

"More than you care to think," he added guardingly.

I looked at him long and hard as we sat there in an awkward silence, each one waiting for the next move. I took out his note about the parcel he wrote to me and put it on the table.

"Thank you for this."

"Oh, you're most welcome, Mr Jackson."

"And these too," putting the five handwritten single word notes on the table, three of them written by the hand of an old person.

"Yes, those," he replied with a sly grin on his face. "I was sure you would eventually work it out."

"But why? What have you got to do with all of this?"

"Yes, Mr Jackson, what has a mere gardener got to do with all of this? I hate moles and molehills."

"Of that I have no doubt."

"But it is not only because of their annoying hills, it's to do with what they do and, more importantly, what they stand for."

I now became extremely suspicious about the direction of this conversation. "What they do?" I questioned him.

"Come now, Mr Jackson. I know what they really do down there, and I have no desire to join them. Not in the next years at least."

I choked, completely bewildered he knew about the secret world of moles, as I thought only a few people knew about it.

"My father and I were gardeners and had full access to the grounds and mansion. We repaired things in the house too. According to my father, everything was just fine when Beaumont was in charge of things, but this changed when the nasty George took over and his three older sisters disappeared. There are secret tunnels and listening points in the house which we used to spy on the family, so I know a lot, Mr Jackson. And I know about the Eternity Project too."

"You have names?" I prompted, absolutely astounded about what I was listening to.

"Only some. You see, before Beaumont died, he had that wooden box made as a family heirloom. Each compartment has a name of one of his three daughters engraved on it: Annabelle, Agnes and Beatrice. They all went into hiding, and have never been heard of since. The box was given to my father, and I inherited it from him. The keys for each compartment were handed to the relevant child and by now handed down to their children. The secrets of the Eternity Project also followed the eldest into hiding."

"This is unbelievable. And the whole time you have been sitting next to me with this knowledge. What's in the box?" I asked, standing up and going to the mantlepiece to look at the box again.

"I have no idea what this box is hiding. My father never knew and was given explicit instructions that each compartment should only be opened by those possessing the keys. Maybe one day, someone will come along and knock on my door."

"Well, what made you send me the notes, Mr Lawnsworthy? Why now? If you have known about the family for so long, what prompted you to act?"

"I saw the power Felicity Forsythe-Twyke was amassing and what she was doing with the Food Factory. I also understand how the system of allocations work and knew she was destroying our planet. It was time for action, Mr Jackson, and I knew you were the man to do it."

"My goodness, you were using me too?"

"Sure. You see, I knew all about Oldfield Thomas and his experiences in Siam as I used to listen to George talk about it when I was a child. He was absolutely obsessed with the myths and convinced everything was true, making control over the mole world and uncovering the secrets of a garden his main purpose in life. This obsession was passed down to his children and they are now extremely powerful, so I guessed that with a little prompting and the correct information, you would also make this journey and hopefully assist in destroying the Forsythe-Twykes from within."

"I did my bit as best as I could, Mr Lawnsworthy, but certainly not alone."

"Yes, that's true. I have actually been quite busy," he said, smiling at me. "I sent you the notes, yes, but I also wrote letters to Jessica Walsh, Sergeant Dawson, Mr Cross, Mr Scribbler and Mr Kowalczyk. I realised you alone could not defeat them; therefore, I enlisted help from others. I formulated a plan over many years and was just waiting for the right moment. I wanted revenge for everything they've done to me and the village," his face became red in anger whilst spilling out his feelings. "They treated me badly, I lost my daughter, and our beautiful village suffered. No more, I told myself."

"You set all of this in motion. I wondered all the time who did it and you were the last person I thought of. You have really stayed under the radar!"

"Yes, and for many years," he added proudly. "And I've been safeguarding the box here for a long time so can do it a little longer I suppose."

"But Mr Lawnsworthy, I don't mean to be rude, but you are not the youngest and …," I started, but he then finished my sentence for me.

"Yes, who will I hand it over to one day? I suppose you also want to ask me about the baby in the picture?"

"Only if you want to tell me?"

"I do. I've been hiding this for so long and it's now time for the truth to come out. We were never a well-off family, and how could we be, working for George and then Felicity, but, thankfully, Beaumont gave my father this house. I married a lovely woman called Margaret and we had a baby together. Unfortunately, my wife died giving birth and left me alone with our daughter. I was not able to provide for her and reluctantly had to give her up for adoption. She never knew my name, but I knew what happened to her, following her every movement and still do today."

"Then why have you not made contact?"

"I was ashamed that I gave her away and too scared to do it."

"But I think you should. I think she would want to know who her father is."

"After all these years, you think I should do it, Mr Jackson?" he asked me, looking sad.

"Yes, of course you should. She would want to know."

I returned to my house quite emotional after what I had just learnt. Mr Lawnsworthy had, in fact, revealed more to me about the Forsythe-Twykes than I had discovered before, and he would certainly have more to tell me when we had the chance to chat again. It was time to pay a visit to my boss.

***

Jemima Kingston was sitting in her office, smiling smugly as she read Timothy Scribbler's latest news article over and over again. He had the exclusive rights to all the stories in the Food Factory and every day wrote about something new, keeping all the residents in the Molehamptons abreast of the situation. Jemima had not heard from Felicity Forsythe-Twyke for some time now. So much for being friends, she thought, but wasn't disappointed one little bit. With a huge grin, she looked around her office feeling happy with herself.

A knock on the door brought her out of her delighted state. "Good afternoon, Mrs Kingston," I said, poking my head around the door. "May I come in?"

"Mr Jackson, good afternoon to you too. What can I do for you? Do you have anything to add to your report?"

I had already debriefed her about my visit and there were things she could know about, but categorically things best kept to myself. You understand!

"Well, actually I do. I told you I had nothing to do with the events in the Molehamptons whilst I was away."

"Mr Jackson, that is quite hard to believe, but please go on."

"Yes, but somebody else was orchestrating things and I believe I know who. It's best if you came with me as I have something to show you."

"Something to show me?" she asked. "Can't you show me here in the comfort of my office?"

"Actually not. Please trust me and just come." I tried to be convincing.

Jemima Kingston, quite rightly suspicious, followed me to my car and we drove to Trout Lane, parking in the driveway of my house.

"Why are we going to your house, Mr Jackson?"

"We're not. Follow me please, Mrs Kingston," and I walked the few steps to my neighbour at number four, Mr Lawnsworthy. He promptly opened the door and the three of us stood there, looking at each other with blank expressions on our faces.

"I don't understand," blurted Jemima genuinely.

Tears rolled down Mr Lawnsworthy's cheeks as he stood there with a nervous smile.

"I think you might," I added softly. "I'll leave the two of you together," and then left them alone.

***

As an observant reader, you may wonder about the memory stick and the identity of the secret minister. Me too! Headphones on, I sat in my room and set about solving these two loose ends. The memory stick was, in fact, in the parcel I collected from Mr Lawnsworthy and had information recorded on it from just before my kidnapping, and also other things I had picked up after my return. Can you remember this stick? Well, I had not forgotten about it and sent it to a friend for analysing before going to Thailand. It was now time to see what information it revealed. My colleague was good and, whilst I was in Thailand, she filtered out sounds, leaving something quite startling.

"That wasn't what I expected!" I said out loud, then removed my headphones and blew out in surprise. It was time to confront Colonel Pickle.

***

The ex-President sat in his office, sadly looking at the pictures on the wall. Life in the mole world had returned to relative normality, the streets cleaned up and some of the damage repaired.

There was a knock on the door. "Good evening, Mr President."

"I should address you as President now."

"All in good time," the Colonel replied seriously. "We need to talk."

"The secret minister?" he asked. "Do you know who it is?"

"Yes, I do. Connor Jackson suspected me all along."

"Oh, did he!"

"He was wrong, because it's you," he spat out. The ex-President didn't answer, just sat there staring at Colonel Pickle. "Aren't you going to say anything?"

"No. I'm quite relieved it's all over, and I can stop the charade. Colonel Pickle, how did you find out?"

"Mr Jackson recognised the tapping of your umbrella from recordings he made and that's what gave you away. Mr Jackson is a very clever man. But why? Why did you do it?"

"I don't expect you to understand and I'm not asking for sympathy. Colonel Pickle, I have been blackmailed for many years now and I didn't, or couldn't, do anything about it. I should have told, and maybe none of this would ever have happened."

"Then tell me now," replied the Colonel sadly.

"Cromwell used his position down here to work out who my family members are, and when I mean family, I mean those still alive on the surface. The Forsythe-Twyke family threatened bad things against them if I did not do what they told me. That Ormerod up there is a bad person, and he has members of my family held somewhere. I was once a human like you, you know?"

"I just can't believe this story. You were far too involved on our side when the Professor's memory was stolen. You should have been uncovered a long time ago."

"Normally yes, but the horrid family have their tentacles everywhere and the dreadful affair was planned in minute detail. I'm not sure anyone who may have tried to work it out would have known who was who. The Forsythe-Twykes masterfully choregraphed everything to make it look like I was on your side but in reality, I was doing their bidding."

"Who do they have hostage."

"Felicity Forsythe-Twyke's husband is my son, Farquhar Ogulburt-Dilingbrush."

***

You already know a lot about the Forsythe-Twyke family and their strange family intrigues so no need to repeat myself. I was, of course, assigned to investigate them by my boss but what came out about her was most startling.

Professor Wingnut was none other than Jemima Kingston's much-loved stepbrother as she was adopted at birth by the Wingnut family. Her real parents were the Lawnsworthys, but do you know who Mr Lawnsworthy married? You might remember her name was Margaret and she died giving birth to Jemima, but you don't know what her maiden name was. After many discussions with Mr Lawnsworthy in the weeks and months after my return from Thailand, he revealed his mother was Margaret Pickle, none other than Colonel Pickle's sister. He knew her when he was young, but they lost contact when he was sent to a military college and never knew she married Gerald Lawnsworthy then died whilst giving birth to Jemima. This was all now getting a little complicated for me. Jemima was born a Lawnsworthy, adopted by the Wingnuts then married Robert Kingston. Therefore, she was related to some of the key personalities in this mind-boggling story: Gerald Lawnsworthy, President Pickle and Professor Wingnut. Best have a look at the family tree just in case you are as confused as I am.

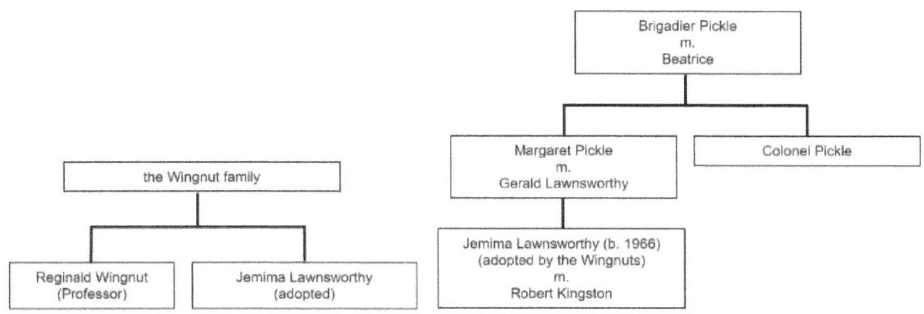

But what are the Forsythe-Twyke family members doing now? Ormerod was sitting in a container somewhere in the Pacific Ocean, whilst Bartholomew had been recalled to London for a right dressing-down by the Prime Minister. And then there was the sad story of Farquhar Ogulburt-Dilingbrush, drugged and held as a prisoner, but now kept company by Felicity. She was a gibbering wreck after all of the events, but at least both of them were being cared for by Clementine. Anyway, she seemed to be the only normal person in the family. Don't worry, I haven't forgotten about Vanessa, and you can find out very soon what she has been up to!

I was now sitting on the couch enjoying a cup of tea with Jemima Kingston and Mr Lawnsworthy whilst the handbag with Cromwell was on the kitchen table well out of earshot. I looked at the wooden chest again and wondered about the three names engraved—Annabelle, Agnes and Beatrice—and who or when the owners of the keys might come forward to open the contents. What was hiding in there?

Jemima was showing a picture of her late husband to her father, one of the sad stories in her life. Another sad story was the loss of Professor Wingnut, her half-brother. I sat there feeling rather uncomfortable, knowing her half-brother's memory was in my house.

For obvious reasons, I could not inform Jemima Kingston that Colonel Pickle, a mole living under the Molehamptons, was her uncle, I definitely did inform the new President about his family. He sadly didn't know much about his childhood except his father, Brigadier Pickle, who died when he was a toddler and his mother disappeared. As I have already mentioned, he lost contact with his sister many years ago, not even realising she had died. But now he had gained a niece, Jemima, whom he now followed her every step. Jemima's garden had never had too many molehills but, ever since the President found out about her, it was now festooned with large brown earth mounds. She might usually have been annoyed about this fact, but now having won a father, she just let it go. President Pickle at long last had a family and he was extremely grateful to me for finding it out.

***

Everything was normal in Trout Lane. Earl Pickle was riding my old bicycle; the Khans were unloading shopping from their car and Mr Lawnsworthy was dusting his rockery. What about the Kennedy brothers then? I heard through my official sources they had enrolled in a Buddhist monk program instead of going to prison in Thailand. The price was revealing everything they knew about the Forsythe-Twyke activities in Thailand, which was actually not too much. The Thai authorities never truly believed the brothers were capable of doing any of this and were quite keen to rehabilitate them rather than punishing them for crimes they definitely could not have committed.

If only the people here knew what I had been up to. Connor Jackson, the boring civil servant and memory thief had met a god who wanted me to hunt down a secretive cult. I knew where the Sanctuary of Epidaurus was, who lived there and the location of the Elixir of Life. The quest for Azoth was most certainly not over.

And then there he was again—the monk appeared next to the Kennedy brothers' house, looked towards me, waved and walked away. I had a funny feeling something soon was going to happen again.

***

The story is not quite over as Sergeant Dawson had just invited me over to give me a present. In excited anticipation as everyone loves presents, I quickly walked into the village centre and noticed the lights shining out of the molehills in front of the police station. On his desk was a gift-wrapped box and a beaming Colonel Pickle standing next to it.

"Mr Jackson, this is for you in recognition for your efforts."

"Oh my, that is most thoughtful."

"Go on, open it then," stammered Sergeant Dawson enthusiastically.

I ripped off the paper and eagerly opened the lid, absolutely amazed at what awaited me—my red tartan slippers! So much effort had been put in to make them as good as new again. Well, nearly. The rips had been sewn together and the holes repaired with green tartan material. They looked funny but quite exceptional. Nobody else's slippers had such a story to tell.

"Time for a celebration then!" grinned Sergeant Dawson and walked across to his new tea trolley.

Before President Pickle could stop him, he had opened the door to the storeroom and pulled out the plug.

***

And in the world below the Molehamptons, there was a loud thud as the lights went out.

Chapter Twenty-Six
Victory by the Courageous Few

Timothy Scribbler sat in the front row of the conference room, awaiting Vanessa Forsythe-Twyke's entrance for her long-awaited press conference. The room was full of excited journalists, chattering away in eager anticipation of what she would tell them. They didn't have to wait long as she walked in to greet them. I watched as she approached the table with an air of self-assured confidence. This was a different Vanessa to the one I had met first, now fully mature and taking on a tremendous responsibility.

"Ladies and gentlemen," she exclaimed, as the clicking of cameras began. "Thank you for coming to my first press conference as Chief Executive of the Food Factory. Not too long ago, I promised my mother a legacy we will never forget!" She stopped and looked at the eager listeners to build up the suspense. "You will all have noticed some changes in the last weeks: the production has stopped, government agencies allowed in, and local farmers invited. Moreover, we have closely consulted with animal rights organisations and also with Jessica Walsh, without whose brave action we might not be sitting here today to hear what I have to say."

All eyes flashed to Jessica, sitting proudly next to Timothy Scribbler.

"We are still at the beginning of our plans, but I can inform you about our new strategic aims." The scraping of chairs and rustling of paper was loud in the room as the journalists changed their positions to start writing. "First, the number of animals here will be drastically reduced."

"But Mrs Forsythe-Twyke," shouted a journalist from the back.

"Questions afterwards please. Second, only animals from local farmers will be accepted here. Third, all animals will be held in the best possible conditions. Fourth, we ask the government to set sensible and ecological quotas on the number of animals bred for the food industry. Fifth, we will be transparent. No longer will we lock the gates and no longer will there be any secrets. Ladies and gentlemen, we are open to visitors. And, lastly, my sixth point, we will increase awareness that when eating meat, you are eating an animal and not just a product in a plastic bag."

Vanessa stopped and looked at the people gathered, all oddly silent, shocked at her news. Slowly the journalists started chatting and the noise level rose until it reached a loud crescendo, all of them putting up their hands to be the first to ask a question.

"That, ladies and gentlemen, is our initial six-point plan, and I hope you can see it is a radically different approach. And now I will welcome questions."

Shouting immediately burst out, the journalists competing to be heard and residents nodded in excited agreement.

"You first," Vanessa said, pointing to Timothy Scribbler.

"Miss Forsythe-Twyke, thank you for your six-point agenda. I understand you are a vegetarian. How can someone like you run a meat processing plant?"

"Good question, and I expected this. I haven't always been a vegetarian, but a certain experience opened my eyes, not about what I was eating but who I was eating. Eat meat, yes, but please with respect because you are eating a living member of this planet. And now you," stabbing her finger at another journalist.

"Why only meat from local farmers?"

"Because we want to show transparency from the field to the plate and this is better done locally. I have formed a working group with local farmers, Mr Rye taking the lead. He will arrange a program where we can trace individual animals from a farm, then here, to shops and restaurants. You will know which animal you eat."

"Isn't that grotesque?" shouted a journalist.

"Grotesque? No, far from it. If you make the conscious decision to eat an animal, then you should have the courage to follow its journey to your plate. Grotesque is producing meat like cars in a mass-production plant," Vanessa confidently replied, as people in the room started to applaud. "And now you, please," pointing again.

"You say you will still slaughter animals but talk about ethics. How does that work?"

"You have a good point. Let's be clear about this—there is no nice way to dress up the fact that when you eat meat, an animal dies. I want to have some respect in this business, so if we are to slaughter animals, then maybe we should consider a new business model. The animals' sole purpose on this planet should not be only to eat them. How often have you seen a pig, a cow or a sheep just enjoying their life as we do? I do not suggest they should roam around freely but I do suggest the only reason they are here is not for us to eat them. Therefore, I also intend to introduce some large fields where animals can live without the fear of slaughter. Already, local residents have signed up to help me in this project and have offered fields and gardens for animals to graze freely."

"Are you not going against our free-market values which have given us so much wealth?"

"In a way, yes I am. But a free market driven by consumer demand can only function up to a certain point. Humans are greedy by nature and if there is no control, we will just take more and more and more. Free-market values are fine with products like smartphones, but how can a creature we share this planet with be categorised as a product, free for us to do with as we like? Governments cannot turn a blind eye, shirk their responsibilities and blame the consequences on consumer demand. Governments must take regulatory control in this industry. And now a final question from you."

"How will the consumers see the effects of this?"

"We will sell to any outlet in the region complying with our transparency criteria from the field to the plate. For example, a restaurant offering steak must be able to provide information about the source animal like pictures and a name."

"But isn't this all rather costly?" questioned a journalist.

"Yes, it will be. My inheritance is rather large as you can imagine, and I intend to use it wisely to make a stand and a new start. Surely, it must be wrong when meat costs less than vegetables?" she posed the question to a silent room, pausing to look around. "It will come at a personal financial cost to me, but someone has to start, and I have the resources to do so. I hope, along with movements like Jessica's," she said looking at her, "we can promote awareness of consumer habits and the whole meat industry may gradually change. Looking about this room, I see the press from around the world, so this subject has hit a chord. It is time for change, and we are going to start here in the Molehamptons and maybe, just maybe, it will be copied in other places."

"Well said!" shouted a voice from Sergeant Dawson's helmet, who immediately started wildly applauding to cover up Colonel Pickle's presence.

I was also standing at the back, proudly observing the scenes as a confident Vanessa left the room. If you thought Vanessa had double-crossed me earlier in our adventure, and just wanted power for herself, you are quite wrong. We planned this all along and everything we did was just a smokescreen to lure the Forsythe-Twykes into a trap. We were most successful, and Vanessa now delighted to turn over a new leaf in her family's devious history and return to what her great-grandfather, Beaumont, and Oldfield Thomas planned from the beginning. She had just pressed the reset button!

Vanessa left the stage and handed over to her newly appointed publicity manager, whom she had known for many years—Mrs Grae de Vole.

***

The Molehamptons changed soon after my return. First, Mr Rye was elected mayor by a large majority, and it didn't take long for him to stamp his mark. One of his first acts was to reintroduce Mr Cross's ferry service, much to the delight of residents and tourists alike who welcomed the clanking of the chain once again. Then, a farmers' market opened on the bridge twice a week promoting regionally sourced produce, attracting visitors and bringing the community together. Also, Mayor Rye initiated an environmental program to rejuvenate the banks of the River Angler, wildlife soon returning including ducks, otters, dormice, badgers, weasels and water voles, just to name a few.

Vanessa's newly designed Food Factory also brought its fair share of visitors, with Mr Walsh, loyal as ever, now running company tours. He was proud to work under new management, and this made his daughter extremely happy. And what about Jessica Walsh? What was she up to now? She didn't stop with her success at the Food Factory, and she set up a political party for the voice of the youth. It had an appealing message, the future being in the hands of young people. Her party's aims were quite simple—force the government into action about transparency in what we eat. The interesting thing about her party was the truly global aspect of it—borders, nations, religions and race were not important anymore. Branches sprouted up all over the world under the name *#openthedoors*.

Seen by many as a stroppy teenager, Jessica Walsh had now proven her potential and showed that not everyone is what they appear to be. Some are good at mathematics, others not. Some are organised and some are just a nightmare. But everyone has something special in them, even though it is sometimes difficult to identify. All Jessica needed was the trigger and if only she knew it came from the least likely of characters—Mr Lawnsworthy. People can really be full of surprises!

Gertrude Lawnsworthy was also full of surprises, and she was a lot more than just a chef. She played a key role in the new local activities, and her small village café, Gertrude's Pasty and Pie shop, became the focal point of the field-to-plate policy. All recipes and ingredients were locally sourced, and everything listed fully on the menu. In fact, it wasn't a big difference from before, but she now bought meat from the Food Factory, convinced of its high quality and standards. Gertrude went further, and along with Jessica Walsh, organised rural cooking courses with the aim of inspiring the residents from the Molehamptons. Bookings came in thick and fast, especially from young people keen to try out traditional dishes. Gertrude only cooked one dish per day, which was advertised in advance, and if the dish contained meat, the name and picture of the animal was on display. I heard some people argue that if demand grew, so would the slaughter of animals. But this was not the case, as she only cooked one batch and when it was finished, then it was finished. But I didn't quite tell the whole truth as she didn't always cook herself. School children were invited to come in, read and understand the recipes, then do the cooking themselves. And everything under the loving and caring supervision of Gertrude Lawnsworthy. It even sometimes happened that some children would go to the guests' tables and show them pictures of the animal they were eating and its name. If this wasn't raising awareness, then I don't know what was. The children also made the odd mistake; with some dishes just a tad burnt, or a wrong ingredient used. The guests never complained, simply smiling at the children, and chomping on their food. Life as the celebrity chef of Lower Molehampton was a far cry from her job at the Forsythe-Twyke mansion.

The fall of the greedy old order of the Forsythe-Twykes had now led to a natural order returning under the wise direction of President Pickle managing everything below the ground. Jessica Walsh naturally had no idea about the role of moles, so the President worked silently and fortuitously whilst Jessica ensured the government kept to their promises above the ground. She put them under permanent and maximum pressure and had constant contact with the new Minister for the Food Standards Agency—thankfully not a Forsythe-Twyke!

***

It was the acts of a courageous few who forced change in the Molehamptons and none more so than Sergeant Dawson, immensely proud of what they had achieved and inspired to have actively taken part in special operations. Despite having case files on his desk and being unable to officially close them, he now knew the moles were responsible for everything. Nobody, well nearly nobody, knew what was going on below the ground, and, moreover, he was now personal friends with the President of the mole world, even though he still called him Colonel Pickle.

It was, however, a mutually beneficial relationship. Sergeant Dawson had always been bothered about rubbish lying around in the streets, for example socks or blocks of salt. The moles of course were to blame for this, as they so often did not tidy up after themselves. Sergeant Dawson now provided a service and a special one. The moles gave him a list of their requirements and he provided the location. All scavenged items were now deposited in his storeroom for temporary safekeeping instead of the risk of using molehills around the Molehamptons and the resulting litter of failed missions: individual socks, shoes and salt blocks often being left lying around. The moles, in return, were responsible for clearing litter away and repairing anything broken in the villages at night-time, keeping the Molehamptons prim and proper. Little did the villagers know that, whilst they were fast asleep, teams of military engineer moles armed with tools would work their way around repairing broken streetlights, small potholes in the streets and many more things. It was a win-win situation for everyone involved. Sergeant Dawson did not only have a special relationship with the President below the ground but also with the key personalities above the ground, fostering a wonderful community with crime at an all-time low. The mayor, proud of the villages, did not know that Sergeant Dawson was assisted in his duties by the mole police, keeping a thorough watch on the Molehamptons and informing the Sergeant of any possible incident. Everything was just as he liked it.

The moles even constructed a playground game which was quite basic—just a grid with molehills popping up in random squares. The kids had great fun stamping down on the mounds but never managed to beat the moles who were always quicker. Then, the moles went one stage further and installed different coloured lights and a sound system which played when the molehills popped up. The kids absolutely loved it, and the ingenious moles provided hours of fun and exercise for all involved.

***

Basil was the last to imagine he would now be gliding across the surface of the River Angler, collecting food for his family. He had little recollection of his last days in the Food Factory, but one memory kept on returning and that was of Ludwig trying to free him. It didn't take Basil too long to recover, having had excellent care at the animal shelter. He was cleaned, fed properly, and, when he was strong enough, returned to the river and his family. Despite being a bit larger and overweight owing to the fattening process, he was delighted to be back in his natural habitat. Even his neighbours and old friends started coming back along with an influx of new river animals not seen for some years.

Basil swam majestically in the middle of the river and took in the scenes he so loved. He looked towards his home under the willow tree and saw Mr Rye walking Ludwig along the river. He turned a little towards the bridge and saw Mr Lawnsworthy walking with a younger woman, deep in conversation together. He also saw Vanessa talking to an older woman at a market stall who was selling pies and pasties.

But the real hero in this story was Ludwig. He had always been loyal, a pre-programmed characteristic in his breed of dog, but now he displayed much more than loyalty alone. He showed the utmost bravery, never giving up on his best friend, Basil. Where most would have thrown in the towel, Ludwig tried again and yet again. Admittedly, he wanted to eat Basil when they first met, but relationships have a habit of taking funny turns.

He was walking along the river with Mr Rye, and saw Basil sitting contentedly on the surface, taking in the beautiful view around him. Ludwig barked, Basil understanding what he said but not Mr Rye. They walked together to the market on the bridge where Mr Rye in his new role as the mayor used the opportunity to talk to stallholders and local residents. He was most certainly very popular, unlike the previous incumbent.

Vanessa first gave Ludwig a most succulent bone to chew on, something she often did in recognition of his bravery. This was, of course, the equivalent in the dog world to the highest medal of honour for humans. Suddenly, his attention was ripped away as the most beautiful dog he had ever seen walked past, Ludwig's head panning around to follow. It was a chocolate brown labradoodle, its fur so soft and curly that it looked just like a cuddly toy. Ludwig went into automatic affection mode and started barking loudly and sniffing in the direction of the love of his life. Mr Rye had a real job holding on to the leash as Ludwig pulled away in an attempt to make contact. The brown dog turned its head and appeared to smile and wink at the drooling Ludwig before walking off with her master.

"My name's Bonnie," she shouted out.

Vanessa was standing on the bridge enjoying the lovely surroundings and chatting with Gertrude Lawnsworthy about next week's menu plan. She looked down the river and saw a duck swimming majestically until her attention was caught by something else. The monk from Wat Suthat was standing at the end of the bridge, observing the whole scene. He smiled at Vanessa, waved, and was gone.

But Vanessa wasn't the only person observing events on the bridge. Mrs Grae de Vole was also standing there, keeping her beady eye on everyone and everything.

Epilogue

Cromwell Forsythe-Twyke was angry after being defeated yet again, destined to remain a prisoner between used tissues and uncomfortable objects. Head poking out of Jemima Kingston's handbag, he saw a duck swimming in the river, gnarled at Ludwig and flashed his teeth at Sergeant Dawson. Then something quite out of place in the rural Molehamptons caught his eye—a monk in an orange robe. Strange, he thought to himself. Who can he be?

But there was still some hope for him when he saw a friendly face. Mrs Grae de Vole winked at him, a very comforting gesture considering his current circumstances. Good that she had gone undetected and will undoubtedly prove useful in the future.

The vibrating of a phone suddenly interrupted his devious thoughts. A sound of a ship's horn and the clatter of metal against metal blasted into his ear before he heard a voice competing against the din.

"Cromwell, my son, I have a plan!" cried Ormerod Forsythe-Twyke

THE END

(highly likely not)